They ...

They are ...

They are ...*ble,*

They are—

100% Male

Self-proclaimed permanent
bachelors, these men fall hard—
when they fall in love!

Dear Reader,

We welcome you to the new 2-in-1 Desires. Each month we'll bring you three new 2-in-1 volumes from all your favourite authors. A double helping of the most rugged, gorgeous heroes around and all in one value-priced book!

This month kicks off with the first story in a new trilogy from Leanne Banks—MILLION DOLLAR MEN—and a wonderful stand-alone story from Joan Hohl in *Tempting the Boss*; these are two office romps sure to satisfy.

Next, we have the latest book in the SONS OF THE DESERT series from Alexandra Sellers—with a super, sexy sheikh hero—and a fantastic story from Peggy Moreland, too, in *100% Male*. You'll need lots of ice to cool you off after meeting these two strong, stubborn yet loveable rogues.

Finally, *Brides-To-Be* has two stories with a modern twist on the classic fairytale wedding fantasy written by fabulous authors Katherine Garbera and Kate Little. Wedding bells are definitely ringing for these couples.

Do tell us what you think of the new format for Desire™ and do look out for our wonderful new line—Superromance™—which is on the shelves now!

The Editors

100% Male

ALEXANDRA SELLERS
PEGGY MORELAND

™
SILHOUETTE
DESIRE
®

*Silhouette, Silhouette Desire and Colophon
are registered trademarks of Harlequin Books S.A.,
used under licence.*

*First published in Great Britain 2001
Silhouette Books, Eton House, 18-24 Paradise Road,
Richmond, Surrey TW9 1SR*

100% MALE © Harlequin Books S.A. 2001

The publisher acknowledges the copyright holders of the
individual works as follows:

Sheikh's Woman © Alexandra Sellers 2001
The Way to a Rancher's Heart © Peggy Bozeman Morse 2001

ISBN 0 373 04731 2

51-1101

*Printed and bound in Spain
by Litografia Rosés S.A., Barcelona*

SHEIKH'S WOMAN

By
Alexandra Sellers

ALEXANDRA SELLERS

is the author of over twenty-five novels and a feline language text published in 1997 and still selling.

Born and raised in Canada, Alexandra first came to London as a drama student. Now she lives near Hampstead Heath with her husband, Nick. They share housekeeping with Monsieur, who came in through the window one day and announced, as cats do, that he was staying.

What she would miss most on a desert island is shared laughter.

Readers can write to Alexandra at PO Box 9449, London NW3 2WH.

For my sister Joy,
who held it all together in the bad times
and makes things even better in the good.

Prologue

She crouched in the darkness, whimpering as the pain gripped her. He had made her wait too long. She had warned him, but he'd pretended not to believe her "lies." And now, in an empty, dirty alley, nowhere to go, no time to get there, her time was upon her.

Pain stabbed her again, and she cried out involuntarily. She pressed a hand over her mouth and looked behind her down the alley. Of course by now he had discovered her flight. He was already after her. If he had heard that cry...

She staggered to her feet again, picked up the bag, began a shuffling run. Her heart was beating so hard! The drumming in her head seemed to drown out thought. She ran a few paces and then doubled over again as the pain came. Oh, Lord, not here! Please, please, not in an alley, like an animal, to be found when she was most helpless, when the baby would be at his mercy.

He would have no mercy. The pain ebbed and she ran on, weeping, praying. *"Ya Allah!"* Forgive me, protect me.

Suddenly, as if in answer, she sensed a deeper darkness in the shadows. She turned towards it without questioning, and found herself in a narrower passage. The darkness was more intense here, and she stared blindly until her eyes grew accustomed.

There was a row of garages on either side of a short strip of paving. Then she saw what had drawn her, what her subconscious mind—or her guardian angel—had already seen: one door was ajar. She bit her lip. Was there someone inside, a fugitive like herself? But another clutch of pain almost knocked her to her knees. As she bent double, stifling her cry, she heard a shout. A long way distant, but she feared what was behind her more than what might be ahead.

Sobbing with mingled pain and terror, she stumbled towards the open door and pushed her way inside.

One

"**C**an you hear me? Anna, can you hear my voice?"

It was like being dragged through long, empty rooms. Anna groaned protestingly. What did they want from her? Why didn't they let her sleep?

"Move your hand if you can hear my voice, Anna. Can you move your hand?"

It took huge effort, as if she had to fight through thick syrup.

"That's excellent! Now, can you open your eyes?"

Abruptly something heavy seemed to smash down inside her skull, driving pain through every cell. She moaned.

"I'm afraid you're going to have a pretty bad headache," said the voice, remorselessly cheerful, determinedly invasive. "Come now, Anna! Open your eyes!"

She opened her eyes. The light was too bright. It hurt. A woman in a navy shirt with white piping was gazing at her. "Good, there you are!" she said, in a brisk Scots accent. "What's your name?"

"Anna," said Anna. "Anna Lamb."

The woman nodded. "Good, Anna."

"What happened? Where am I?" Anna whispered. She was lying in a grey cubicle on a narrow hospital trolley, fully dressed except for shoes. "Why am I in hospital?" The hammer slammed down again. "My head!"

"You've been in an accident, but you're going to be fine. Just a wee bit concussed. Your baby's fine."

Your baby. A different kind of pain smote her then, and she lay motionless as cold enveloped her heart.

"My baby died," she said, her voice flat as the old, familiar lifelessness seeped through her.

The nurse was taking Anna's blood pressure, but at this she looked up. "She's absolutely fine! The doctor's just checking her over now," she said firmly. "I don't know why you wanted to give birth in a taxicab, but it seems you made a very neat job of it."

She leaned forward and pulled back one of Anna's eyelids, shone light from a tiny flashlight into her eye.

"In a taxicab?" Anna repeated. "But—"

Confused memories seemed to pulsate in her head, just out of reach.

"You're a very lucky girl!" said the cheerful nurse, moving down to press her abdomen with searching fingers. She paused, frowning, and pressed again.

Anna was silent, her eyes squeezed tight, trying to think through the pain and confusion in her head. Meanwhile the nurse poked and prodded, frowned a little, made notes, poked again. "Lift up, please?" she murmured, and with competent hands carried on the examination.

When it was over, she stood looking down at Anna, sliding her pen into the pocket of her uniform trousers. A little frown had gathered between her eyebrows.

"Do you remember giving birth, Anna?"

Pain rushed in at her. The room suddenly filling with people, all huddled around her precious newborn baby, while she cried, "Let me see him, why can't I hold him?" and then...*Anna, I'm sorry, I'm so very sorry. We couldn't save your baby.*

"Yes," she said lifelessly, gazing at the nurse with dry, stretched eyes, her heart a lump of stone. "I remember."

A male head came around the cubicle's curtain. "Staff, can you come, please?"

The Staff Nurse gathered up her instruments. "Maternity Sister will be down as soon as she can get away, but it may be a while, Anna. They've got staff shortages there, too, tonight, and a Caes—"

A light tap against the partition wall preceded the entrance of a young nurse, looking desperately tired but smiling as she rolled a wheeled bassinet into the room.

"Oh, nurse, there you are! How's the bairn?" said the Staff Nurse, sounding not altogether pleased.

The bairn was crying with frustrated fury, and neither of the nurses heard the gasp that choked Anna. A storm of emotion seemed to seize her as she lifted herself on her elbows and, ignoring the punishment this provoked from the person in her head who was beating her nerve endings, struggled to sit up.

"Baby?" Anna cried. "Is that *my baby?*"

Meanwhile, the young nurse wheeled the baby up beside the trolley, assuring Anna, "Yes, she is. A lovely little girl." Anna looked into the bassinet, closed her eyes, looked again.

The baby stopped crying suddenly. She was well wrapped up in hospital linen, huge eyes open, silent now but frowning questioningly at the world.

"Oh, dear God!" Anna exclaimed, choking on the emotion that surged up inside. "Oh, my baby! Was it just a nightmare, then? Oh, my darling!"

"It's not unusual for things to get mixed up after a bang on the head like yours, but everything will sort itself out," said the Staff Nurse. "We'll keep you in for observation for a day or two, but there's nothing to worry about."

Anna hardly heard. "I want to hold her!" she whispered, convulsively reaching towards the bassinet. The young nurse obligingly picked the baby up and bent over Anna. Her hungry arms wrapping the infant, Anna sank back against the pillows.

Her heart trembled with a joy so fierce it hurt, obliterating for a few moments even the pain in her head. She drew the little bundle tight against her breast, and gazed hungrily into the flower face.

She was beautiful. Huge questioning eyes, dark hair that lay on her forehead in feathery curls, wide, full mouth which was suddenly, adorably, stretched by a yawn.

All around one eye there was a mocha-hued shadow that added an inexplicably piquant charm to her face. She gazed at Anna, serenely curious.

"She looks like a bud that's just opened," Anna marvelled. "She's so fresh, so new!"

"She's lovely," agreed the junior nurse, while the Staff Nurse hooked the clipboard of Anna's medical notes onto the foot of the bed.

"Good, then," she said, nodding. "Now you'll be all

right here till Maternity Sister comes. Nurse, I'll see you for a moment, please.''

The sense of unreality returned when she was left alone with the baby. Anna gazed down into the sweet face from behind a cloud of pain and confusion. She couldn't seem to think.

The baby fell asleep, just like that. Anna bent to examine her. The birthmark on her eye was very clear now that the baby's eyes were closed. Delicate, dark, a soft smudging all around the eye. Anna was moved by it. She supposed such a mark could be considered a blemish, but somehow it managed to be just the opposite.

"You'll set the fashion, my darling," Anna whispered with a smile, cuddling the baby closer. "All the girls will be painting their eyes with makeup like that in the hopes of making themselves as beautiful as you."

It made the little face even more vulnerable, drew her, touched her heart. She couldn't remember ever having seen such a mark before. Was this kind of thing inherited? No one in her family had anything like it.

Was it a dream, that memory of another child? Tiny, perfect, a beautiful, beautiful son...but so white. They had allowed her to hold him, just for a few moments, to say goodbye. Her heart had died then. She had felt it go cold, turn to ice and then stone. They had encouraged her to weep, but she did not weep. Grief required a heart.

Was that a dream?

She was terribly tired. She bent to lay the sleeping infant back in the bassinet. Then she leaned down over the tiny, fragile body, searching her face for clues.

"Who is your father?" she whispered. "Where am I? What's happening to me?"

Her head ached violently. She lay back against the pillows and wished the lights weren't so bright.

* * *

"My daughter, you must prepare yourself for some excellent news."

She smiled trustingly at her mother. "Is it the embassy from the prince?" she asked, for the exciting information had of course seeped into the harem.

"The prince's emissaries and I have discussed the matter of your marriage with the prince. Now I have spoken with your father, whose care is all for you. Such a union will please him very much, my daughter, for he desires peace with the prince and his people."

She bowed. "I am happy to be the means of pleasing my father…. And the prince? What manner of man do they say he is?"

"Ah, my daughter, he is a young man to please any woman. Handsome, strong, capable in all the manly arts. He has distinguished himself in battle, too, and stories are told of his bravery."

She sighed her happiness. "Oh, mother, I feel I love him already!" she said.

Anna awoke, not knowing what had disturbed her. A tall, dark man was standing at the foot of her trolley, reading her chart. There was something about him… She frowned, trying to concentrate. But sleep dragged her eyes shut.

"They're both fine," she heard when she opened them next, not sure whether it was seconds or minutes later. The man was talking to a young woman who looked familiar. After a second Anna's jumbled brain recognized the junior nurse.

The man drew her eyes. He was strongly charismatic. Handsome as a pirate captain, exotically dark and obviously foreign. Masculine, strong, handsome—and impossibly clean for London, as if he had come straight from a massage and shave at his club without moving through the dust and dirt of city traffic.

He was wearing a grey silk lounge suit which looked impeccably Savile Row. A round diamond glowed with dark fire from a heavy, square gold setting on his ring finger. Heavy cuff links on the French cuffs of his cream silk shirt matched it. On his other hand she saw the flash of an emerald.

He didn't look at all overdressed or showy. It sat on him naturally. He was like an aristocrat in a period film. Dreamily she imagined him in heavy brocade, with a fall of lace at wrist and throat.

She blinked, coming drowsily more awake. The junior nurse was glowing, as if the man's male energy had stirred and ignited something in her, in spite of her exhaustion. She was mesmerized.

"Because he's mesmerizing," Anna muttered.

Suddenly recalled to her duties, the nurse glanced at her patient. "You're awake!" she murmured.

The man turned and looked at her, too, his eyes dark and his gaze piercing. Anna blinked. There was a mark on his eye just like her baby's. A dark irregular smudge that enhanced both his resemblance to a pirate and his exotic maleness.

"Anna!" he exclaimed. A slight accent furred his words attractively. "Thank God you and the baby were not hurt! What on earth happened?"

She felt very, very stupid. "Are you the doctor?" she stammered.

His dark eyes snapped into an expression of even greater concern, and he made a sound that was half laughter, half worry. He bent down and clasped her hand. She felt his fingers tighten on her, in unmistakable silent warning.

"Darling!" he exclaimed. "The nurse says you don't remember the accident, but I hope you have not forgotten your own husband!"

Two

Husband? Anna stared. Her mouth opened. "I'm not—" she began. He pressed her hand again, and she broke off. Was he really her husband? How could she be married and not remember? Her heart kicked. Had a man like him fallen in love with her, chosen her?

"Are we married?" she asked.

He laughed again, with a thread of warning in his tone that she was at a loss to figure. "Look at our baby! Does she not tell you the truth?"

The birthmark was unmistakable. But how could such a thing be? "I can't remember things," she told him in a voice which trembled, trying to hold down the panic that suddenly swept her. "I can't remember anything."

A husband—how could she have forgotten? Why? She squeezed her eyes shut, and stared into the inner blackness. She knew who she was, but everything else eluded her.

She opened her eyes. He was smiling down at her in deep concern. He was so *attractive!* The air around him seemed to crackle with vitality. Suddenly she *wanted* it to be true. She wanted him to be her husband, wanted the right to lean on him. She felt so weak, and he looked so strong. He looked like a man used to handling things.

Someone was screaming somewhere. *"Nurse, nurse!"* It was a hoarse, harsh cry. She put her hand to her pounding head. "It's so noisy," she whispered.

"We'll soon have her somewhere quieter," said the junior nurse, hastily reassuring. "I'll just go and check with Maternity again." She slipped away, leaving Anna alone with the baby and the man who was her husband.

"Come, I want to get you out of here," he said.

There was something odd about his tone. She tried to focus, but her head ached desperately, and she seemed to be behind a thick curtain separating her from the world.

"But where?" she asked weakly. "This is a hospital."

"You are booked into a private hospital. They are waiting to admit you. It is far more pleasant there—they are not short-staffed and overworked. I want a specialist to see and reassure you."

He had already drawn Anna's shoes from under the bed. Anna, her head pounding, obediently sat up on the edge of the trolley bed and slipped her feet into them. Meanwhile, he neatly removed the pages from the clipboard at the foot of her bed, folded and slipped them into his jacket pocket.

"Why are you taking those?" she asked stupidly.

He flicked her an inscrutable look, then picked up the baby with atypical male confidence. "Where is your bag, Anna? Did you have a bag?"

"Oh—!" She put her hand to her forehead, remembering the case she had packed so carefully...and then had carried out of the hospital when it was all over. That long, slow walk with empty arms. Her death march.

"My bag," she muttered, but her brain would not engage with the problem, with the contradiction.

"Never mind, we can get it later." He pulled aside the curtain of the cubicle, glanced out, and then turned to her. "Come!"

Her head ached with ten times the ferocity as she obediently stood. He wrapped his free arm around her back and drew her out of the cubicle, and she instinctively obeyed his masculine authority.

The casualty ward was like an overcrowded bad dream. They passed a young man lying on a trolley, his face smashed and bloody. Another trolley held an old woman, white as her hair, her veins showing blue, eyes wild with fear. She was muttering something incomprehensible and stared at Anna with helpless fixity as they passed. Somewhere someone was half moaning, half screaming. That other voice still called for a nurse. A child's cry, high and broken, betrayed mingled pain and panic.

"My God, do you think it's like this all the time?" Anna murmured.

"It is Friday night."

They walked through the waiting room, where every seat was filled, and a moment later stepped out into the autumn night. Rain was falling, but softly, and she found the cold air a relief.

"Oh, that's better!" Anna exclaimed, shivering a little in her thin shirt.

A long black limousine parked a few yards away

purred into life and eased up beside them. Her husband
opened the back door for her.

Anna drew back suddenly, without knowing why.
"What about my coat? Don't I have a coat?"

"The car is warm. Come, get in. You are tired."

His voice soothed her fears, and the combination of
obvious wealth and his commanding air calmed her. If
he was her husband, she must be safe.

In addition to everything else, being upright was making her queasy. Anna gave in and slipped inside the luxurious passenger compartment, sinking gratefully down
onto deep, superbly comfortable upholstery. He locked
and shut the door.

She leaned back and her eyes closed. He spoke to the
driver in a foreign language through the window, and a
moment later the other passenger door opened, and her
husband got inside with the baby. The limo began rolling
forward immediately. Absently she clocked the driver
picking up a mobile phone.

"Are we leaving, just like that? Don't I have to be
signed out by a doctor or something?"

He shrugged. "Believe me, the medical staff are ter-
minally overworked here. When they discover the empty
cubicle, the Casualty staff will assume you have been
moved to a ward."

Her head ached too much.

The darkness of the car was relieved at intervals by
the filtered glow of passing lights. She watched him for
a moment in light and shadow, light and shadow, as he
settled the baby more comfortably.

"What's your name?" she asked abruptly.

"I am Ishaq Ahmadi."

"That doesn't even ring a faint bell!" Anna exclaimed. "Oh, my head! Do you—how long have we been married?"

There was a disturbing flick of his black gaze in darkness. It was as if he touched her, and a little electric shock was the result.

"There is no need to go on with this now, Anna," he said.

She jumped. "What? What do you mean?"

His gaze remained compellingly on her.

"I remember my—who I *am,*" she babbled, oddly made to feel guilty by his silent judgement, "but I can't really remember my *life.* I *certainly* don't remember you. Or—or the baby, or anything. How long have we been married?"

He smiled and shrugged. "Shall we say, two years?"

"Two years!" She recoiled in horror.

"What of your life do you remember? Your mind is obviously not a complete blank. You must have something in there…you remember giving birth?"

"Yes, but…but what I remember is that my baby died."

"Ah," he breathed, so softly she wasn't even sure she had heard it.

"They told me just now that wasn't true, but…" She reached out to touch the baby in his arms. "Oh, she's so sweet! Isn't she perfect? But I remember…" Her eyes clenched against the spasm of pain. "I *remember* holding my baby after he died."

Her eyes searched his desperately in the darkness. "Maybe that was a long time ago?" she whispered.

"How long ago does it seem to you?"

The question seemed to trigger activity in her head. "Six weeks, I think…."

You're going to have six wonderful weeks, Anna.

"Oh!" she exclaimed, as a large piece of her life suddenly fell into place. "I just remembered— I was on my way to a job in France. And Lisbet and Cecile were going to take me out for a really lovely dinner. It seems to me I'm…" She squeezed her eyes shut. "Aren't I supposed to be leaving on the Paris train tomorrow…Saturday? Alan Mitching's house in France." She opened her eyes. "Are you saying that was more than two years in the past?"

"What sort of a job?"

"He has a seventeenth-century place in the Dordogne area…they want murals in the dining room. They want—wanted a Greek temple effect. I've designed—" She broke off and gazed at him in the darkness while the limousine purred through the wet, empty streets. Traffic was light; it must be two or three in the morning.

"I can remember making the designs, but I can't remember doing the actual work." Panic rose up in her. "Why can't I remember?"

"This state is not permanent. You will remember everything in time."

The baby stirred and murmured and she watched as he shifted her a little.

"Let me hold her," she said hungrily.

For a second he looked as if he was going to refuse, but she held out her arms, and he slipped the tiny bundle into her embrace. A smile seemed to start deep within her and flow outwards all through her body and spirit to reach her lips. Her arms tightened. Oh, how lovely to have a living baby to hold against her heart in place of that horrible, hurting memory!

"Oh, you're so beautiful!" she whispered. She shifted her gaze to Ishaq Ahmadi. He was watching her. "Isn't she beautiful?"

A muscle seemed to tense in his jaw. "Yes," he said.

The chauffeur spoke through an intercom, and as her husband replied, Anna silently watched fleeting expressions wander over the baby's face, felt the perfection of the little body against her breast. Time seemed to disappear in the now. She lost the urgency of wanting to know how she had got to this moment, and was happy just to be in it.

When he spoke to her again, she came to with a little start and realized she had been almost asleep. "Can you remember how you came to be in the taxi with the baby?"

Nothing. Not even vague shadows. She shook her head. "No."

Then there was no sound except for rain and the flick of tires on the wet road. Anna was lost in contemplation again. She stroked the tiny fist. "Have we chosen a name for her?"

A passing headlight highlighted one side of his face, the side with the pirate patch over his eye.

"Her name is Safiyah."

"Sophia?"

"Yes, it is a name that will not seem strange to English ears. Safi is not so far from Sophy."

"Did we know it was going to be a girl?" she whispered, coughing as feeling closed her throat.

He glanced at her, the sleeping baby nestled so trustingly against her. "You are almost asleep," he said. "Let me take her."

He leaned over to lift the child from her arms. He was gentle and tender with her, but at the same time firm and confident, making Anna feel how safe the baby was with him.

Jonathan. "Oh!" she whispered.

"What is it?" Ishaq Ahmadi said, in a voice of quiet command. "What have you remembered?"

"Oh, just when you took the baby from me...I..." She pressed her hands to her eyes. Not when he took the baby, but the sight of him holding the infant as if he loved her and was prepared to protect and defend the innocent.

"Tell me!"

She lifted her head to see him watching her with a look of such intensity she gasped. Suddenly she wondered how much of her past she had confided to her husband. Was he a tolerant man? Or had he wanted her to lie about her life before him?

She stammered, "Did—did—?" She swallowed, her mouth suddenly dry. "Did I tell you about...Jonathan? Jonathan Ryder?"

But even before the words were out she knew the answer was no.

Three

"Tell me now," Ishaq Ahmadi commanded softly.

She wanted to lean against him, wanted to feel his arm around her, protecting her, holding her. She must have that right, she told herself, but somehow she lacked the courage to ask him to hold her.

She had always wanted to pat the tigers at the zoo, too. Now it seemed as if she had finally found her very own personal tiger...but she had forgotten how she'd tamed him. And until she remembered that, something told her it would be wise to treat him with caution.

"Tell me about Jonathan Ryder."

Nervously she clasped her hands together, and suddenly a detail that had been nagging at her in the distance leapt into awareness.

"Why aren't I wearing a wedding ring?" she demanded, holding both hands spread out before her and staring at them. On her fingers were several silver rings of varied design. But none was a wedding band.

There was a long, pregnant pause. Through the glass panel separating them from the driver, she heard a phone ring. The driver answered and spoke into it, giving instructions, it seemed.

Still he only looked at her.

"Did I...have we split up?"

"No."

Just the bare syllable. His jaw seemed to tense, and she thought he threw her a look almost of contempt.

"About Jonathan," he prompted again.

If they were having trouble in the marriage, was it because he was jealous? Or because she had not told him things, shared her troubles?

She thought, *If I never told him about Jonathan, I should have.*

"Jonathan—Jonathan and I were going together for about a year. We were talking about moving in together, but it wasn't going to be simple, because we both owned a flat, and...well, it was taking us time to decide whether to sell his, or mine, or sell both and find somewhere new."

Her heart began to beat with anxiety. "It is really more than two years ago?"

"How long does it seem to you?"

"It feels as if we split up about six months ago. And then..."

"Why did you split up?"

"Because...did I not tell you any of this?"

"Tell me again," he repeated softly. "Perhaps the recital will help your memory recover."

She wanted to tell him. She wanted to share it with him, to make him her soul mate. Surely she must have told him, and he had understood? She couldn't have married a man who didn't understand, whom she couldn't share her deepest feelings with?

"I got pregnant unexpectedly." She looked at him and remembered that, sophisticated as he looked, he was from a different culture. "Does that shock you?"

"I am sure that birth control methods fail every day," he said.

That was not what she meant, but she lacked the courage to be more explicit.

"Having kids wasn't part of deciding to live together or anything, but once it happened I just—knew it was what I wanted. It was crazy, but it made me so happy! Jonathan didn't see it that way. He didn't want..."

Her head drooped, and the sound of suddenly increasing rain against the windows filled the gap.

"Didn't want the child?"

"He wanted me to have an abortion. He said we weren't ready yet. His career hadn't got off the ground, neither had mine. He—oh, he had a hundred reasons why it would be right one day but wasn't now. In a lot of ways he was right. But..." Anna shrugged. "I couldn't do it. We argued and argued. I understood him, but he never understood me. Never tried to. I kept saying, there's more to it than you want to believe. He wouldn't listen."

"And did he convince you?"

"He booked an appointment for me, drove me down to the women's clinic.... On the way, he stopped the car at a red light, and—I got out," she murmured, staring at nothing. "And just kept walking. I didn't look back, and Jonathan didn't come after me. He never called again. Well, once," she amended. "A couple of months later he phoned to ask if I planned to name him as the father on the birth certificate.''

She paused, but Ishaq Ahmadi simply waited for her to continue. ''He said…he said he had no intention of being saddled with child support for the next twenty years. He had a job offer from Australia, and he was trying to decide whether to accept or not. And that was one of the criteria. If I was going to put his name down, he'd go to Australia.''

His hair glinted in the beam of a streetlight. They were on a highway. ''And what did you say?''

She shook her head. ''I hung up. We've never spoken since.''

''Did he go to Australia?''

''I never found out. I didn't want to know.'' She amended that. ''Didn't care.'' She glanced out the window.

''Where are we going?'' she asked. ''Where is the hospital?''

''North of London, in the country. Tell me what happened then.''

Her eyes burned. ''My friends were really, really great about it—do you know Cecile and Lisbet?''

''How could your husband not know your friends?''

''Are Cecile and Philip married?''

He gazed at her. ''Tell me about the baby, Anna.''

There was something in his attitude that made her uncomfortable. She murmured, ''I'm sorry if you didn't know before this. But maybe if you didn't, you should have. ''

''Undoubtedly.''

''*Did* you know?''

He paused. ''No.''

Anna bit her lip. She wondered if it was perhaps because she hadn't told him that she had reverted to this memory tonight. Had it weighed on her throughout the new pregnancy? Had fears for her new baby surfaced and found no outlet?

"Everything was fine. I was pretty stressed in some ways, but I didn't really have doubts about what I was doing. At the very end something went wrong. I was in labour for hours and hours, and then it was too late for a Caesarean...they used the Ventouse cap."

She swallowed, and her voice was suddenly expressionless. "It caused a brain haemorrhage. My baby died. They let me hold him, and he was...but there was a terrible bruise on his head...as if he was wearing a purple cap."

No tears came to moisten the heat of her eyes or ease the pain in her heart. Her perfect baby, paper white and too still, but looking as if he was thinking very hard and would open his eyes any moment...

She wondered if that was how she had ended up giving birth in the back of a cab. Perhaps it was fear of a repetition that had made her leave it too late to get to the hospital.

"Why weren't you there?" she asked, surfacing from her thoughts to look at him. "Why didn't you take me to the hospital?"

"I flew in from abroad this evening. And this was six weeks ago?"

"That's how it feels to me. I feel as though it's the weekend I'm supposed to be going on that job to France, and that was about six weeks after the baby died. How long ago is that, really?"

"Did you ever feel, Anna, that you would like to— adopt a child? A baby to fill the void created by the death of your own baby?"

"It wouldn't have done me any good if I had. Why are you asking me these questions now? Didn't we—"

"Did you think of it—applying for adoption? Trying to find a baby?"

"No." She shook her head. "Sometimes in the street, you know, you pass a woman with a baby, or even a woman who's pregnant, and you just want to scream *It's not fair,* but—no, I just…I got pretty depressed, I wasn't doing much of anything till Lisbet conjured up this actor friend who wanted a mural in his place in France."

She leaned over to caress the baby with a tender hand, then bent to kiss the perfectly formed little head. "Oh, you are so beautiful!" she whispered. She looked up, smiling. "I hope I remember soon. I can't bear not knowing everything about her!"

He started to speak, and just then the car drew to a stop. Heavy rain was now thundering down on the roof, and all she could see were streaks of light from tall spotlights in the distance, as if they had entered some compound.

"Are we here?"

"Yes," he said, as the door beside her opened. The dark-skinned chauffeur stood in the rain with a large black umbrella, and Anna quickly slipped out onto a pavement that was leaping with water. She heard the swooping crack of another umbrella behind her. Then she was being ushered up a curiously narrow flight of steps and through a doorway.

She glanced around her as Ishaq, with the baby, came in the door behind her.

It was very curious for a hospital reception. A low-ceilinged room, softly lighted, lushly decorated in natural wood and rich tapestries. A row of matching little curtains seemed to be covering several small windows at intervals along the wall. There was a bar at one end, by a small dining table with chairs. In front of her she saw a cluster of plush armchairs around a coffee table. Anna frowned, trying to piece together a coherent interpretation of the scene, but her mind was very slow to function. She could almost hear her own wheels grinding.

A woman in an Eastern outfit that didn't look at all like a medical uniform appeared in the doorway behind the bar and came towards them. She spoke something in a foreign language, smiling and gesturing towards the sofa cluster. She moved to the entrance door behind them, dragged it fully shut and turned a handle. Still the pieces refused to fall into place.

Anna obediently sank down into an armchair. A second woman appeared. Dressed in another softly flowing outfit, with warm brown eyes and a very demure smile, she nodded and then descended upon the baby in Ishaq Ahmadi's arms. She laughed and admired and then exchanged a few sentences of question and answer with Ishaq before taking the infant in her own arms and, with another smile all around, disappeared whence she had come.

"What's going on?" Anna demanded, as alarm began to shrill behind the drowsy numbness in her head.

"Your bed is ready," Ishaq murmured, bending over her and slipping his hands against her hips. At the touch of his strong hands she involuntarily smiled. "In a few minutes you can lie down and get some sleep."

His hands lifted and she blinked stupidly while he drew two straps up and snapped them together over her hips. Under her feet she felt the throb of engines, and at last the pieces fell together.

"This isn't a hospital, this is a plane!" Anna cried wildly.

Four

"Let me out," Anna said, her hands snapping to the seat belt.

Ishaq Ahmadi fastened his own seat belt and moved one casual hand to still hers as she struggled with the mechanism. "We have been cleared for immediate take-off," he said.

"Stop the plane and let me off. Tell them to turn back," she cried, pushing at his hand, which was no longer casual. "Where are you taking us? I want my baby!"

"The woman you saw is a children's nurse. She is taking care of the baby, and no harm will come to her. Try and relax. You are ill, you have been in an accident."

Her stomach churned sickly, her head pounded with pain, but she had to ignore that. She stared at him and showed her teeth. "Why are you doing this?" A sudden wrench released her seat belt, and Anna thrust herself to her feet.

Ishaq Ahmadi's eyes flashed with irritation. "You know very well you have no right to such a display. You know you are in the wrong, deeply in the wrong." He stabbed a forefinger at the chair she had just vacated. "Sit down before you fall down!"

With a little jerk, the plane started taxiing. "No!" Anna cried. She staggered and clutched the chair back, and with an oath Ishaq Ahmadi snapped a hand up and clasped her wrist in an unbreakable hold.

"Help me!" she screamed. "Help, help!"

A babble of concerned female voices arose from behind a bulkhead, and in another moment the hostess appeared in the doorway behind the bar.

"Sit down, Anna!"

The hostess cried a question in Arabic, and Ishaq Ahmadi answered in the same language. *"Laa, laa, madame,"* the woman said, gently urgent, and approached Anna with a soothing smile, then tried what her little English would do.

"Seat, madame, very dingerous. Pliz. seat."

"I want to get off!" Anna shouted at the uncomprehending woman. "Stop the plane! Tell the captain it's a mistake!"

The woman turned to Ishaq Ahmadi with a question, and he shook his head on a calm reply. Of course he had the upper hand if the cabin crew spoke only Arabic. Anna had a dim idea that all pilots had to speak English, but what were her chances of making it to the cockpit?

And if it was a private jet, the captain would be on Ishaq Ahmadi's payroll. No doubt they all knew he was kidnapping his own wife.

Ahmadi got to his feet, holding Anna's wrist in a grip

that felt like steel cables, and forced her to move towards him.

The plane slowed, and they all stiffened as the captain's voice came over the intercom—but it was only with the obvious Arabic equivalent of "Cabin staff, prepare for takeoff." Ishaq Ahmadi barked something at the hostess and, with a consoling smile at Anna, she returned to her seat behind the bulkhead.

Ishaq Ahmadi sank into his seat again, dragging Anna inexorably down onto his lap. "You are being a fool," he said. "No one is going to hurt you if you do not hurt yourself."

She was sitting on him now as if he were the chair, and his arms were firmly locked around her waist, a human seat belt. The heat of his body seeped into hers, all down her spine and the backs of her thighs, his arms resting across her upper thighs, hands clasped against her abdomen.

Wherever her body met his, there was nothing but muscle. There was no give, no ounce of fat. It was like sitting on hot poured metal fresh from the forge, hardened, but the surface still slightly malleable. The stage when a sculptor removes the last, tiny blemishes, puts on the finishing touches. She had taken a course in metal sculpture at art college, and she had always loved the metal at this stage, Anna remembered dreamily. The heat, the slight surface give in something so innately strong, had a powerful sensual pull.

She realized she was half tranced. She felt very slow and stupid, and as the adrenaline in her body ebbed, her headache caught up with her again. She twisted to try to look over her shoulder into his face.

"Why are you doing this?" she pleaded.

His voice, close to her ear, said, "So that you and the baby will be safe."

She was deeply, desperately tired, she was sick and hurt, and she wanted to believe she was safe with him. The alternative was too confusing and too terrible.

The engines roared up and the jet leapt forward down the runway. In a very short time, compared to the lumbering commercial aircraft she was used to, they had left the ground.

As his hold slackened but still kept her on his lap, she turned to Ishaq Ahmadi. Her face was only inches from his, her mouth just above his own wide, well-shaped lips. She swallowed, feeling the pull.

"Where are you taking me?"

"Home." His gaze was steady. "You are tired. You will want to lie down," he murmured, and when the jet levelled out, he helped her to her feet and stood up. He took her arm and led her through a doorway.

They entered a large, beautifully appointed stateroom, with a king-size bed luxuriously made with snowy-white and deep blue linens that were turned down invitingly. There were huge, fluffy white pillows.

It was like a fantasy. Except for the little windows and the ever-present hum you would never know you were on a plane. A top hotel, maybe. Beautiful natural woods, luscious fabrics, mirrors, soft lighting, and, through an open door, a marble bathroom.

"I guess I married a millionaire," Anna murmured. "Or is this just some bauble a friend has loaned you?"

"Here are night things for you," he said, indicating pyjamas and a bathrobe, white with blue trim, that were lying across the foot of the sapphire-blue coverlet. "Do you need help to undress?"

Anna looked at the bed longingly and realized she was

dead on her feet. And that was no surprise, after what she had apparently been through in the past few hours.

"No," she said.

She began fumbling with a button, but her fingers didn't seem to work. Even the effort of holding her elbow bent seemed too much, so she dropped her arm and stood there a moment, gazing at nothing.

"I will call the hostess," Ishaq Ahmadi said. And that, perversely, made her frown.

"Why?" she demanded. "You're my husband, aren't you?"

His eyes probed her, and she shrugged uncomfortably. "Why are you looking at me like that? Why don't you want to touch me?"

She wanted him to touch her. Wanted his heat on her body again, because when he touched her, even in anger, she felt safe.

He made no reply, merely lifted his hands, brushed aside her own feeble fingers which were again fumbling with the top button, and began to undo her shirt.

"Have you stopped wanting me?" she wondered aloud.

His head bent over his task, only his eyes shifted to connect with hers. "You are overplaying your hand," he advised softly, and she felt another little thrill of danger whisper down her spine. Her brain evaded the discomfort.

"Did you commission work from me or something? Is that how we met?" she asked. She specialized in Mediterranean and Middle Eastern designs, painting entire rooms to give the impression that you were standing on a balcony overlooking the Gulf of Corinth, or in the Alhambra palace. But what were the chances that a wealthy Arab would want a Western woman to paint trompe l'oeil fifteenth-century mosaic arches on his palace walls when he probably had the real thing?

"We met by accident."

"Oh." She wanted him to clarify, but couldn't concentrate. Not when his hands were grazing the skin of her breasts, revealed as he unbuttoned her shirt. She looked into his face, bent close over hers, but his eyes remained on his task. His aftershave was spicy and exotic.

"It seems strange that you have the right to do this when you feel like a total stranger," she observed.

"You insisted on it," he reminded her dryly. He seemed cynically amused by her. He still didn't believe that she had forgotten, and she had no idea why. What reason could she have for pretending amnesia? It seemed very crazy, unless...unless she had been running away from him.

Perhaps it was fear that had caused her to lose her memory. Psychologists did say you sometimes forgot when remembering was too painful.

"Was I running away from you, Ishaq?"

"You tell me the answer."

She shook her head. "They say the unconscious remembers everything, but..."

"I am very sure that yours does," Ishaq Ahmadi replied, pulling the front of her shirt open to reveal her small breasts in a lacy black bra.

She knew by the involuntary intake of his breath that he was not unaffected. His jaw clenched and he stripped the shirt from her, his breathing irregular.

She wasn't one for casual sex, and she had never been undressed by a stranger, which was what this felt like. The sudden blush of desire that suffused her was disconcerting. So her body remembered, even if her conscious mind did not. Anna bit her lip. What would it be like, love with a man who seemed like a total stranger? Would her body instinctively recognize his touch?

She realized that she wanted him to make the demand on her. The thought was sending spirals of heat all through her. But instead of drawing her into his arms, he turned his back to toss her shirt onto a chair.

"What will I remember about loving you, Ishaq?" she whispered.

He didn't answer, and she turned away, dejected, overcome with fatigue and reluctant to think, and lifted her arms behind her to the clasp of her bra. She winced as a bruised elbow prevented her.

Her breath hissed with the pain. "You'll have to undo this."

She felt his hands at work on the hook of her bra, that strange, half electrifying, half comforting heat that made her yearn for something she could not remember. She wondered if they *had* been sexually estranged. She said, "Is there a problem between us, Ishaq?"

"You well know what the problem between us is. But it is not worth discussing now," he said, his voice tight.

She thought, *It's serious.* Her heart pinched painfully with regret. To think that she had had the luck to marry a man like this and then had not been able to make it work made her desperately sad. He was like a dream come to life, but…she had obviously got her dream and then not been able to live in it.

If they made up now, when she could not remember any of the grievances she might have, would that make it easier when she regained her full memory?

As the bra slipped away from her breasts, Anna let it fall onto the bed, then turned to face him, lifting her arms to his shoulders.

"Do you still love me?" she whispered.

His arms closed around her, his hands warm on her bare skin. Her breasts pressed against his silk shirt as her arms cupped his head. He looked down into her upturned face with a completely unreadable expression in his eyes.

"Do you want me, Ishaq?" she begged, wishing he would kiss her. Why was he so remote? She felt the warmth of his body curl into hers and it was so right.

A corner of that hard, full mouth went up and his eyes became sardonic. "Believe me, I want you, or you would not be here."

"What have I done?" she begged. "I don't remember anything. Tell me what I've done to make you so angry with me."

His mouth turned up with angry contempt. "What do you hope to gain with this?" he demanded with subdued ferocity, and then, as if it were completely against his will, his grip tightened painfully on her, and with a stifled curse he crushed his mouth against her own.

He was neither gentle nor tender. His kiss and his hands were punishing, and a part of her revelled in the knowing that, whatever his intentions, he could not resist her. She opened her mouth under his, accepting the violent thrust of his hungry, angry tongue, and felt the rasp of its stroking run through her with unutterable thrill, as if it were elsewhere on her body that he kissed her.

Just for a moment she was frightened, for if one kiss could do this to her, how would she sustain his full, passionate lovemaking? She would explode off the face of the earth. His hand dropped to force her against him, while his hardened body leapt against her. She tore her mouth away from his, gasping for the oxygen to feed the fire that wrapped her in its hot, licking fingers.

"Ishaq!" she cried, wild with a passion that seemed to her totally new, as the heat of his hands burned her back, her hips, clenched against the back of her neck with a firm possessiveness that thrilled her. "Oh, my love!"

Then suddenly he was standing away from her, his hands on her wrists pulling her arms down, his eyes burning into hers with a cold, hard, suspicious fury that froze the hot rivers of need coursing through her.

"What is it?" she pleaded. "Ishaq, what have I done?"

He smiled and shook his head, a curl of admiring contempt lifting his lip. "You are unbelievable," he said. "Where have you learned such arts, I wonder?"

Anna gasped. He suspected her of having a lover? Could it be true? She shook her head. It wasn't possible. Whatever he might suspect, whatever he might have done, whatever disagreement was between them, she knew that she was simply not capable of taking a lover while pregnant with her husband's child.

"From you, I suppose," she tried, but he brushed that aside with a snort of such contemptuous disbelief she could go no further.

"Tell me why you won't love me," she challenged softly, but nothing was going to crack his angry scorn now.

"But you have just given birth, Anna. We must resign ourselves to no lovemaking for several weeks, isn't it so?"

She drew back with a little shock. "Oh! Yes, I—" She shook her head. He could still kiss her, she thought. He could hold her. Maybe that was the problem, she thought. A man who would only touch his wife if he wanted sex. She would certainly hate that.

"I wish I could *remember!*"

He reached down and lifted up the silky white pyjama top, holding it while she obediently slipped her arms inside. He had himself well under control now, he was as impersonal as a nurse, and she tasted tears in her throat for the waste of such wild passion.

Funny how small her breasts were. Last time, they had been so swollen with the pregnancy...hadn't they? She remembered the ache of heavy breasts with a pang of misery, and then reminded herself, *But that's all in the past. I have a baby now.*

"Do you think I'll remember?" she whispered, gazing into his face as he buttoned the large pyjama shirt. It seemed almost unbearable that she should feel such pain for a baby who had died two years ago and not remember the birth of the beautiful creature who was so alive, and whose cry she could suddenly hear over the subdued roar of the engines.

"I am convinced of it."

"She has inherited your birthmark," she murmured with a smile, touching his eye with a feather caress and feeling her heart contract with tenderness. "Is that usual?"

He finished the last button and lifted his eyes to hers. "What is it you hope to discover?" he asked, his hands pulling at her belt with cool impersonality. "The... Ahmadi mark," he said. "It proves beyond a doubt that Safiyah and I come of the same blood. Does that make you wary?"

"Did you think I had a lover?" she asked. "Did you think it was someone else's child?"

His eyes darkened with the deepest suspicion she had yet seen in them, and she knew she had struck a deep chord. "You know that much, do you?"

Somewhere inside her an answering anger was born. "You're making it pretty obvious! Does the fact that you've now been proven wrong make you think twice about things, Ishaq?"

"Wrong?" he began, then broke off, stripped the suede pants down her legs and off, and knelt to hold the pyjama bottoms for her. His hair was cut over the top in a thick cluster of black curls whose vibrant health reflected the lampglow. Anna steadied herself with a hand on his shoulder and stifled the whispering desire that melted through her thighs at the nearness of him.

They were too big. In fact, they were men's pyjamas.

"Why don't I have a pair of pyjamas on the plane?" she asked.

"Perhaps you never wear them."

He spoke softly, but the words zinged to her heart. She shivered at the thought that she slept naked next to Ishaq Ahmadi. She wondered what past delights were lurking, waiting to be remembered.

"And you do?"

"I often fly alone," he said.

It suddenly occurred to her that he had told her absolutely nothing all night. Every single question had somehow been parried. But when she tried to formulate words to point this out, her brain refused.

Even at its tightest the drawstring was too big for her slim waist, and the bunched fabric rested precariously on the slight swell of her hips. Ishaq turned away and lifted the feathery covers of the bed to invite her to slip into the white, fluffy nest.

She moved obediently, groaning as her muscles protested at even this minimal effort. Once flat on her back, however, she sighed with relief. "Oh, that feels good!"

Ishaq bent to flick out the bedside lamp, but her hand stopped him. "Bring me the baby," she said.

"You are tired and the baby is asleep."

"But she was crying. She may be hungry."

"I am sure the nurse has seen to that."

"But I want to breast-feed her!" Anna said in alarm.

He blinked as if she had surprised him, but before she could be sure of what she saw in his face his eyelids hooded his expression.

"Tomorrow will not be too late for that, Anna. Sleep now. You need sleep more than anything."

On the last word he put out the light, and it was impossible to resist the drag of her eyelids in the semi-darkness. "Kiss her for me," she murmured, as Lethe beckoned.

"Yes," he said, straightening.

She frowned. "Don't we kiss good-night?"

A heartbeat, two, and then she felt the touch of his lips against her own. Her arms reached to embrace him, but he avoided them and was standing upright again. She felt deprived, her heart yearning towards him. She tried once more.

"I wish you'd stay with me."

"Good night, Anna." Then the last light went out, a door opened and closed, and she was alone with the dark and the deep drone of the engines.

Five

"Hurry, hurry!"

The voices and laughter of the women mirrored the bubble of excitement in her heart, and she felt the corners of her mouth twitch up in anticipation.

"I'm coming!" she cried.

But they were impatient. Already they were spilling out onto the balcony, whose arching canopy shaded it from the harsh midday sun. Babble arose from the courtyard below: the slamming of doors, the dance of hooves, the shouts of men. Somewhere indoors, musicians tuned their instruments.

"He is here! He arrives!" the women cried, and she heard the telltale scraping of the locks and bars and the rumble of massive hinges in the distance as the gates opened wide. A cry went up and the faint sound of horses' hooves thudded on the hot, still air.

"They are here already! Hurry, hurry!" cried the women.

She rose to her feet at last, all in white except for the tinkling, delicate gold at her forehead, wrists, and ankles, a white rose in her hand. Out on the balcony the women were clustered against the carved wooden arabesques of the screen that hid them from the admiring, longing male eyes below.

She approached the screen. Through it the women had a view of the entire courtyard running down to the great gates. These were now open in welcome, with magnificently uniformed sentinels on each side, and the mounted escort approached and cantered between them, flags fluttering, armour sending blinding flashes of intense sunlight into unwary eyes.

They rode in pairs, rank upon rank, leading the long entourage, their horses' caparisons increasing in splendour with the riders' rank. Then at last came riders in the handsomest array, mounted on spirited, prancing horses.

"There he is!" a voice cried, and a cheer began in several throats and swelled.

Her eyes were irresistibly drawn to him. He was sternly handsome, his flowing hair a mass of black curls, his beard neat and pointed, his face grave but his eyes alight with humour. His jacket was rich blue, the sleeves ruched with silver thread; his silver breastplate glowed almost white. Across it, from shoulder to hip, a deep blue sash lay against the polished metal.

The sword at his hip was thickly encrusted with jewels. His fingers also sparkled, but no stone was brighter than his dark eyes as he glanced up towards the balcony as if he knew she was there. His eyes met hers, challenged and conquered in one piercingly sweet moment.

Her heart sprang in one leap from her breast and into his keeping.

As he rode past below, the white rose fell from her helpless hand. A strong dark hand plucked it from the air and drew it to his lips, and she cried softly, as though the rose were her own white throat.

He did not glance up again, but thrust the rose carefully inside the sash, knowing she watched. She clung to the carved wooden arabesques, her strength deserting her.

"So fierce, so handsome!" she murmured. "As strong and powerful as his own black destrier, I dare swear!"

The laughter of the women chimed around her ears. "Ah, truly, and love is blind and sees white as black!" they cried in teasing voices. "Black? But the prince's horse is white! Look again, mistress!"

She looked in the direction of their gesturing, as the entourage still came on. In the centre of the men on black horses rode one more richly garbed than all. His armour glowed with beaten gold, his richly jewelled turban was cloth of gold, ropes of pearls draped his chest, rubies and emeralds adorned his fingers and ears. His eyebrows were strong and black, his jaw square, his beard thick and curling. He lifted a hand in acknowledgement as those riders nearest him tossed gold and silver coins to the cheering crowd.

Her women were right. Her bridegroom was mounted on a prancing stallion as white as the snows of Shir.

"Saba'ul khair, madame."

Anna rolled over drowsily and blinked while intense sunlight poured into the cabin from the little portholes as, *whick whick whick whick,* the air hostess pulled aside the curtains.

Her eyes frowned a protest. "Is it morning already?"

The woman turned from her completed task and smiled. "We here, madame."

Anna leapt out of the bed, wincing with the protest from her bruised muscles, and craned to peer out the porthole. They were flying over water, deep sparkling blue water dotted with one or two little boats, and were headed towards land. She saw a long line of creamy beach, lush green forest, a stretch of mixed golden and grey desert behind, and, in the distance, snow-topped mountains casting a spell at once dangerous and thrilling.

"Where on earth are we?"

"Shower, madame?"

"Oh, yes!"

The hostess smiled with the pleasure of someone who had recently memorized the word but had produced it without any real conviction and was now delighted to see that the sounds did carry meaning, and led her into the adjoining bathroom.

Anna waved away her offer of help, stripped and got into the shower stall, then stood gratefully under the firm spray of water, first hot, then cool. This morning her body was sore all over, but her headache was much less severe.

Her memory wasn't in much better shape, though. It still stopped dead on the night before she had been due to leave for France. Now, however, she could remember a shopping expedition with Lisbet during the afternoon, going home to dress, meeting Cecile and Lisbet at the Riverfront Restaurant. Now she could remember leaving the restaurant, and almost immediately seeing a cab pull up across the street. "You take that one, Anna, it's fac-

ing your direction,'' Lisbet had commanded, and she had
dashed across the street...

She could remember *that* as if it were yesterday.

Of the two years that had followed that night there
was still absolutely nothing in her memory. Not one image had surfaced overnight to flesh out the bare outline
Ishaq Ahmadi had given of her life since.

When she tried to make sense of it all, her head
pounded unmercifully. The whole thing made her feel
eerie, creepy.

Last night's dream surfaced cloudily in her mind. She
had the feeling that the man on the black horse was Ishaq
Ahmadi.

She wondered if that held some clue about her first
meeting with him. Had she seen him from a distance
and fallen in love with him?

That she could believe. If ever there was a man you
could take one look at and know you'd met your destiny,
Ishaq Ahmadi was it. But he was definitely keeping
something from her. If once they had loved each other,
and she certainly accepted that, there was a problem
now. It was in his eyes every time he looked at her. His
look said she was a criminal—attractive and desirable,
perhaps, but not in the least to be trusted.

Anna winced as she absently scrubbed a sore spot.
The accident must have been real enough. Her body
seemed to be one massive bruise now, and she ached as
if she had been beaten with a bat.

That thought stilled her for a moment. Panic whispered along her nerves. Suppose a man had beaten his
pregnant, runaway wife and wanted to avoid the con-
sequences...

Anna reminded herself suddenly that they would be
landing soon and turned off the water. In the bedroom

mirror she stared at herself. She was still too thin, just as she had been after losing her baby two years ago. There were dark circles under her eyes to match the bruising on her body.

She had a tendency to lose weight with unhappiness. Anna sighed. By the look of her, she had been deeply unhappy recently, as unhappy as when she had lost Jonathan's baby. But the question was—had she lost the weight *before* she left Ishaq, or *after?*

Her clothes were lying on the neatly made bed. The shirt had been mended, the suede pants neatly brushed. Anna's breath hissed between her teeth. *It's terrific, Anna. Stop dithering and buy it!*

She had bought this shirt on that Friday afternoon and worn it that night to dinner in the Riverfront. These were the clothes that she could remember putting on that night. Her jacket was missing, that was all.

Anna stood staring, her heart in her throat. With careful precision she reached down and picked up the shirt. The tag was completely fresh. Either she was confusing two separate memories in her mind...or she and Lisbet had bought this shirt yesterday.

"Ah, I was just coming for you," Ishaq Ahmadi said, as she opened the door. "We are about to land. Come and sit down."

He sank into an armchair as Anna obeyed. Beside him the nurse sat with the baby in her arms. The air hostess was behind the bar. Anna could smell coffee.

"I'll take the baby," she said, holding out her arms.

To her fury, the nurse glanced up at Ishaq Ahmadi.

"Give me the baby," she ordered firmly.

Ishaq Ahmadi nodded all but invisibly, and the nurse passed the baby over. Safiyah was sleeping. Anna stroked her, the hungry memory of the son who had not lived assuaged by the touch of the tiny, helpless body, the feather-soft skin, the curling perfect hand. Her mouth, full, soft and tender, was twitching with her dream, as were her dark, beautifully arched eyebrows.

Anna glanced up at Ishaq Ahmadi and thought that he had probably once had the same mouth. But now its fullness was disciplined, its softness was lost in firmness of purpose, its tenderness had disappeared.

She wanted to believe that he was telling the truth. That he was her husband and that this was the child of their mutual love. She wanted to believe the evidence of the shirt was somehow false. Her heart was deeply touched by the baby, the man. It was possible, after all. She might have packed the shirt away, left everything with friends, perhaps, and then, fleeing to those friends from her husband, had recourse to her old clothes.

Or confusing the memory of two different shopping trips might be a sign that her more recent memory was returning.

"Where are we?" she asked, watching out the window as the wheels touched down in the familiar chirping screech of arrival.

Palm trees, sunlight, low white buildings, the name on the terminal building in scrolling green Arabic script, the red Roman letters underneath moving past too fast for her to read…

"We are in Barakat al Barakat, the capital of the Barakat Emirates," he said.

"Oh!" She had heard of the Emirates, of course. But she knew almost nothing about the country except that it was ruled by three young princes who had inherited jointly from their father. "Is it—is it your…our… home?"

"Of course."

"Are you Barakati?"

"Of course," he said again.

She had some faint idea that amnesia victims didn't forget general knowledge, only personal. So how was it that she couldn't remember anything about the country that was her home? Her skin began to shiver with nervous fear.

A few minutes later the door opened. Bright sunshine and fresh air streamed into the aircraft, bringing with it the smell of hot tarmac and fuel and the sea and...in spite of those mundane odours, some other, secret scent that seemed full of mystery and magic and the East.

An official came deferentially aboard in an immigration check that was clearly token, and her lack of a passport wasn't even remarked on. Anna flicked a glance at Ishaq as the men spoke. Well, it wasn't surprising that he was as important as that. She could have guessed it just by looking at him.

Down below a sparkling white limousine waited, and the chauffeur and a cluster of other people were standing on the tarmac.

"Give the baby to the nurse," Ishaq Ahmadi said when the official departed with a nod and smile. Anna immediately clutched Safiyah tight.

"She's sleeping," she protested, with the sudden, nameless conviction that if she obeyed him she would never see the baby again.

"Give the baby to the nurse," he repeated, approaching her.

Anna evaded him, and stepped to the open doorway of the aircraft. "If you try to take her away from me, I'll scream. How far does your influence go with the people out there?"

Out on the tarmac her appearance in the doorway caused a little stir. People were gazing her way now.

Ishaq's jaw tightened and his eyes flashed at her with deep, suspicious anger. "How cunning you think you are. So be it."

He came up beside her and, with an arm around her waist, stepped with her through the door onto the top step. He stopped there, and to Anna's utter amazement, two of the men below produced cameras and began snapping photos of them.

"What on earth—?" she exclaimed.

She heard him murmur what sounded like a curse. "Smile," he ordered, with a grimness that electrified her. "Smile or I will throttle you in front of them all."

"What is it?" she whispered desperately. "Who are you?" and then, crazily, after a beat, "Who am I?"

"You will not say anything, anything at all, to the journalists."

"Journalists?"

She stared at the photographers in stunned, stupid dismay. What was going on? What could explain what was happening to her?

Ishaq went down the narrow stairs one step ahead of her, turning to guide her down. His hand was commanding, and almost cruel, against her wrist. In crazy contradiction to her feelings, the sun was heaven, the breeze delicious. Light bounced from the tarmac, the car, the plane with stupefying brilliance.

A man with a camera jumped right in front of them, and Anna recoiled with a jolt. "Excuse me!" she murmured, outraged, but he only bent closer. "Please, you'll disturb the baby!"

"Ingilisiya!" someone cried. *"Man hiya?"*

"Louk these way, pliz!"

The chauffeur had leapt to open the door of the limousine, and Ishaq shepherded her quickly to it. Before Anna's eyes could adjust to the blinding sunlight she was in the dimness of the car, the door shutting her and the baby behind tinted glass.

The voices were still calling questions. She heard Ishaq's deeper voice answer. A moment later he was slipping into the seat beside her. The nurse got into the front seat. The chauffeur slammed the last door and the limousine moved off as a cameraman bent to the window nearest Anna and snapped more pictures.

She turned to Ishaq.

"What's going on?" she said. "Why are there journalists here?"

"They are here because they permanently stake out the airport. The tabloids of the world like to print photographs of the Cup Companions of the princes of Barakat as they come and go in the royal jets. Usually it does not matter. But now—" he turned and looked at her with a cold accusation in his eyes that terrified her "—now they have a photograph of the baby."

Too late, she realized how foolish she had been to defy him when she knew nothing at all.

Six

The limousine turned between big gates into a tree-lined courtyard and swept to a stop in front of a two-storey villa in terra-cotta brick and stone with a tiled roof. The facade was lined with a row of peach-coloured marble pillars surmounted with the kind of curving scalloped arches Anna was more used to painting on clients' walls than seeing in real life.

Anna's heart began beating with hard, nervous jolts.

"Are we here?" she murmured, licking her lips.

It was a stupid question, and he agreed blandly, "We are here."

The door beside her opened. Anna got awkwardly out of the car, the baby in one arm. She stood looking around as Ishaq Ahmadi joined her. The courtyard was shaded with tall trees, shrubs and bushes, and cooled with a running fountain, and she had a sudden feeling of peace and safety.

"Is this your house?"

He bowed.

The baby woke up and started making grumpy noises, and the nurse appeared smilingly at Anna's side. She clucked sympathetically and made an adoring face at the complaining baby, then glanced up at Anna.

Anna resolutely shook her head and, with a defiant glance at Ishaq Ahmadi, shifted the baby up onto her shoulder. The baby wasn't going out of her sight till she understood a lot more than she did right now.

But he merely shrugged. A servant in white appeared through one of the arches, and they all moved into the shade of the portico.

Her eyes not quite accustomed to the cool gloom, she followed Ishaq Ahmadi into the house, through a spacious entrance hall and into the room beyond. There the little party stopped, while Ishaq Ahmadi conversed in low tones with the servant.

Anna opened her mouth with silent, amazed pleasure as she gazed around her. She had never seen a room so beautiful outside of a glossy architectural magazine. An expanse of floor patterned in tiles of different shades and designs, covered here and there with the most beautiful Persian carpets she had ever seen, stretched the length of a room at least forty feet long.

There were low tables, sofas covered in richly coloured, beautifully woven fabric like the most luscious of kilims, a black antique desk, and ornately carved and painted cabinets. Beautiful objets d'art sat in various niches, hung on the walls, stood on the floor.

A wall that was mostly window showed a roofed balcony overlooking a courtyard, in which she could see the leafy tops of trees moving gently in the breeze. The balcony was faced with a long series of marble pillars supporting sculpted and engraved stone arches and walled with intricately carved wooden screens. Beyond the treetops, she saw a delicious expanse of blue sky and sea.

Anna closed her eyes, looked again. Heaved a breath. She felt the deepest inner sense of coming home, as if after interminable exile. She belonged here. She sighed deeply.

She turned to Ishaq Ahmadi. "Why was I in London?" she asked.

He raised his eyebrows in enquiry.

"I've been doubting you and everything you told me," she explained. She closed her eyes and inhaled, letting out her breath on another deep sigh of relief. "But I *know* this is home. Why did I leave, Ishaq? Why did you have to bring me home by force?"

He looked at her with an unreadable expression.

"Do you tell me you remember the house?"

She shook her head. "No...not really *remember*. But I have the feeling of belonging."

"You are a mystery to me," he said flatly. "Give Safiyah to the nurse, and let us have something to drink."

The manservant was waiting silently, and Ishaq turned to him with a quiet order. With a slight bow the man moved away.

Meanwhile, with a caress, a kiss and a lingering glance, Anna let the nurse take Safiyah from her arms. The woman smiled reassuringly and disappeared through a doorway, leaving Anna alone with Ishaq Ahmadi.

Who was opening a door onto the magnificent balcony. "Come," he said, in a voice that instantly dispelled her more relaxed mood. "We have things to discuss."

He slipped off his suit jacket and tossed it onto a chair. She hesitated.

"My dear Anna, I assure you there is nothing to fear on the terrace," he said. "No one will throw you over the edge, though it is undoubtedly what you deserve."

What she deserved? Well, there was no answer she could make to that until she remembered more.

"Do I—have I left any clothes here?" Anna asked, rather than challenge him, feeling she could hardly bear any more wrangling. She couldn't remember ever having felt so tired. "Because if so, I'd like to change into something cooler."

"I am sure there is something to accommodate you. Shall I show you, or do you remember the way?" Then, correcting himself, "No, of course, you remember nothing."

She followed without challenging that mockery as he closed the door again and led her along half the length of the room and down a flight of stairs. There they walked along a hall and he opened a door.

If she had been hoping that the sight of her bedroom would trigger memories, that hope died as she entered the utterly impersonal room. For all the feeling that the room had been inhabited for centuries, there was not one photograph, one personal item on view. A few bottles of cosmetics on a dressing table were the only evidence that a woman slept here.

Well, she had known from the beginning that her marriage was troubled, so there was no reason to weep over this confirmation. Anna opened the door of a walk-in closet. Inside there were empty hangers, a few items in garment bags, a pair of sandals on the floor, a case neatly placed on a shelf.

So she had left him. She had preferred to run to Lon-

don to have her baby in the back of a cab rather than
stay with her handsome, passionate husband. Anna bit
her lip. And he had come and kidnapped her and brought
her back.

And she had no idea what that meant. Was she to be
a prisoner now? Would he keep the baby and banish her?
Or did he mean to try again to make a troubled marriage
work?

She heaved a sigh, but there was nothing to be gained
in trying to second-guess him. She was desperately dis-
advantaged by her memory loss, utterly dependent on
him for any description of what had gone wrong between
them.

Anna stripped, found some clean underwear in a
drawer. Bathing her face and wrists in cool water, she
paused and stared at her reflection. The face that looked
back at her was not the face of a woman who was happy
about having left her husband. Her eyes, normally a deep
sapphire blue, looked black with fatigue.

Or perhaps it was the marriage itself that had done
that to her.

The bra was too large for her. So she had been away
some time? She abandoned the bra, slipping into briefs
and a pale blue shirt and pant outfit in fine, cool cotton.
The shirt was long, Middle Eastern fashion. It was size
medium, and she had always bought petite. Anna shook
her head. Nothing fit, in any sense of the word. One of
the thong sandals was broken and she decided to go
barefoot.

Ishaq, having changed his suit for a similar outfit to
her own in unbleached white cotton, and wearing thong
sandals, was waiting for her outside the door.

He led her up to the main room again.

"What time is it?" she asked as he opened the balcony door. He obediently consulted the expensive watch on his wrist.

"Eleven."

"It feels more like six in the morning to me," she remarked, yawning and stepping outside. "I feel as if I've hardly slept."

From here she could see that the house was built in a squared C shape, and the broad balcony she was on ran around the three sides. One storey below, the courtyard was deliciously planted with trees and shrubs around a fountain. Beyond that there were other levels of the terrace, connected with arches and stone staircases, but mostly hidden from view by the greenery.

"It is seven in the morning in London. We have travelled east four hours," he replied.

She laughed at her own stupidity. "Oh, of course! Well, it just goes to show how confused I am!"

"No doubt."

The balcony was partitioned with beautiful wooden arches in the most amazing scrollwork. As they walked through one of these archways, Anna paused to touch the warm, glowing wood. "I paint arches like this on the walls of rooms," she observed. "But I've never before seen the real thing at first hand." Then she turned with a self-conscious laugh. "Well, but except—"

"Except for the fact that you live here," he said blandly.

They strolled through another arched partition, past windows leading to magical rooms. The house seemed very old, the brick and tiles well-worn by time and the tread of generations. Flowering plants tumbled in the profusion of centuries over the balcony and down to the terrace below, others climbed upwards past the opening towards the roof.

"Is this your family's house?"

"I inherited it from my father early this year."

"Oh, I'm sorry," she murmured, and then shook her head for how stupid that must sound to him—his wife, who must have attended the funeral with him, formally commiserating with him months after the fact.

"Sorry," she muttered. "It's hard to…"

Past the next archway a group of padded wicker chairs and loungers sat in comfortable array by a low table near a tiny fountain. Anna sighed. Her weary soul seemed to drink in peace so greedily she almost choked. There were flowers and flowering bushes everywhere. The breeze was delicious, full of wonderful scents. The sound of running water was such balm. The whole scene was luxuriously, radiantly, the Golden Age of Islam.

"This is beautiful!"

As he paused, Anna stepped to the scrollwork railing and glanced down. She could hardly believe that any normal process of life had brought her to such a magnificent home.

The villa was not small. That was an illusion at the entrance level. Below her on various levels now she had a clearer view of the stepped terraces full of flowers and greenery, and discovered that the courtyard led to a terrace with an inviting swimming pool unlike any she had ever seen. It was square, set with beautiful tiles both around the edge and under water.

The house was built on a thickly forested escarpment above a white sand beach that went for miles in both directions. Straight ahead of her, across the bay, she saw the smoky blue of distant hills. To the left, several miles away around a curving shoreline, she could just catch sight of the city. Beyond the bay the sea stretched forever, a rich varied turquoise that melted her anxiety and fatigue with each succeeding rush of a wave onto the sand.

The murmur of voices told her that the servant had reappeared, and she turned to see him pushing a trolley laden with a large cut-glass pitcher of juice and a huge bowl of lusciously ripe fruit. All the glass was frosted, as if everything had been chilled in a freezer. In a few deft movements, the man transferred the contents of the trolley to the table, and at a sign from his master, retired.

As she sank onto a lounger Ishaq poured a drink and handed it to her without speaking. She put the ice-cold glass to her lips and drank thirstily of the delicious nectar, then lifted her feet onto the lounger and leaned back into a ray of sun that slanted in. The breeze caressed her bare toes. Behind her head a flowering shrub climbed up a pillar and around an arch, a carpet of pink blossoms. Anna smiled involuntarily as the heavy tension in her lifted. For a moment she could forget her fears, could forget how he had brought her back home, and simply be.

He sank into the neighbouring chair, facing her at an angle, leaned back and watched her over the rim of his glass. His gaze set up another kind of tension in her, that warred with the peace she was just starting to feel.

"So, Anna," he said. She closed her eyes against the intensity she felt coming from him.

"Ishaq, I'm tired. Can't we leave this for another day?"

"Delay would suit you, would it? Why?"

"I really am at a loss to understand you," she sighed. "I'm here, the baby's here, what else do you want?"

He smiled. "You have no idea what it is I want?"

"If I don't even remember being married to you, how can I possibly be expected to guess what you want?"

she exploded. She could feel that she was very near breaking point.

"All right," he said. "Let us deal with what you do remember. As far as you remember, six weeks ago you gave birth and the child died."

She closed her eyes. There was no softness in his tone, and she wondered what kind of fool she had been to tell him, when she remembered nothing about what kind of man she had married. She must have had good reason for not telling him.

"That's how it feels."

"You were distraught over this loss."

"Yes, of course I was." She gave him a steady look, desperately hoping she would be able to hold her own against him. "And I remind you that you were not then part of my life, Ishaq."

"You wondered about the possibility of adopting a baby, but as a single woman you were not eligible through conventional channels."

"What?" She blinked at him. "I never said that! Why are you putting words in my mouth?"

"Anna, time is short. I intend to find the truth."

"The truth of *what?*" she exploded. "You keep telling me different things! How can you expect me to remember anything when you keep changing your story? What is it you want? Why is time short? Why are you playing these games? Why does the past matter now? It's over, isn't it?"

"You wanted a baby very much," he continued, as if she hadn't spoken.

"Ishaq—"

"You wanted a baby very much?"

"No, I did not want 'a baby' very much!" she said through her teeth. "I wanted *my* baby. My baby, Noah, who had every right to be born healthy and strong. I wanted him. I still do. You're going to have to face it, Ishaq. It's not something that gets wiped out by time. He's there in my heart, and he will never leave. Safiyah joins him there, but she won't replace him. Noah will always be in my heart.''

It was the first time she had spoken of the baby in such a way. Her urgency meant she spoke without defending herself against the pain, and her breath trembled in her throat and chest. She felt the lump of stone in her chest shift, and thought, *Six weeks of hiding from the hurt is one thing. But what kind of marriage can it be if I've been keeping this inside for two years?*

He was leaning forward, close to her, but staring down into the glass he held loosely between his spread knees.

"What drew us together?" she asked.

He lifted his eyes without moving his head.

"Have I never been able to be open about my feelings before? Is our relationship entirely based on sex or something?"

His eyes took on a look of admiration laced with contempt. "In spite of having no memory of me, you feel sexual attraction between us?"

"Don't you?" she countered.

His look back at her was darkly compelling, and her skin shivered. There *was* a strong sexual pull. And if that was the centre of their bond, it would be foolish to pretend to exclude it from their negotiations.

He reached out and ran a lean finger along her cheek, and the little answering shiver of her skin made her heart race. "Have you forgotten this?"

She gulped. Oh, how had she ever, ever managed to attract him? He was so masculine, so attractive, and yet with an air of risk, of danger. Like the powerful muscles under the tiger's deceptively furry coat, under Ishaq Ahmadi's virile masculinity there was a threat that he would make a bad enemy.

"It seems rather wasteful on my part," she agreed with a crazy grin, wanting him to smile without any edge. "But I'm afraid I have."

"Then I will have the pleasure of teaching you all over again," he said lazily. His hand cupped her cheek and he looked searchingly into her face. "Yes?"

She had no argument with that. She bit her lip, smiling into his eyes, nearer now. "It might even be the thing to bring back my memory."

"Yes, of course! That is the most ingenious excuse for making love that I have heard. But you always were imaginative, Anna."

His lips were almost touching hers, and her skin was cold and hot by turns. His hand cupped her neck and his fingers stroked the skin under the cap of hair.

She felt the rightness of it. She wanted to lean against him and feel the protection his strength offered, feel his arms clasp her firmly, feel herself pressed against his chest again. For in his arms, just as in this house, she knew she was home.

He moved his mouth away from hers without kissing her, moved to her eyelid. She closed her eyes in floating expectation, feeling the sun's heat and Ishaq's warmth as if both derived from one source.

He trailed light kisses across her eyelids, brushed her long curling lashes with his full lips, trailed a feathery touch down the bridge of her nose. His thumb urged her chin upwards, and her head fell back in helpless longing.

She felt starved for the touch, as if she had been longing for it for months. Years. Her arms wrapped him, her hand on his neck delighting in the touch of the thick hair.

At last he kissed her lips, and it was right, so right. As if some deep electrical connection had been made. She felt it sing against her mouth and melt her heart, and she felt his hand tighten painfully on her arm and knew that he felt it, too. Whatever had gone wrong between them, it was not this.

He was gnawing on her lower lip with little bites that sent shafts of loving and excitement through her. His other hand came up and encircled her throat, too, and he held her helpless in his two hands while his mouth hungered against hers, stealing and giving pleasure.

Anna pressed her hand against his chest, thrilling to the strength of heart and body she felt there. It was both new and old. She felt as if she had loved him in some long-distant past, some other life, and at the same time that it was all totally new. She seemed never to have been warmed with such delight by a kiss, never yearned so desperately for a man's love.

He wrapped her tight in his arms and drew her upper body off the lounger and across his knees with a passion that made her tremble. Now his mouth came down on hers with uncontrolled longing, and he kissed her deeply and thoroughly until her bones were water and her heart was alive with wild, wild need.

His mouth left hers, trailed kisses across her cheek to her ear, down her neck to the base of her throat, and slowly back up the long line of her throat.

"Ishaq!" She cried his name with passionate wonder before his kiss could smother the sound on her lips. "Ishaq!"

His lips teased the corner of her mouth and moved up towards her ear.

"Tell me the truth, Anna," he whispered. "Tell me, and then let me love you."

"Tell you?" She would tell him anything, if only he would carry on kissing her. But she had nothing to tell. "Tell you what?" He did not answer, only stared compellingly at her, and she slowly turned away her head. "I don't remember," she protested sadly, feeling the passion die within her. "Why won't you believe me? What have I done to forfeit the trust you must once have had in your wife?"

His eyes squeezed shut, and she felt how he struggled for control of himself and bit by bit gained it. Then he lifted her to rest in the lounger again, took his hands away, and sat looking at her. She saw burning suspicion in his eyes.

"What is it?" she pleaded. "What do you want me to tell you? What have I forgotten?"

He shook his head, reaching for his glass, and nervously she picked up her own. He drank a long draft of juice, and set the glass down carefully.

"What have you forgotten, you want to know?" He looked at her levelly. "You have forgotten nothing, Anna. Except perhaps the humanity that is the birthright of us all. Tell me where Nadia is."

Anna closed her eyes, opened them. Swallowed.

"Nadia?" She repeated the name carefully. "Who is Nadia?"

Ishaq smiled. "Nadia, as you very well know, is the mother of the baby you kidnapped and have been pretending is your own."

Seven

The storm of passion he had raised in her body was now a dry emptiness that left her feeling sick. "What?" An icicle trailed along her spine. She blinked at him, mouth open, feeling about as intelligent as a fish. "What are you talking about?"

He watched her in silence. When she moved, it was to set her glass down on the table very carefully.

"I don't know anyone nam...the mother of the baby? Of Safiyah?" Her voice cracked. "She's not my baby?"

He was silent. She stared into his face. Was this the truth, or some kind of mind game?

"You're trying to break me," she accused hoarsely. "Tell me the truth. If you have any humanity at all, if you have one ounce of human feeling in you, tell me the truth. Is Safiyah our baby?"

"You know very well that she is not," he said. "Will

you never come to the end of your play-acting? What can you stand to gain from this delay?''

Anna heard nothing except *she is not.*

"She's not?'' she repeated. ''She's not?''

He sat in silence, watching her, his sensual mouth a firm, straight line.

''If she's not mine, then...I haven't forgotten two years of my life, either,'' Anna worked out slowly. She wrapped her arms around her middle and looked away from his gaze, rocking a little. ''And we aren't married, and this is not my home. It was all lies.''

She looked into his face again, saw the confirmation of what she had said, and turned hopelessly to gaze around her. A quiver of sadness pierced her. It had seemed so right. Being here, the baby, the man—it had felt real to her. She shook her head. ''But how...is one of us crazy?''

He looked like someone sitting through a badly acted play. ''You, if you imagined you could get away with it,'' he offered.

Her mouth was bone-dry. One hand to her throat, she tried to swallow, and couldn't. ''I don't know anyone named Nadia,'' she began, with forced calm. ''I was in an accident and I woke up in hospital and they told me my baby was okay. You said you were my husband and I had amnesia. That's all I know. That is literally all I know.''

Ishaq Ahmadi—if that was his name—leaned back in his chair. ''You knew enough to pretend the baby was your own,'' he pointed out dryly.

She shook her head in urgent denial. ''My memory was a complete jumble. You can't know what it's like unless you've experienced it. First I thought I was back at the time I was in hospital for...when my baby died.

When they said, 'Your baby's fine,' I thought..." She stopped and swallowed. "I thought Noah's death had been a bad dream. I thought I'd dreamt the whole six weeks since. I thought I had another chance."

She forced down the taste of tears at the back of her throat.

"And then you came along," she said, in a flat voice. "You turned everything on its head."

It was all so crazy, so horrible, she could hardly take it in. She put a hand to her aching forehead. "Where did the baby come from? Why did you tell me we were married?" she demanded, fighting to keep sane. He'd be convincing her the world was flat next.

"For the same reason you pretended to believe me."

"No!" she cried. "No! You know perfectly well—" She broke off that argument, knowing it was futile. "What is this? Why are you doing this?"

"You can guess why."

She shook her head angrily. "I can't guess anything! How dare you do this to me! Messing with my mind when I was concussed, telling me I was suffering from amnesia! What do you want? What can you possibly want from me? Why, *why* did you say she was our baby?"

"Because husbands have rights in such cases that others do not have."

She blinked at the unexpectedness of it. It was perhaps the first time he had given her a straight answer to any question.

"Are you the baby's father?"

He paused, as if wondering how much to tell her. "No. Nadia is my sister. "

"How did I come to be in the hospital with her baby? Did you plant her on me somehow?"

One eyebrow lifted disbelievingly. "Not I. That's what I want you to tell me. I found you there together."

Anna shook her head confusedly. "I don't understand. Then how do you know this is your sister's baby?"

"By the al Hamzeh mark." He rubbed his eye unconsciously.

"By the—*what?*" She jerked back in her chair. "Are you telling me that you abducted a baby and a total stranger from a hospital and brought us across four time zones on the strength of the baby's *birthmark?*" she shrieked incredulously.

He gazed at her for a moment. Anna shifted nervously.

"Nadia was in labour and on her way to the hospital when she disappeared. A few hours later you turned up in another, nearby hospital, pretending to be the mother of a newborn baby with the al Hamzeh mark."

"How did you know I *wasn't* her mother? The nurses told me it was my baby. So how did you know better? Is there really nobody else in the world with that mark except you and Nadia?"

"The nurse who examined you knew very well it was not your baby. She had written notes on your chart to that effect. You may read the notes, if you doubt me. I have them. She made a note for the hospital to check with the police for any reported incidents of baby stealing from maternity wards and to keep you in for observation till the matter was investigated."

Anna blinked and opened her mouth in amazed indignation. "But then why—but they—I *told* them my baby died, and they said, No, here's your baby, she's alive!"

He shrugged.

Anna couldn't fit any one piece of the puzzle with another. She shook her head helplessly, feeling how slowly her mind was working. "Anyway, if you knew I wasn't Safiyah's mother, why bother to abduct me? Why didn't you just take the baby? I wouldn't be likely to complain, would I, if I was faking it?"

"I wanted information from you. And you were in no state to—"

"Information about what?" she interrupted.

"About how you got possession of Safiyah."

This was unbelievable.

"Like for example?" she demanded. "What are you suggesting? That I—jumped Nadia while she was in labour, dragged her off somewhere, and then stole her baby when it was born?"

"That is one possible scenario, of course. Is that what happened?"

"Well, thank you, I'm starting to get a picture here," Anna said furiously. "On no evidence whatsoever, you have decided that I am a baby snatcher. And that gives you the right to treat me like a criminal. You don't owe me an iota of respect, or the decency of truth. Nothing. Because of what you *suspect*. Have I got that now?"

Now she understood the reason for his questions earlier. The ugliest doubt of her own sanity brushed her. Was it possible? Had grief made her crazy enough to want a baby at any cost? Could she have done such a thing and forgotten all about it? Was that even the reason for her amnesia? No. *No.*

"And what do you imagine I did with Nadia?" she went on, when he didn't speak.

"That is one of the things I want you to tell me," he said.

Anna leapt to her feet. "How dare you talk to me like this? I did not do it! You have absolutely no grounds *whatsoever* for making such an appalling accusation!"

"I have not accused you. But you were in that cab with a newborn baby who is not your own. That needs some explaining."

She was not listening. She stormed on. "How dare you take such extreme action on no evidence at all...lying, abducting me, making me believe I'm half crazy! Telling me...my God, and we almost made love!" she raged, her cheeks blazing as she suddenly remembered the scene.

"Was that my doing?" he asked dryly. "Or was that your attempt to get my guard down?" He was speaking as if this were only another such attempt. As if he believed nothing she said.

The flame of rage enveloped her, licking and burning till she felt something almost like ecstasy.

"Don't *you* accuse *me!*" she stormed. "*I've* never said anything but the truth! All the manipulation has come from your corner! You even lied about your name, didn't you? Last night it was the Ahmadi mark. Just now you called it the al Hamzeh mark!"

Ishaq Ahmadi looked bored. "Never lied to me? You lied to me not half an hour ago."

"I have not lied to you!"

He got to his feet, facing her over the lounger, and Anna stepped back, but not fast enough to prevent his grasping her wrist.

"What do you call it? You told me you recognized this place, that you knew you had come home! You have not been within a thousand miles of this place."

Her eyes fell before the searching gaze. "Why did you say it?" he prodded.

She was silent. She had felt a sense of homecoming, probably only because she wanted to feel it. Wanted the baby to be hers, wanted him to be her husband. So desperately wanted all the sorrow and anguish of her terrible loss to be years in the past. There had certainly been enough clues that he was lying, if she had wanted to put them together.

"What did you hope to gain?" he pressed.

"Suppose you tell me!" she blazed, pain fuelling her anger in order to hide from him. She wrenched her wrist from his hold. "What advantage could there possibly be in saying something like that?"

"Perhaps you hoped to lower my guard and make your escape?"

"By sleeping with you, I suppose! Sexually amoral, too. That's quite a charming list you've made up there."

"You lied. You must have had a reason."

"Dear Kettle, yours sincerely, Pot!" she exclaimed mockingly. "I have only your word for what's going on, you know. And your word hasn't exactly proved unassailable. You..."

She stopped. "Why did you think I would believe you in the hospital, if things are as you say? You must have known I had amnesia. You must have been deliberately playing on the fact. Otherwise, why wouldn't I just tell the nurse you were an impostor?"

"I did not imagine that you would believe me. I thought you would prefer to pretend to do so, however, rather than run the risk of being revealed as a kidnapper and arrested by the police." Now she remembered that curious, warning pressure on her hand as she lay so dazed in the casualty ward. "And I was right. You could not afford to make a stand, because that would mean an immediate inquiry. And any inquiry would have shown that the baby could not be yours."

"If I hadn't been totally out of it I would have made a stand soon enough," she said. She suddenly felt too weak to support her own anger. All her energy had been used up; she was empty. She had no more strength for holding pain at bay.

Her baby seemed to reach for her heart, the touch of that tiny soul unlocking the deepest well of grief in her. She shook her head and forced herself to confront Ishaq, to cloak her weakness from this dangerous adversary.

"If you hadn't lied about absolutely *everything*... If a lie is big enough, they'll believe it! Are you proud to be taking your lead from a monster?

Anger flickered in his eyes.

"I do what is necessary to protect those I love," he said coldly. She believed him. She saw suddenly that he was a man who would make a firm friend as well as an implacable enemy and, in some part of her, she could grieve for the fact that she was destined to be his enemy.

"Well, bully for you!" she cried, her voice cracking with fatigue. "I want to get out of here and go home to my life. So suppose you tell me what you want from me?"

Ishaq Ahmadi inclined his head. "Of course. You have only to tell me where Nadia is and how you got her baby. Then you are free to go. I will of course pass the information and your name on to Scotland Yard."

With a grunt of exasperation that almost moved into tears, Anna whirled to stride away from him. Against the wall of the house a railing protected a worn brick staircase running down to the courtyard below, and again she felt that crazy sense of belonging. *I have gone up and down that staircase a hundred times.*

She shook her head to clear it, stopped and turned to face him.

"Why don't you believe me?" she demanded. He lifted an eyebrow, and she fixed her eyes on his. "No,

I really mean it. My explanation of events is as reasonable as anything else in this—'' she lifted her hands ''—in this unbelievable fantasy, so why won't you even give it a moment's consideration? You absolutely dismiss everything I tell you. Why?''

A sudden, delightful breeze whipped across the terrace, stirring her hair and the leaves, whipping the cloth on the table, snatching up a napkin and carrying it a few yards. Her nostrils were suddenly filled with the heady scent of a thousand flowers. The servant appeared as if from nowhere to chase down the napkin.

''Because what you tell me has no logic even of its own. How did you come to be in the hospital with this baby?''

''Funny, that's exactly why I *believed* you,'' she said on a desperate half laugh. ''How did I get there? That's the question, all right.''

''Your story has no foundation. It rests on sand.''

''What about the cab driver?'' she exclaimed. ''What did he say about it?''

''He was quite seriously hurt. He cannot yet be questioned.''

''Where did the accident happen?''

''The taxi pulled into the path of a bus on the King's Road at Oakley Street,'' he replied, as if she already knew. ''You were in the back with the baby. There can be no doubt of that.''

She damned well was not, but she didn't waste time on what he thought he knew. She wanted to sort this out.

''Oakley Street. That's only a couple of minutes from the Riverfront.'' The Riverfront Restaurant was moored near Battersea Bridge. ''What time was the accident?''

"Not long after midnight, according to the police report."

She wondered how he had got access to the police report, but didn't waste time asking. "We asked for our bill around midnight, I'm pretty sure."

She squeezed her eyes shut. That meant her memory loss covered a very short period. If only a few minutes had elapsed from the time she got into the cab till the accident...

"If you're right, the only possible explanation is that the baby was in the cab when I got into it," Anna said, and as she said it, the truth finally pierced her heart. That darling baby whom she already loved was not to be hers to love...any more than her son had been.

Ishaq Ahmadi snorted. "Excellent. If only you had thought of this explanation a few hours ago."

Anna shook her head, swallowing against the feeling that was welling up inside her, a flood of the deepest sadness. She had no right after all to hold and love that beautiful, perfect baby, no matter how empty her arms were, how much she yearned.

"Perhaps a little later you will remember this. At a convenient time you will perhaps remember getting into a cab and discovering a baby cooing and kicking there."

His words hurt her. *Noah,* she thought. *Oh, my baby! You never kicked and cooed....*

Suddenly all her defences were gone. She felt like a newborn herself. She dropped her arms to her sides.

"Maybe I didn't catch that cab. I don't actually remember getting into it. Drivers change shift around midnight, don't they? Maybe he wouldn't take me and we went up to the King's Road to try and get cabs there. Maybe..."

She was babbling. She didn't know if she was making

sense. She blinked hard against the unfamiliar tears that threatened, against the sudden pressure on the wall that had held down her feelings for so long. She wanted to put her head back and howl her loss to the whole mad world that had let it happen, let her perfect baby die.

"Yes?" he prompted.

"I don't know," she said, despair welling up. How could she sort anything out when she could not remember? It was boxing in the dark. Was it possible she had forgotten some horrible conspiracy? Had her grief driven her to the madness of taking someone else's baby to fill her empty heart? Women did such things.

Tears began to slip down her cheeks. She couldn't seem to control them. Her head was pounding; it must be the heat. She staggered a little.

"I'm tired," she realized suddenly. "Really tired." She put out her hand to an arch for support, but it was further away than it seemed. A sob came ripping up from her stomach, bringing with it bile and the juice she had just drunk, and feeling came surging on its heels.

"Oh!" she cried. "Oh, I can't..." Her fingers caught at something, a branch, perhaps, but she couldn't hold on, and at the next sob her knees gave way.

The branch was Ishaq's arm. He caught her around the waist when she buckled, supporting her as grief and bile spilled from her amid howls of anguish.

"My baby!" she cried desperately, as the image of Safiyah blended with that of her own darling son, and seemed to be torn anew from her arms and her heart. Her throat opened, and at last she howled out the uncomprehending, intolerable misery that had been her silent companion for so many days and weeks. "Oh, my baby! My baby! Why? *Why?*"

Eight

"*Princess, it is too dangerous!*" pleaded the maidservant. She stood wringing her hands as her mistress, gazing into the mirror, tweaked the folds of the serving girl's trousers she wore.

She glanced up, eyes sparkling in the lamplight. "He is a brave man, the Lion. He will admire bravery. If I could, I would challenge him in the field of battle."

"If anyone discovers you—"

"I will flee. And you will be waiting for me, with my own raiment," she said firmly.

She admired herself one last time in the mirror. The short jacket just covering her breasts, the pants caught tight below the knee, the delicate gold chain around her ankles fanning out over her feet to each toe, the circlets of medallions around her waist and forehead, the glittering diaphanous veil that did not hide the long dark curls...*the costume of her father's winebearers suited a woman well.*

A smile pulled at her dimpled cheek as she turned away and kissed her maid. "Fear not," she said. "I am quick of mind and fleet of foot and I shall elude all save him I would have capture me." A delicious thrill rushed through her and she picked up the white rose that lay waiting and tucked it into her waist.

A few minutes later the two women crept together down the dark, secret passages of the palace towards the sounds of revelry in the great banqueting hall.

Inside the hall, the narrow doorway was hidden by a large carpet hung upright to provide a narrow passage against the wall, but as they glided in behind it, light from the banquet beyond revealed more than one spy hole in the fabric. She pressed her eye to one and gazed hungrily.

The men sat and lay around the laden cloth on cushions and carpets, drinking and eating, laughing, toasting the bridegroom, who sat beside her father. At the far end of the room musicians played. Serving men moved about the room, carrying huge platters massed with food. A whole roast sheep was being set down before the bridegroom.

But she had no thought for her intended. Her eyes searched the faces of the men seated nearest the prince, looking for the one they called al Hamzeh. The Lion. The birthmark made her search easy, even at such a distance, and her heart thudded in pain and delight as her eyes found him.

She took the golden pitcher from her frightened maidservant's hands then and glided stealthily out into the room, her movements measured by the bell-like tinkle of her jewellery. She walked down the room towards the

Lion, as if in answer to a summons, as she had watched the cup bearers do.

He sat cross-legged on the carpet, leaning against a mound of silken cushions at his elbow, listening as someone described some feat of the bridegroom's at the hunt. His dark hair, glowing in lamplight, fell in tousled curls over the glittering gold embroidery of his jacket. On his fingers heavy carved gold held rich rubies and emeralds; high on his arm she noted the seal of his office, a signet in gold and amber. He seemed to glow independent of the lamplight. She watched in a fever of desire as he bit into a sweetmeat and his tongue caught an errant morsel of powdered sugar from his full lower lip.

She approached, and bent over to fill the cup that he held in one strong careless hand. The scent of him rose up in her nostrils, spices and musk and camphor from his clothes, and from his skin the clean perfumed smell of a man just come from the hammam.

As if he sensed something in the winegirl, the Lion lazily turned his head and let his eyes follow the smooth arms up to her white breast, her half-hidden cheek. Instead of turning her face demurely away, she met his gaze with a look of passionate challenge. He started, his lips parting with questing amaze.

She let fall the white rose by the goblet, the little note fluttering like a lost petal from its stem. His eyes flicked to the rose, and she saw by his stillness that he understood. He turned and looked up at her, and now his gaze devoured the sweet face so passionately that her own eyes fell.

His hand moved possessively to gather up the rose before it could be noticed by anyone else—enclosing it jealously to keep it from other eyes, crushing it in a signal of all-consuming passion. She melted into answering passion as she felt his gesture on her own skin.

A thorn pierced his flesh and he smiled, as if a little pain was no more than to be expected from love.

Anna awoke in a strange bed and gazed around her.

Her headache was gone, and she felt deeply refreshed, as if she had made up for all the lost sleep of weeks past in one go. But the sunlight filtering through the shutters was still bright.

She had wept till she was completely drained and exhausted. She had wept it all out, for the first time, and then had fallen into a deep sleep. And now a burden had lifted from her. The heavy weight was gone.

Now healing could begin.

And of all people it was Ishaq Ahmadi who had sat beside her and witnessed her grieving. He had not said much, but his quiet presence had been exactly right. Someone to listen without feeling driven to reassure. Someone to hear and accept while understanding that nothing could be done to change her world for her.

With more interest in life than she had experienced for weeks past, Anna leaned up on one elbow and gazed around her.

She was in a different bedroom entirely from the one she had changed her clothes in. This was a very spacious room, beautifully decorated in blues and dark wood, with a door leading to the terrace. There were two other doors, and in the hopes that one of them led to a bathroom, Anna sprang out of bed and crossed an expanse of soft silk carpet woven in shades of blue and beige.

She got the bathroom first time, and when she returned to the bedroom, there was a smiling maid waiting for her. The bed was made as neatly as if Anna had never slept in it, and on the bed were laid clothes, as if for her choice.

"Saba'ul khair, madame," the maid murmured, ducking her head.

Anna smiled. *"Salaam aleikum,"* she offered. It was the only phrase she knew in Arabic.

It was a mistake, because the woman immediately burst into delighted chatter, indicating the terrace beyond the windows and the clothes on the bed.

Laughing, Anna shook her head. "I don't speak Arabic!" she said, holding up her hands in surrender, but when she saw that among the offered outfits were several swimsuits, she turned towards the windows. The woman was opening the slatted wooden shutters so she could see more clearly what was out there.

The room was at one of the tips of the C. On the far side of the broad terrace was the swimming pool she had seen from above. Ishaq Ahmadi was sitting at a table in a beach robe, reading a newspaper. A meal was being served to him.

Anna's stomach growled. She turned to the bed and picked up a swimsuit in shades of turquoise. It was beautifully cut and looked very expensive. Underneath that was another one, identical except for the size. With a frown of interest Anna picked up a few other items. Everything had been supplied in two sizes.

It might be conspicuous consumption, but as for refusing to accept his casual largesse, well, Anna was dying for a swim. So she stripped off her clothes and inched into one of the blue suits. It had an excellent fit, and she turned to examine herself briefly in a large mirror. She was thin, but the antique mirror was kind. Her shape was still unmistakably feminine. The suit emphasised her slender curves. The gently rounded neckline produced a very female cleavage, and her back, naked to the waist, had an elegantly smooth line. Her legs were lean but shapely, even if the large purple bruise on one thigh showed cruelly against her too-pale skin.

It was a long time since she had examined her reflection for femininity and attractiveness. Now it was perhaps a sign of her return to feeling that she was anxious to look attractive.

The maid held a cotton kaftan for her, and she slipped her arms into the sleeves with a murmur of thanks. It was plain white with an oriental textured weave and wide sleeves, and she knew without looking at the label that it had cost a small fortune. She chose a purple cotton-covered visor and a pair of sunglasses from a small spread of accessories.

He had thought of everything. He must have phoned a very exclusive boutique—or had one of his servants do so. Well, she would be glad if the utter stupidity of her trip here was relieved by a few hours of sun before she flew back to a wintry Europe. And though the items would be beyond her budget, they wouldn't amount to much for a man who owned a house like this.

The maid drew open the door for her, and Anna stepped out under the arched overhang and into the luscious day and walked across the tiled paving, past shrubs and flowers, past palm trees and small reflective pools, towards the swimming pool.

The air was cooler, and the sun had moved in the opposite direction to what she would have expected. She had thought the courtyard faced south, but in that case the sun was setting in the east.

Before she could reorient herself she had arrived at Ishaq's table beside the pool in a corner where the house met the high perimeter wall, nestled attractively under an arching trellis thick with greenery and yellow blooms.

He closed his paper as the servant pulled out a chair for her. A second place had been set.

"Good afternoon," she said, sinking down into it.

"Afternoon?" Ishaq queried with a smile, and she simultaneously took in the fact that his meal was composed of fruit and rolls.

"Café, madame?" murmured the servant, and she smelled the strong, rich odour and demanded, "What time is it?"

"Just after nine," said Ishaq Ahmadi.

"In the morning!" A breathless little laugh of comprehension escaped her. "Have I slept an entire day?"

"I am sure you needed it. You must be hungry."

"Ravenous!" She flung down her sunglasses, then leaned back out of the shady bower so that the sun caught her face, and felt that she was happy in spite of everything. "Oh, this is heaven! What a wonderful place!"

He smiled. He had lost some of the hard edge of suspicion he had carried since they first met. And she— well, she had shown him things about herself that no one else in the world had seen. So it was only natural that she felt closer to him now.

He offered the basket of rolls. "Perhaps you would like what you call a full English breakfast?"

Taking a roll, Anna smiled up at the servant who was setting cream and sugar just so by her coffee cup. "I could devour a plate of bacon and eggs," she told Ishaq, then checked herself. "Oh, but—"

"I am sure the cook has some lamb sausage."

"That sounds delicious."

Ishaq translated her wishes to the servant. As the man

slipped away, he said, "I do not ask my staff to cook pork for non-Muslim guests. I hope you will not object to doing without it during your stay."

"My *stay?*" She looked at him. "I want to go home. Are you planning on forcing me to stay here beyond today?"

"Force you? No," he replied calmly. "But you might reconsider when you look at this."

His hand was resting on the arm of his chair, holding the newspaper he had been reading. He lifted it to present her with the paper, front page up.

Trahie Par Son Milliardaire De Cheikh! screamed the French headline, which she could vaguely translate as *Betrayed By Her Millionaire Sheikh,* and Anna only shook her head. But then her eye was drawn further down the page, to a large photograph.

"That's me! That's you and me!" she cried in astonishment, snatching the paper without apology and spreading it under her horrified nose.

It was a photo taken at the airport, of herself, holding Safiyah, and Ishaq Ahmadi with one arm around her, guiding her to the limousine. An inset photo showed a sultry, big-lipped blonde whose face Anna vaguely recognized.

Very clearly marked—and too dark, so someone had obviously retouched the photo—was the al Hamzeh mark on the eye of Ishaq and of Safiyah.

"Oh, good grief!" Anna cried weakly. "Is this…" She glanced at the stack of papers on the table beside him, knowing the answer even as she asked. "Is it in the English papers?"

"Very much so," he agreed lazily.

She jumped up and ran to the stack. Of course, today

was Sunday. The English Sunday tabloids were notori-
ous for their love of scandal among the rich and famous.

Sheikh Gazi's Secret Baby!

Sheikh's Mistress In Baby Surprise!

Mystery Beauty Has Playboy Gazi's Baby!

All the tabloids save one had run it on the front page,
with a variant of the photograph she had already seen.
Every headline insinuated or said outright that the
woman in the photo was the sheikh's mistress and the
mother of his child. Worst of all, in virtually every photograph Anna's face was clear and unmistakable. She
looked exactly like herself. And her arms were around
the baby in a firm maternal hold that spoke louder than
the headlines.

Still in a state of stunned disbelief, Anna chose one
of the papers and returned to her seat, sinking slowly
into it as she read the story.

Sheikh Gazi al Hamzeh, the wealthy, jet-setting
Cup Companion and trusted confidant of Prince
Karim of West Barakat, startled the world yesterday
with the revelation that his long-time English mistress has given birth to his child.

The infant is thought to be over a month old.
''The birth was kept secret till Gazi could gain the
prince's approval to acknowledge the child,'' said
a source close to the sheikh.

Prince Karim, whose own son was born in July,
is understood to be urging the sheikh to marry his
so far unidentified mistress, seen here with the
sheikh on arrival at Barakat al Barakat.

''Sheikh Gazi has gone to extraordinary lengths
to protect the privacy of his mystery girlfriend,''
says our own society columnist, Arnold Jones

Bremner. "Virtually no one outside his circle knows who she is."

Although the couple have been seen in some of London's most exclusive private clubs over the past year, they use a service entrance. This is the first photograph of them together.

Insiders say the couple are unlikely to marry.

Anna lifted her eyes to "Ishaq Ahmadi."

"'*Long-time mistress!*'—where did they get this?" she demanded. Her gaze hardened. "Is this what you told them?"

He laughed. "They did not trouble to ask me. The truth might have got in the way of invention. Suppose you had been the baby's English nanny! Where would their front page be then?"

"They asked you questions at the airport," Anna said stonily. "I heard them. And you answered."

His jaw tightened. "Recollect that it was you yourself who insisted on presenting them with the tantalizing sight of the baby. But for that our arrival would have been unremarkable."

"What does *Paris Dimanche* say?" she asked, to catch him out. If the stories matched, surely that meant there had been one source?

He looked as if he saw right through her suspicious mind, but made no comment, merely lifted the paper and negligently began to translate.

"Sheikh Gazi al Hamzeh, the Hollywood-handsome, polo-playing millionaire considered one of the world's most eligible bachelors, has dashed the hopes and broken the heart of beautiful model/actress Sacha Delavel, his close friend, with the revelation that he is on the point of marrying the mother of his child. 'It comes as a total shock,' Mademoiselle Delavel reportedly told friends from the privacy of a villa in Turkey, where she is said to have fled as the news broke. 'I never knew of her existence until today.'"

He tossed the paper aside as Anna's breakfast was placed before her. He deliberated over the fruit in the bowl and chose a ripe pomegranate as if he had nothing else on his mind. Then he neatly began to slice into the rind.

For some reason this story was much more infuriating than the other.

"I suppose when you're next seen with Sacha Delavel *I'll* be the one billed as having the broken heart," Anna snapped.

Ignoring her, he delicately, patiently prised open the pomegranate to reveal the luscious red rubies within. Anna shivered as if she were watching him make intimate love to another woman.

"Sacha Delavel and I danced together at a charity ball given for Parvan war relief a few months ago in Paris. They have searched their picture library and found some nice photos of the two of us, which are on page seven. The rest is invention."

She watched as he sank strong white teeth into the red fruit. Liquid spurted from the seeds over his hands and mouth, but he was concentrated on his pleasure. A thrill of pure sensation pierced her, and with a little gasp Anna dropped her eyes to her own breakfast.

"Did they get your name right? You're Sheikh Gazi al Hamzeh?"

"In the West I commonly use that name," he admitted wryly.

"Oh!" she remarked with wide-eyed sarcasm. "*It's not your real name, either?*"

"My name is Sayed Hajji Ghazi Ishaq Ahmad ibn Bassam al Hafez al Hamzeh," he said, reeling the name off with the fluency of poetry. "But this is difficult for English speakers, who do not like to take time over other people's names. Nor do they trouble to pronounce consonants that don't appear in English."

She couldn't think of any comeback to that. They ate in silence for a few minutes. With little flicked glances she watched him enjoy the pomegranate, and marvelled that anyone could believe that ordinary Anna Lamb was the mistress of such a powerful, virile, attractive man, or that he had dropped someone as beautiful as Sacha Delavel for her.

But she was pretty sure that people *would* believe it, now. It had been in the papers, after all. Probably even her own friends would wonder. Not Cecile or Lisbet, of course. But others less close to her.

"What do we do about this?" she finally asked, indicating the papers.

"Do?" Sheikh Gazi shrugged and wiped his hands and mouth with a snowy napkin. "Ignore it."

"*Ignore* it? But we have to make them retract. We could sue."

"And sell more papers for them."

"But it's all lies!"

Sheikh Gazi smiled at this indignation. "People will soon forget."

"But—aren't you going to do *anything?*"

"The editors hope that I will. Then they would have something to run with. A story denied is a story. Do you really want to see *Sheikh Gazi Denies Baby* as next Sunday's headline? Or do you prefer *Gazi Is Not The Father, Says Anna*?''

"But people will think—it says that you and I are...''
She licked her lips and faded off, startlingly aware of
the day, the heat, the luscious taste of fruit in her mouth,
the smell of the sun on his skin. *They think we're lovers.*
The thought hovered between them, shimmering like
heat.

"And the more you say now, Anna, the more they
will go on thinking it,'' he said.

"But I—I have to go back to London immediately.
To France,'' she amended. "What if the papers find out
my name?''

"They will certainly do so,'' he warned her softly.
"As soon as the papers are read in London this morning—'' he glanced at his watch "—it is nearly six
o'clock there now—someone who knows you will call
a journalist and name you.''

They were reading the story before most people in
England were awake. She realized he must have some
mechanism for getting the Sunday papers as soon as they
rolled off the presses at midnight and flying them out to
Barakat.

"Your price per copy must be astronomical,'' she observed dispassionately. "Do you have a regular Sunday
delivery of the European papers?''

"No,'' he said.

The servant came with a new pot of coffee. He
whisked their half-drunk cups away and poured fresh
coffee into clean cups. Even with her worries, Anna had
attention to note the luxury of that.

"Today was special, huh?'' She had always dreamed
of being famous one day, but for her work, not for some-

thing like this. "Well, so some friend or client will spill the beans. Then what? Will they phone me?"

"Phone you? They will phone you, they will phone your friends, they will come to your front door. At least one paper will offer you money for an exclusive, and if you accept, the editor will do everything to convince you to make the story of your sheikh lover more extreme and exciting."

"What do you mean?"

"Before they are through you will be tricked or persuaded into confessing that we have made passionate, death-defying love in the back of a limousine as it drove through London and Paris, in moonlight on the deck of my yacht, high in the air in the royal jet, on the magical white sand beach down there, and even on the back of my favourite polo pony as it galloped through the forest. Naturally we have been insatiable lovers. And of course they will publish photos of you posed in my favourite piece of sexy underwear."

His words sent electric twitches all across her scalp and down her spine, and Anna sat up abruptly and sugared her coffee. Was he being assailed by the same treacherous thought she was—that since everyone believed it anyway, they might as well make it the truth?

Nine

"**I**'m not going to be selling anyone any story," she said, setting the spoon in the saucer with a little snap. "Your polo pony's reputation is safe from me."

He lifted his hands in a shrug.

"But it really burns me that everyone I know is going to half believe I had your baby. What am I going to tell *them?*"

"That the story is false."

Her anger exploded on a little breath. "Oh, sure! You seem to forget that I actually have been pregnant. Only my close friends know my baby died. I haven't told anyone. I've hardly seen anyone since it happened. Everybody is going to wonder."

He looked at her. "I see."

"And what happens when I don't have the baby with me? People are going to think I walked away and let you keep her."

"Is it so bad? Fathers do get custody," he pointed out, so offhand she gritted her teeth. "And you have a career that takes you—"

She ground out, "I would no more give up my baby to its father for the sake of my career than—" She broke off with an exasperated sigh.

"Blame it on me," he suggested. "Everybody knows Arabs are an uncivilized bunch of barbarians who kidnap their own children."

"Will you stop laughing at me?" she demanded hotly.

"I will stop laughing when you stop being foolishly outraged by something so unimportant. It is not the end of the world, Anna. People will accept that the story was false when you tell them, or they will not. Either way they will cease to care within a week. These things—" he flicked the pile of newspapers with a gesture of such deep and biting contempt she flinched "—they feed the lowest tastes in humans, and like any junk food the purveyors of it make it addictive and completely without nutrition in order to create a constant demand for more. One story runs into another in people's minds. It is a taste for scandal and outrage this feeds, not a desire for factual information."

"I want to make them print a retraction," she said doggedly.

"Anna, by next Sunday, if we give them no more fuel for their fire, no one will remember whether you had a sheikh's baby or bribed a government minister, and no one will care! Do you know how many times my picture has appeared in these rags? Do you think anyone who gobbles such stories along with their Sunday toast remembers my name? I am 'that sheikh' if they think of me at all, and they confuse me with half a dozen other Cup Companions, or even with the princes themselves.

Even with something like the al Hamzeh mark to distinguish me, people say to me, *Oh, you were in the paper, weren't you? What was that about again?* when the story was about the ex-Sultan of Bagestan.''

''You just told me a minute ago that they're going to chase me down like dogs,'' she said irritably.

''*Yes*, if you put yourself in their way.'' He gazed compellingly at her, lifting his closed fist, the first knuckle extended towards her, for emphasis. ''*Yes*, if you give them fodder by complaining. This is a story that has another one or two headlines in it at most—*if* we give it to them! If not, it will die now. This is not, as they say, a story with legs.''

''What does that mean?'' she asked doubtfully, half convinced. He seemed to know so much about it.

''To have legs? It is newspaper jargon. It means a story that is going to run under its own steam.''

She sat in silence, her chin in her hands, absorbing it.

''There is nothing to be gained by issuing a denial, Anna. The best you can do, if you wish it to go no further, is stay out of sight for a while.''

She tried again. ''It's not as though I'm a celebrity, is it? It's you they're really interested in. If I can just get to France, I'll be fine. Alan's house is pretty remote.''

''Let me offer you an alternative to France, Anna.'' His gaze was now utterly compelling. Although he was trying to disguise it, she realized that he wanted something from her, and the butterflies in her stomach leapt into a dance so wild she was almost sick.

She licked her lips. ''And what would that be?''

''You could stay here with me until the heat dies down,'' he said.

* * *

A long moment of stillness was interrupted by the shrill cry of a bird in a nearby tree. Anna dropped her napkin by her plate with a matter-of-fact gesture.

"I—" she began, and then broke off. Her blood pounded in her stomach, making it feel hollow in spite of the meal she had just eaten.

"Do not turn me down without giving it some thought, Anna. There is advantage to you in staying away from the press for the moment. And I assure you I will do everything in my power to make your stay enjoyable."

Anna licked her lips. What was he really offering her here? A mere bolt-hole, or her very own Club Med holiday complete with dark lover? With any ordinary man, she would be in no doubt, but he was a man whose interest would flatter the most famous and beautiful women in the world. Why should he want her?

"For how long—a week?" she asked.

He shrugged and lifted a hand. His hands were graceful and strong, and she wondered if he played a musical instrument. Or perhaps a man got hands like that playing music on women's bodies...she stomped on the little flames that licked up around her at the thought.

"Perhaps a week, a few weeks. It depends."

On what? she wondered. Not on newspaper interest, obviously, when he had already assured her that would scarcely last till next Sunday.

Was he imagining that he would put her through her paces and see how long she kept him interested? She was unlikely to keep a millionaire playboy sheikh who hung out with the likes of Sacha Delavel interested for long. She had never studied sex as an art, and she would bet that he had.

"But people would find out I was here, wouldn't

they? It would just confirm the story. So whenever I went back I'd have to face journalists wanting me to talk about it. Wouldn't I?''

He shrugged and plucked a grape from the bowl. She had the feeling again that he was hiding something.

"Where's the advantage in delaying the inevitable? At least if I go back now I can deny it. If I stay here even for a week no denial is ever going to sound credible.''

It suddenly occurred to her that she sounded like someone wanting to be convinced, and she shut up.

"Can you think of no advantage from such a holiday? Barakat is a very exclusive holiday destination. No package tours come here. We have only a few resorts. That beach is as crowded now as it ever gets.''

She couldn't refrain from a glance in the direction he indicated. The strip of white sand curving around the bay in front of them was virtually deserted. So it actually wouldn't be stretching credibility too far to suggest that they had made love there, she found herself thinking absently...

Some part of her urged her to simply capitulate, and let nature take its course. But a little voice was warning her to be wary. Sheikh Gazi was not disinterested. What purpose would her staying serve for him? Was he really attracted to her, or was he deliberately letting her think so to disguise his real motives? And if he *didn't* want her sexually, what did he want?

Had he in fact been offering *her* sex as a bribe? He wanted her to stay and he knew she was attracted. Plenty of women would jump at the chance for a holiday in this paradise with a man like Gazi—and a sheikh, too!— devoting himself to them. Was he assuming she was one of them?

Anna, examining the grape between her fingers with minute fixity, blushed to the roots of her hair. After a moment she slipped it into her mouth.

"I would of course reimburse you for your time," he said, and that certainly proved the suspicion. He was simply trying whatever was handy by way of a bribe. If sex wasn't enough, he would throw in cash. God, what that said about his opinion of her!

"Really," she observed, her voice distant, almost absent.

"At your professional rate, of course."

She flicked him a look. "Which profession would that be?"

He chose to ignore the irony. "Which profession? I don't—you are an artist, you say. Artist, designer, interior decorator, whatever fees are your usual fees."

"Since you're doing me the big favour by allowing me to hide here, I don't really see why *you* should pay *me*," Anna said sweetly. "Isn't the shoe on the other foot? Or perhaps you have some reason of your own for wanting me to stay?"

He sat for a moment tapping a thumb on his cup, considering.

"Yes," he said at last. "I also have reasons for wishing it."

"Well, well! And what would those reasons be?"

"I cannot discuss it with you," he said. The look in his eyes was an assessment, but a long way from sexual assessment. She realized abruptly that he did not trust her, or fully accept her version of events, even now. But he might be willing to make love with her if that was what it took to keep her here. Rage swept her, with a suddenness that astonished her.

"Suppose I take a stab at guessing?"

He watched her.

"Let's see, now," she began. She tilted her head and looked at him. "You're sure about that judgement, are you—that this story hasn't got legs, as you call it?"

"That a Cup Companion has a child with his mistress may offend the religious in Barakat, but for a Western audience it means nothing. You must be aware of the truth of this. As you pointed out, you are not a celebrity yourself. That gives the story only limited interest."

She nodded thoughtfully. "That's okay as far as our affair and our secret baby go, but that's all lies anyway. But there's something you're leaving out of the calculation, isn't there? I mean, that's not the only story here, not by a long way."

She saw a flicker of feeling in his eyes, instantly veiled. He fixed her with a dark, impenetrable gaze. "And what else is there?"

Anna did not stop to consider how unwise it might be to show such a man how thoroughly she understood his motives.

"You abducted a baby from an English hospital, Sheikh Gazi—and according to the papers, you're one of the trusted Cup Companions of Prince Karim. That's got legs, don't you think? You also abducted an Englishwoman. And you got us out of England and into Barakat without passports. That's got legs, too. In fact, it's got so many legs it's a centipede.

"And forgive me if I suggest that you wouldn't have done any of that just for sheer amusement. So the real reason you took such risks, Sheikh Gazi, whatever it is—that's a story that'll have legs, too."

He was silent when she finished, and her ears were suddenly filled with the thunder of her own agitated

heartbeat. Too late, Anna reflected that perhaps her reasoning processes hadn't fully recovered from her accident. What on earth had made her challenge the man
here on his own ground?

"How well you grasp the facts," Sheikh Gazi said
softly, tossing his napkin down beside his plate. "But I
advise you to consider a little longer before you try to
blackmail me, Anna."

His eyes were absolutely black. His gaze stabbed her,
and her heart pounded hard enough to make her sick.

"I am not trying to blackmail you!" she shouted, re-
jecting her own dimly realized understanding that her
little summation might well have sounded like it. "Why
are you constantly accusing me of the lowest possible
crimes?"

"What, then?" he said, his lips a tight line in a face
that suddenly seemed sculpted from stone. "Just a pleasant little gossip to pass the time of day with me?"

She gritted her teeth. "Tell me, is it your wealth and
position that give you the right to trample over other
people, or is it just that women in general are beneath
contempt?"

"I do not hold women in contempt," he said in flat
repudiation.

"I have a life," she interrupted rudely before he had
finished. "Forgive me if I find it offensive to be offered
a holiday on the casual assumption that my career can
be put on hold in order to save you from the conse-
quences of your own actions." She tilted her head.

"I also resent being taken for such a fool. It's not me
who's going to suffer if I deny this ridiculous story, is
it? It's you. I have nothing at all to fear from the truth.
Now—" She held up her hands. "I have no intention
of telling anyone anything, except that you are not my

lover and I am not the mother of your baby. But I do intend to get out of here and back to my own life. So unless you're considering adding forcible confinement to the list of your crimes—''

''You are annoyed because I have underestimated your intelligence,'' he interrupted with a sudden return to reasonableness that secretly irritated her. ''Fair enough, but if you can see so far, a little more thought will tell you—''

''Please don't spell out anything more for poor little me,'' Anna snapped, lifting a hand. ''I really think I understand enough. The rest I don't want to know. You might decide at some future date that I am a danger to you if I learn any more now.''

His face closed, and she saw that he could be deeply ruthless when he chose.

''You are determined to consider only your own convenience.''

''Me?'' She could hardly speak for outrage. With biting sarcasm, she began, ''I quite understand that *you* feel your concerns should come first with everyone you meet, Sheikh Gazi—no doubt it follows from having more servants than is good for you. But forgive me if *I* consider it quite reasonable that I should put myself and my clients first.''

He gazed at her for a moment. ''My concern is for my sister,'' he said quietly. ''Let me—''

She lifted her hands, pushing the palms towards him. ''Well, that's admirable! But I have already told you I know nothing about your sister. She is a total stranger to me. And my life has been quite disrupted enough on her behalf, thank you! Now I'd like to get it back on the rails.''

Sheikh Gazi acknowledged this with a hard, business-like little nod. "Let us hope that future generations consider such devotion to your art a worthwhile sacrifice."

"It's no sacrifice on my part, believe me!" Anna exclaimed explosively, if not quite truthfully. "Not that I would *begin* to suggest that you rate your claims too high!"

He went absolutely still with fury. For a moment they stared at each other. Anna's skin twitched wildly all over her back and breasts as emotion flared in him, and she wondered what her reaction would be if he reached for her. If he started to make love to her, it was entirely possible she'd end up agreeing to anything he asked her to do, short of murder.

As if in answer to her thoughts, Sheikh Gazi shoved back his chair and got to his feet. He shrugged out of his bathrobe, letting it fall onto the chair. Then he stood there, naked except for a neat black swimsuit in body-hugging Lycra. She could not avert her fascinated gaze.

Wind seemed to blow up out of nowhere, seducing all the flowers on the trellis overhead to give up their perfume, tousling her hair and robe, caressing her skin, so that all at once her whole body came alive.

He was gorgeous—there was just no other word. Beautifully proportioned legs, powerful thighs, neat-muscled waist curving up to a very male expanse of chest with just the right amount of curling black hair, broad shoulders that were held with the minimum of tension, strong arms.

Probably she would never get another chance at such death-defying sexual excitement as he had just offered. When she was an old woman probably she would look back on this day and call herself seventeen kinds of fool for turning him down.

Her gaze locked with his, her heart jumping, her stomach aquiver. She was acutely aware that the bed she had spent the night in was only yards away across the terrace.

He could convince her to stay. Even knowing his passion was totally calculated, a payment for services rendered, she would still burn up if he touched her. The thought of him using his sexual expertise to reduce her to willing cooperation in his plans, whatever they were, made her legs weak.

Sheikh Gazi al Hamzeh's lips parted. "Then you will not wish to avail yourself of my offer," he said, with bone-chilling politesse. "I will arrange for your return to London as soon as possible." Then he turned, stepped to the edge of that delightful pool, and dove in.

Ten

It wasn't as easy as that. Anna would of course not be allowed to re-enter Britain without a passport. Her passport was in London, however, in her flat. The keys to her flat were in her handbag, which was presumably still at the hospital. Before anything else, someone had to be nominated to go to the hospital and pick up her belongings, then go to her flat, find her passport, and send it to her.

Anna wanted to ask Lisbet to do it, but Sheikh Gazi frowned when she suggested it. "The hospital must be dealt with very diplomatically. And anyone going into your flat may be questioned by journalists," he warned.

"Lisbet's an actress. She'll know how to handle that."

"*Allah!*" he murmured in horrified tones. "You surely do not want someone to whom publicity is the breath of life being asked by the press about your private life?''

''Lisbet won't say anything. If anyone is going to be rooting around my flat in my absence, I'd rather it was Lisbet,'' she said doggedly.

''And your other friend—Cecile?''

''If Cecile was challenged by a reporter, she'd collapse and give them my entire life back to when I sucked my thumb, and be under the impression that she had handled them very well. I love her, but really, she just has no idea.''

''There must be another way,'' said Sheikh Gazi. ''I will consider.''

Anna had to insist on being allowed to call her client to explain her delay. ''What is the point? You will be there in a day or two,'' Sheikh Gazi argued.

''The point is I was due there yesterday,'' Anna said, thinking how different the perception of time was in the Barakat Emirates. It was true there was no one at the villa to worry, but what if Alan phoned from London and got no answer? A day or two was plenty of time to get worried.

Sheikh Gazi gave in very gracefully when she explained how Sunday meant Sunday to the English, and a delay till Tuesday or even Wednesday was significant.

''Of course, darling. Whenever,'' Alan Mitching said when she tried to explain. ''You relax and enjoy yourself. The villa's not going to disappear. No one's using the place till Christmas. You can get the keys from Madame Duval anytime.'' She had the feeling that Alan was sitting there with a tabloid leaning against his breakfast teapot, avidly reading about her and Gazi.

''Will you tell Lisbet that I'll be in touch?''

''Of course.''

Having won this argument, Anna found it harder to press the other. So when Sheikh Gazi suggested that it would be best for someone from the Barakati Embassy in London to get her passport, since they could put it in the diplomatic pouch, she felt almost obliged to be as gracious as he had been in giving in.

He insisted on her being examined by a specialist, in spite of the fact that she would be back in London within a day or two and could see her own doctor. Although the man spoke German and French, he knew so little English Gazi had to translate for him.

"He says you are well, there is no lasting damage," Gazi told her, and she suddenly discovered, by the depths of her own relief, how frightened she had been, and was grateful to him for insisting.

Two days later, when she was expecting to hear that her passport had arrived in that day's diplomatic pouch, word came through that the hospital would not give up her handbag without a signed authorization.

It seemed things were going to move at a Middle Eastern speed. It was hard to find the energy to push for a faster conclusion, though, especially as the surroundings were so blissful. Her fatigue seemed to be taking this opportunity to catch up with her. Anna found she had no physical energy for anything but swimming, lying in the sun, or wandering around the beautiful house, and no mental energy at all.

She signed a permission and Sheikh Gazi sent it off by special messenger, and another day drifted past like the others.

The desert sky was black as a cat, with a thousand eyes. The wind blew, hot and maddening, around the turrets, driving her thin robe against her body, biting sand against her cheeks and into her eyes. She crept precariously along the parapet, feeling how the wind clutched at her, trying to fling her down.

He was there before her with a suddenness that made her gasp, his arms around her, dragging her against himself.

"You came," he whispered hoarsely.

The wind whipped at her, but not so harshly as his passion. Her back arched over his arm as her eyes glowed up into his. "How could I not?" she half laughed, half wept. "Am I not lost, and are not you the polestar? Am I not iron, and you the lodestone?"

Holding her with one powerful arm, he bent over her and tenderly drew the scarf from her mouth to gaze at her face in the moonlight. He drank in her beauty with a hunger that melted her, his eyes burning with desire.

"How beautiful thou art," he murmured, and his hand captured one of hers and drew it to his mouth. He pressed the fingers, then the palm, against his burning lips, water in the desert.

He kissed her throat, white in the moonlight, and she trembled with her first taste of such passion. His eyes pierced hers again. "Thou art no slave girl!" he said.

She smiled. "No. No slave girl."

"Tell me thy father's name, and I will send to him for thee. I will make thee my wife."

She shook her head. "Thou art the trusted companion of a prince," she whispered. "And truly, I am no better than a slave. Do not seek to know my father, but only know that I willingly give up all for one taste of thy love. The world holds nothing for me."

He bent his head and his mouth devoured hers with a violence of passion. The wind gusted with a sudden fury, dashing sand cruelly against them. He tore his mouth from hers.

"Your lips are nectar. Tell me thy father's name, for I will not take thee like a slave, but wed thee in all honour."

"Ah, do not ask, Beloved!" she pleaded, but when he insisted, she smiled sadly and said, "Mash'Allah! My father is King Nasr ad Daulah."

He stared at her. "But the king has only one daughter! The Princess Azade, and she—"

"True, oh Lion! Three days hence the Princess Azade is destined to become the wife of the prince to whom you are sworn in allegiance. But for one taste of your love she forsakes all."

The baby was a source of deep delight. Safiyah seemed to have cast off the trauma surrounding her birth completely. She was a happy, deep-thinking spirit who loved to lie with Anna on the terrace under a flowery, shady trellis and watch the blossoms just overhead dance in the constant, cooling breeze.

"There couldn't be a better crib toy," Anna told Sheikh Gazi. Because, whatever their differences, they were united in a deep fondness for the baby. "It's even got musical effects." The birdsong from the trees planted around the terrace and the forest beyond was nearly constant, and it was clear from Safiyah's expression that she loved to listen.

Anna was picking up a little Arabic from the nurse, in the usual women's exchange of delight and approval with a baby. *Walida jamila* was the first expression she learned. She was pretty sure it meant *pretty baby,* and she and the nurse could say it back and forth to each other, and to the baby herself, with endless delight.

And every day she felt a little more of her long-standing fatigue and unhappiness being leached out of her body and self by her surroundings.

The only fly in the ointment was Sheikh Gazi himself. His job had to be very fluid, because he worked from home, and he was almost constantly around. He sat beside the pool in his trunks, tapping away at his laptop or talking into a dictaphone or telephone, while Anna swam and sunned and played with the baby. She was constantly aware of him.

They ate together at nearly every meal. He had a powerful radio, on which he regularly listened to the news from several countries, and in different languages. They often discussed what was happening in the world, and although he was insightful and seemed very informed, he always listened to her opinions with respect.

He talked only a little about himself, though. When she asked, he told her that his job was to coordinate the publicity and public relations side of West Barakat's trade relations with the world, but spoke little more about it. Instead he talked about Barakat's history and culture.

He played music softly as he worked. Anna, who had rarely listened to Middle Eastern music, found it haunting, and in some mysterious way perfect for her surroundings. At intervals, too, could be heard from the city the wail of the muezzin, the Islamic call to prayer, and it all seemed to fit into one marvellous whole.

Sometimes it seemed as if the accident had been a doorway to another reality. A curious little space-time warp had appeared, and she had been shunted through— into some other life stream, where she joined up with a different Anna. An Anna who had made a different choice long ago, and now belonged here. Sometimes it seemed just as if Gazi had been telling the truth—as if they had been married for years.

Except for one thing.

However delicious the weather, however exotic the food his servants brought them, however sexy he looked emerging from the pool, his strong body rippling and his smoky amber skin beaded with water, however electrically she felt his presence—he never again suggested to Anna, by word or by deed, that her holiday out of time might include him as a lover.

He seemed totally immune to her physical presence. Whatever had made him kiss her with such passionate abandon on two occasions, he wasn't interested now.

She had never before met a man who had given up a pursuit of her after one little rejection, but that was what Gazi had apparently done. Or maybe it was simply that, in turning down his request to stay, she had lost her chance at the free lovemaking. In short, since she had refused his actual invitation to stay and was here only from necessity, he didn't feel obliged any longer to pretend he wanted to make love to her.

In every other way, they were practically the ideal family.

The fact that the constant delay getting her passport meant she had ended up staying after all never was mentioned between them. Anna sometimes wondered what his reaction would be if she made the suggestion that since she was, however inadvertently, acceding to his demands, he ought to live up to the original offer.

If you left out of the reckoning a teenage crush on a rock star, it was the first time in her life that she had felt such powerful romantic interest in a man who felt none in return, and it wasn't a sensation she enjoyed. Half the time she was determined not to accept even if he did change his mind, and the other half she had to restrain herself from making a clear pass.

He really was moving heaven and earth in the effort to understand her concept of time, and when she reminded him that another day was passing, he shook his head in frustration with his own stupidity and picked up the phone at once. But unfortunately, he was met with the same lack of focus at the other end. He ended up shouting in outraged impatience down the phone to a Barakati Embassy employee and hung up cursing.

"They understand nothing, these government employees!" he exploded. "To them nothing can be done without the correct documentation and by following established procedure! The person who collected your keys from the hospital put them in the safe last night, and today there is no one in the embassy to give permission for opening this safe." He glanced at her hesitantly. "I can phone Prince Karim, Anna. He is very absorbed with certain affairs of state, but...if I explain, he would call and order them to open the safe. Shall I do this?"

Anna blushed. "No, no, of course not! You can't bother the prince for that!" she exclaimed. And although he hid his relief, she could tell that it was not a request he had wanted to make.

And so another day slipped away.

Though she had told him she wouldn't be here long enough for it to be necessary, Gazi had been adamant about providing her with clothes suitable for the climate. So she had chosen a small but lovely wardrobe of mixed Middle Eastern and Western clothes from a selection sent in for her approval by a couple of city boutiques.

During the day she often wore nothing more than a bathing suit under a cotton kaftan. She never left the house, but for the moment she had no desire to do so, and it was great to be able just to slip off the kaftan any time and dive into the delicious pool.

The water was salt because the pool was, in accordance with Barakati law, Gazi told her, supplied by the ocean and not from the limited fresh-water resources of the country. So there was no smell of chlorine hovering over the garden or on her skin, and it felt like bathing in a natural pool.

She loved the sun, and although in this climate she was careful with exposure, she knew it was a source of deep healing. Her pale skin was a mark of her unhappiness and ill health, and she was delighted when it turned a soft brown.

The healthier she felt, the more physically she responded to Sheikh Gazi's constant presence, reading, tapping into the computer, talking on the phone. Sometimes she would lie on her lounger feeling the sun's hot caress and feel such a surge of desire for him she was convinced he was on the point of coming over to her, but when she glanced over he usually wasn't even looking at her. Or if he was, his face was tight with disapproval.

Every evening Anna dressed for dinner with the casual elegance her new clothes allowed. Made herself as beautiful as she could, without ever fooling herself she was competition for anyone like Sacha Delavel. She was being a fool, she knew, but she couldn't help wanting to see in his eyes, if only once, that she was attractive enough to disturb him.

Sometimes she would remember those moments when he had kissed her. She had felt such passion in his arms and his mouth, seen such burning desire in his eyes, that she had responded by going almost out of her skull with delight.

But now she had to wonder if that had been entirely faked. If he had merely been offering her a sample of the treats on offer. No doubt he could fake the whole thing if necessary. But she never felt that intensity in him now...and she found that was what she really wanted. She wanted to know she could touch his mind, his heart, his feelings. Not simply that he could perform a sexual service like a gigolo, if she insisted. That was how she stopped herself making a move.

They talked and laughed together over the delicious, candlelit meals until she was weak with wanting him. She was almost sure that the dark fire she sometimes surprised in his eyes held admiration.

Sometimes she couldn't believe that things he said could be anything other than a prelude to lovemaking. But if so, his feeling never lasted more than a brief moment. Although she was somehow kept in a constant fever of anticipation and wishing, he never touched her. And if she touched him, even with a spontaneous pat on the arm as she spoke, he would stiffen and look at her with an unreadable look that made her lift her hand.

It didn't help her get a handle on her feelings to discover Gazi was the best listener she had ever met in her life. He drew her out as if he was really interested in her life and her opinions, her experiences and her dreams. He showed particular interest in her art, wanting to know what had drawn her to want to reproduce Middle Eastern art on the walls of England's houses.

The house itself was like the magician's cave, with masterpieces of ancient scrollwork and sculpture in every corner. The patterned tilework was unbelievably artistic, the colours from a palette of magic. Anna spent hours wandering and examining the treasures.

At her request Gazi would explain the significance of

certain symbols, read and translate the beautiful calligraphic designs, so thoroughly she felt she was in a personal tutorial with a professional expert.

"How do you know so much about it?" she asked him in amazement when he had described how certain tiles had been painted and fired, and he threw her a look.

"This is my people's culture and history and art," he said, in a voice like a cat's tongue on her skin. "It is some of the greatest artistic and architectural achievement in the history of the human race. How should I not be familiar with it? Every Barakati is familiar with such things, as familiar as an English person with Shakespeare. But in addition it is my job to know such things."

She was certainly learning more about her area of interest than she had ever learned at art college, and bit by bit she was packing in a wealth of inspiration that could probably carry her for years.

If only she didn't feel that she was also packing in future heartbreak.

"Something has to give," Anna muttered after several days of inaction.

Sheikh Gazi was on the phone trying to get through to the Barakati Embassy in London.

"Yes, today I will insist—why does no one answer?" Gazi said, exasperatedly listening to a recorded message. "It is noon in London, where is everyone? Ah, of course!" He lifted a hand. "Today is Friday, *juma,* they are all at the mosque." He put down the phone. "I will try again later."

"Friday?" she murmured, almost unable to believe that so much time had passed.

"The Friday prayer is the minimum required act of

worship in the week. It is my own fault, I should have remembered.''

He had certainly remembered earlier in the day, Anna thought absently. A bit before noon, he and the entire staff had left the house in a minivan, everyone dressed in their best. She and Safiyah had been left alone for an hour, and when the van returned only Gazi and the nurse were in it.

''Is that where you all went earlier? To the mosque?'' Anna asked.

''Yes, all of my household who wish it have the right to be driven to the mosque for *juma*. It is far to walk. Then they go home to their families. Tonight you and I will eat at the hotel.''

A little later Anna poured a subtle, spicy perfumed oil into her bath and afterwards dressed with care in a flowing, ivory silk *shalwar kamees* embroidered at breast and sleeve with deep blue thread and flat beads of lapis lazuli. Her tiny silver ear studs and silver rings were all the jewellery she had, but they at least suited the outfit. A gauzy navy stole and pair of navy leather thongs on her bare feet completed her outfit.

In the early evening she joined him at the front door, where a sports car was waiting. He drove them up the road to the Hotel Sheikh Daud for dinner in luxurious elegance on a balcony overlooking the sea. From here the view was much more open; she could see the whole stretch of the shoreline around the shallow bay, out into the water of the Gulf of Barakat.

Lights twinkled from the city, on the yachts out in the bay, and in the sprinkling of houses nestled in the forest along the shore. The sea and the sky were one deep, rich black, so that it seemed to her that the sky itself rushed onto the shore and retreated again, with that hypnotic roar and hiss.

A young woman sang haunting Barakati love songs, the food was deliciously cooked, and Gazi's eyes were on her almost constantly. Anna found herself floating away on a dream. A dream that was composed of Gazi's mouth, Gazi's eyes…

He watched her, knowing what she wanted. Her wide mouth stretching in a tremulous smile, her head tilting back to offer her slim throat, as if she knew how that posture in her excited him. His own mouth was tight with control.

"This song is so beautiful," she said dreamily, at the end of the meal, when their coffee cups were drained and the singer sang again. "Tell me what the words mean."

He unlocked his jaw. "They mean that a man is refusing to fall into a trap that a woman has set for him," he replied. "A woman he desires but does not trust. She dresses in beautiful jewels and robes, she perfumes her hair, she smiles, until he is driven mad with passion. But he cannot give in."

In a brief pause in the music, his voice rasped on her ears, and Anna pressed her lips together. "He can't?"

"He knows that she is forbidden to him."

The music resumed on a haunting, wailing note, like a woman in the act of love. She made a little face of disappointment, and he thought that she would not look so if he made love to her.

"Why?" Her eyes, inviting him, were dark as the night sky, her face beautiful as the moon.

"Because she is a cheat," Gazi said harshly.

The singer's voice joined the music again with a keening plaint. Fixed by his narrowed gaze, Anna could not turn away.

"So what happens?"

"He decides to make her admit her betrayal," Gazi said softly. "He will pretend to love her, so that she will confess."

"And he calls *her* a cheat?" she asked.

"The song is about how the man fools himself as to his own motives. He is lying to himself. It is not for the reason he gives himself that he is going to make love to her, but because she has succeeded—before he even began."

The music stopped, amid applause from the restaurant patrons.

"You are beautiful, Anna," he told her in a voice like gravel. "You tempt me, with your soft looks, your willing mouth. I lie awake at night, wishing I were fool enough to believe that I could make love to you without danger. But it is not to be, Anna. You will not succeed."

Eleven

At first, hearing the word *danger,* her heart thrilled, because she believed he meant that he was in danger of falling in love with her. But his voice and the expression in his eyes were so hard...and suddenly she understood.

She drew back into her chair, her brain sharp with suspicion. "My God, you still think—!" Suddenly it all fell into place. "I've been here a *week* now, waiting for someone to perform a simple errand that Lisbet could have done in an hour! You've been delaying deliberately! What is going on?"

"I thought this way would be easier," he said, but she knew it was a lie.

"Easier for you!" she stormed. "Easier for you to keep me here against my will. Did you call back the embassy today, when the staff returned from the mosque?"

Gazi slapped a hand to his head. "Ah! I forgot!" He

lifted his wrist and glanced at his watch. "Too late now. It is past seven o'clock in London."

"You forgot. And today's Friday, and I suppose the Barakati Embassy in London closes over the weekend?"

"All embassies in London, I believe, do so. I am sorry, Anna."

Anxiety choked her. Most of a week had gone by. He had manipulated her into doing exactly what he wanted, and fool that she was, she had spent the time dreaming.

"Is there a British Embassy in Barakat al Barakat?" she demanded.

"But of course!" he assured her blandly. "The British have always been on excellent diplomatic terms with Barakat, even though they never conquered us. The embassy is in Queen Halimah Square."

"If my passport isn't here by Monday, I want to go to the embassy and ask them to issue me a temporary travel document so I can go home," Anna told him sternly.

"Very wise," he said, nodding. "Yes, an excellent solution."

"I want to stay here in the hotel tonight," she said.

He shrugged. "As you wish. Will you go now and check in?"

Anna half got to her feet. "Yes, I—" She stopped, one hand on the back of her chair, and a nearby waiter came to her aid. She stood up because she had to, but stayed looking down at Gazi al Hamzeh. "I don't have a credit card or anything."

"Perhaps if you explain your situation, they will give you credit. Foreigners need passports to register in hotels here, but I am sure you can convince them to wait until you can apply to your embassy on Monday."

Before she could come to any decision he was on his

feet beside her, and the maître d' was hurrying over to bow his distinguished guest out.

Anna had always believed she had her fair share of courage. But she could not summon enough to make a stand now. The thought of trying to make herself understood, in a foreign language, a foreign country, while making a charge of abduction against a leading citizen— a Cup Companion of the ruling prince! And Gazi, as if knowing exactly what she was trying to get the courage for, remained deep in friendly conversation with the man, all the way to the door.

And only she knew, and he knew, that the dark expression in his eyes as he smiled at her was the look of a watchdog guarding a criminal.

They did not speak on the drive back to his house. Anna went straight to her own room, without a word.

She spent a restless night. Only the fact that, thanks to the tabloids, half the world knew where she was kept her from complete panic. She tossed and turned and looked back over the week and realized how easy a mark she had been. Time had slipped by, with sun and food and good talk…. He had her exactly where he wanted her. He had accused her of trying to tempt him. But it was Gazi who had been using constant temptation to keep her brain muddled.

How easily manipulated she had been by his interest in her! He had let her talk and talk. *It's a known brainwashing technique!* she reminded herself disgustedly. *It's what cults do with their marks—give them massive doses of attention. Love-bombing.* And even knowing that, how easily she had fallen for it.

And his Arab incompetence, his lack of appreciation of Western ideas of time—she began to blush for how easily she had fallen for the stereotype. Of course he had been faking all that. She had never met a man with a more incisive, better-informed mind. He spoke at least three languages! What could have possessed her to fall into the trap of believing that he could be so inefficient and ineffectual, could lack a basic understanding of Western culture?

She saw now that he had begun this act only after she refused his invitation. He had deliberately become a caricature Arab. Anna snorted. It must have taken an extremely efficient organization to effect the abduction of her and the baby. That was a plan he had certainly conceived on his feet, and it had been flawlessly executed. From the time he found her in the hospital to the time the plane took off scarcely two hours had elapsed.

Clearly he had a crack team. Yet somehow he had fooled her into believing he couldn't organize getting her *handbag* from the very hospital he had abducted her and the baby from!

And still she had no idea why. What did he want from her? Why did he continue to think she was engaged in some kind of dishonesty? And above all, what was his reason for wanting to keep her here?

"Fly with me!"

"Willingly would I fly with thee, Beloved. But where can we fly, that is not ruled by your father or my prince?"

"India," she breathed.

He smiled at her, knowing she knew nothing save the name. "India is far, very far."

"For you I would suffer any hardship!" she cried.

"Beloved, if they catch us before we reach India, they will not let us live."

She smiled. "Choose fleet steeds, then, my Lion!"

He stood gazing out over the far horizon. "And if I say, stay here and live thy life as thy destiny demands—"

"I will fling myself from this parapet tomorrow night rather than wed him."

He turned and caught her to his chest, and stared into her eyes, his love a torment, because he was destined never to enjoy her beauty. But he could not tell her so. He put his lips on hers and tasted their deaths.

"Why then, we will fly to India," he said.

The dreams were profoundly disturbing, though she never quite remembered them. She would awaken suffocating with love and anguish, her heartbeat pounding through her system, yearning for him so desperately she could almost feel her dream lover beside her, as if his arms had only now let her go.

Her dream lover was Gazi al Hamzeh. And the dream seemed another reality, one that she half watched, half lived…always yearned for.

"I have had a phone call," Gazi said at breakfast. "Your passport has been picked up from your apartment. Today, if you wish, you can fly back to London. I will arrange for someone to meet you at the Immigration desk at Stansted airport with your passport."

She looked at him, one eyebrow raised. "If I wish? Of course I wish."

"You are determined to return?" he said softly. They were at a table on the balcony, looking out over the sun-kissed courtyard in the cool of the morning.

"Has not my home seemed to you like a good place to recuperate from your accident and restore yourself after your sorrows?" he asked, gesturing out to the paradise below them.

"In case you haven't noticed, I've had a week of that," she said. All her hackles were rising as she scented danger. Did he mean to prevent her again?

Gazi took another sip of the perfectly brewed coffee, set the cup in the saucer, and with an almost invisible flicker of his eyes, dismissed the attentive serving man, who nodded and slipped away.

"Anna, I would like to tell you...to explain something to you."

"With a view to changing my mind about leaving?"

He hesitated. "Perhaps. No—not necessarily. But in hopes that what you learn may change your mind about other things that you might plan to say or do."

"Such as talk to the media."

"And other things."

Anna was curious, but she hesitated. "Suppose you tell me what you want to tell me and it turns out you don't change my mind about anything at all?"

Gazi shrugged. "Then of course you will do whatever suits you."

She wondered if that was the truth. He had already kept her here a week against her will. What new ploy might he come up with? But, she reflected, at least she would know more about why. That had to be an advantage.

"Fire away," she said, with a casualness she was far from feeling.

"Nadia, my sister, the mother of Safiyah, is missing. This you know. We are very worried about her."

"Who is 'we'?"

"I and my family. If you permit, I will tell you Nadia's story from the beginning," he said, and waited for her nod before beginning. "Three years ago, my father announced that he had chosen a husband for my sister.

None of us knew until that moment that he was even considering such a step. It was an even greater surprise when we learned that he had chosen a man named Yusuf Abd ad Darogh. This was not a man my sister had any admiration for. She begged my father to go no further in it.''

''Oh,'' she murmured.

''I tried to reason with my father.'' Anna picked up the echo of frustration and sorrow in his voice and tried to stop her heart softening towards him. ''But my father was of the old school. In spite of all that we said, in spite of her deep unhappiness, Nadia was married to Yusuf.''

He gazed down at his coffee cup, which his hand absently clasped in a strong, loose embrace. Following the direction of his abstracted gaze, Anna had to close her own eyes. Something in the incipient power of the hold made her want to feel it close around her arm, her body....

''Yusuf's job then took him to the West,'' he was saying as she surfaced. ''He works for a large Barakati company, and he and Nadia moved to London. I am in London frequently, and of course I visited or spoke to Nadia on each visit. One of my brothers also.

''For the first year or so, things were apparently not intolerable. Then time went by, and Nadia did not become pregnant. She was becoming more and more anxious about it. We suspected that Yusuf was blaming her for it.''

Anna was listening now with her mouth soft, her eyes fixed on him, her sympathies entirely with Nadia. She heard an anxiety in his tone that proved that he loved his sister, and she couldn't help wanting to help him.

''Then at last Nadia became pregnant. But it made

Yusuf no happier. It became difficult for us to get any reading on how Nadia was. More and more there was some excuse why visits were not convenient just at the moment, or she could not come to the phone. When we did visit we somehow were never allowed time with Nadia alone. And we gradually came to understand that she was only allowed to speak to any member of her family on the phone when Yusuf was in the room with her.''

Anna shivered. "She must have felt totally helpless," she said.

"I am sure you are right, but if so, she was never able to express it.''

He paused and cleared his throat. "My father died. When they returned to Barakat for the funeral, Nadia was wearing *hejab*. Here in Barakat even a simple headscarf is not worn outside of the mosque except by the religious old women. Nadia was wearing full black robe and scarf, no lock of hair showing, which is extreme by Barakati standards, and nothing she herself would have wished. It is certain that she was made to do it by Yusuf.

"Shortly after this, when they returned to England, Nadia became ill with the pregnancy. Too ill to speak to us when we phoned. Or there were other excuses."

Gazi paused, and an expression of self-reproach tightened his mouth for a moment. "There was a great deal to see to about my father's estate. I was here in West Barakat virtually full-time for weeks. One day my brother and I realized that neither of us had been allowed to speak to Nadia for almost two months."

Anna was listening too hard to be capable of making a sound.

"We knew it was fruitless to try to phone again. Yusuf would only put us off. My brother and I flew in together on Friday last week and arrived unannounced at their apartment. We found—we found Yusuf running around the streets like a wounded animal, screaming for Nadia and saying that she had disappeared.

"He said that she had gone into labour shortly before our arrival, and he had gone out to the garage—it is in a mews behind the house—for the car. When he drew up at the front door, it was open and Nadia was gone. That is what he said."

Anna bit her lip. "Was it—do you think he was lying?" she whispered.

"There is no way to be sure," Gazi replied. "It is possible he had warning that we were on our way and staged a show for our benefit. What reason could Nadia have for running away at such a time? She would want to go to the hospital to have her baby safely."

"You don't think she was desperate and it was maybe—her only chance to escape?" Anna offered quietly.

At this, Gazi bent forward, his hands clasped between his knees. "Perhaps it is so, Anna, perhaps it is so. But now do you see how important your involvement is? You are the only lead we have. The question we must ask is, how did you come to be in a taxi with Nadia's baby? The answer to this may tell us much."

She gazed at him, feeling how strong the pull was. He had half hypnotized her, made her want to declare she was on his side. It was like pulling a tooth to stand up and walk away, out of his potent orbit. But she needed to think clearly, and she couldn't sitting so close to him. She had to do it.

Moving a little distance from the table towards an archway covered with greenery, she turned and said, "Well, thank you for telling me that. But it's *still* not the whole story, is it?"

"Why do you think so?" asked Sheikh Gazi. His gaze was just slightly wary, but she noted the change, and it proved her right.

She lifted her hands. "Because it's got more holes than a sponge! Excuse me, but there you are out combing the streets for your pregnant sister, and you just happen to search the casualty ward of the Royal Embankment Hospital, is that what I hear?"

He was watching her with steady disapproval. "There was an item on the radio that made me think I would find Nadia and her baby there. Instead I found you."

"On the radio?" she demanded disbelievingly.

"Yes, Anna," he said, and she was glad to make him understand how it felt to have his word doubted. "A silly item, meant to be amusing—'mother, baby *and* cab driver all in hospital and doing well.'"

"Ah! Okay, you found me. And you found a baby you were instantly convinced was Nadia's. And what do you do? Do you call the police and tell them your suspicions? Do you claim the baby and take it home to Papa? No, strangely enough, you *kidnap* me and this infant you are convinced is your niece, and you immediately cart us off to Barakat! Now, that needs a little more explaining than the current version of your story offers. Because even a man with your influence and connections, it seems to me, and no doubt they reach to the very top, isn't going to risk breaking the laws of two countries without a very substantial reason.

"Unless, of course, your contempt for women runs so deep you forgot that Safiyah and I had any human rights at all. You're quick to condemn your brother-in-law for keeping your sister a prisoner, but have you noticed that you are at this moment doing exactly the same thing to me?"

She saw that he was angered by that. "I do not keep you prisoner!" he exploded.

"What do you call it?" Anna cried. She suddenly doubted whether the best course after all was challenging him. Her safest alternative probably had been to pretend to go along with whatever he suggested and then, when his guard was down, make good her escape. But she was too late.

"Why don't you tell me the truth, Sheikh Gazi?"

"I have told you the truth, so far as it goes." His eyes were hard. "Recollect that you have still offered no coherent account of how you came to be in possession of my sister's baby."

"Recollect that you have offered no convincing proof that the baby *is* your sister's!"

"There can be no question of it. My brother remains in London, pursuing enquiries. If any woman had reported her child missing, he would have discovered it."

"How do you know that some past girlfriend of your own hasn't given birth and abandoned the baby? Maybe I found her!"

"You are being ridiculous," he said, his face hard. "The baby was in a satchel that had obviously been prepared for a hospital maternity visit. In that satchel, which has now been picked up from the Royal Embankment Hospital, were items recognizably my sister's."

"All right, let's assume Safiyah is your sister's baby, then. What do you suspect *me* of? Your little team has had the keys to my apartment for the best part of a week by now," she told Gazi coldly. "Don't you feel that if there was anything at all to connect me with your sister they'd have found it?"

Gazi took a breath, trying for calm. "Nevertheless, it

is very difficult to imagine any scenario in which you are completely uninvolved. You must see that. What am I to guess? That the hospital mistakenly mixed up two casualties, leaving Nadia with no baby? That Safiyah was abandoned at the precise place where you had your accident?''

''As far as I'm concerned, either of those is more likely than that I went out of my tiny mind and kidnapped a baby, all during the one half hour of my life that I don't happen to have any memory of.''

''All right.'' Gazi's full, usually generous mouth was drawn tight. ''I will tell you more. Nadia's husband, Yusuf, may suspect that the baby is not his. In Yusuf's mind his suspicion would be enough. In such a case, it is not easy to guess what he intended to do, but it is almost certain that he would not allow Nadia to keep the child and raise it as his own.''

She felt a little chill in the warm breeze, and shuddered.

''It was in the hopes of preventing Yusuf discovering that we had found Safiyah that we rushed her out of the country in the way we did. This would have succeeded, but for your actions. The press has created huge potential risk by running photos of me arriving in Barakat al Barakat with a baby. Yusuf of course now suspects that the child is Nadia's.''

His voice was hard with suspicion. Anna frowned and took a step back towards the table where he sat. ''You thought I deliberately showed the baby to the cameras to let Yusuf know you had her?''

He was sitting in a casual but not a relaxed posture, one elbow on the chair arm, his hand supporting his cheek. ''There seemed very little other excuse for such wanton disregard of the baby's safety.''

Anna gasped indignantly. "I did it to protect the baby from *you*!" she informed him hotly, flinging herself back into her chair. "I didn't know the paparazzi were even there. You had convinced me the baby was ours, but you sure hadn't convinced me you had any affection for me! I thought you were going to try to snatch her! You told me nothing but lies! How was I supposed to guess what was going on?"

He raised an eyebrow, but did not comment, merely said, "Fortunately the press blunted the damage by printing that the baby is ours, and even hinted that Safiyah is several weeks old."

She laughed in irritation. How stupid did he think she was? "Fortunately? You told them that, didn't you? You've already admitted that your job is in press relations, so you've got all the necessary contacts."

He waited for her to finish and then went on. "It was of crucial importance in deflecting Yusuf's suspicions. Yusuf will believe what he sees in print if we reinforce it. Or at least, don't contradict it. That is why I hoped that you would agree to remain unavailable for a while. Not to deny the press stories."

"And when I refused, you forced my compliance through trickery."

"There are lives at stake," Sheikh Gazi said.

"Why the hell didn't you tell me there were lives at stake, then, instead of trying to bribe me with sun and fun and money and sex?"

"Sex?" he asked, his eyebrow up. "Do I try to bribe you with sex, or has that been the other way?"

Suddenly danger of a different sort whispered on the breeze. Anna snapped, "What reason could you possibly have for suspecting that I would want to bribe you with sex? What would I hope to achieve?"

"That is something only you know!" he bit out, his own anger flaring suddenly, making Anna jump. "I find you with my sister's baby, you can give no reasonable explanation, you deliberately show her to reporters after I have successfully smuggled her out of England—" He broke off. "Did you give me any reason to trust you? You threatened me with exposure for having abducted Safiyah! What—"

"I *never* threatened you! I told you I had no intention of exposing you! I said I would do nothing more than deny—"

They were by this time almost shouting.

"To go back to England and to deny that Safiyah is our child is to send Yusuf a notarized declaration that she is Nadia's daughter," Gazi said coldly. "Now, if you are involved with Yusuf in any way, I ask you to tell me what your involvement is. And if you are not involved, I ask you to go on with the charade that has been created until we find the truth.

"For the love of God, Anna!" he cried as she hesitated. "My sister may be at this moment her husband's prisoner. Or hiding in some alley, snatching food from rubbish tins. Have you a heart, Anna, to appreciate what she may be suffering, and to help her?"

Twelve

She met him at the stables, in her disguise as a page, while the sounds of revelry still rose on the air from the palace. He dared use no light, nor kiss her, but only turned silently to lead her through dark, tortuous passages to the great city wall.

She climbed the rope ladder ahead of him, bravely, without a murmur of fear, and he thought what a wife she would have made him, if things had been otherwise.

On the other side, still without speech, he led her to the outcrop within which he had tethered two horses. With one quick embrace only, one whispered word of courage, he tossed her into the saddle.

They rode out towards the dawn.

They arrived in London at midmorning, and it was only when she felt the wheels touch down and saw the familiar landmarks that Anna started breathing again.

She had agreed to return to London and make her arrangements as quietly as possible, to head straight to France and hide out at the villa of her clients without speaking to the media.

At Immigration, they were met as promised, by an escort of three bodyguards, one of whom handed over her passport. Sheikh Gazi, she noticed, was travelling on a Barakati diplomatic passport, and they were allowed to enter Great Britain with barely a nod. No one even questioned why or how she had left the country without a passport.

Then they came through the doors into the terminal and were faced with a crowd of excited paparazzi.

Anna stopped as if she had walked into a wall. She could hear the noise of clicking cameras, but the shouted questions might as well have come from the Tower of Babel for all she could understand. She swayed.

"How on *earth* did they find out we were arriving?" she cried, astonished at the sheer numbers.

"Anna, Anna!" "Can you look this way?" "Smile for the folks, Anna!" "Are you happy? How's the baby, Anna?" "Did the baby come with you?" "What's your baby's name, Anna?"

Then a strong arm was around her, and Sheikh Gazi's hand was gripping her arm above the elbow, urging her forward. He leaned into her ear and murmured, "Walk quickly but on no account run. Let me handle them."

This was a command she was only too relieved to obey.

His voice was low and for her ear alone, and in spite of everything it raised yearning in her heart, and heat in her blood. "Look at me."

She looked nervously over her shoulder into his face, and met a glance of such lazy, sexy approval her stomach rolled over. Anna stumbled, and his strong embrace steadied her. She smiled involuntarily, her whole self stretching and basking in his unexpected admiration like a cat in a sunbeam.

The photographers cried out their satisfaction. "Kiss her, Gazi!" someone cried, and Anna's heart thumped. But the sheikh only laughed lightly and shook his head.

They moved quickly after that, his bodyguards doing no more than create a little breathing space as the group of journalists ran beside them through the terminal to the exit, calling questions.

"How do you feel about the baby, Sheikh Gazi?"

"What do you think, Arthur?" he called, as if it should be obvious.

"Did you get Prince Karim's approval?"

"He has never disapproved, to my knowledge."

"When's the wedding? Have you set the date?"

"No," the sheikh's deep voice responded above her ear.

"Are you going to?"

Sheikh Gazi threw the last questioner a smile. "Julia, you'll be the first to know."

Questions and answers were following each other in such a rapid-fire way it was a moment before Anna took it all in. She blinked and turned to him. "What are you—?" she began, but he put a warning grip on her arm.

"Let me handle it, Anna!" he said again.

It terrified her. He was doing it again. Forcing her into compliance through circumstance. She had not agreed to look the press in the eye and pretend it was true, and now she was frightened. Had he ever told her the truth? Was she a pawn in something she didn't know about? Suddenly she doubted the truth of everything he had

said. He had a much deeper reason for this constant manipulation of her. He must.

Anna swallowed, coughed and forced herself to turn
to the nearest man with a notebook.

"I am not Sheikh Gazi's mistress," she said.

"Great!" he said, scribbling. "Can I say fiancée?"

"No! Don't say I'm his fiancée! And the baby is
not—"

"The baby is not with us!" Gazi cried over her,
drowning her out. "The doctor thought it better."

His arm went tight around her and he was swooping
her through the main exit to where a limousine waited
by the curb, the rear door already open.

Anna threw one wild look along the half-deserted
road. Wherever she ran now, she would be chased by
all these journalists, and would certainly catch up
with her. What would she say then, what could she do?
She could not simply deny that she was his mistress and
that the baby was hers and then expect to disappear.
They would hound her unmercifully for the whole story.
And if she told it…Gazi had powerful friends.

Feeling like every kind of coward, Anna got into the
limousine. Gazi quickly followed. One of the bodyguards got into the back with them, the other two in front
with the driver, and a second later they were pulling
away from the happy mob of journalists.

She turned to Sheikh Gazi al Hamzeh. "How did they
know we were arriving?" she demanded furiously.

"In a moment," he said, then turned to the other man.
"Anything?" he asked.

The man shook his head. He looked younger than the
sheikh, and she thought she could detect a facial resemblance between them. "Still not a trace," he said. "She
has evaporated into air, Gazi. Yusuf insists he knows

nothing, and unless we're willing to show our hand with him, there's no saying if that's the truth or not.''

He had none of the air of a man talking to his employer. As if in confirmation of this judgement, he turned suddenly to Anna. "Hi, Anna," he said, with an engaging smile. "I'm Jafar. People here call me Jaf."

"Hello," she said slowly. She glanced back and forth between the two men.

"Jafar is my brother," Sheikh Gazi said quietly.

"It's great of you to play along, Anna," said Jaf. "We really appreciate it."

Anna didn't return his smile. "Thank your brother," she said. "I had nothing to say about it."

She seemed to herself not to start breathing again until the familiar sights of Chelsea met her eyes and she could believe that Gazi was going to do what he said and take her home.

There were a few journalists on the street in front of the ramshackle Victorian house where she had an apartment, and as the three went up the walk there were more shouted questions.

Anna left it to Gazi to talk to them, already rooting for her keys in the little shoulder bag Jaf had given back to her at the airport. But no key chain met her searching fingers. Anna clicked her tongue and lifted the bag to eye level, just as Gazi produced her keys and unlocked the door.

So Jaf had passed over her keys to Gazi instead of herself.

They all moved inside the small front hall and closed the outer door on the paparazzi. Then she held out her hand and said sharply, "My keys, please."

She waited, staring at him, until Gazi put her keys in her hand. A moment later she stepped through her own door, followed by Jaf and Sheikh Gazi, and led the way upstairs.

The phone was ringing. Anna moved into the main room as the answering machine picked up. She stood looking around her for a moment, trying to orient herself in her own life.

The room was long, with windows at each end. The south-facing half, overlooking the street, was her sitting room, with a fireplace, sofa and chairs; the north, whose windows overlooked an overgrown courtyard with a tree, was her studio, with trestle tables, trolleys, rolls of paper, a couple of painted screens that she was working on for a client. Two broad expanses of wall down both sides of the room were covered with sketches, paintings, photos, colour swatches and other bits and pieces of her working life.

Underneath them, painted on the plaster, was a series of arches not unlike those she had seen for real in Gazi's house. Anna blinked and wondered if it was merely her own mural that had given her the idea she was at home there.

It just did not feel like only a week since she had dressed for her meal with Cecile and Lisbet. She felt strange, removed from her old life, as if she hadn't been here for months.

"Hello, Anna. This is Gabriel DaSouza from the *Sun*...."

She mentally shut out the voice coming from the answerphone, and moved towards the sofa. On the table in front of it was spread the week's mail, including a few scribbled notes from the press.

Anna frowned, wondering who had placed them there, and just then heard a step in the kitchen. She whirled, her heart jumping into her throat.

"Hi!" said Lisbet. "I made the coffee while I was waiting. Jaf figured we'd all need it."

Lisbet kicked off her shoes and under Jaf's interested gaze slid her long, black-stockinged legs behind Anna on the sofa as she accepted the cup of coffee Anna had poured for her.

"Frankly, it's a mystery to me, too," she told Anna. "You ask what happened—absolutely nothing. Someone pulled up in a cab and got out, you got in. The cab drove off. It took Ceil and me a couple of minutes to flag another one. Ceil dropped me at home. That was all I knew until someone phoned me at sparrow's peep Sunday morning to say was that Anna Lamb in this morning's *Sun?* I said it couldn't possibly be you. And then Alan said you'd called him...."

Jaf leaned forward, taking his own cup from Anna's hand. "Someone got out of the cab, you say. Did you notice who?"

Lisbet pursed her lips and shook her head. "It was on the other side of the street and I wasn't really paying attention."

"Try to think back. You may have seen something. One person, a couple?"

Lisbet obligingly closed her eyes and tried to visualize the scene. "There was a tree just there—someone came past it, but whether that was whoever got out of the cab or not...one person, I think. Dressed in black, maybe, with street lighting it's—wait! There was someone in black a couple of minutes later, too. I wonder if it was the same person? By the bridge."

Lisbet opened her eyes. "I noticed her because she seemed to be wearing one of those black things that cover a woman from head to foot and I thought it was strange to see a Muslim woman by herself there at night.''

''Battersea Bridge?'' Jaf prompted.

Lisbet nodded. ''Yes, the Riverfront isn't far from there, and we were sort of strolling in that direction after Anna left, looking for a cab. This woman crossed the road ahead of us and went onto the bridge. But I don't know that she was the person who got out of the cab Anna caught. There was something about her that drew my eye, I can't really say what it was.''

Anna, meanwhile, put her hands up to her face. A woman in black. She smelled the scent of the river at night, autumn leaves.... She dropped her hands again and found Sheikh Gazi's eyes on her.

''What have you remembered?'' he asked softly.

She shook her head sadly. ''Nothing.''

They sat drinking coffee without speaking for several minutes. Lisbet was lost in thought. She surfaced and said, ''Unless something completely weird and incredibly unlikely happened after you got into that cab, Anna, the accident must have happened within a couple of minutes. He turned the corner, drove straight along Oakley to the King's Road and smashed into the bus. Five minutes max.''

''That's what I think.''

''So either someone walked up to the accident scene and slipped the baby into the crashed cab knowing that an ambulance would be coming, which, let's face it, is pretty far-fetched, or...or you got into a cab with a baby already in it.''

''Yes.'' Anna nodded.

''Or else some completely off-the-wall thing happened in the hospital.''

As her friend put into words just what she herself had

been trying to say to Sheikh Gazi, Anna felt what a huge relief it was to have her integrity reaffirmed after his suspicions. She glanced at him to see how he was taking this, but his face gave nothing away.

Lisbet went on, ''So putting myself in Nadia's place...I'm running away from an abusive husband, but I'm already in labour, right? So I—what? Give birth in the back of a cab? But then the driver would have radioed an emergency call to get an ambulance to the scene, wouldn't he? Was there such a call?''

''No,'' said Jaf, sitting forward. Lisbet was certainly convincing while she was getting into a part.

''Or he would get her straight to a hospital. What he *wouldn't* do is pull up on the Embankment and drop his passenger, with or without her baby. So, let's assume for the moment that Nadia was the person who got out of the cab that you got into, Anna, and that she left the baby in it. Doesn't it follow that she had already given birth, and *then* flagged the cab to take her somewhere?''

''Yes...'' Anna said slowly, the excitement of discovery building in her. This was starting to feel right.

Jaf said, ''The baby was absolutely newborn, wrapped in a woman's bathrobe and laid inside a satchel. She had not been washed. The hospital guessed that the driver had stopped to assist in the birth and then had hastily wrapped the baby and resumed the journey to the hospital, when the accident occurred. He is still not able to be questioned.''

Anna glanced at Gazi. ''She might have given birth in the apartment, and when he went for the car, she just ran out into the streets.''

Lisbet pursed her lips.

''You and your brother were both out of town, right?

Who in London could Nadia go to, with her baby? Who could she trust not to call her husband?''

Jaf shook his head. ''She had no childhood friends in London, only those she had met since moving here three years ago. And we think her social life was very restricted.''

''So maybe something like a women's shelter would have been her only option. Was she on her way to one? Have you checked whether there are any shelters in the neighbourhood of Battersea Bridge?''

Jaf smiled. ''We have not before thought about concentrating on this area, of course. I will see what can be done, but women's shelters are very secretive.''

''The big question is, what changed Nadia's mind? Why did she leave the baby in the cab? If she *was* going to a shelter, surely...'' Lisbet faded off thoughtfully.

Sheikh Gazi intervened at last. ''That is the flaw in an otherwise excellent argument. If she went to a women's shelter, why not take the baby with her? And in addition, whether she went to such a place, or to friends we know nothing about, why has she not called us?''

Lisbet hesitated. ''I hate to—uh.'' She glanced at Anna for guidance. Anna, catching her meaning, shrugged.

Lisbet turned to Gazi. ''I have one advantage over you here. I *know* that Anna isn't involved in the way you suspect. I know that she doesn't know any guy named Yusuf, and that she wouldn't be involved in anything like baby-snatching if she did,'' she said firmly, and Anna suddenly felt like crying. ''I also know that if she says she was confused after the accident and has amnesia about a critical moment, that's the exact truth. So.''

She heaved a breath. No one else spoke. ''I don't want

to distress you, and please forgive me if this suggestion is way off beam, but is it possible that…I mean, unhappy people have been known to…do you think Nadia went to the bridge because jumping seemed the only way out?''

Thirteen

"I've got to go," Lisbet said, looking at her watch a few minutes later. "We've got a night shoot up on Hampstead Heath tonight and I'm due in Makeup in an hour." She turned to Anna. "Do you want to come and hang out for a while?"

The question was put casually, but Anna knew that it was her friend's way of extricating her from a difficult situation. If she went with Lisbet, Sheikh Gazi and his brother would have no option but to leave.

But she found herself shaking her head. "I've got to get to France, Lisbet. I'm only half packed and I have to organize my ticket."

Lisbet lifted an eyebrow as if she understood more than Anna was confessing. "Well, phone me on my mobile later. I'll probably be hanging around doing nothing most of the night."

"All right."

Lisbet slipped into her shoes and a smart little jacket, put sunglasses on her nose.

"Would you allow me to take you where you have to go?" Jaf offered, and Lisbet's mouth was pulled in an involuntary, slow smile.

"Sure," she said easily.

"They will photograph us," Jaf warned, gesturing towards the windows and the photographers still waiting in the street below. "Do you mind?"

Lisbet laughed. "I'm an actress, Jaf. Publicity is everything."

A moment later Gazi and Anna watched from the windows as Lisbet and Jaf braved the journalists and slipped into the back of the limo. As the limo pulled away she turned to look at him, and all at once the silence weighed very heavily in the room.

"Well," Anna said. "Sorry we couldn't be more help."

Sheikh Gazi took her hand, but not in a handshake, and stared into her eyes. "You can be of more help," he said, in a rough, urgent voice. She felt a surge of energy from him travel up her arm to her throat and chest.

"I really—" Anna coughed to clear her throat. "I really can't, you know, unless I remember something. But I do think Lisbet's right. The baby had to be in the cab when I got into it."

"That is not what I mean, Anna."

Her heart began a wild dance in her breast. She stared at him, licked her lip unconsciously and, taking her hand from his, turned away to hide the heat she felt burning up in her cheeks.

He was mesmerizing, he really was. He had the most extraordinary ability to turn himself off and on. A few

minutes ago, listening to Lisbet, he had gone to low
voltage, Anna thought wildly, effacing himself in some
mysterious way to watch and listen. Now he was high-
powered again.

"I'm almost afraid to ask," she joked, nervous of her
own deep response.

He looked at her with a frown and turned her towards
him, his eyes searching her face till she felt exposed and
vulnerable, was trembling. She had never felt so emo-
tionally fragile just at a man's look. Almost shaking with
nerves, she lifted her hands up and placed them against
his chest. She felt his body react to the jolt of the connection, and his eyes darkened suddenly, like a cat's.

And then his arms were around her, and he was staring down into her upturned face. "Anna," he murmured,
his lips inches from her own. She felt him tremble and
with fainting pleasure recognized in him a mixed desire
to cherish her and yet crush her against himself.

Then he closed his eyes, and she felt him tense with
a huge effort of will. In the next moment she was released. He dropped his arms and stepped back.

"We must talk," he said.

A little laugh of bitter disappointment escaped her. So
she was still the woman who was a cheat, whose temptation he must resist.

"Must we?"

"Anna, what your friend said has changed the picture.
You must see this."

"Yes, and how does it affect me?" she asked,
blowing air out hard and turning away as she tried to
get a grip on the passionate ache her arms felt to hold
him.

"It is no longer enough, Anna, that you agree simply
to disappear to France and say nothing to the press."

She turned to look over her shoulder at him with deep hostility. "Why not?" she demanded.

"They are out there, Anna. They know you now—they will chase you for the story."

"And whose fault is that? Are you suggesting it was *not* your brother who notified everyone and his dog of our arrival time?"

"No, you are right. It was Jaf who did this. I am sorry. We thought only to take one last advantage of your presence, to get one more story that might convince Yusuf. But now things are more desperate."

"But Lisbet didn't tell you anything you didn't already know—or guess."

"Yes," he contradicted. "May we sit down again?"

It was a command, and her reaction was to turn towards a chair. A sudden draft made her feel how the temperature was dropping outside—or perhaps it was inside her own heart—and Anna stooped and flicked on the gas fire in the fireplace before flinging herself into an armchair on one side of it.

The gas ignited with a whoosh. Sheikh Gazi took the chair opposite her, on the other side of the fireplace. Then for a moment he turned his gaze to blink thoughtfully at the flames leaping up around the fake coal.

She watched him. The bone structure of his face was emphasized by the firelight flickering over it in the gathering dusk, revealing sensitivity at temple and mouth. In this light he looked like an old portrait of a saint, sensuous and ascetic together. She suddenly saw, behind the playboy handsomeness, that he was a man used to the rigours of self-discipline. And he was exerting it now.

Sheikh Gazi stared into the fire. He began speaking slowly. "Ramiz Bahrami has been my close friend most of my life. His family is from one of the ancient tribes in the mountains of Noor, but his father moved to the capital to serve the old king. Ramiz and I went to school in the palace and later to university together. He is a close, personal friend of Prince Karim. Highly trusted."

Anna blinked, her lips parting in surprise, and he flicked his eyes from the fire to her face. She saw open pain in them, and her heart hurt for him.

"My sister Nadia and Ramiz fell in love. She could not have chosen a better man. It was when Ramiz approached my father to ask for permission to marry Nadia that we were all rocked by the information that my father had already chosen Yusuf for her.

"I told you I argued with my father. I tell you now I never pleaded so strongly with him about anything before or since. But he would not give in. Ramiz was a university-educated, moderate Muslim with political ambitions, and Yusuf was mosque-educated, ignorant of the world, devout. It was one thing for my father to let his sons be educated at university. It was another thing entirely to give his daughter to such a man."

He was silent for a moment, staring into the flames.

"How did Ramiz react to his refusal?" she prompted softly.

"They both took it hard. Very hard. Ramiz appealed to the prince to intervene, but although Prince Karim did make a request, he knew very well that a father cannot be ordered even by a prince in such a matter.

"Ramiz wanted to run away with her. I would have assisted them, but Nadia was raised with a strong sense of religious duty. She felt it right to obey my father, even in this. And she knew that such a thing in any case would ruin Ramiz's political career."

He breathed. "She said no. I was sorry for it, and yet I knew she was right."

If he was trying to get her onside with this recital, he was succeeding. Anna's heart was deeply touched.

"Ramiz left the country before the wedding—Prince Karim kindly sent him on some mission abroad. He did not return until Yusuf and Nadia had come here to London."

"Has Ramiz married?" Anna asked softly.

He looked at her, shaking his head once. "No. He devoted himself to work. Karim trusts him absolutely. For the past year he has been engaged on something that took him to various countries. For a while he was in Canada.

"It is only since Nadia's disappearance that I have learned from the prince that Ramiz spent part of the past year here in London."

She gasped. "Do you think they met?"

"Now that the pieces come together a little, I begin to believe that they met. I think that this was the root of Yusuf's jealousy, of his suspicion that Nadia's baby was not his own."

"Did Yusuf know that Ramiz and Nadia were in love?"

"It is possible that my father confided something to Yusuf. I cannot say it is not so. My father might have hoped in this way to prevent trouble by alerting Yusuf to the danger."

She could say nothing. What a wholesale betrayal of a daughter.

Gazi took a breath. "Anna, the story is not over. Ramiz disappeared several months ago, and Prince Karim cannot be certain where he was at the time of his disappearance. But it is very possible that he was in England."

"Are you...are you saying Yusuf killed him?"

Again pain was mirrored on his face. "We can't be certain. Ramiz may even be alive. But it seems more of a possibility now that Ramiz's disappearance, rather than being connected with his secret work for Prince Karim, was because of his personal life."

"Do you think that Yusuf is right? Is Safiyah Ramiz's baby and not his own?"

"How can I be certain unless we have tests done? It will be some time before this can be arranged. And time is something we do not have.

"Anna, if your friend is right, and it was Nadia she saw that night…if Nadia is dead and Ramiz also, then it is possible that Safiyah is the only heir either of them will ever have.

"As things stand, as the legal father under English law, Yusuf has the right to custody of Safiyah. I cannot give up custody of the only child my sister and my friend will ever have to such a man as this, and with such a motive to hate her.

"Anna, I ask you, as a woman who knows the value of one child's life, to go on with the pretence we have started. Let the world think we are lovers. Pretend Safiyah is our child. Stay with me until we have discovered the fate of Nadia and Ramiz."

He wasted no time acting on her capitulation. By the time she had hastily thrown a few things into a bag, completed her half-made arrangements for leaving the flat unoccupied for a few weeks, and written a note for the downstairs tenant, another limousine was waiting to sweep them off to London's most prestigious hotel.

There they went to a huge suite on the top floor, with wonderful views overlooking Hyde Park. "We must give the press as much fodder as we can," he told her.

"The more Yusuf reads about us in the papers, the more he will believe."

Before anything else, Gazi insisted that Anna should be examined by another medical expert on head injury. The surgeon, who seemed to be a personal friend, however, was as cheerful as his counterpart in Barakat had been.

"It's not uncommon for accident victims to experience amnesia such as yours," he reassured Anna. "The period of time immediately surrounding the trauma is lost. In fact, it's unlikely you'll ever regain those minutes. But there is absolutely nothing to worry about."

After that she went to the private Health Suite, where she had a steam bath and a massage, and emerged feeling totally pampered. Then she went downstairs to see a top hairdresser, and then a makeup artist.

She returned to the suite to find that several outfits had been sent up from a boutique downstairs for her choice.

"Choose something for tonight," Gazi ordered her. "We will have dinner in a club. Tomorrow we will go shopping in the stores."

She chose a simply cut, utterly luxurious full-length coat and spaghetti-strap dress in black velvet. She had never worn anything so expensive in her life. The outfit clung to her, emphasizing her fashionable thinness.

She emerged from her bedroom, feeling she had never looked so stylish in her life, to find Gazi at a desk in the sitting room of the suite. He looked up, and for an instant his eyes burned her. Then he dropped his eyes and snapped open one of several cases on the desk.

"Diamonds, perhaps," he said with forced casualness, offering it to her.

Anna gasped when she looked inside. "Oh, goodness, where did these come from?"

He raised an eyebrow. "From the jeweller down-stairs." He lifted from its silky bed a fabulous necklace that seemed to burn with cold fire, and when he slipped it around her neck she was almost surprised that it didn't scorch her skin. "Do you like diamonds, Anna?"

She laughed, delighted at the utter madness of her life, and turned to the mirror above the fireplace. "I've never really been on speaking terms with diamonds," she said. "But I'm quite happy to wear a necklace like this to-night, I promise you!"

Later, sitting at the table beside her on an intimately small, semicircular bench seat in a place so famous Anna had to pinch herself to believe it, Gazi observed, "Di-amonds are too cold for you. You should wear coloured stones. Sapphires, to match your eyes."

Anna only laughed, shaking her head, and fingered one of the earrings.

"You must wear a variety of jewels over the next day or so," he said. "Then, it will please me if you will choose the set you like best to keep. As a gift of grati-tude."

Anna almost choked on the tiny garlic mushroom she was eating as a starter. "Choose a *set* of jewels?" she exclaimed, putting a hand to her throat, and feeling the diamonds glowing there. "You're joking! These must be worth a fortune!"

"What you are doing for Nadia is worth much more to me," Gazi said.

Anna gazed down at the beautiful diamonds encircling her wrist, shaking her head. "Thank you. Not that I have anything against jewellery, Sheikh Gazi, but there's something else that I'd much rather have.'' She looked up. ''It would be a real favour, if you—''

His face darkened with an unreadable expression. His gaze raked her with an intensity that held more fire than the diamonds, leaving her gasping for air. Anna breathed and thought, *God, he thinks I'm going to ask him to make love to me*— But before the thought was completed, the sheikh was in control of himself again.

''Whatever you ask for, if I can,'' he said levelly.

She could hardly speak, for the thought of what that unguarded moment had told her was choking her. Desire pulled at her, drew her lips into a trembling smile. She could not control that, for what else could his look mean, but that he wanted her, and for some reason known to himself, was exercising rigid control?

In the moment when that control had slipped, she had felt a powerful passion emanating from him. Her whole body seemed to be made of butterflies now, all fluttering, so that nothing but thought held her being together. She was so fragile she would dissolve in the smallest gust of wind.

She knew that he could not remain in control if she challenged him. The thought was like champagne to her system, making her drunk.

She swallowed and tried to speak.

''Tell me,'' he commanded, and Anna struggled to bring her own thoughts back in line.

''I just—it just occurred to me that you could maybe mention to people that I'm a mural artist, specializing in Middle Eastern themes. It would be such fabulous publicity for me. And if as a result I got even one commission from—'' she lifted a hand and gestured around the room, where more than one table had recognizable faces

"—from someone like this, well, I'd be muralist to the stars, wouldn't I?"

He stared at her, his eyes narrowed. "And you would rather have this than precious stones?"

Anna smiled, biting her lip. "It would be a lot more useful over the long term."

"You are a very unusual woman."

Jealousy clawed her, and she didn't think before she spoke. "But then I suppose the favours I'm providing are a little different than what you're used to, too."

His eyes went black as he got it, and his hand found hers on the table between them and crushed it as he stared into her eyes. All the breath left her body in one grunting moan at the suddenness of the change in him. She thought, *I've done it, he's lost control,* and the thought made her blood wild.

"It will not be a favour, Anna, from me or from you, when it happens," he growled between his teeth, and kissed her hand with a mouth drawn tight with passionate control. "It is a necessity between us. You know it."

She felt passion like burning heat in his touch, saw it in his eyes, felt it rush through her body so powerfully she was dimly grateful she was not standing. Gazi was trembling as his hand released hers and came up to stroke her temple, her cheek. She shivered.

"Is it not so? Do you not feel it so?"

She couldn't have said a word to save her life, she was so swamped with feeling. She tried to swallow, but her throat was choked.

"I have seen it in your eyes, Anna! In every move you make!" he insisted. "Do you deny it?"

She opened her mouth and dropped her head back, trying to catch her breath. Electric sensuality roared through her, setting every part of her alight.

"I have wanted you until I was mad," he whispered hoarsely. "Your perfume, your mouth, your body stretched out in the sun…what it cost me, hour after hour, day after day, to see you there, to feel how you wanted to tempt me—*ya Allah!* how I wanted you!"

"Gazi!" she whispered helplessly.

"And do you challenge me now with talk of favours? Favour?" His voice grated over her charged nerves, blinding her with sensation, making her faint. "Shall I ask you for this as a favour, and offer you jewels in return? How much will you ask, I wonder? A diamond for each kiss, Anna? Another for every thrust of my tongue into your sweet mouth, to make us both mad with wanting more? And what, to touch your breasts? A bracelet of sapphires?"

His voice dropped to a tiger's hungry growl. She could feel his breath against her neck. "To open your legs for me, Anna, what for this favour? A necklace, a tiara? I give it to you, yes! If it were necessary I would bury you in jewels, make love to you on a bed of diamonds and rubies and then give them all to you."

His eyes burned her, heat licking through her body, melting everything into wild need.

"But it will not be necessary, Anna—will it? Do you think I do not know that to make you open your legs I need only ask with my tongue for entry? If I press my kiss on you there, Anna, who does whom the favour? Tell me that you too do not want this, if you can. Tell me the thought of my tongue on your body is not part of your dreams as it is of mine."

"Stop," she moaned helplessly. "My God, Gazi, stop, I'm—"

"Think of opening your legs to my kiss, Anna," he commanded, watching how desire burned her and made her tremble, devouring her need. "Think of my tongue, my mouth, think how the heat will stir you, make you need what only I can give you. How you will cry out, and beg for more."

"Gazi," she pleaded. "Gazi, I can't take it."

"Yes," he said, deliberately misunderstanding her. "Yes, you can take more than this. You must. Do you think I can stop there? No, once we start, Anna—"

He lifted her hand to his mouth again, and bit the fleshy part of her palm between strong white teeth. A thousand nerves leapt into wildest reaction, and she could scarcely stifle the moan that rose to her throat.

"What comes next, Anna? Who will beg whom for the favour of my body inside you, hmm? Will we not beg each other for it? Say it!" he commanded.

She wondered dimly how she would survive. She opened her eyes and mouth at him, struggling for control.

"Tell me!" he commanded again.

She licked her dry lips, opened her mouth for air. "Tell you what?"

"Tell me whether you will ask me for the favour, Anna. Tell me that you will want it, too. Or will it be a favour you grant me when I ask?"

Feeling coursed up and down her body, through every cell.

She dropped her head. "You know I want you," she said, scarcely getting the words out.

It was as if she struck him with all her strength. She saw his back straighten with a jolt, his head turn to one side. His eyes never left hers, and she saw blackness like the centre of a storm, and realized that he had, at last, been driven beyond his strength.

Fourteen

It was at that moment that their lobsters arrived. She saw Gazi flick an unbelieving glance at the waiter, and at the plate, saw his hand clench. Then his eyes moved from the deliciously steaming lobster slowly up to her face, and he smiled a smile that sent little rivulets of sensation all over her.

They were silent as the pepper grinder made its ritual pass over both plates and then Gazi picked up a claw of the lobster between his strong fingers. His hands clenched till the knuckles showed white, and she quivered where she sat, knowing it was a sign not of exertion, but control. The shell broke open to reveal the tender white meat.

His hand not quite steady, he dipped the triangular wedge of flesh in butter, lifted it and held it out invitingly to her mouth. Anna tried to speak, failed, licked her lips and then submitted, leaning forward a little to

take the meat between her teeth and pull it delicately
from the shell.

He watched her chew and lick the butter from her
mouth, with a smile that took her breath away. She
dropped her eyes to her own plate, picked up the cracker
and broke a piece of shell, then did as he had done,
dipping the tender juicy flesh into butter, and holding it
for him to eat.

When his teeth closed firmly on the meat, biting it,
drawing it out, and then eating it with sudden, uncontrolled hunger, a shaft of purely sexual sensation went
through her. Anna grunted, and his eyelids flickered.

The meal that followed was torment, the torment of
overcharged senses. Anna had never experienced a sensuality to equal it in all her life. They fed themselves
and each other without plan, with their bare hands, with
forks, biting, chewing, licking, and fainting with delight
at each touch of lips and tongue on buttery flesh.

And all the time he talked to her, in a low, intimate
voice that was another charge on her drunken senses.
"You lay in the sun, Anna, the sweat breaking out on
your skin, on your thighs, till I could think of nothing
but my tongue licking it off, till I could taste the salt of
you actually in my mouth…and you knew it and I knew
you knew it."

"No," she whispered.

"How I wanted to punish you for tempting me. I
dreamed of how I would do this, how I would make you
weep with desire and wanting. How my hands and
mouth would touch you, caress you, stroke you…my
hands on your damp skin, stroking your feet, your
thighs, your stomach, your breasts. Sometimes, when
you lay on your back, it was like death, the wanting to

walk over to you, to put my hand on the fabric of your suit and draw it aside and kiss you there.

"I told myself my tongue would torment you till you wept for the thrust of my body, and then I would refuse, so that you should know what torment was mine.

"But I knew I was a fool. If once I had touched you, I would have lost all. If I made you beg, at the first pleading I would have to thrust into you. I could not have resisted then."

"Gazi," was all she could whisper.

"Yes, I dreamed of you saying my name in this way," he said roughly, as if the sound of her voice was too much, and held another delicate morsel up to her lips. "And you will say it again for me, in every way that I dreamed."

He looked down at her body, at the bare, soft brown shoulders, the slender curved arms, the soft folds of the fine velvet that covered her breasts. Her nipples pressed against the delicate velvet cloth, announcing her sexual arousal.

She was constantly half fainting. Her blood ran between head and body with a wild rushing that drowned her. She saw him looking down at her body, saw his eyes darken.

He offered her another buttery bite. Looking into his stormy, hungry eyes, she thought of how she would kiss his flesh, too, and gently took what he offered onto her tongue, half smiling at him in sensuous promise.

The breath hissed between his teeth. "You drive me to the edge," he said in a voice like gravel.

When the meal was over, Anna could scarcely stand. She staggered, her knees turned to butter, and was sure she must look drunk, if anyone were watching them, but she didn't want to find out. Gazi took the coat from the attendant and held it for her, and she could feel his arms like iron with the effort it took not to pull her into his embrace as she slipped her arms inside the sleeves.

Neither of them even noticed the photographers' cameras as they went, hand in hand, his grip so possessive it hurt her, out to the waiting car.

His control lasted until the limousine door shut them in. With a steady hand he pressed a switch, and a blind hummed up to cover the glass between the passenger compartment and the driver's. Another switch plunged them into darkness. Music was already softly playing. Outside the black-tinted windows, the city lights began to slide past.

He reached for her, passion tearing at them both, and with a cry she was in his arms. He drew her across his lap, her head in one possessive hand, his other arm wrapping her waist under the velvet coat, and lifted her up to his mouth for the wildest, hungriest kiss either of them had ever experienced. They were pierced with passionate sweetness, and moaned their pent-up need against each other's lips.

Never had a kiss sent so much pleasure through her body, so that she trembled and clung, shivering with desire. Never had his mouth been so hungry for a woman, so that no matter how he drank, he could not get enough of her. Her arms wrapped his head, her fingers threaded the dark curls, while her mouth opened to his wild demands.

The car stopped, a door slammed, and at last, heaving with breath, they broke apart. She lay looking up at him, seeing nothing but the glint of light on his curling hair; he stared blindly down at her. Like two animals, scenting each other in the darkness.

"We are at the hotel," he murmured.

Her hand was clenched in his hair and Anna had to command her fingers to let him go. She felt the hard, uncomfortable pressure from his groin against her side and smiled as he helped her to sit up.

"All right?" he asked, and she heard the click as he unlocked the door. The chauffeur opened it, and a moment later they were inside the hotel and stepping into the luxurious, golden-lighted elevator that carried them upwards.

In the darkened sitting room, two lamps cast soft pools of light, and a fire had been lit in the grate. They moved towards it without speaking. Beside the fireplace a small table held a decanter and glasses.

"Will you have a brandy?" Gazi asked as he helped her out of her velvet coat. The silky lining brushing her skin was almost more than she could bear. She nodded mutely as he tossed the coat onto a sofa, and he turned to the table.

He lifted the stopper out of the decanter and set it down with a small sound that seemed to resonate around them. The slight gurgling of the liquid, even, was another branch laid on the erotic fire.

He handed her the goblet, the brandy a glowing, rich, warm amber in the bottom. Picking up his own, he swirled, drank, and set the glass down again. Then he bent and hungrily kissed her.

The taste of brandy hit all her senses as he kissed it into her mouth, onto her tongue. Anna felt shivers of sensation from her brain to her toes, and with her free hand clutched at his jacket front, her head going back to allow him the fullest access to her mouth.

His hands enclosed her, one arm around her waist, one hard on her naked shoulder. He lifted his mouth from

her mouth, and moved hungrily down the line of her
throat. The taste of brandy on her tongue smoked
through her system, and hot on its trail little flames of
sensation licked their way.

His hand found the little velvet buttons at her back,
and one by one began to undo them. Her eyes closed
dreamily, the better to follow the progress of his determined fingers down her spine, from between her shoulder blades, down and down along her spine to her waist,
while her skin became ever more sensitive.

The buttons stopped below her waist, leaving the
whole long stretch of her back naked and accessible to
his teasing, tasting hands, and he stroked and caressed
the bare skin while his mouth sought hers again.

The room was warm. All her shivers arose in his
touch, a curious heated chill running crazily all over and
through her. She buried her hand in the thick curls of
his head and obediently bent backwards as he pressed
her body tight against him.

Her glass was slipping from her grasp, and as he
straightened he took it from her and set it down. Then
he stood close, looking down at her. The straps of her
dress had loosened and were slipping off her shoulders,
and she instinctively bent her elbows up, placing her
hands against her throat.

"Let it fall," Gazi commanded softly, and his voice,
too, was all erotic sensation, compelling her obedience.
She dropped her arms to her sides, and the velvet whispered slowly, slowly down over her breasts, leaving
them naked to the touch of the fireglow.

He closed his eyes, opened them again, and that, too,
created sensation in her. The dress rested precariously
on her hips for a moment, clung there, and then, as he

reluctantly, slithered down the gentle curve and fell with a little swoop to her feet.

She stood revealed in tiny black briefs, smoky lace-top stockings, delicate high-heel mules, and the diamond circlets at throat and wrist.

His hands reached out to slide with possessive heat down her back and encircle her rump, and he drew her against him, gazing into her eyes with a hotter, brighter flame than the fire provided.

"You will drive me out of my mind," he growled, and as her head fell helplessly back he pressed his lips against the pulse at the base of her throat. Her hands wrapped his neck, slid down his back onto the silky fabric of his jacket.

"Take this off," she murmured, as her hands moved to his chest and slipped inside and against his shirt, pushing the jacket down his arms. He shrugged out of it and let it fall, and now she flirtatiously pulled at his neat black bow tie, untied it, and with a hungry, teasing smile, slowly pulled it away.

He smiled, his eyes dark, and let her work on the tiny buttons, one by one, of his shirt. His chest was darkly warm in the firelight, and as she pulled the shirt down his arms, she laid a line of kisses in the neat curling mat of hair, up and across his shoulder to his throat.

"You have not taken off my cuff links," Gazi murmured protestingly, as his mouth smothered hers in a kiss so hungry she moaned.

Anna smiled. "You're at my mercy, then," she whispered, drawing the shirt further down his arms to pinion him.

He smiled a smile, and lifted his arms, the muscles bulging for a moment of exertion, and then she heard the sound of tearing fabric and the distant clink of but-

tons hitting somewhere, and his arms were free, each
wrist carrying a tattered half shirt. He stopped a moment
to tear himself free, tossing the remnants of the shirt
wildly away. Then his arms wrapped her tight, dragging
her against him with a ruthlessness that told her she had
released a demon in him, and swung her up to carry her
to his bedroom.

"A little further, Beloved, before we rest."

*"Ah, how weary I am with riding! How far to India
now, my Lion?"*

*He looked over his shoulder at the cloud in the dis-
tance. "Not far, my princess. Courage."*

*But her eyes followed his, and now she, too, saw the
signs of pursuit. "Riders!" she cried. "Oh, Lion, is it
my father?"*

*"A caravan," he lied. "On its way, like us, to India.
We shall join them."*

*She spurred her mount to a gallop again, and bit her
cheek not to cry out against the pain and weariness.
They rode in silence, as those behind grew steadily
closer.*

"Will they catch us, Lion?" she asked.

He did not answer.

Anna awoke from the dream just before dawn, still in
his arms. Rain drove against the windows and she lay
listening to the music of it.

Never in her life had she been held with such passion
as she had felt in Gazi's hands, never had she experienced such a wild storm of pleasure and need as had
swept her in his embrace.

When he entered her, it was all fresh, all new, for the
joy she experienced had touched a part of her that no

one had ever touched in her. Everything that had gone before was like a sepia photograph in comparison. She had clung to him, accepting the thrust of his body from the depths of her self, weeping as pleasure suffused her.

She loved him. She looked into his face now, the faint glow of dawn showing her the mark on his eye, and a passion of tenderness overwhelmed her. Her heart melted in its own burning, and was reborn stronger, surer, understanding things that until yesterday she had only dimly glimpsed.

Of course he did not love her. He was attracted, but for a man like him sexual passion was more a part of his being than her effect on him. She had no illusions about ordinary Anna Lamb's ability to touch his heart.

It would break her heart when her time with him was over. Maybe it would have been better for her if she had resisted the temptation of his lovemaking...but Anna had the feeling that, however much this affair cost her in the end, when she was an old woman she would look back on her moments with Sheikh Gazi as something she was glad to have experienced.

She felt chilly suddenly, and instinctively slipped closer to him. Still asleep, he reached for her, and drew her in against his warm, naked body as if that was where she belonged.

The Sunday papers were delivered to the suite, and as they sat over their breakfast at a table set cozily in front of a bright fire, Gazi and Anna glanced through them.

The story of their arrival in London was not extensively reported, though it had got a few mentions in gossip columns. Only one paper ran a picture on the front page. It was a shot of her looking up at him, and

she thought the look between them should set the paper
on fire.

Gazi glanced from the paper to her with a look that
made her heart jump with sadness, though she couldn't
have said why. Perhaps because her pictured face was
that of a woman deep in love, and that troubled him.

He shook his head over the favourite story, a rehashed
royal scandal. "We must do better than this," he said
matter-of-factly, tossing the last tabloid aside and picking up his coffee. "Yusuf cannot be counted on to read
gossip columns."

Anna gazed at him. "Do better, how?"

"First things first," Gazi said, with a smile that
stopped her heart. "I must take you shopping."

Anna had only ever dreamed of the kind of shopping
trip that followed. He seemed to want to buy her everything he saw. She protested several times that he was
buying too much, but he simply ignored her.

"Never has so much been purchased by so few in so
short a time," she joked, as he signalled his approval to
yet another outfit, one only suitable for a yacht cruise.
At last he said, in a bored voice, "Anna, you must have
clothes if we are going to carry this off."

"But where will I ever wear these?"

"On my yacht," he said with surprise.

"But, Gazi—" she began again, and he made an impatient sound.

"Anna," he told her in a low voice. "I ask you to
remember that you are the pampered darling of a rich
Arab, and the mother of his only child. Please, Anna!
Cannot you find it in you to be capricious, difficult to
please, even a little greedy? You should be saying
'Can't I have both, darling?' not 'Gazi, you are spending
too much on me!' You are doing me a great favour

much more than you know, and it is only right that I should reward you according to my means. Do you think a few thousands spent on clothes means anything to me?''

Then she gave herself up to it—total, guilt-free shopping.

''Can I buy one for Lisbet?'' she asked, when he encouraged her to buy several fashionable pashminas in a variety of colours. Gazi shrugged his approval. ''Buy her a dozen, Anna,'' he said.

His cellphone rang several times as they shopped, and he had brief discussions with the callers. When they had finished their shopping at one famous store, Anna was surprised to hear Gazi say that they would take everything with them.

The store produced several uniformed footmen to carry their packages. Gazi chose a medium-sized shopping bag and handed it to Anna. ''Carry this, Anna,'' he said, and took two small boxes under his own arm.

Followed by the footmen, whose arms were full, he led the way to the exit. Outside they were met by two or three photographers, who snapped their cameras as the little procession, the image of conspicuous consumerism or remnant of a vanished era, depending on your point of view, walked along the pavement to the limousine waiting a few yards away.

When they got into the car, she grinned at Gazi. ''You're really good at this!'' she said.

''It is a part of my job to be good at it. In any case, it is not difficult to manipulate something like the media,'' he said. ''Greed is the biggest weakness anyone has, whether an institution or an individual.''

She eyed him. ''Do you think it's right to manipulate people?''

"Anna, if I said to the editors of those papers, 'In the hope of saving my sister's life I need you to run a certain story,' do you think they would agree?"

She thought. "I don't know. Wouldn't they?"

"It is possible. But it is also possible that one of them at least would consider the fact that I am afraid for my sister's life at her own husband's hands a much better story. I do not wish to see a headline tomorrow reading *Save My Sister, Pleads Arab Playboy*."

She was silenced.

They returned to the hotel, where they had a few hours to prepare for a black-tie function in the evening. Anna had the full treatment again, massage, manicure and pedicure, and professional makeup job.

By the time she was ready for the party she was feeling utterly pampered, and she knew she had never looked better in her life. Her hairstyle wasn't violently different from her old one, but it was a thousand times better cut. Little locks of hair tumbled this way and that over her scalp and down the back of her neck in charming confusion, with half a dozen sapphire-and-diamond trinkets nestling artistically among them, which seemed to reveal a dark sensitivity in her sapphire eyes. Her individual looks and fine bone structure had been dramatized with subtle shading and black eyeliner, and her wide, expressive mouth was coloured dark maroon.

She wore an ankle-length coat dress with a stand-up shirt collar, bodice snugly fitted to the waist, and slightly flaring skirt that was open at the front to well above the knee. It was made of soft-flowing midnight-blue and creamy tan silk brocade that matched both her skin and the deep blue of her eyes. It gave the impression that she was naked under a covering of lace. For warmth she carried one of her new cashmere pashminas, in matching midnight-blue.

She was all blue, black and tan. With clear nail varnish on her short artist's nails, and stockings that matched the navy of the dress, the only flash of real colour was her wine-dark lips. Anna looked dramatic and sensational and, staring at herself in the mirror, she thought that, although she would never be a beauty, perhaps tonight it was just a little less unbelievable that she might be the consort of a man like Sheikh Gazi al Hamzeh.

He was looking extremely rich and handsome himself, in a black dinner jacket with diamond cuff links and diamond button studs nestling among the intricate pleats of an impeccable white silk shirt.

He lifted his head from the contemplation of the fire as she entered the room, and his eyes found her in the huge slanted mirror just above the mantel. His glance darkened in a way that sent blood rushing to her brain, and for a moment neither moved.

Formal wear seemed to emphasize the patch around his eye. He really was a swashbuckler tonight. Anna shivered with a frisson of pure sexual excitement.

"Hi," she said, lifting a hand to shoulder height and waggling her fingers at him, a crazy grin splitting her face.

He turned. "Hi," he returned, smiling with one corner of his mouth, his eyes still intent. "You are very lovely tonight, Anna."

"Amazing what money can do, isn't it?" she quipped, to hide from both of them what admiration in his voice could do to her heart.

"Money can do many things, Anna, but it cannot invent beauty like yours in a woman."

His tone was not consciously caressing, but there was a timbre to his voice that always drew a reaction from her, and coupled with a comment like this, it made her mouth soften tremulously. She couldn't think of anything to say.

"Come and see if you like these," he commanded softly, and opened another jeweller's box to reveal a breathtaking spangle of diamonds and sapphires to match those in her hair. She chose a large square-cut sapphire ring and diamond teardrop earrings, and waved her hands airily.

"I could get used to this!" she joked.

He was watching her with a smile that turned her insides to mush. "Good," he said.

Fifteen

It was a party at a very exclusive private address, with a long line of limos waiting in the sweep drive to disgorge celebrities, and several photographers snapping continually. Anna realized just how exclusive it was, though, only as they moved through the rooms, sparkling with glowing chandeliers, brilliant conversation and an array of jewels on nearly every inch of bare skin. She recognized numerous faces—from film, from television, and even one or two from *Parliamentary Question Time*.

"Gazi, how fabulous of you to come!" a glamorous redhead exclaimed exuberantly. She was covered head to toe with glittering gold and had an accent Anna couldn't quite place. "And this is Anna! Hellooo!" she crooned, grabbing Anna's hands and kissing her on both cheeks.

"Hello," Anna returned, unable to place her.

"Gazi says that you paint wonderful murals of Moorish palaces that he can't tell from the real thing," the woman said, her eyes searching the crowd for a waiter and summoning him over to offer a tray of champagne. "I hope you will paint something for me. You must come to see me, Anna, and I will show you my small dining room and you will tell me if you can do something Greek with it."

As Anna expressed her enthusiastic willingness, a photographer ambled over. "Can I get one of all three of you?" he called, and the redhead struck a pose, smiling a practised smile. Anna tried to do the same, wishing she had asked Lisbet for a few pointers.

"Of course, we want the publicity," the hostess murmured to Anna. "The editor has given us a two-page photo spread in the weekend magazine."

"Thank you, Princess," the photographer said, moving away again.

"My God, that was, that was Princess...Princess..." Anna muttered in a low voice, groping for the name of one of the uncrowned heads of Europe, as they moved on a few minutes later. Gazi smiled down at her.

"She is the patroness of the charity," he said.

"Charity?" Anna repeated, and then threw a glance around the glittering assembly. "Is this a *charity* function?"

Her sense of humour was sparked, and she flicked a look up into his face, trying to suppress a smile, an effort that only added to the charm of her expression. As she met the appreciative glow in his own eyes she bit her lip and her head went back, and a crack of delighted laughter burst from her throat, causing a few heads near them to turn.

"Sheikh al Hamzeh, my dear chap! What a very great pleasure!" a white-haired man cried in the crusty tones of the Establishment, and a moment later they had been absorbed into the group and Anna was talking to a famous television host.

The evening that followed was one she thought she would always remember. Gazi was blandly informing everyone who asked—and everyone did—that they had met when he bought a painted screen from her to put in his Barakat home.

So Anna was asked for her business card by several people who said they were in the middle of redecorating or about to redecorate and would love to have her do something, and also by the television host, who seemed to have a more personal interest in mind. That boosted her sexual confidence amazingly, because Gazi gave the man a look that would have quick-frozen strawberries in June.

Then she reminded herself that he was here to manipulate people into believing he cared. She must be careful not to fall for the act herself.

But the whole evening was made delicious by his constant attendance, the possessive brush of his hand over her back, the look of sometimes lazy, sometimes urgent desire in his eyes. She knew it was only partly true, but then it was only partly false. And it was headier than the champagne.

They stayed till after midnight. Then, as they left the party, she discovered just how much Sheikh Gazi al Hamzeh was a master of media manipulation.

"The first editions have now gone to bed," he explained quietly as they moved to the door. "They now would like something new for the later editions. Will you play along with me, Anna?"

"All right," she said nervously. "What are we going to do?"

"We are going to have a spat and make up," he murmured.

The temperature had dropped while they were inside, and when they emerged on the pavement the waiting photographers were huddled under the awning, looking miserable and stamping their feet against the cold. Most of them only eyed the couple. They had pictures of them going in, and there was nothing to be gained by another identical shot of them coming out.

Gazi paused to tip the doorman. "Don't be stupid!" he murmured over his shoulder to her in low-voiced masculine irritation, as if continuing an argument begun inside.

The lights showed a driving wet snow coming down at an angle, and although the doorman had clearly been busy with the broom on the red carpet that covered the pavement under the awning, snow was settling again.

"Why is it stupid?" Anna muttered furiously. Her blood was singing with mingled nerves and excitement. He looked so handsome and powerful in his navy cashmere coat, his white silk scarf over the black bow tie, mock anger flashing in his eyes. "It's not stupid!" She turned away from him towards the curb.

"Anna!" he commanded, striding after her, and reaching a hand to clasp her arm. Anna whirled and snatched her arm away.

"I don't appreciate being called stupid!"

The gusting wind suddenly cooperated. It whipped the split skirt of her dress out behind her, revealing all the length of her slim legs, thighs bare above her lace-top stay-ups, and incidentally freezing her where she stood. The photographers, who had slowly been waking up, now snapped to attention.

As she whirled, Anna accidentally put her foot straight

onto a little mound of cold slush. She slipped, half gasped, half screamed, and instinctively clutched at Gazi. A second later she felt her feet go entirely out from under her as electric warmth embraced her. Gazi was scooping her up in his arms.

"Excellent, Anna!" he murmured in her ear, and she felt the heat of him rush through her chilled blood.

He had his arm under her bare knees. As he lifted her, the skirt fell away, revealing her legs right up to the hip. Her shoes dangled from her toes. The photographers were scrambling now, calling encouragement and approval, as Anna, freezing, futilely groped for the panels of her skirt.

"Don't cover your legs! You will soon be warm," Gazi whispered in her ear in a firm command that was suddenly charged with an erotic nuance, and set her heart racing. "Look at me, Anna, and relent!"

Her breath catching in her throat, she lifted one arm to his shoulder and glanced uncertainly into his face. He paused for a few moments, smiling down at her with sexy promise, as if his imagination, too, had suddenly moved into high gear. Cameras clicked and flashed all around them, and then Gazi stepped to the limousine that was just purring up the drive, and after a moment she was inside.

Instantly she was locked in his arms, being ruthlessly kissed. His hand slid up her stockinged thigh with a touch like cold fire, because his flesh was chilled but still heated her blood.

Haunting music played, the windows were all covered, and recessed light glowed softly, enclosing them in their own little world. Anna was half sprawled on the luxurious leather under him, her legs angled, her dress up around her hips, revealing everything as Gazi lifted his mouth, straightened and gazed at her. But as she made a move to sit, he pushed her back with one hand, while the other unerringly found its way to the lace at the top of her stockings, traced its way over the bare skin above, and then, with ruthless precision, to a spot behind the lace of her bikini panties.

Anna gasped. She found she could make no move, no protest, to prevent what he intended. Sensation shot through her, as much from the look in his eyes as from his touch, as he carefully stroked and stroked the potent little cluster of hungry nerves.

They responded obediently to his dictates, as if instantly recognizing their master. A breathless little grunt escaped her, and her hips moved hungrily. She saw the corner of his mouth go up, and one strong arm was on her thigh then, lifting her leg over his head as he sat, and resting it on his other side—spreading her wide for his eyes, his hands…his mouth.

She understood his intent as he bent forward. His hand stopped its delicate stroking and instead his fingers slipped under the lace of her briefs and pulled it to one side, and then, just as he had promised, his mouth was against her, his tongue hot, teasing, hungry.

Her hands clenched in his hair. She could do nothing, say nothing. She was completely at his mercy, melted into submission by the shafts of pure, keening pleasure that his mouth created in her.

"Gazi!" she cried, hitting the peak with a suddenness that made her heart thump crazily. Honeyed sweetness poured through her as her back arched and her muscles clenched.

"Another," he urged her in soft command, and she felt how expertly his fingers toyed with her and his tongue rasped her to pleasure again. She felt completely open, completely helpless, as if the pleasure he gave her put her in his power. "Again," he said, and like an animal going through a hoop, her body had to obey.

After an endless time in a world of pleasure, she found him relenting. He restored her clothing, and drew her body up so that she sat in his embrace, her back against his chest, his face in her hair.

"What's happening?" she begged, hardly knowing where she was.

"We are almost at the airport," he murmured, and she could still shiver as his voice whispered against her ear.

"Oh!" she exclaimed. She had completely forgotten that tonight he had said they would fly back to West Barakat. She lifted a bare foot. "My shoe's gone," she said stupidly.

He felt behind him and eventually found it, and Anna marvelled that she had the muscle coordination necessary to slip it onto her foot. Then the limousine rolled to a stop and it was only moments before they were back on the private jet again, very like the first time, except that this time, Gazi was looking at her with a promise in his eyes that tonight she would not spend the hours in that bed alone.

They weren't long in the air when the hostess approached them with a small tray of Turkish delight and a low-voiced query. Gazi turned to Anna. "Would you like a nightcap or a hot drink, Anna? Or do you prefer to go straight to bed?"

She did not like being offered a choice. She wanted him to want to take her to bed as much as she wanted to go. So perversely, she said, "Oh, let's have some coffee."

She bit into a deliciously soft sugary cube and then stared absently at the shiny green inside of the half still between her fingers.

"Of course," he said, and she couldn't read his expression. "How much sugar?"

"Sweet, please."

He spoke to the hostess, who smiled, nodded, and disappeared into the galley.

Meanwhile Anna unbuckled her seat belt and settled more comfortably in the big plush armchair. With a little whisper of silk, her dress slithered away to reveal all the length of one leg, encased in the dark cobweb of expensive stocking he had bought for her.

Gazi's gaze was instinctively drawn, then moved up to her face, with a look that abruptly reminded her of what had taken place in the limousine. The heat of the memory invaded her body, burned her cheeks.

As the hostess set a little cup of thick sweet liquid in front of her, Gazi reached for a powdery cube of Turkish delight and put it in his mouth with a lazy hand. Anna felt electricity in the air, felt her eyes forced up to his face. He tilted his head and met her gaze, and Anna's heart kicked as if it wanted to kill her.

"I am glad you do not want to sleep," he said.

She yearned towards him, body and soul; she was almost weeping with love and desire. She said, half meaning it, "I don't intend to waste a moment of my allotted time, Gazi."

His eyes darkened with dramatic suddenness, and only then did she realize with what an iron hold he was controlling himself. He reached to imprison her hand, took the little cup from her fingers with his other, and set it down.

"Then let us not waste a moment," he told her

through his teeth, and a moment later he had pulled her to her feet and was leading her to the stateroom.

The bed with its snowy linens was inviting, the room luxuriously intimate, with the ever-present hum of the engines seeming to cut them off from the world.

She melted into passionate hunger as he unbuttoned her dress and drew it off her shoulders, and kissed him with little hungry bites as she in turn unbuttoned his shirt, his trousers, and stripped everything except his underwear off. Then at last, with desperate hungry kissing, they fell onto the bed and their hands began a passionate roaming over each other's body.

He stroked her silken legs, stripped the fine lace from her breasts, while her hungry hand found his sex and pressed it in demand.

Their blood raced up, too needy to wait, and when he stripped off the last of the lace that hid her from him, and tore off the cloth from his own hips, she cried little cries of encouragement and need, and spread her legs, her body ready for the hard, hungry thrust of his.

It was as much pleasure as he could bear, thrusting so suddenly into her, and he drew out and thrust again, to see the grimace of pleasure on her face. Neither of them knew how long they went on, crying out their pleasure, until desire and love and sensation exploded into a fireball of sweetness that burned new pathways all through their being.

They bathed their faces at the little spring, and then turned towards the dust cloud that told them how close their pursuers approached.

"It is not a caravan, Lion," she said sadly. "It is my father."

"It must be so, Beloved."

"They will kill us," she said. *"I am sorry for one thing only,"* and he marvelled at her bravery, for her voice held no quiver, no doubt.

"What, then, Beloved, do you have regrets? I for myself have none," he said.

"Only one, my Lion. That we had nor time nor place to taste each other's love before we die."

"Ah, that," he said.

"Give me your small sword," she commanded. *"For my life will cost them almost as dear as yours."*

He pulled the little blade from his belt. *"Beloved, do you indeed wish it so?"*

"What, shall I die a coward's death at my lover's hands? How would we face each other in the other world, if I asked this of you?"

His heart wept to see her so stalwart.

"One day," she said. *"One day, we shall meet. Somewhere, somehow. Do not you feel it?"*

He was silent.

"It is so!" she swore. *"If we but wish it! Swear to me that it shall be so!"*

The Lion drew his sword and laid his hand upon the blade. *"As God is my witness, though we die here, I will wander a lost soul until your words are fulfilled, Beloved."*

"So be it," she said. *"And when we have found each other, then we will live all the life we lose now. For God rewards true lovers for their constancy. How can He do else?"*

Sixteen

It was early afternoon at the villa, and they were sitting over a late lunch on the terrace by the pool when the call came through.

Nadia was alive. Jaf had already been to see her. Gazi told her that much before embarking on a long conversation with his brother, while Anna sat waiting in anxious impatience for the details.

"She jumped off the bridge," he told her when at last he put the phone down. "The water level in the Thames was high that night. That saved her."

Anna bit her lip and tried to find the right things to say. He took her hand and kissed it.

"Someone in one of the moored houseboats saw her go. They rescued her. She begged them not to go to the police, told them if her husband found her he would kill her. The man was a surgeon. He admitted her to a private hospital. Since then she has been too ill to say anything.

When she recovered a little, she phoned the only number she could remember. Fortunately it was the number of our apartment in London and Jaf was there.''

He sat in silence, contemplating it, until she prompted him. ''What about Ramiz?''

A shadow crossed his face. ''The reason she felt hopeless enough to jump was—when Ramiz discovered she was pregnant, he promised to return here to West Barakat and ask us to begin divorce proceedings on her behalf. She never heard from him again.

''Yusuf must have suspected something, for suddenly she was a prisoner in her own home. She knew nothing of Ramiz's disappearance, but she knew that if Ramiz had spoken to me she would have heard. She thought Ramiz had proved faithless. Yusuf became more and more jealous, till she was frightened for her life and her child's. You were right, Anna. She went into labour and saw it as her only chance. She fled, and gave birth in a garage.

''Only then did she understand she had nowhere to flee to. We were not in town, and our apartment is the first place Yusuf would look for her. After months of bravery, Nadia broke. She caught a cab, left the baby in the cab without letting the driver know, walked onto the bridge and jumped.''

They were silent, trying to understand her despair.

''And I got into the cab,'' Anna murmured at last.

''Yes, Nadia said a woman was there as she got out. She said she looked at you, silently entrusting her baby to you.''

Anna shook her head. ''I still don't have any memory of it. She must be very relieved to know that you have Safiyah safe.''

''Yes, of course. She regrets very deeply what she

tried to do, and we will bring her home here as soon as possible to be with her baby.''

"But you're still worried," Anna said. "Is it something about Ramiz?"

Gazi looked at her, weighing his words, and the look in his eyes made her sad with fear. "Yes, partly about Ramiz. It concerns more than Nadia, or Safiyah, or Ramiz. It is personal, but also much more than personal. It may involve the national security of the Barakat Emirates.''

Her breath came in on a long, audible intake.

"If I tell you, Anna, it will put a burden of secrecy on you. You can never mention it to anyone, not even your friend Lisbet. Can you accept this? Will you hear me?''

"Are you working for Prince Karim?"

"I am his Cup Companion. Of course I work for him. In this matter, for all the princes.''

"Are you a spy?"

"It is not my usual job. But we all do whatever is necessary.''

Anna gazed out over the terrace to the blue sea and wondered how it was possible for a life to change so dramatically in such a short time. How had it happened that she was sitting here in this fabulous villa, whose existence she had known nothing about two weeks ago, being invited to hear the state secrets of the Barakat Emirates?

"If you tell me all this, you're then going to ask me to do something?"

He swallowed, and her heart clenched nervously. "Yes, I will ask you something. But I want to tell you, not to persuade you to anything, but because I am tired of secrecy between us.''

Her heart began to thud. "From the beginning I have
been forced always into a position of suspecting you
against my natural inclinations, Anna. I could not do or
say the things I wished, because so much more than my
personal happiness or even my sister's life was at stake.
If I was indeed blinded to your true self, the whole country might suffer. Now I ask your permission to tell you
the truth."

Anna swallowed against the lump of fear and nerves
that choked her. "Yes," she said. "Please tell me."

"You know already that Ramiz was on an undercover
assignment for the princes. What I did not tell you was
that his mission was to infiltrate, if possible, a secret
group trying to overthrow the monarchy here."

Anna silently opened her mouth. She could hardly
breathe.

"We think that it was not by his own design that
Ramiz met Nadia again. We have suspected that his in-
vestigations led him to Yusuf. What Nadia says seems
to confirm this."

"Oh, my God! You mean Yusuf is part of the conspiracy?"

"Yusuf must not have known that Nadia was in love
before her marriage. My father kept her secret. If he had
known, it is impossible to believe that he would have
brought Ramiz home to meet his wife, as she says he
did. But Ramiz—Ramiz knew who Yusuf was. Pity
Ramiz, whose mission required that he accept the invitation!"

"How dreadful!" she breathed, and bit her lip, feeling
how totally inadequate that was.

"Do you now understand, Anna, why I was forced to
lie to you and abduct you and accuse you? It is not
merely the princes' lives that are at risk from this con-

spiracy. A move to overthrow their rule would bring
certain civil war to Barakat. Tribe against tribe, brother
against brother. It would bring to the surface many ri-
valries now in abeyance. The repercussions would last
beyond this generation, whatever the outcome. Our personal lives were less important than this.

"Can you accept that I thought and acted in this way,
Anna?"

She nodded, her head bent, not daring to hope for
what might be coming next. "To have you here, to be
falling more and more under your spell with every moment that passed, to understand how faulty my own
judgement might be...to have to suspect that you did
this to me deliberately...to be forced to lie—I hope you
did not suffer so much at my hands that you cannot also
pity me, Anna."

Still she could not lift her head.

"Look at me," he commanded in a firm, quiet, lover's
voice, and her heart kicked protestingly and then rushed
into a wild rhythm as she looked at him.

"I love you, Anna. When you are here, this house,
the house of my ancestors, is complete for me. Wherever
I am, when you are there, too, I am home. Stay with me.
I don't ask you to give up your art. Anna, I live more
than half my time in Europe—we can work it out.

"You already love me a little, I think. You would not
look at me with such eyes when I make love with you,
if you did not love me a little. Is it not so?"

She bit her lip and gazed at him. "Oh, Gazi!" she
whispered.

"Let me finish," he pleaded. "I see you with my
sister's child and I know that you are the mother I want
for my own children. I know that somehow, you got in

that taxi that night because we had to meet, you and I.
And we did meet.

"Don't make me let you go. Marry me, and I will
make your love grow. If ever a man could make a
woman love him, Anna, I know that I can make you
love me."

His urgency impelled him to his feet, and he drew her
up into his arms. They stood in the nook formed by the
ancient arch, against a trellis spread with flowers and
thick greenery, his strong arms protectively around her.
A delicate perfume drifted down as their bodies made
the flowers tremble.

"Gazi," was all she could say, but that word told him
everything.

* * * * *

In summer 2002, look for
SONS OF THE DESERT : THE SULTANS,
as Alexandra Sellers's sensuous series
continues...with surprise twists and turns.

Forthcoming titles include:

THE SULTAN'S HEIR
UNDERCOVER SULTAN
SLEEPING WITH THE SULTAN.

THE WAY TO A RANCHER'S HEART

By
Peggy Moreland

PEGGY MORELAND

published her first romance with Silhouette® in 1989 and continues to delight readers with stories set in her home state of Texas. Winner of the National Readers' Choice Award, the Golden Quill, and a finalist for the prestigious Romance Writers of America RITA Award, Peggy's books frequently appear on numerous best-seller lists. When not writing, she enjoys spending time at the farm riding her horse, Lo-Jump. She, her husband and three children make their home in Florence, Texas. You may write to Peggy at PO Box 1099, Florence, TX 76257-1099, USA.

This book is dedicated to my editor, Lynda Curnyn, with heartfelt thanks for all the guidance and support offered to me…and my apologies for forcing her to learn a new language, Texas-ese. Thanks, Lynda!

One

There was tired, then there was *tired*, the boot-shuffling, butt-dragging, bleary-eyed kind of exhaustion that followed too many nights without enough sleep and too many days filled with nonstop activity. Jase Rawley's current physical state fell into that latter category.

After parking his semi-rig and trailer filled with stocker calves he'd hauled from Kansas to Texas beside the loading chute attached to his corral, he trudged wearily through the inky darkness to his equally dark house in the distance. Once inside, he toed off his cowboy boots by the kitchen door, left them there for easy access the next morning, then tugged his shirttail from the waist of his jeans and headed down the hall to the master bedroom, unbuttoning his shirt along the way. At the side of his bed, he stripped off the shirt, leaned to set the alarm on the bedside table for 6:00 a.m., then, all but limp with exhaustion, fell face-first across the king-size bed. He was instantly asleep.

Three hours later he awakened to the irritating electronic beep of his alarm clock. Groaning, he made a fist, whacked it against the alarm, then buried his face against the mattress again. He inhaled deeply, wearily, weighing the pros and cons of putting off unloading the calves for a few more hours. But the rich, nutty smell of coffee brewing had him slowly lifting his head again.

Bracing his palms against the mattress, he lifted himself higher, sniffing the air. "Sis," he murmured almost reverently as he heaved himself from the bed and to his feet, "you're a saint."

With his nose lifted high like a radar device, guiding him to the coffeepot, he padded his way down the hallway, still dressed in the jeans and socks he'd slept in. A yawn took him as he stepped into the kitchen, and he closed his eyes, giving in to it, as he passed by the island, rubbing a wide hand over his burly chest. "Mornin'," he grumbled as he drew a bead on the coffeemaker and headed for it.

"Good morning. Would you like your eggs fried or scrambled?"

He froze at the question, then slowly turned, focusing in on the woman who stood on the opposite side of the island calmly rolling out biscuits. Above a pert nose sprinkled with a light spattering of freckles, bright, cheery green eyes met his, while full lips curved upwards in a not-normal-for-this-time-of-morning smile. Brown hair, the color of roasted chestnuts, spilled over slim shoulders and framed an oval, youthful face…a face that looked nothing like his sister's.

"Who the hell are you?" he asked in dismay.

Her smile widened and she wiped a palm across the bib of her apron as she rounded the island. "Annie Baxter," she said and held out the hand, now free of flour. "I'm your new housekeeper and nanny."

He stared at the flour streaks her hand had left on the apron's bib, the T-shirt and cut-off jeans the apron didn't quite hide, then moved his gaze farther down to the length of long, tanned legs beneath the apron's hem, the bare feet, the toenails painted a putrid shade of blue. Slowly he lifted his gaze back to hers, without making a move to accept the hand she offered. "Housekeeper?" he repeated dully.

Her smile turned curious. "Well, yes. Your sister hired me. Penny Rawley?" she offered helpfully, as if hearing his sister's name might prod his memory. "You were aware that she planned to hire someone, weren't you?"

He gulped, then swallowed, remembering, vaguely, a conversation with his sister a couple of weeks earlier in which she'd told him she was moving out. He seemed, too, to remember her saying something about hiring someone to take her place in his home. But he hadn't taken his sister seriously. Had thought she was bluffing. She had more than once over the years. Penny had *always* lived with him. Had ever since their parents had died more than fifteen years before. He hadn't thought she'd really leave. Ever. Hadn't even considered the possibility. Penny was a fixture, a solid rock of dependability that he'd relied on heavily since his wife's death two years before.

"Yeah," he said and swallowed again. "I seem to remember her mentioning something about that." Realizing she still held her hand extended, he closed his fingers around hers and slowly pumped her hand.

"Whew," she said, laughing softly. "That's a relief. I thought, for a minute, that either you or I were in the wrong house." She withdrew her hand to move back to the opposite side of the island. "Penny told me that you'd be returning today, although I didn't realize it would be quite this early."

"I decided to drive straight through," he murmured, still having a hard time absorbing the fact that Penny was gone and had left a stranger in her place. "How long have you been here?"

"Six days. Penny hired me on Monday, stayed until Thursday to make sure I had settled in well and the children had accepted me, then she left."

And Jase knew why his sister had cleared out before he'd returned from his trip. If he'd been home, he never would have allowed her to take the first step out the front door...at least not without him first putting up one hell of a fight. "Did she say where she was going? How she could be reached?"

"Well, of course she did," she replied, as if surprised by his question, then wiped her hands across her apron again and turned to the desk behind her. Snagging a pad between the tips of a flour-dusted finger and thumb, she turned and held it out to him. "She said that she was staying with Suzy for a couple of days. You do know who Suzy is, don't you?"

He frowned at her skeptical tone, though he could

hardly blame her for questioning him. Not when he hadn't even known that his sister was planning on moving out or that she was hiring him a new house-keeper and nanny. "Yeah," he grumbled. "I know Suzy." Tearing off the top piece of paper, he stuffed it into his jeans pocket, then tossed the pad on the island before heading for the coffeemaker.

"You never did say how you liked your eggs," she reminded him, dropping plump rounds of dough into a pie tin. "Fried or scrambled?"

He filled a mug with coffee and turned, gulping a swallow, praying that the caffeine would clear his brain, and he'd realize that this was all a bad dream. Something he'd imagined. Hell, a full-blown night-mare!

But when the strange woman didn't disappear in a cloud of mist as he'd hoped, but kept right on cutting dough into rounds and dropping them into the pie tin, he muttered, "fried," and headed for the door that led to the hallway. "I've got to make a few calls," he called over his shoulder. "Holler when breakfast is ready."

The first—and only—call Jase made was to Suzy's house and to his sister.

He waited impatiently through four rings before his sister's childhood friend answered.

"Hello?" Suzy mumbled sleepily.

"Put Penny on the phone," he growled.

"Well, good morning to you, too, Jase," she snapped peevishly, then dropped the phone with a clatter and yelled, "Penny! Phone! It's the bear."

Scowling at the nickname Suzy had tagged him

with years before, he drummed his fingers impatiently on the top of his desk while he waited for his sister to pick up the phone.

"Jase?"

"What the hell were you thinking!" he shouted as soon as he heard her voice. "Running off and leaving these kids with a complete stranger."

"Annie's not a stranger," she said defensively, then added, "Well, not totally, anyway. I interviewed her thoroughly and checked her background and references before offering her the position. She's perfectly safe and more than capable of taking care of the children."

"I don't give a good goddamn if she's Mary Poppins's trainer. You get your tail back home where you belong, and I mean *now!*"

"I'm not coming home, Jase. I've already accepted a job in Austin."

"You've *what!*"

"I've accepted a job in Austin. Quite a good one, in fact. I'll be the executive secretary to the owner of a large computer security company."

"Quit," he said, tossing up an angry hand. "Resign. Do whatever you have to do, but you get yourself back here where you belong. I don't want some stranger raising my kids."

"Then *you* raise them!"

Jase jerked the receiver from his ear and stared at it, shocked by the anger in his sister's voice, and even more so that she would defy him. Scowling, he slapped the phone back against his ear. "Is Suzy behind all this? Is she the one who put these crazy ideas into your head?"

A heavy sigh crossed the phone lines. "No, Jase. Suzy had nothing to do with my decision to leave the ranch."

"Oh, that's right, Jase," he heard Suzy mutter in the background. "Blame everything on me."

"Well, she's usually the one who fills your head with these crazy notions," he snapped irritably. "This isn't like you, Penny. Running off half-cocked. Leaving the kids with a complete stranger. Hell! What if this woman doesn't work out? What if she decides to up and leave? Who's going to take care of the kids then?"

"You," she informed him firmly. "They're *your* children, not mine, and it's high time you pulled yourself together and assumed your responsibilities as their father."

He sprang from his chair. "I've never shirked my responsibilities as their father! I've provided for these kids, haven't I? I've seen that they have everything they need."

"You give them everything but yourself. Oh, Jase," she said, suddenly sounding tearful. "They need you. Can't you see that? They not only lost their mother when Claire died, they lost their father, too."

After showering and dressing, Jase returned to the kitchen, still furious with his sister for abandoning him and sticking a stranger in his house without discussing it with him first. He heard the sound of his six-year-old daughter's laughter from the hallway as he pushed open the swinging door. "What's so funny?" he asked, pausing with a hand still braced against the door.

Four heads turned from the table to peer at him.

In the blink of an eye, Rachel was up and racing across the room to throw her arms around his waist. "Daddy!"

He dropped an awkward hand on her head and scrubbed, frowning. "Hey, dumplin'."

She caught his hand and gave it a tug. "We've got a new nanny. Annie. She's really cool."

His frown deepened at the term Rachel used to describe the new nanny, suspecting that she had picked it up from her older brother and sister. "Yeah. So I hear."

He clapped a hand on his thirteen-year-old son Clay's shoulder, then dropped down onto the chair at the head of the table. He nodded a greeting to Clay's twin sister, Tara, and pulled his napkin from beside his plate. He draped it across his thigh while carefully avoiding making eye contact with the new nanny. "Shouldn't you kids be getting ready for school?" he asked gruffly.

Tara rolled her eyes dramatically, her newest way of expressing what a "dweeb" she thought her father was. "It's not even seven yet, Dad. We've got lots of time."

Jase reached for the basket of biscuits. "Don't want you missing the bus," he informed her. "I've got a trailer full of calves to unload and don't have time to cart you kids' butts to school."

Tara tossed her napkin down and shoved back her chair. "Since when do you have time to do anything with us?" she snapped and stormed from the room.

Jase watched her leave, noting the hiking boots, the low-waisted, baggy-legged, faded jeans and the inch

of bare skin her cropped T-shirt exposed. "Change
into something decent!" he yelled after her. "No
daughter of mine is going to school dressed like some
tramp."

He heard her sass something in return, but couldn't
make out her words. Scowling, he spread a heavy
layer of butter over his biscuit and remembered his
sister's comments about him assuming responsibility
for his kids. Well, he *was* responsible, he told himself.
He had let go of a lot of things over the last couple
of years, but he'd never let go of his responsibilities
to his kids. To prove it, he asked, "Did you kids do
all your homework?"

"Yes, Daddy," Rachel said obediently.

As he took a bite, he angled his head to look at
Clay, who had remained conspicuously silent. Butter
dripped down his chin, as he gave it a jerk in his son's
direction. "What about you? Did you get yours
done?"

Clay shoved back his chair. "Didn't have any," he
mumbled and headed for the door and the hallway
beyond.

Jase snatched up his napkin and wiped it across his
mouth and chin. "I better not be getting any calls
from your teachers," he called after his son. He
shifted his gaze to Rachel, who remained at the table,
staring at him, round-eyed. "Well? Are you planning
on going to school today, or not?"

"I'm goin'," she replied quickly and slid from her
chair. "Thanks for breakfast, Annie," she said, giving
the new nanny a shy smile. "It was real good."

Annie graced her with a radiant smile in return.

"I'm glad you enjoyed it. Don't forget your lunch," she reminded the girl.

Rachel sidled to the side of Annie's chair, winding a finger through a pigtail. "Did you pack me a surprise like you did on Friday?"

Annie draped an arm around Rachel's waist and hugged her to her side. "You bet I did. But don't peek," she warned, tapping a finger against the end of the child's nose. "It won't be a surprise if you do."

A pleased smile spread across Rachel's face. "I won't," she promised and skipped to the counter to collect her lunch sack. "See you this afternoon, Annie," she called cheerfully as she raced for the back door.

"Not if I see you first," Annie teased, waving.

Jase frowned, more than a little surprised by his children's obvious approval of the new nanny—and maybe a little jealous, if he were willing to admit to the emotion. And now, with all the kids gone, only he and the nanny remained at the table and he wished he hadn't been so quick to hustle them off to school. Uncomfortable with the silence that suddenly seemed to hum around him, he cleared his throat. "I guess Penny informed you of your duties."

"Yes. She was very thorough."

Unsure what else to say, he quickly slathered butter over another biscuit. "I'm outside most of the day, but if you should need anything, I have a cell phone in my truck. The number is on the wall by the phone," he added, gesturing with the biscuit toward the wall.

"Penny explained everyone's schedules to me and

showed me where to find everything.'' She propped her elbows on the table and leaned forward, studying him, her chin resting on her hands. "The children miss you when you're gone."

Feeling heat creep into his cheeks, Jase shoveled a forkful of eggs into his mouth. "I'm seldom away. When I am, it's never for more than a week at a time."

"Just the same, they miss their daddy."

He cleared his throat again and reached for his cup, gulped a drink of coffee, then shoved back his chair. "I've got calves to unload."

She kept her gaze on his face as he rose. "Do you plan to come in for lunch?"

He was tempted to tell her no, just to avoid being alone with her again, but thought better of it. It was a helluva long time until dinner. "Yeah. But you don't have to cook. I can make a sandwich or something."

She rose, too, and started gathering plates. "I don't mind cooking. In fact, I really enjoy it. Is there anything special you'd like me to prepare?"

Jase snagged his hat from the countertop where he'd dropped it the night before and glanced her way as she headed for the sink, juggling dirty plates. He couldn't help noticing that the bibbed apron she wore didn't cover her rear end or hide the sway of a very delectably shaped butt. He cleared his throat yet again when his gaze lit on her bare feet, and heat climbed up his neck, burning his cheeks. "I'm not a picky eater," he mumbled and tore his gaze away from what shouldn't have been a erotic sight. "Whatever you put on the table is fine with me."

She glanced over her shoulder and warmed his face even more with a smile. "Good. I'll surprise you, then. Should I expect you about noon?"

Flustered, he rammed his hat over his head and turned for the back door. "Yeah, noon," he muttered, and wondered if the surprise she had in store for him was anything like the one she'd secreted in his daughter's school lunch.

Annie strolled through the small fenced area, studying the ground and the barely discernable rows that lay beneath the high weeds, enjoying the feel of the sun warming her skin. A garden, she thought dreamily. She could imagine rows of tomato plants, their branches sagging with fat, juicy tomatoes; cantaloupe vines crawling across freshly hoed rows, their plump, succulent rounds of yellow- and green-veined rinds peeking between the plants' velvety, scalloped leaves.

Oh, how she'd love to plant a garden, she thought, sighing wistfully. It had been years since she'd worked a garden, dug her fingers in rich, fertile soil, feasted on a garden's bounty. Four years to be exact. The summer before her grandmother passed away.

With another sigh, one filled with bittersweet memories this time, she walked on, deciding she might just ask her new boss for permission to clear out the weeds and plant a few vegetables. There was time yet before spring arrived fully.

She frowned as she thought of her new boss. Penny Rawley certainly hadn't exaggerated when she'd said that her brother was a little reserved, perhaps might even appear a bit gruff. Gruff? She snorted at the mild description. The man was positively sour. Frowning all the time. All but growling at his children.

But, my, oh my, she thought with a lusty sigh, he was one prime hunk of man.

She shivered just thinking about the way he'd looked when he'd walked into the kitchen that morning, his eyelids still heavy with sleep, rubbing a wide hand over the soft mat of dark hair that swirled over a muscled chest. She wondered if he realized that the first button of his jeans had been unfastened. She wondered, too, if he realized how sexy she had found that glimpse of navel shadowed by dark hair, the equally dark V that seemed to point below the waist of his jeans and to the soft column of flesh that lay beneath a strip of fabric faded a slightly lighter shade than the rest of the denim.

With a delicious shiver, she leaned to pluck a bachelor's button from the tangled weeds and straightened to tuck the bloom behind her ear.

"What are you doing?"

She jumped, startled, and turned to find her new employer standing behind her watching her, his arms folded across his chest, his hat shading his eyes. She huffed a breath. "Mercy! You might warn a person before you slip up on them unsuspecting. You scared a good ten years off my life!"

He narrowed an eye. "How old are you, anyway?"

She snatched the flower from behind her ear, sure that it was her foolishness that made him question her age. "Twenty-six."

He snorted a disbelieving breath. "Try again."

Mindful of the stickers that might be hiding beneath the tangle of weeds, she made her way carefully back to the gate. "I *am* twenty-six. If you don't believe me, I can show you my driver's license." She reached the gate and opened it.

He stepped back, eyeing her suspiciously as she passed by. "You don't look a day over eighteen."

She chuckled, not sure whether to be pleased or insulted. "Thanks...I think." Flipping her hair back over her shoulder, she tipped up her face to smile at him, having to squint against the glare of the sun to do so. "How old are you?"

He stared down at her a long moment, making her aware of the skimpy tank top she wore, the Daisy Duke cutoffs, her bare legs and feet. Then he dropped his arms from his chest, stuffed his hands into the pockets of his jeans and turned for the house. "Old enough to stay clear of young girls like you."

She sputtered a laugh. "Young girls like me?" she repeated, following him. "And what is that supposed to mean?"

He lifted a shoulder as he opened the screen door, then stepped back to let her enter the house first. "When I was younger, we called 'em jailbait. But I guess now I'd just call 'em trouble."

"Trouble?" When he didn't offer an explanation, she stopped in front of him, folding her arms beneath her breasts and arching a brow, stubbornly refusing to enter until he had clarified that last comment. His gaze dropped to her chest and breasts that strained against her tank top's fabric. She bit back a smile as a blush rose to stain his cheeks.

"*Trouble,*" he repeated, emphasizing the single word, as if it alone explained everything, then gave her a nudge with his shoulder, urging her through the door ahead of him.

"Okay," she said and crossed to the sink to wash her hands. "Granted I'm younger than you. Even I can see that. But what's wrong with a young woman, and why do you consider one trouble?"

"Woman?" He snorted at her choice of word. "I said *girl*. I would hardly classify you as a woman."

She snagged a dish towel from the hook above the sink and dried her hands as she turned to peer at him. "And what does a *girl* have to do," she asked, placing emphasis on the word as he had, "in your opinion, before she is classified as a woman?"

He elbowed her aside and hit the faucet's handle, then stuck his hands beneath the water. "Live. Get some years on her. Some experience."

Enjoying the conversation, but unsure why when she knew she should be insulted by his chauvinistic attitude, she rested a hip against the counter and watched as he scrubbed his hands. "And what do you consider experience?"

He scowled and hit the handle with his wrist, shutting off the water. He stood, dripping water into the sink, and Annie pushed the towel into his hands. He shot her a look, his scowl deepening. "Live," he repeated. "Life offers its own form of experience."

She angled her body, watching as he crossed to the refrigerator. "Oh, really?" she posed dryly.

"Yeah, really," he muttered, his reply muffled by the interior of the refrigerator. He pulled a gallon jug of milk from inside, closed the door, then lifted the jug, drinking directly from the container.

Clucking her tongue at his lack of manners, Annie

pulled a glass from the cupboard, crossed to him and snatched the milk jug from his hand.

Scowling, he wiped the back of his hand across his mouth, removing a white moustache. "What did you do that for? I'm thirsty."

She filled the glass and handed it back to him. "Unsanitary," she informed him prudently and opened the door to replace the jug of milk. "And a bad example for the children. Now I know where Clay picked up the habit." She pulled out a bowl and crossed to the table. "I hope you like pasta, because that's what I made for lunch."

Still frowning, he followed her to the table and sat down in his chair at the head of it, eyeing the bowl's contents with distrust. "What's in it?"

"Pasta curls, grilled vegetables, some herbs, a little olive oil and balsamic vinegar."

He reared back, curling his nose and eyeing the bowl warily. "I'm a meat and potatoes man, myself."

"Really?" she asked, nonplused, and sat down in the chair at his right. "I'd think after working around those smelly old calves all morning that you'd have lost your taste for beef."

He jerked his head up to glare at her. "I'll have you know those smelly old calves help pay the bills around here."

She lifted a shoulder and spooned a generous serving of pasta onto his plate. "If you don't eat the merchandise, then that just means more profit, right?"

His thick brows drew together over his nose. "What the hell kind of thinking is that?"

She lifted a shoulder as she served her own plate. "Rational. The less you eat, the more beef you have to sell." She lifted her shoulder again as she set the bowl back on the table. "Makes sense to me."

He huffed a breath and picked up his fork, shaking his head. "Yeah. I guess to a *girl* like you, that would make sense."

Heaving a long-suffering sigh, she turned to look at him. "Are we back to that topic again?"

He scooped up a forkful of pasta and shoveled it into his mouth. "Yeah, I guess we are."

Stretching across the table for the breadbasket, she tore off a section of the still-warm loaf and dropped it onto his plate before tearing off a piece for herself. "If that's all you can think to talk about, your conversational skills are lacking. You really should work on that."

"Nothing wrong with my conversational skills," he informed her and lifted his fork for another bite. "You're just pissed because I called you a *girl*."

She shook her head and sank back in her chair, watching him wolf down the pasta. And he'd said he was a meat and potatoes man, she thought, biting back a smile. "I'm not insulted because you referred to me as a girl. I am a girl. A female. And proud of it. But I *am* a bit surprised that you'd make an assumption on my level of experience, based on your definition of the term," she added pointedly, "considering you know absolutely nothing about me."

He cocked his head to peer at her, then waved his fork in her direction before returning his attention to his meal. "Okay. I'll bite. Tell me about yourself."

She reached for her glass of water and took a sip, then propped her elbows on the table, cradling the glass between her hands. "I'm a graduate of the University of Texas where I majored in art and minored in secondary education. I obtained my master's degree in December.''

He lifted an eyebrow, obviously impressed. "A college graduate, huh? So what's a woman with that much education doing working as a housekeeper and nanny?"

It was her turn to lift an indifferent shoulder. "I like to eat. When you graduate in December, teaching jobs are a little hard to come by."

"You plan to teach?"

"Yes, and I hope to do some freelancing on the side."

"What kind of freelancing?"

"Photography. I plan to supplement my income by selling photos, and possibly accompanying articles, to magazines and journals."

"Sounds like you've got your future all planned out nice and tidy."

"Yes," she agreed, but was unable to resist the urge to dig at him a little. "So does that make me mature, more experienced? By your definition, a woman, rather than a *girl?*"

He snorted and laid down his fork, then reared back in his chair and leveled his gaze on her. "Experience comes with knocks. The hard kind. That's where I got my degree. The school of hard knocks."

"And what kind of knocks have you had in your life?"

His gray eyes, once intent upon hers and filled with something akin to humor, took on a hooded look, as if a black cloud had swept across them, hiding his emotions. He rose and carried his glass to the sink to rinse it out and refill it with water, then stood, staring out the window.

"My parents died in a car wreck when I was nineteen," he said after a moment, his voice roughened by the memories. "I was a freshman at Texas A&M. Had to come home and take over the ranch. My sister, Penny, was thirteen. The courts appointed me her legal guardian." He stood a moment longer, staring out the window, then angled his head to narrow an eye at her. "My wife died two years ago. Brain aneurysm. Gone like that," he said, with a snap of his fingers. "Without any warning. Left me with three kids under the age of eleven to raise on my own."

"You had Penny," she reminded him, fighting back the swell of sympathy that rose.

Scowling, he turned to face the window again. "*Had* being the operative word."

"You still have her," she insisted. "Just because she chose to pursue her own life doesn't mean that she's extracted herself permanently from yours."

He shot her a glare over his shoulder. "Sure you didn't get that degree in psychology?"

She shook her head. "No. Art. But I'm a people watcher. It's a hobby of mine. And do you know what I see when I look at you?"

"What?" he asked drolly.

"A man who feels sorry for himself."

He slammed the glass down on the counter so hard that water shot above the lip like a geyser. He spun to face her, his face flushed with anger. "I don't feel sorry for myself. I've taken the cards I've been dealt and played them as best I could. Nobody can question that. Least of all *you*."

She rose and crossed to him. "Maybe I don't have the right, but I *do* think I'm correct in assuming you feel sorry for yourself. And now you're blaming your sister for leaving you to take care of your children alone."

He grabbed her by the shoulders, his eyes boring into hers as he glowered down at her. "You listen to me little *girl*," he grated out through clenched teeth. "I don't blame Penny for anything, other than taking off without giving me any warning."

Undaunted by his anger, by the dig of his fingers into her flesh, she met his gaze squarely, maybe a bit stubbornly. "She warned you she was leaving. You told me so yourself just this morning."

He continued to glower at her, a muscle ticking on his jaw, then he released her, pushing her away from him as he turned back to face the window. "I didn't believe her. She'd said before she was going to leave, but she never went through with it."

"And you're angry with her because this time she did what she said she was going to do."

He whirled to face her, his gray eyes hard as steel. "The kids need her. They depend upon her. And she walked out on them."

"They need *you*," she argued. "Their father."

He thrust his face close to hers. "And what makes you an authority on what a kid needs? Huh? What the hell makes you think you know better than I do what my own kids need?"

She drew in a long breath, never once moving her gaze from his. "Because I was a kid once myself. My father died of a heart attack when I was five. My mother never got over the loss. She committed suicide when I was six. I *needed* my father," she said, and blinked back the unexpected tears that rose. "And I needed my mother, too. But she wimped out. Left me all alone." She hitched a breath but refused to let the tears fall. "That's how I know," she said, her voice growing as steely as the eyes that met hers. "You want to talk about hard knocks?" She tapped a finger against his chest. "Mister, I'll compare lumps with you any day of the week."

Two

Annie experienced a brief stab of remorse for the sharp words she'd exchanged with her employer…but, thankfully, it didn't last long. She dispensed with it by assuring herself that he'd deserved the tongue-lashing she'd given him.

Calling her a *girl,* she reflected irritably as she stripped the sheets from the children's beds. And carrying on as if he were the only person in the world who had suffered any losses. Well, she had suffered her share of losses, too. But she had *dealt* with her losses, accepting them as natural occurrences in life, situations totally out of her control, and had gone on living, which was more than she could say for Jase Rawley. Instead of dealing with his grief, it appeared he had dug himself a hole and climbed inside where he continued to lick his wounds, shutting out his children and anyone else who tried to get too close.

But his children needed him, she thought, feeling the frustration returning. Couldn't he see that? She certainly could and she'd only been living in his home for a week. Well, he was going to have to climb out of that hole, she told herself as she stuffed the linens into the washing machine. Even if it meant her throwing a stick of dynamite into the hole he'd dug for himself and blasting him out.

Pleased with the image that thought drew, Annie started the first load of laundry, then went to the master bedroom to remove the sheets from Jase's bed. Though she'd been in his room several times during the week, she hadn't entered her employer's private quarters since his late-night return. She noticed immediately the changes his presence made in the room. The sharp, spicy scent of aftershave lingered in the air, as did the faint odor she'd learned to associate with the corral and the livestock herded in and out of it almost daily.

She stooped to pick up a pair of socks from the floor and held her nose, grimacing, as she deposited them in the hamper in the master bath where she noticed more signs of her employer's presence. A wet towel lay on the floor, discarded after his morning shower, she was sure. A toothbrush was angled over the edge of the sink and an assortment of coins were scattered over the tile countertop where he'd obviously emptied his pockets before dropping the jeans to the floor. She nudged a fingertip through the pile of loose change, finding a rusty nail and a crumpled receipt amongst the coins, as well as a tattered package of antacids.

Shaking her head at the odd accumulation, she picked up the jeans and dropped them in the clothes hamper before returning to the bedroom. She frowned slightly as she noticed that the bed, though rumpled, was already made. Had he made it up himself? she wondered, then snorted a laugh when she noticed the imprint of his body on the comforter and realized that he hadn't even bothered to turn down the bed when he'd arrived home, but had opted to sleep on top of the covers instead.

With a rueful shake of her head, she ripped back the comforter and quickly stripped off the sheets. Wadding them into her arms, she headed for the laundry room, but slowed in the hallway, her attention captured by the gallery of framed pictures hanging there. Though she'd looked at the photos before, she found her curiosity heightened after her earlier, heated conversation with her employer.

Pictures of Rachel and the twins dominated the wall, monitoring the children's growth from birth to present day, but Annie found herself skimming over them in search of pictures of Jase. She smiled as she recognized a picture of him with Penny, taken when his sister was probably about Tara's age. Jase stood apart from Penny, yet there was an unmistakable protectiveness in his posture that indicated he took his responsibilities as his sister's guardian very seriously.

Though he was much younger in the picture, Annie noticed that Jase hadn't changed much over the years. In fact, she was sure she recognized the grim scowl and the steely-eyed impatience as the same expression he'd graced her with at breakfast and again at noon.

With a sigh, she shifted her gaze to Penny. Plain, but by no means unattractive, in the photograph Penny projected an image of solemnity unnatural for one so young. Annie supposed it was due to the tragedies Penny had suffered so early in life, the responsibilities she'd been forced to assume.

Though she'd only known Jase's sister a short span of time, Annie suspected she knew Penny better than her own brother did. She attributed that advantage to her fondness for studying people, noting their mannerisms and habits, the little quirks that spoke volumes about their personalities. Too, people tended to tell her things about themselves, guarded little secrets that they wouldn't dream of sharing with another. She wasn't sure why that was so, though she suspected it was simply because she was willing to listen. For whatever reason, throughout her life she had found herself serving as a sounding board and vault for the problems and dreams of countless others, just as she had for Penny in the short week they had spent together before Penny's departure.

Penny Rawley was way past spreading her wings a little, Annie reaffirmed as she moved farther down the hallway. From what Penny had told her, the woman had dedicated herself and her life to Jase and his family. Especially so after the death of Jase's wife.

Reaching a wedding portrait framed in gilt, Annie stopped in front of it, tilting her head slightly as she studied the couple pictured there. So young, she thought with a twinge of sadness as she focused on the bride smiling radiantly and lovingly up at her husband, a bouquet of white roses clutched beneath her chin. And what a scar her passing had left on Jase, she reflected with regret, noting the devotion with which he gazed down upon his wife and remembering the bitterness of his expression when he'd snapped his fingers, demonstrating the quickness of her passing. That he'd loved his wife was obvious in the gesture. That he still harbored resentment, maybe even anger over her loss was even more obvious.

Pensive, she moved on to the laundry room, stuffed the dirty linens into the washing machine, then headed outside with a basket loaded with those she'd already washed. The warmth of the sun and the sound of birds singing in the centuries-old oak tree at the corner of the backyard chased her concerns for Jase and his family from her mind and drew a cheerful smile. Humming an accompaniment to the birds' warbled songs she drew a sheet from the basket, caught it by its corners and clipped it to the clothesline, then reached inside the basket for another.

"We have a clothes dryer."

Annie jumped, then sagged weakly, clutching the damp sheet against her chest as she turned to frown at Jase. "You've got to quit doing that," she scolded.

"Doing what?"

"Sneaking up on me like that."

He lifted a shoulder. "Wasn't sneaking. Was on my way to the house." He gestured to the sheet she still held against her chest. "Thought I ought to let you know we have a clothes dryer and save you the trouble of hanging the sheets on the line."

She huffed a breath as she turned. "I know there's a clothes dryer," she replied, thinking of the mountains of dirty laundry she'd washed since her arrival in his home. She plucked a clothespin from the line and clipped it over the sheet, securing it in place. "I just happen to prefer sun-dried linens."

He lifted an indifferent shoulder. "It's your back."

"Yes, it is," she agreed and squatted down beside the basket to dig through the remaining linens for the matching pillowcases to hang. "And speaking of my back, would you mind if I strained it a little more by cleaning out the garden and planting a few vegetables?"

When he didn't respond immediately, she glanced up and found that he'd turned and was staring at the garden plot, his eyes narrowed, his jaw set in a hard line. Seeing the slow bob of his Adam's apple, she quickly rose. "If you'd rather I didn't—"

He shook his head and walked away. "Do what you want with it," he muttered.

She stared after him, wondering what it was about her request that he found so upsetting.

Still puzzling over Jase's strange reaction to her request to plant a garden, Annie whacked at the weeds choking the small piece of ground. She'd cleared a space about three feet by three feet when the hairs on the back of her neck prickled. Sensing that she was being watched, she glanced up and saw Jase standing in the opening of the barn's loft, shirtless, his hands braced high on the opening's frame. Sweat gleamed on his muscled arms and chest and darkened the waist of his jeans.

Though his hat shadowed his face, she felt the intensity of his gaze, the unmistakable heat in it. As he continued to stare, she drew a hand to the hollow of her throat, suddenly feeling exposed, as if he'd somehow managed to strip her of her clothing and left her standing naked in the garden.

An awareness passed between them, something primitive and sexual that had Annie's pulse pummeling her palm, her mouth going dry as dust. She wanted to look away...but found she couldn't. She could only stare in slack-jawed fascination at the virile image he created standing high in the loft, one knee slightly bent, one hip cocked a little higher than the other. He looked so commanding, so utterly masculine, so bone-meltingly sexual. And when he dropped a hand to rub it lazily across the dark, damp hair on his chest, she closed her eyes, suddenly feeling weak, sure that she could feel the damp heat on her lips, taste on her tongue the salt from his skin.

Anxious for another look, she opened her eyes, but he was already turning away. Stifling the moan of disappointment that rose, the sense of loss, she slowly caught up the hoe and began to chop half-heartedly at the weeds again, her movements sluggish now, her strength drained by the attraction that churned low in her belly.

Her thoughts were so scattered, her senses so dulled, it took a moment for her to become aware of the rumble of the school bus. Straightening, she drew the hoe up, propped her hands on its handle and inhaled a deep, steadying breath, pushing back her lustful thoughts of Jase as she watched the bus near.

It stopped in front of the house and the door folded back. Rachel, always seated at the front of the bus, came tumbling down the steps, dragging her book bag behind her, and headed straight for the house.

"Hey, Rachel!" she called, lifting a hand in greeting. "Over here. How was school?"

A grin spreading from ear to ear, Rachel raced toward the garden, waving a paper above her head. "Annie! Look! I made a hundred on my spelling test!"

"Why, that's wonderful, sweetheart!" Annie stepped from the garden and leaned the hoe against the low fence, then knelt and wrapped an arm around the girl's waist, drawing her to her side. "And look," she said pointing, "your teacher gave you a gold star, too."

"That's 'cause my penmanship was so good."

"And it is," Annie agreed, hugging the girl to her.

"What's for dinner?"

Annie glanced up at the question and saw Tara headed her way, followed closely by Clay. She widened her smile to include the twins. "Dinner isn't for a couple of hours, yet, but there are fresh vegetables in the refrigerator and some dip, if you'd like a snack."

Tara rolled her eyes and did a neat U-turn, heading for the house. "Rabbit food," she muttered under her breath.

Surprised by the teenager's sour expression, Annie rose, staring after her.

"Ignore her," Clay said. "She's in one of her moods."

"It certainly appears that way," Annie replied, wondering if the mood was a carryover from the teenager's brief but heated confrontation with her father that morning. "And how was your day?" she asked, turning to smile at Clay.

"Okay."

"Kiss any girls?" she teased.

He ducked his head, blushing, and chipped the toe of a boot against the ground. "Nah."

Annie laughed. "Well, there's always tomorrow."

He glanced up at her, then quickly away, his blush deepening, then shifted his gaze to the garden. "What are you doing out here?"

"Getting the soil ready to plant." She glanced at the garden and sighed wearily, disappointed by the small amount of progress she'd made. "But it's turning out to be a much bigger chore than I anticipated."

"Does Dad know you're working in here?"

"Well, yes," Annie replied, puzzled by his question. "Why do you ask?"

He shrugged and hitched his backpack higher on his shoulder. "No reason. It's just that...well, nobody's planted a garden since Mom died."

"Oh," she murmured, understanding now why Jase had seemed so upset when she'd asked his permission to plant a garden. "I didn't know."

Clay shrugged again. "No big deal. It's just dirt."

Annie stared at the weed-clogged clods she'd managed to overturn, suspecting that, though the garden might be nothing more than dirt to Clay, it represented a great deal more to the boy's father.

Feeling the guilt nudging at her for the painful memories her request must have drawn for Jase, she shrugged it off and forced a smile as she turned to Clay. "Are you hungry?"

He reared back and patted his stomach, grinning. "Starving."

Annie caught Rachel's hand, then slung an arm over Clay's shoulders, heading both children toward the house. "How about some rabbit food?" she teased.

"Just call me Thumper," he replied, grinning.

"Clay!"

Clay spun, his grin fading when he saw his father standing in the barn's doorway, scowling, his arms folded across his chest. "Yeah, Dad?" he called.

"You've got chores waiting."

"But couldn't I eat something first?"

When his father merely angled his head and arched a brow in warning, Clay heaved a sigh. "Yes, sir," he mumbled, then turned to Annie. "Sorry. Guess I'll have to grab something later."

Offering him a sympathetic smile, Annie slipped the backpack from his shoulder and lifted it to her own. "I'll save some dip for you," she promised.

As she watched Clay trudge toward the barn, she glanced Jase's way and saw that he waited in the doorway still wearing the now-familiar scowl...and wondered how much of the man's gruffness was direct fallout from the loss of his wife.

"Could I crank up the rototiller and plow up the garden for Annie?"

Hunkered down beside the engine he was working on, Jase glanced up at Clay's question, then frowned and turned his attention back to the spark plug he was adjusting. "You've got chores to do."

"But afterwards?" Clay persisted. "It wouldn't

take me long and it'll take her forever to clean out all those weeds using just a hoe.''

''There's more important work that needs to be done than tilling a garden.''

''Like what?''

At the frustration he heard in his son's voice, Jase dropped the wrench to his knee and glanced up, his frown deepening. ''Like the fence that needs mending down in the bottom. The new calves I hauled in last night that need feeding and watering. The well house that needs painting.''

Ducking his head, Clay scuffed the toe of his boot at the loose hay in the alleyway. ''There's *always* work that needs doing around here,'' he mumbled.

Jase pushed his hands against his knees and rose. ''And there always will be,'' he said, tossing the wrench to the workbench, ''so long as you complain about your chores instead of just doing them.''

''I'm not complaining,'' Clay argued. ''I just wanted to help Annie out.''

''If the new nanny wants a garden, then she'll have to do the work herself.''

''You won't let me help her because you don't like her.''

Jase dug through the tools, reluctant to admit there might be some truth in his son's accusation. ''I didn't say that.''

''You didn't have to. But *we* like her. She's nice. And she's really funny, too. She's always saying stuff or doing stuff that makes us laugh.''

Yeah, Jase thought, keeping his back to his son. He'd noticed those qualities in her, too. As well as a few others. "Whether she's nice or not, isn't the point. Getting your chores done *is*."

Clay's voice took on a pleading tone. "Don't run her off, Dad. Please? We like her."

Jase spun to look at his son. "Run her off? Where'd you get a crazy notion like that?"

Clay lifted a shoulder. "I don't know. But if you're mean to her, she won't want to stay around here long."

Which might be best for them all, Jase affirmed silently, then narrowed a suspicious eye at his son. "You wouldn't have a crush on the new nanny, would you?"

Heat flamed on Clay's cheeks. "Heck no! She's way too old for me."

Jase turned back to the workbench. "You wouldn't be the first male to fall head over bootheels for an older woman. She's young and fairly attractive. "

"*Fairly* attractive?" Clay echoed. "Dad, she's a hottie!"

Jase angled his head to look at his son, his brow furrowing. "Hottie?"

"Well, yeah," Clay said, his cheeks turning a brighter red. "A looker. You know…a babe."

Shocked to discover that his son was aware of the finer points of the opposite sex, Jase picked up a wrench, and began to clean it. "You shouldn't be noticing things like that," he said gruffly.

Chase snorted a laugh. "Shoot. I'd have be to blind *not* to notice."

Irritated by his son's obvious attraction to the nanny, but unsure why, Jase gave his chin a jerk toward the door. "Best get after those chores."

Clay stuffed his hands in his pockets and turned away. "Yes, sir," he mumbled dejectedly.

Jase angled his head to watch his son pull the feed bucket from its nail on the wall and noticed for the first time the slight swell of muscles on the boy's arms, the length of his stride as he headed for the barn door.

Frowning, he stared after him, wondering what had happened to the pint-size kid with the gangly legs and the too-long arms. The one who had always claimed girls were stupid.

The one who had once looked up at his daddy with hero worship in his eyes.

Jase had never considered his house small. Fact was, his home was a spacious two-story built by his parents prior to his own birth, and could adequately accommodate a family of ten or more without putting a hardship on anyone in the house.

But ever since the new nanny's arrival, his house seemed to have shrunk to the size of a cracker box, as had the rest of his ranch. He couldn't take a step without running into her. Literally.

He couldn't count the number of times he'd bumped into her in the house or when stepping out of the barn, which invariably led to physical contact of some description. A hand on her arm to steady her, or one of her hands braced against his chest to prevent him from mowing her down on those occasions when he'd round a corner unaware of her presence.

And those brief, physical contacts were beginning to get on his nerves.

He'd known he wasn't going to like having a

stranger in his house. He'd known, too, that having one who was so young and who was...well...such a *hottie* as his son had described her, might create a problem or two. But he *hadn't* been prepared for the amount of time he would waste thinking about her instead of working, wondering where she was, what she was doing, what she was wearing.

As far as he'd been able to determine, her wardrobe consisted of cutoff jeans, tank tops and other equally revealing articles of clothing. If that wasn't distracting enough, he'd discovered she had a habit of humming while she worked that never failed to draw his gaze...and usually to a part of her anatomy that he had no business looking at.

And tonight was no exception.

With the kids already in bed for the night, he and Annie had the downstairs to themselves. And, though he kept his face hidden behind the newspaper he was reading, he was painfully aware of her exact location, which was, at the moment, less than five feet from his recliner and the tips of his boots. A laundry basket at her side, she sat on the floor folding towels...and humming an irritatingly cheerful little tune.

She glanced up, caught him staring and cocked her head, a questioning smile curving her lips. He quickly ducked his head behind the paper again and flipped the page, pretending to be engrossed in the day's news.

After a moment, he worked up the courage to peek over the top of the newspaper again and caught her just as she rocked up on one hip to stretch to place a folded towel onto the growing stack at her side. At the movement, the hem of her shorts crawled higher on her leg, revealing the thin, white elastic band of her panties and a peek of the lighter-toned skin on her rump that the sun hadn't seen. A low moan rose in his throat, as he stared, all but strangled by the sight.

"Did you say something?"

He snapped his gaze to hers, unaware that he'd let the sound escape. He jerked the paper back in front of his face to hide the heat crawling up his neck. "No," he mumbled. "I…I was just commenting on the weather report for tomorrow. Supposed to be in the high eighties again."

"Eighties," she repeated and sank back on her elbows with a long-suffering sigh. "Hard to believe it's only March. I can't imagine what the temperatures will be by the time summer gets here."

If the temperatures proved to be anything like the heat currently registering in his body, Jase couldn't imagine, either.

Aware of the uncomfortable swell in his jeans, he knew he'd best leave while he was still able to walk.

She glanced up as he rose. "Are you going to bed?" she asked in surprise.

"Yeah," he growled and pivoted quickly, heading for his room.

"Sweet dreams," she called after him.

Yeah, right, he thought irritably. As if his dreams would be anything but X-rated, an affliction he could trace directly back to the day he'd arrived home and found the new nanny in his house.

Annie knew she had a let-me-kiss-it-and-make-it-better tendency that had gotten her into trouble more than once over the years. But knowing that about herself didn't stop her from trying to think of ways to resolve the problems she saw building in the Rawley household.

In the week since Jase's return home, she had watched Tara go from a talkative and spirited young girl to a sullen-faced, headed-for-trouble teenager, who spent more time in her room than she did with her family. While Clay, on the other hand, had metamorphosed from an easygoing, if a bit shy, teenaged boy into a bundle of tightly wound nerves who jumped at the slightest noise, as if he expected a bomb to go off at any minute. And, Rachel, bless her heart, who had tagged Annie's every step since Annie's arrival, soaking up every smile sent her way, every bit of praise, had begun to cling to Annie's legs as if she expected Annie to disappear, leaving her all alone.

Though Annie tried to find another explanation for the sudden changes in the children's behavior, she could find nothing to attribute them to other than their father's return, a realization that both saddened and frustrated her.

Not having a family of her own, Annie knew the value of familial relationships and hated to see Jase and his children not taking advantage of all they had to offer each other. But what could she do to wake them up to what all they were missing?

"You're not God," she reminded herself as she checked her camera for film. "You're just the nanny."

Hoping to find some subjects or scenes to photograph that would take her mind off the Rawleys' problems, she slipped her camera strap over her head and headed outdoors.

Jase stepped inside the barn, paused a moment to let his eyes adjust to the sudden change in light, then headed straight for his workbench. Finding the tool he needed to adjust the carburetor on his truck, he curled his fingers around it, then paused, listening, when he heard a rustling sound above. He glanced up at the rafters that supported the hayloft, then swore, dropping his head and blinking furiously when dust and bits of hay showered down on his face.

Dragging an arm across his eyes, he rammed the wrench into his back pocket and strode for the ladder to the loft, muttering under his breath, "If that damn skunk is back again..."

He climbed the ladder and poked his head through the narrow opening that led to the loft, glancing around. Seeing nothing out of the ordinary, he carefully navigated the last few steps, trying to keep his movements as quiet as possible, so not to frighten the skunk. It would be just his luck to get sprayed by the varmint, he thought irritably.

Tiptoeing, he made his way along the narrow pathway created by the tall stacks of baled hay he'd stored there the previous summer, peering into the shadowed crevices. When he reached the end without finding a sign of the critter, he started back, but stopped when he heard a soft whirring sound.

Frowning, he turned and retraced his steps, then paused, listening again. Sure that the sound had come from behind the last row of hay, he wedged himself into the space between the hay and the barn wall, and edged his way to the end, silently cursing the loft's oppressive heat that had his shirt sticking to his skin. When he reached the opposite end, he peered out...and nearly choked at the sight that greeted him. Annie lay sprawled on her stomach on the loft floor, her bare feet kicked up in the air, holding a camera before her face.

"What the hell are you doing!"

"Sshh!" she hissed, flapping a warning hand behind her.

Scowling, he stooped to keep from bumping his head on the low rafters and moved to hunker down at her side. He followed the direction of the camera lens to the far corner of the loft where dust motes danced a slow waltz in a slanted beam of sunlight.

"Well, I'll be damned," he murmured as he met the unblinking scrutiny of a mama cat who lay curled on a busted bale of hay.

Easing down to his hips, he drew up his knees, dropped his forearms over them and watched, enchanted by the squirming mass of kittens that suckled greedily at the mama cat's swollen teats. The camera continued to click and whir at his ear, recording the event, frame by frame.

A hand grasped his and he glanced up, surprised to discover that Annie had risen. Smiling, she pressed a finger to her lips to silence him, then tugged him to his feet and led him back through the tunnel of hay.

When she reached the loft's opening, she released his hand to grasp the ladder's braces and grinned up at him as she started down. "Wasn't that just the coolest thing you've ever seen?"

Coolest? Jase shook his head at her choice of adjective as he followed her down. "Yeah, it was cool all right," he muttered wryly, thinking the comment sounded more like something his thirteen-year-old daughter would say than a twenty-six-year-old woman.

"Do you think we should bring them a blanket and some food?" she asked, her eyes all but glowing with excitement, as he dropped down onto the alleyway beside her.

"She's a mouser," he said, scowling. "A barn cat. She knows how to take care of herself."

"But—"

"No," he ordered firmly.

Sighing her disappointment, she lifted the camera over her head, shaking her hair free of the strap. With her arms stretched up high over her head, Jase couldn't help but notice that her T-shirt was damp with perspiration and clung to her skin. Once he noticed that, it was impossible for him not to look closer and see that she wasn't wearing a bra, an absence clearly discernable by the jut of rigid nipples centered over twin mounds of flesh that strained against the T-shirt's damp fabric.

Weakened by the sight, he could only stare, unable to move, unable to think, unable to breathe.

"The light was absolutely perfect," he heard her say as she dropped to a knee to clamp the cover back over her lens. "And those kittens! Weren't they just the most adorable things you've ever seen?"

Jase swallowed hard, weakened further by the glimpse of bare breasts she'd unknowingly revealed when she'd dropped down at his feet to fiddle with her camera. Unable to tear his gaze away from the enticing sight, but knowing that a response of some kind was required, he murmured absently, "Yeah, adorable," then clamped his lips together to stifle the moan that rose as he watched a thin trickle of sweat begin to slowly wind its way down between her breasts.

She glanced up at the mournful sound, caught him staring, then looked down at her front. Obviously aware of what held his attention so raptly, she heaved a sigh and pushed to her feet. "Well, I guess I won't have to worry about you entering me in any wet T-shirt contests."

Distracted by the bob of her breasts as she rose, he shifted his gaze to hers and frowned. "What?"

She chuckled self-consciously and shoved the camera strap over her shoulder. "I said, I guess I won't have to worry about you entering me in any wet T-shirt contests. No big deal," she said with a shrug. "Literally," she added, then laughed.

"Personally, I've always considered anything more than a handful a waste."

Jase wasn't sure what made him state his preference, but when Annie replied with a sassy, "lucky me," he realized that her cheekiness was a front to hide her self-consciousness over her less-than-voluptuous breasts. He stepped closer and slipped his fingers beneath the camera strap, angling it higher on her shoulder. "No," he corrected and arched a brow as he met her gaze. "Lucky *me.*"

He watched her green eyes sharpen, then darken, and felt the heat that all but crackled between their bodies. With his fingers still curled around the strap at her shoulder, he slid his gaze to her mouth. Her tongue darted out to slick slowly over her lips and his groin tightened in response.

He wet his own suddenly dry lips and wondered what it would be like to kiss her, what taste and textures he'd find on that impudent mouth of hers. Mortified by the direction of his thoughts, he glanced up...but found the same question burning in her eyes.

He wasn't sure who moved first—him or Annie—but the point became moot when their lips touched. Lightly at first, hesitantly, then slamming together with an urgency that rocked him to the soles of his boots. Was it him, he wondered dazedly, who pushed for more? Or was it Annie?

Didn't matter, he told himself as he closed his hands around her upper arms, intending to push her way, to end this madness before it got out of hand. And he would have ended it, too, if she hadn't chosen that exact moment to wind her arms around his neck and slip her tongue between his lips.

He inhaled sharply as her flavor shot through him, her tongue dancing over his. This is wrong, he told himself even as he gathered her into the circle of his arms. She was young, his children's nanny. He had no business messing around with her in this way.

But no amount of reasoning could bring him to release her, could persuade him to drag his mouth from hers. It had been too long since he'd held a woman, felt feminine softness pressed against the rigid length of his sex. Too long since he'd sipped at a woman's unique sweetness, grown drunk on her flavor alone.

He roamed his hands over her back, down along her curves, stunned by the varying terrains he encountered, in the silkiness of her skin, in the heat that rose from her body to warm his hands. He drank from her like a man rescued from a desert after being lost there for weeks. Greedily. Hungrily. Desperate to satisfy a ravenous thirst.

And when a moan of frustration rumbled low in her throat and she pressed herself more insistently against him, he thrust his tongue deeply into her mouth, seeking a release from the need that ripped through him like a flash of summer lightning.

He wanted her, he realized with a suddenness that had him gripping her more tightly. All of her. And nothing short of dragging her to the barn floor and taking her would satisfy that want.

The realization brought reality crashing down upon him, making him aware of what he was doing, and who he was doing it with. He tore his mouth from hers and stumbled back a step, his chest heaving as he stared down at her flushed face, her passion-glazed eyes. Dropping his arms from around her, he whirled away from the sight of her lips, swollen from the demanding pressure of his own. He dragged the back of his hand across his mouth, wanting to rid himself of her tempting taste. "I'm sorry," he said and curled his traitorous hands into fists at his sides.

"I'm not."

He spun, startled by her reply. "What?"

She tucked her fingers around the camera strap and lifted her shoulder in a shrug. "I'm not sorry."

"But...why?"

"You're a good kisser," she said simply, then smiled and added with a wink, "And I've always appreciated a man who really knows how to cut loose and kiss a woman.''

As he stared, dumbstruck, she headed for the barn door. "By the way," she called, turning and walking backwards. "If you ever want to cut loose again, just give me a holler. I'll be around." Waggling her fingers at him, she turned and strode from the barn, humming that same disgustingly cheerful tune.

Three

Jase had never had trouble sleeping...or at least he hadn't since he'd figured out that physical exhaustion was an excellent cure for the particular form of insomnia he had suffered since his wife's death. But on this particular night, and in spite of the fourteen hours of backbreaking labor he'd put in on his ranch, his cure didn't seem to be working. He hadn't even taken a break for dinner, convinced there was no way in hell he could face his housekeeper across the dinner table. Not after what had transpired between them that afternoon. Not after he'd kissed her. Not after he'd felt that hard, firm body of hers pressed against his.

Not after her assurance that she'd be around if he ever felt the need to kiss a woman again.

Swearing, he rolled from his bed and paced across the room, dragging a hand over his hair. He had to quit thinking about her. Had to shake the images that kept leaping to mind. The feel of her in his arms. Plump, moist lips that surrendered beneath his, even as they demanded a satisfaction of their own. The little muffled whimpers of pleasure that hummed low in her throat. The small, firm breasts flattened against his chest, the prod of desire-thickened nipples. The feel of her buttock muscles tightening in his—

He spun, swearing again. He had to quit thinking like this! About *her!* She was trouble with a capital T. He'd known that from the first moment he'd laid eyes on her. For two long years he'd managed to suppress his need for physical release with a woman, but after little more than a week with the new nanny in his house, all he could think about was getting her into bed.

Grabbing his jeans, he jerked them on. There was only one way to handle this, he told himself as he headed for the bedroom door, yanking up his zipper. He had to fire her. Get her out of his house. If he didn't, he was going to go stark raving mad...or have her. And he refused to fall prey to either of those possibilities.

A man on a mission, he marched down the hall, through the darkened kitchen and bounded up the staircase. At the landing, he made a sharp turn to the right and rapped his knuckles against her bedroom door.

He heard a rustling sound from the other side and a mumbled "Just a minute." Scowling, he folded his arms across his chest and waited.

Seconds later, the door opened and Annie appeared, shrugging on a robe.

Framed by the golden light of the bedside lamp she'd switched on, she squinted sleepily up at him. "Is something wrong?" she asked as she tugged the belt of her robe around her waist.

"Yeah," he said, infuriated to discover that she could sleep, when he could do nothing but toss and turn and think about her. "We need to have a talk."

She swept a hand over her hair, holding it back from her face as she peered up at him curiously. "What about?"

He glanced down the hallway and to the rooms where his children slept, then returned his gaze to hers. "Can we talk inside? I don't want to wake the kids."

"Well, yes," she said clearly puzzled by the odd request, but stepped aside, allowing him to enter.

After casting another nervous glance down the hallway, he closed the door behind him. He paused, watching as she crossed to the bed and sat down. He bit back a frustrated groan as all the images he'd tried to block returned, flashing across his mind like freeze frames from an erotic movie. She shouldn't look this good, he told himself. It just wasn't normal. Hell! He'd awakened her in the middle of the night from a dead sleep, yet she looked good enough to eat, sitting there in a ratty terry bathrobe with those toenails of hers, still painted a putrid blue, peeking from beneath its hem. "You're going to have to leave," he blurted out.

Her eyes widened in surprise. "What?"

He waved a frustrated hand. "You're going to have to leave. This just isn't working out."

She rose slowly, her cheeks flushing with anger,

her green eyes snapping with it. "For who? You? Or the children?"

"For anybody!" he cried, his voice rising in frustration. "I'll give you a month's severance pay and a good reference, if you need one, but I want you out of here first thing in the morning."

She drew the folds of her robe's collar together high on her neck, and lifted her chin. "I don't want any more from you than what is owed me, and you can keep your reference, good or bad."

Seeing the tears gleaming in her eyes and knowing he was responsible for them, Jase dragged a hand over his head, mussing his wild hair even more. "Look," he said, feeling like a heel. "Don't take this personally."

Her nostrils flared. "If my termination isn't personal, then I'd like to know what it is. I've done my job. You certainly can't find fault with me there. I've cared for the children and supervised their activities, just as your sister instructed. I've cooked for them, done their laundry, settled their disputes and managed to keep the house clean and neat, as well."

Though he tried, Jase couldn't find an argument in there anywhere. "You're young," he said, digging for a reasonable excuse she might accept, and bit back a groan when her chin shot higher. "Well, hell, you *are* young!" he shouted.

"There isn't that much difference in your sister's and my ages, and you didn't seem to have a problem leaving your children in her care."

"That's because she's my sister, dammit, and I was never tempted to throw my sister down on the barn floor and have my way with her!"

"Dad?"

Jase whirled to find Clay standing in the doorway, a pair of cotton pajama bottoms riding low on his hips, his hair spiked from sleep. With his eyes narrowed suspiciously, the boy leaned to peer around his father at Annie.

Jase immediately took a step sideways to block his son's view, wondering how much of their conversation Clay had overheard. "What are you doing out of bed?" he snapped. "You should be asleep."

Clay jerked his gaze to his father's, his expression turning accusing. "Why are you in Annie's room?"

"We're talking."

"You were yelling at her," Clay argued. "I heard you."

Annie stepped from behind Jase, touched by the boy's concern. "I'm fine, Clay," she reassured him. "Go on back to bed. I can handle this."

The teenager shifted his gaze from Annie to his father, then back, his reluctance to leave obvious. "Tara's sick," he mumbled.

Annie's eyes shot wide. "What?" she cried, hurrying forward. "What's wrong with her?"

Clay rolled a shoulder and turned away. "I don't know. I heard her in the bathroom puking, but she's got the door locked and won't let me in."

Annie and Jase bolted for the door, shoving impatiently at each other as they both tried to wedge their way through the opening at the same time. Frustrated, Annie managed to twist her way past him and ran down the hall. At the bathroom door, she stopped and pressed her ear against the wood, listening.

"Tara?" she called softly. "Sweetheart, it's Annie. Are you ill?"

Jase shouldered her aside and lifted a hand to pound his fist against the door. "Open up, Tara!" he shouted. "Now!"

Annie pressed her lips together and shot him a disapproving look. "You're only going to upset her with your shouting," she whispered angrily.

"That's too damn bad." He closed a hand over the doorknob and gave it a hard twist. "You have exactly three seconds to open this door, Tara," he yelled, "or I'm getting my tools and taking it off its hinges. One. Two. Thr—"

The door flew open and Tara stepped out, her arms folded over her chest in a belligerent stance Annie had grown accustomed to since Jase's return.

"Are you sick?" Jase demanded to know.

"What do you care?" she muttered and turned for her room.

Jase caught her by the arm and spun her back around. "Clay said you were sick. Are you?"

Tara shot her brother a murderous look. "Tattletale."

Jase gave her arm a shake. "Are you sick or not?"

Slowly, Tara turned her gaze to her father, her eyes flat with resentment. "No."

"But I heard you puking," Clay argued.

Tara shot him another dark look. "So I threw up. Big deal. Something I ate probably didn't agree with me, because I feel fine now."

Annie listened to the exchange, an ugly suspicion rising in her mind when she saw a toothbrush lying on the floor near the base of the toilet.

Jase, on the other hand, seemed relieved by his daughter's reassurance that she wasn't ill. "Good," he said and released her arm. "Y'all get back to bed and go to sleep."

He waited until the twins had returned to their rooms and closed their doors, then turned to Annie, his scowl returning. "We'll finish our discussion downstairs."

Annie darted a worried glance at Tara's door. "I'll be down in a minute. I just want to check on Tara first and make sure she's all right."

"Make it snappy," Jase muttered and headed for the stairs.

Annie slipped into the bathroom, retrieved the toothbrush, then crossed to Tara's door. She tapped softly, then waited, praying she was wrong.

Tara opened the door, still wearing the same belligerent expression. "What do you want?"

Annie opened her hand, revealing the toothbrush. "I found this on the floor in the bathroom."

A look of alarm flashed across Tara's eyes before she hid it behind a mask of indifference. "I probably knocked it off the basin when I was sick." She snatched the toothbrush from Annie's hand and, with a muttered thanks, slammed the door in her face.

Annie stared at the door for a moment, then turned and marched downstairs and to the kitchen where Jase waited, slouched in his chair at the head of the table. She crossed to her own chair opposite his and sank down. Unable to keep her suspicions to herself a moment longer, she said, "She's lying."

He peered at her in confusion. "Who's lying?"

"Tara." Annie sank back against her chair and

pressed a hand against her stomach, feeling a little bit sick herself at the thought of the harm the girl could be doing to her body if Annie's suspicions were correct.

"Why would she lie about throwing up? She said she ate something that didn't agree with her, threw it up and now she's fine. Sounds reasonable enough to me."

Annie inhaled deeply, searching for the right words, knowing how important it was for her to make Jase understand the seriousness of the situation. "Yes, she threw up," she agreed. "And, yes, she feels fine now. But she didn't throw up because of something she ate. She *made* herself throw up."

"And why the hell would she do a stupid thing like that?"

"To get your attention."

He slumped down in his chair, scowling. "That's the wildest bunch of bull I've ever heard. Who in their right mind would make themselves throw up just to get some attention?"

Annie leaned forward, determined to make him understand Tara's need for him. "A teenage girl who is desperate to make her father notice her, that's who. She's thirteen, Jase. The time in a young girl's life when her hormones are in a constant state of flux. The time when her emotions can run the gamut from ecstatic joy to darkest depression in the blink of an eye. The time," she added pointedly, "when a young girl needs the love and support of her parents the very most."

Jase rocketed from his chair and turned away, pacing from the table. "She's only got one parent," he growled. "Me. And she knows I love her."

"How does she know?" Annie challenged. "Do you tell her?

He yanked open the refrigerator, scowling. "She knows," he muttered as he fished through the refrigerator's contents for a soft drink.

"But do you *tell* her?" Annie insisted.

He slammed the refrigerator door and ripped back the tab on the canned drink. He tipped his head back, guzzling the soda, then dropped his hand to aim the can at Annie's nose. "I don't need you, or anybody else, telling me how to raise my own kids."

"That's not my intent," she replied as she rose. "But are you familiar with bulimia?"

"Tara isn't bulimic. Hell," he said, gesturing wildly with the can, "she's skinny as a rail, as it is. There'd be no reason for her to make herself sick just to lose weight."

"I didn't say she *was* bulimic. But last week she mentioned to me that they were studying eating disorders in her health class and discussed the warning signs for both anorexia and bulimia. She seemed intrigued by the possibility that a person could suffer from bulimia and no one who lived with them would even be aware of the problem."

Annie glanced down at her hands, twisting her fingers nervously, knowing she was overstepping her bounds, but helpless to do anything else. "I think she's testing you," she said quietly, then found the courage to look back up at him. "She's trying to prove to herself that you really don't care anything for her."

"That's ridiculous. I care for my daughter."

"Whether you do or not really isn't the point. It's how Tara *perceives* your feelings that's important. And from what I've observed, she considers your indifference and the time you spend away from the house as a lack of affection for her."

"So what do you suggest I do? Ignore the work that needs to be done on the ranch? Stay in the house all day and play dolls with her?"

"Tara doesn't play with dolls any longer. But, no, that's not what I'm suggesting. I'm simply trying to point out that Tara is a troubled teen who needs her father's love and support more than she ever has before. What concerns me most is the lengths she might go to gain your attention."

He gave his chair an angry shove, slamming it back up to the table. "Well, thankfully, you're leaving and won't have to concern yourself with Tara's welfare any longer."

"Do you really think replacing me at this point in time is wise?"

He braced his hands on his hips and narrowed his eyes at her. "So that's it. It's your own welfare you're concerned about, not Tara's."

Annie fought back the anger that rose, the urge to strike back, and forced herself to focus instead on Tara's needs. "She lost her mother," she reminded him. "And now her aunt is gone, too, the only other woman in her life she felt close to. I don't think it would be in Tara's best interest for me to leave right now. She's accepted me, as have the other children, and I'm afraid another change in the household so soon after Penny leaving would be upsetting for them all. Especially Tara. She might decide to run away or...worse.''

He stared at her, the blood slowly draining from his face, obviously understanding the danger Annie hadn't been able to bring herself to voice. Swallowing hard, he turned away and crossed to the sink, bracing his hands on its edge as he stared blindly at the dark window. ''You really think the situation is that bad?''

''I don't know,'' Annie admitted honestly. ''But she's definitely going through a rebellious stage, and the statistics for troubled teens who attempt suicide are alarming. What she needs right now is stability, close supervision...and love.''

He dropped his chin to his chest, groaning, and the sound tore through Annie's heart. In spite of his obvious dislike for her, his intent to remove her from his home, she found herself wanting to cross to him, wrap her arms around him and offer him her comfort. Before she could give in to the temptation, though, he lifted his head, his expression bleak as he stared at the dark window.

''Stay, then,'' he said in a voice rough with emotion. ''I can't take a chance on losing my daughter, too.''

Annie had the opportunity to question the wisdom of her insistence to be allowed to remain in the Rawley household more than once over the next few days. Ever since the late-night confrontation between Tara and her father, Tara seemed to have withdrawn even more from the family unit, a situation that concerned Annie more and more each day.

And Jase. The man had to be the blindest, most

stubborn man in the world. In spite of Annie's warn-
ings, he continued to spend the majority of his time
out on the ranch, doing whatever he did while away
from the house and all but ignoring his children, as
well as Annie.

But she couldn't give up, she told herself as she
headed outdoors to the garden, intending to take out
her frustrations on the weeds that grew there. It didn't
matter to Annie that Jase avoided *her*. She was a mature woman and could handle rejection, though she
did find his determination to deny his obvious attraction to her puzzling—and a bit frustrating, since she
found him so attractive. But what mattered a great
deal to her was his avoidance of his family. She *had*
to find a way to draw them back together, she told
herself. For their sakes. How she'd go about doing
that, she wasn't sure. But she was confident she'd find
a way.

As she neared the garden, she slowed, then stopped
altogether, her mouth sagging open when she saw that
the weed-choked ground had been plowed under and
turned into neatly aligned rows. She glanced at the
rototiller parked near the fence…and knew who had
done the work.

Jase. He'd plowed the garden for her. But why?

The sound of cattle bawling drew her gaze to the
corral where Jase had worked all morning. Dust hung
like a cloud over the area, stirred by the calves' constant milling inside. She caught a glimpse of Jase
moving among the animals, his hat grayed by a thin
film of dust, his shirt clinging wetly to his back and
chest beneath the relentless afternoon sun. The calves

moved in a tight herd away from him, obviously distrusting the human in their midst.

She strained for a better look, wondering what he was doing, and wondering, too, if she dared interrupt his work long enough to thank him for plowing the garden for her. While she wavered uncertainly, a dog barked and she shifted her gaze to the Australian shepherd dog, sitting at the gate. The animal's posture was tense and expectant, as if anxious to join Jase inside the corral.

As Annie stared, mesmerized by the scene, she realized what a wonderful photo op this would be and raced for the house. She returned minutes later, fitting a zoom lens over her camera. As she neared the corral, she slowed her steps, not wanting to disrupt the action going on inside. Drawing a deep breath to steady her hands, she stooped and placed the camera's lens between the pipes that shaped the corral. She quickly brought the dog into focus and managed to squeeze off several shots before the milling calves blocked her view.

Pleased, she readjusted the angle of the camera and focused in on Jase. The zoom lens brought him within touching distance, giving her an intimate view of the dark stains of sweat on his shirt, the dust that filled the creases on his face, the determined set of his jaw. Rugged, she thought, pressing her finger excitedly over the shutter release time and time again. Man pitted against animal. Contemporary cowboy. Hardworking rancher.

If the pictures turned out nearly as well as she hoped, she would send them to an editor of one of the Western or livestock magazines for consideration.

With the focus for the series and potential markets tumbling through her mind, she kept the camera focused on Jase, recording his movements, the range of emotions that swept across his face. Steely-eyed determination, she thought with a shiver. A sharp wariness in the squint of his eyes when a calf squared off with him, threatening head-to-head battle. Smug pleasure when he managed to separate from the herd the steer he wanted. She clicked off several more shots, only vaguely aware of the flutter of attraction that warmed her belly.

"Roscoe!"

The dog bounded forward at Jase's sharp command, his tongue lolling, his tail wagging.

Jase waved a hand in what Annie assumed was a signal of some sort and the dog dropped to the ground and slunk surreptitiously in a wide circle around the steer, approaching the animal from the rear. With a slow, methodic diligence, the dog pushed the steer toward an open chute. When the steer darted inside, Jase moved quickly to drop the gate into place, successfully penning the animal.

Annie squeezed off a couple of more shots, then straightened. "Wow," she said breathlessly, impressed.

Jase whipped his head around at the sound of her voice, obviously unaware of her presence until that moment. Frowning, he dropped his gaze to the camera she held at her waist. "What the hell are you doing with that?" he asked impatiently.

She smiled, determined not to let his grouchiness chase her away. "Taking some pictures. Great action. Lots of emotion, too."

His frown deepened into a scowl. "It's called work," he muttered and stretched to draw a large stainless-steel syringe from a toolbox on the ground near the chute.

Annie hurried over to peer through the rails. "What are you doing?" she asked, already drawing the camera before her face.

"Vaccinating the calves." Jase rubbed his fingers high on the calf's shoulder, pinched an area of flesh between his fingers, then injected the needle.

Annie clicked a shot, then winced when the calf bawled. "Did you hurt him?" she asked, lowering the camera.

"No. He's just pissed because I separated him from his buddies."

"Oh," she said doubtfully, not at all convinced the calf hadn't experienced a little pain. When Jase picked up a tool that looked something like pliers, she pushed to the balls of her feet, straining for a better view. "What's that for?"

"I use it to notch his ear."

Annie hunched her shoulders, tensing, as Jase positioned the tool over the calf's ear and squeezed. "Surely *that* hurts him," she said, grimacing as Jase removed a small V of flesh.

He tossed a look of disgust over his shoulder, then rammed the tool into his back pocket without bothering to comment.

"Why do you notch his ear?" she persisted, figuring she'd need some factual data for the article she planned to write to accompany the photos.

"It's a way to identify him."

"I thought ranchers branded their cattle?"

He inhaled deeply, obviously annoyed by her questions. "I do, but only those animals I plan to add to my herd. These are stocker calves. I'll feed 'em out, then sell most of 'em before winter comes. Those I keep, I'll brand."

"Oh," she said, absorbing that information. "But—"

Before she could ask the next question, he turned to scowl at her. "Don't you have anything better to do than stand around all day, asking a bunch of stupid questions?"

Annie thought of the work she'd planned to do in the garden and that which awaited her in the house, and slipped her hand behind her back, crossing two fingers. "No. Not a thing," she lied cheerfully.

He jerked his chin toward the truck parked beside the corral. "Then make yourself useful and fetch that clipboard from the front seat."

Excited at the thought of assisting, she tugged her camera from around her neck and jogged for the truck. Placing the camera carefully on the seat, she grabbed the requested clipboard and hurried back to the chute. "Here you go," she said, sticking an arm between the pipes to pass Jase the clipboard.

With his hands occupied with the calf, he gave his head a jerk, motioning her inside. "Bring it over here."

With a nervous glance at the other calves that continued to mill in a tight group in the corral, Annie swung a leg through the rails, then ducked her head and slipped through the space, straightening to stand on the other side. Keeping a cautious eye on the calves, she sidestepped her way to where Jase waited.

"Here," she said and thrust the clipboard in what she hoped was his direction.

"Tag number 12, Black Angus, steer."

Annie whipped her head around to peer at him in confusion. "What?"

"Tag number 12, Black Angus, steer," he repeated impatiently, then ordered, "Write it down."

"Oh," she said and drew the clipboard to her hip, balancing it there as she drew the pen from its holder. She quickly jotted down the information, casting an occasional nervous glance toward the other calves.

"Got it?"

"Yes," she said and exhaled an uneasy breath.

He released his hold on the steer and dragged his hands across the seat of his pants. "Put today's date in the column marked Vaccinated."

She quickly made the entry, then hugged the clipboard to her breasts. "Is that all?"

He gave his chin a jerk in response as he released the gate. "For that one."

Annie's eyes widened as she turned to stare at the herd. There had to be at least thirty or forty calves remaining. "You mean we have to do *all* of them?"

"All," he confirmed, then pulled up the gate on the chute. "Do you think you could stand in this opening and keep that steer from getting out?"

"Well...yes," she said, eyeing the animal warily. "I suppose so."

"When I give the signal, move out of the way and Roscoe will herd the next calf inside."

Swallowing hard, Annie positioned herself in front of the chute, casting an uneasy glance over her shoulder at the steer who stood at the far end. Suppressing a shudder at his intimidating size, she turned back around to see Jase approaching the herd. She quickly forgot about the steer behind her and watched in growing fascination as Jase moved among the animals, studying them, seemingly unafraid of getting stomped on or gored by an occasional budding horn.

"Get ready," he called, obviously having selected the calf he wanted from the herd. "Roscoe!"

Annie watched the dog shoot forward, then screamed when something struck her hard in the middle of her back, knocking her off her feet. She flung out her arms to break her fall, but slammed face first against the ground, her teeth jarring at the impact. The steer leaped over her, grazing her back with one of his sharp hooves.

"Why the hell did you let him get past you?"

Dazed, she slowly lifted her face from the dirt, blinking twice before she realized what Jase had said. "I didn't *let* him get past me," she cried indignantly, then grimaced and spit a collection of foul-tasting dirt from her mouth.

"You were supposed to block the opening!"

She heaved herself up on her elbows as Jase bore down her, his hands fisted at his sides, his eyes dark with anger. "I *was* blocking the opening," she snapped. "He knocked me down and ran right over the top of me."

"Well, you shouldn't have let him get past you."

She pushed herself to her knees, spitting granules of dirt that clung stubbornly to her lips, and glared up at him. "Look, buster," she said, drawing her hands to her hips. "I'm not Calamity Jane. I stood in

he opening, just like you instructed. It isn't *my* fault
he dang calf got out.''

''Then whose fault is it?'' he shouted, gesturing
wildly at the chute behind her. ''*You* were the one
who was supposed to guard the gate.''

Feeling the anger building, Annie pushed herself
he rest of the way to her feet, then gasped, doubling
over, as a pain shot across the middle of her back.

''What's the matter?''

She gulped, then swallowed, fighting back the nau-
ea that rose. ''I think he stepped on me.''

With her head bent toward the ground, her view of
he world was narrowed to the area around her feet.
she saw Jase's boots enter that space, then felt the
weight of his hand on her hip.

''Where?''

She drew in a shaky breath. ''Just above my
waist.''

She felt his fingers catch the hem of her tank top,
hen the brush of his knuckles as he drew it up and
way from her spine. When he didn't offer a comment, she squeezed her eyes shut, fearing the worst.
''Is it bad?''

When he still didn't reply, she angled her head
ack over her shoulder to peer at him. The almost
poplectic look on his face took her by surprise.

''Jase?''

He snapped his gaze to hers, heat staining his
heeks. ''Uh...no,'' he replied and dropped his hand
rom her shirt. ''It's just a scrape.''

She pressed her hands against her waist and
traightened slowly, groaning. ''Tell that to my ach-
ng back.''

"I've got a first aid kit in my truck. I'll get it."

She nodded and walked to the side of the corral. Sinking gingerly to the ground, she waited while he went to collect the kit.

When he returned, she lifted her face, squinting up at him as he opened the box. "This isn't going to hurt, is it?"

He hunkered down beside her, balancing the box on his knee as he dug through its contents. "Might sting a little."

She drew back, watching as he set the box aside and tore open a small packet he'd removed. "What's that?" she asked suspiciously.

"A piece of gauze soaked with hydrogen peroxide. I'll need to clean the wound first."

"Wound?" she repeated, snapping up her head to look at him. "I thought you said it was just a scrape."

He tugged his hat down lower over his brow, hiding his eyes from her. "Wound. Scrape. Same damn thing."

"I bet you wouldn't think so if it was *your* back that was hurt," she replied petulantly.

He drew a circle in the air with his finger, indicating for her to turn around.

Frowning, Annie scooted on her bottom, offering him her back. "Just be gentle, okay?" she requested uneasily.

She felt the pressure of his fingers as he lifted her shirt, then cool air hitting her skin as he shoved it up high on her back and held it between her shoulder blades. A second or two passed without any other movement, and she angled her head slightly over her shoulder. "Well? Are you going to clean it, or not?"

"Yeah," he said, his voice suddenly sounding rusty. "I am." He dropped down to his knees and eased closer, his thighs bumping against her hips.

Squeezing her eyes shut, Annie bowed her back to give him easier access and dipped her chin, prepared to scream if he treated her roughly. But the fingers that swept the gauze across her back were surprisingly gentle, almost tender in their ministrations. She flinched a little as the cold liquid struck her warm skin, and he jerked his hand back.

"Did I hurt you?"

She bit back a smile at the alarm she heard in his voice. "No. It's just cold."

"Oh," he said, releasing a breath. He blotted at the scrape, then tossed the square of gauze aside. "I'm going to put some antibiotic cream on it now."

"Whatever you say, Doc."

She heard him digging through the box, then felt the pressure of his fingers again as he gently smoothed the cream over the scrape. The sensation wasn't all that unpleasant, though she did feel a slight sting when the ointment came in contact with her broken skin. She closed her eyes as he continued to stroke, lulled by the slow, almost hypnotic movement of his fingers.

"You might be a little sore tomorrow," he offered quietly.

"Tomorrow?" she echoed, then snorted a laugh. "How about right now?"

"Where does it hurt?"

She stretched an arm around behind her, pointing at a spot just above her waist and below the scrape. "There."

He pressed the tips of his fingers tentatively against the spot.

"Yeah," she said, and closed her eyes again with a sigh. "Right there."

He increased the pressure of his fingertips, gently kneading at the sore muscle. She arched her back, moaning softly, and leaned forward, hugging her arms around her knees to give him better access. She hummed her pleasure as he increased the pressure of his thumbs on either side of her spine, all but purred at the slow stretch of his fingers across the width of her back and shivered deliciously when his fingers dipped into the curve of her waist and gently squeezed.

She was sure he'd stop the massage then, prayed he wouldn't, and caught her lip between her teeth when he shaped his hands around her waist and began to slowly drag his palms up her sides. There was a dreamlike quality to his movements, a studied slowness that made her wonder if he realized what he was doing or who he was doing it to.

He didn't like her. He'd made no bones about that. And she seriously doubted that he was giving her the massage because of any latent sense of responsibility he felt for her soreness. And he certainly wasn't doing it out of the kindness of his heart! As far as she could tell, he didn't have one.

But as his hands continued to stroke upwards, she decided the why wasn't important. The only thing that mattered was the play of his palms over her skin. She emptied her mind of everything, focusing on the strength in the wide hands that shaped her, the gentleness in them, the sensual chafe of his work-roughened palms over her tender flesh. Heat swirled to life low in her belly, swept out to gently nudge nerve endings from sleep.

She shivered when his palms bumped slowly over the rounded sides of her breasts, then sucked in a breath, her eyes flipping wide, when he slipped his hands around her and covered them.

Tensed, she waited, uncertain what to say, what to do. She could hear the rasp of his labored breathing behind her, feel the tremble in the fingers cupping her, recognized both as his struggle for control. Slowly he increased the pressure of his hands, molding them around her breasts' shape, his fingers sinking deeply into their cushiony softness. She closed her eyes as wave after wave of sensation spilled through her and her nerves skipped into a faster dance beneath her skin. A low moan of pleasure crawled up her throat and slipped past her lips before she could stop it.

At the sound, he snatched his hands from around her and bolted to his feet. Startled—and a little disappointed—she twisted her head around to peer up at him, but the glare of the sun prevented her from seeing his face.

"I finished doctoring your scrape," he mumbled as he stooped to scoop the first aid kit from the ground.

That he would try to pretend the intimacy had never occurred, surprised Annie...and infuriated her. She grabbed hold of a rail, hauled herself to her feet and whirled to face him. "Excuse me? Are you just going to pretend that that never happened?"

He glanced her way, and she stumbled back a step,

stunned by the raw need she saw in his eyes, the rigid set of his jaw.

He quickly turned away. "Go back to the house," he growled. "I'll finish the rest of the calves alone."

Four

Jase made it inside the barn and out of sight of the house—and he hoped, Annie—then stopped and, with a furious growl, hurled the first aid kit against the tack-room door. It bounced off the wood with a loud *crack* and its lid popped open, spilling the box's contents out over the alleyway. He stared at the scattered supplies, his chest heaving as if he'd just run a marathon, his body trembling as if he'd just encountered a ghost.

He'd touched her, he thought, his mind spinning crazily at the memory, his pulse still beating erratically from the contact. Dear God, he'd touched Annie.

He opened his hands to stare at them, still able to feel the silk-like texture of her skin, the heat in it as he'd swept his palms up her sides. The pillowed softness of her breasts giving beneath his hands, the jab of desire-awakened nipples growing rigid against his palms.

Groaning, he curled his fingers inward, digging his fingertips painfully into his palms, trying to block the memory, the shame.

No, he thought in self-reproach. He hadn't *touched* her. He'd *groped* her like some hormone-crazed teenager would a date in the back seat of his father's car.

And what angered him even more was that he wished he could touch her again.

He swore and spun, driving his fingers through his hair. He was crazy. He had to be. There was no other way to explain his actions. He knew better. He'd known he was attracted to her. Hadn't he promised himself that he would stay away from her for that very reason? He didn't want to feel anything for her. Hell, he didn't want to feel anything, at all! Feeling *hurt,* and he'd had a stomach full of hurting.

"Jase?"

At the sound of her voice behind him, he groaned, knotting his fingers in his hair. "What do you want?"

"I forgot to thank you for tilling the garden for me."

He inhaled deeply, then dropped his hands and lifted his head to stare at the far wall. "You've said it. So go."

"Why are you so angry with me?"

"I'm not angry."

He heard her short snort of disagreement and wished fervently that she would accept his answer and just leave him the hell alone.

But he knew she wouldn't. Not Annie.

And she didn't.

"Liar."

He dragged in another long breath, trying to force the tension from his body, the sharpness from his tone, hoping if he succeeded in doing so he could convince her to leave. "I said I'm not angry."

"Then why won't you look at me?"

He turned slowly, curling his hands into fists at his sides as he braced himself for the confrontation. "Okay," he said, enunciating each word carefully and distinctly as he met her gaze. "I'm looking at you, and I'm not angry. *Now* are you satisfied?"

She cocked her head to the side. "No," she said, after moment of quiet deliberation. "I'm not." She folded her arms across her chest and walked around him. "Your hands are fisted, a sure sign of agitation. And there's a little muscle ticking right here—" when she reached to point at the spot, he jerked away, dodging her touch "—on your temple," she finished and infuriated him more by biting back a smile.

"Why don't you just go back to the house like I told you to and leave me the hell alone?"

"Because that's not healthy."

He threw his hands up in the air. "For who?" he shouted.

"For you."

He took a threatening step toward her. "Listen, little *girl,*" he said, leveling a finger at her nose. "If you know what's good for you, you'll sashay that cute little fanny of yours back to the house and keep it there."

Her smile widening, she strained to peer over her

shoulder at her backside. "You really think my fanny's cute?"

Jase dropped his face against his hands, moaning.

"Come on, Jase," she cajoled and cupped a hand over the back of his neck, squeezing softly. "Would it really be so bad to admit that you're attracted to me?"

He tried to ignore the gentle urging of her fingers against his neck...but failed, the same as he'd failed in trying to avoid her.

"Would it help if I told you that I'm attracted to you, too?" she asked softly.

Her face was dipped close to his, so close the moist warmth of her breath fanned the shell of his ear and sent a shiver chasing down his spine. He drew in a deep breath, searching for the strength to resist her, and her scent filled his head, making his mind spin dizzily. But it was her quiet admission that put the tremble in his hands, the throbbing ache in his loins.

She was attracted to him. Oh, damn. How was he supposed to respond to that? How was he supposed to resist her, when all he wanted to do was throw her down on the floor and make love to her? Was this some kind of game she was playing with him? Was she purposely trying to seduce him?

Knowing he had to send her away before he completely lost control, he forced his hands from his face and straightened. He met her gaze, sure that he'd find teasing in her eyes, the coy playfulness of a woman with seduction on her mind. But all he found in the green depths was clear-eyed honesty and warm compassion.

He could have resisted coyness, had before when

other women had plied him with their womanly wiles, but her honesty and compassion rendered him helpless. "Annie—" When her hand slipped from behind his neck to rest against his cheek and she tipped her head to the side, her expression softening in understanding, he shut his eyes on a groan and closed his hand over hers. "Don't," he said and dragged her fingers away.

"Jase—"

"Don't," he said more insistently and turned his back on her.

He heard her sigh of defeat but refused to turn around.

"Okay," she said softly. "But someday you're going to have to let go of all that emotion that's inside you. If you don't, you're going to wind up with an ulcer, for sure."

That afternoon Annie waited for the arrival of the school bus, smug in her new discovery.

In spite of Jase's insistence that the mama cat she'd photographed was self-reliant and could take care of herself and her babies, Annie had taken an old blanket and some food to the loft, only to find the cat and her kittens already snuggled on a horse blanket spread over loose hay and containers of water and food nearby.

Knowing it was Jase who had provided for the cat and her babies, she considered confronting him with her knowledge of his kindness...but quickly decided against it. She knew he'd probably just deny the act or attempt to lessen its significance in some way.

The big softy, she thought with a smile as she

watched the bus screech to a stop with a squeal of
brakes. Jase wanted her to believe he was mean and
callous, but she was beginning to believe that there
was another side to him. One that could possibly grow
with the proper nurturing.

Pleasure spread warmly through her chest as she
watched Jase's children troop toward her, Rachel lag-
ging behind the twins as she stopped to pick wildflowers growing alongside the drive. Heavens, but she
loved these kids, she thought as she hurried to meet
them.

"How was school?" she asked as she accepted the
backpack Clay passed to her.

"Lame," Tara muttered and passed her by.

"Same old same old," Clay replied and turned
wearily for the barn.

"Wait," Annie called to Clay. She held out a paper
bag. "A snack," she whispered and shot him a con-
spiratorial wink.

"Peanut butter cookies?" he asked hopefully,
sneaking a peek inside.

"They are your favorite, aren't they?"

He glanced up at her, a grin spreading from ear to
ear. "Thanks, Annie," he said, then turned and ran
for the barn.

Annie smiled after him, but glanced down when
she felt a tug on her shirttail.

"Do I get peanut butter cookies, too?" Rachel
asked, peering up at her.

"Nope." She laughed at the child's crestfallen expression and dropped to a knee in front of her. Smiling, she tapped a finger against the end of the little

girl's nose. "You get oatmeal, because they're *your* favorite."

"What kind does Tara get?"

Annie rose, her gaze going to the house, watching as Tara stepped inside. "Sugar cookies," she replied, secretly hoping the sweet treat would take some of the sourness out of Tara's disposition.

"Daddy doesn't like us."

Annie glanced up from the sandwiches she was making to look at Rachel in surprise. "Well, of course your father likes you."

Rachel stubbornly shook her head, her pigtails slapping against rosy cheeks. "No, he doesn't. Tara said so."

Annie turned to look at Tara who was standing at her opposite side, wrapping in plastic wrap the sandwiches Annie had made. "Did you tell Rachel that, Tara?"

Tara kept her gaze on her work but lifted a shoulder. "So what if I did?" she replied sullenly. "It's the truth."

Annie laid down her knife and turned, catching Tara's shoulders in her hands and angling the girl around to face her. "But your father loves you," she insisted. When Tara refused to look at her, Annie pressed a finger beneath the girl's chin and forced her face up. "He loves you," she said more firmly. "I know he does."

"Then why doesn't he ever spend time with us?"

Her heart breaking at the tears she saw glistening in the girl's eyes, Annie gathered Tara into her arms. "Because he has so much work to do," Annie replied, hugging her. "It takes a lot to run a ranch of this size." Realizing how weak the excuse sounded, especially to a young girl, she pushed Tara out to arm's length and forced a smile. "But maybe we can change that."

"Yeah, right," Tara muttered, and dashed a finger beneath her nose. "Like Dad would quit working, just because we wanted him to."

"He might," Annie said secretively. "Especially if we lure him with a really tasty picnic lunch."

"A picnic?" Rachel cried and began jumping up and down and clapping her hands. "Can we really go on a picnic?"

"Why not?" Annie asked. "Instead of waiting for Clay to come and pick up the sandwiches, we'll just deliver their lunch to the hayfield." She waved a hand toward the pantry. "Tara, you get the picnic basket and, Rachel, you get that tin of cookies we baked this morning."

Within minutes the three had packed the picnic basket and tossed a quilt into the trunk of Annie's car and were headed for the hayfield where Jase and Clay had worked all morning. As they bumped past the open gate, Annie saw Clay in the distance driving a tractor with a disk attached. Jase followed pulling a machine that broadcast seed.

Steering her car along the fence line until she reached a group of trees, Annie pressed the horn several times, then climbed out.

"Unpack our lunch, girls," she called to Tara and Rachel. "I'll stop them when they make this round."

Stepping out into the field, Annie waited, smiling

as Clay neared. "Hey!" she called, waving a hand over her head. "How about some lunch?"

Clay slowed, grinning, and pulled the lever to raise the blades of the disk. "Don't have to ask me twice."

While he shut off the tractor's engine and climbed down, Annie stepped farther out into the field to stop Jase. She kept her smile in place when she saw his scowl. Fitting her hands at the sides of her mouth to be heard over his tractor's engine, she yelled, "We brought your lunch!"

He slowed, then stopped, his scowl deepening. "Clay was supposed to go to the house and get it."

Pushing her smile higher, Annie replied, "I know, but we thought a picnic might be fun." Before he could argue, she turned and headed back for the trees and the quilt the girls had spread out.

"How about some lemonade, Clay?" she asked and filled a plastic cup from the thermos she'd brought along.

He accepted the cup with a grin. "Thanks, Annie." He plopped down on the quilt and dug around in the basket. "What did you make for us? I'm starving."

Tara slapped his hand away. "Sandwiches, you moron, and keep your skanky hands off. You're dirty."

Clay sat back, still grinning, seemingly willing to let his twin sister wait on him. "What kind?"

"Tuna, pimento cheese or turkey," Tara said, assuming the position of hostess. "Which would you like?"

"All of 'em."

Tara shot him a frown. "Pig."

Clay's grin spread wider. "I'm not a pig. I'm a workin' man and workin' men have big appetites."

Annie laughed, unaffected by the twins' bickering, recognizing it as the harmless teasing that siblings exchanged.

"I want pimento cheese," Rachel piped in as she dropped down to her knees on the quilt.

Tara filled a plate and passed it to her brother, then arranged another for Rachel. "Annie?" she asked. "What about you?"

"Turkey, please," Annie replied, pleased to see that Tara's sullen expression was gone and she was actually smiling. "And one of those pickles, too," she added. She glanced up as Jase approached. "What kind of sandwich would you like, Jase?"

"What are my choices?" he grumbled.

Annie repeated the selections.

"Tuna," he said, and dropped down on the far end of the quilt, as far away from the others as he could possibly get.

Tara quickly arranged several sandwiches on a plate and passed it to her father.

He accepted it without looking up or acknowledging the gesture. Seeing the disappointment on Tara's face, Annie quickly offered, "The girls helped make the sandwiches."

Jase grunted a response and took a bite, while Clay faked a choking sound. "Tara helped cook?" He clutched his stomach dramatically. "I've been poisoned!"

Pursing her lips, Tara slugged him on the arm and Clay fell over as if she'd delivered a knockout punch. Rachel laughed and fell on top of her brother an began tickling him. Tara joined in and, with the two girls teaming up, they quickly pinned their brother to the ground, laughing at the advantage they'd gained.

"You kids settle down," Jase snapped. He waved an impatient hand. "And hurry up and eat. Clay and I have work to do."

The wrestling match came to a abrupt stop and Tara sat up, the laughter in her eyes dying as she looked over at her father. Slowly she shifted off Clay and picked up her plate. Rising, she carried it to the trunk of Annie's car and pitched it into the paper sack they'd brought to collect their garbage, then climbed into the front seat and slammed the door behind her.

Annie watched Tara, her heart sinking.

Later that night, after the children had gone to bed, Annie waited for Jase to return to the house, hoping to talk to him about the picnic and explain to him how he'd spoiled a perfectly wonderful outing and how deeply he'd disappointed his children by doing so.

She watched for him from the back porch, perched on the first step, dressed in her nightgown and robe, her arms hugged around her knees. The night was blessedly cool, a respite from the unseasonably hot afternoon, and Annie tipped up her chin to peer at the sky. Stars blinked overhead, scattered across a field of blue-black velvet, and a sickle-shaped moon hung low in the sky.

In the distance she could hear the low call of cattle and closer the hum of insects darting in and out of the glow of the security light near the barn. Though she'd spent her entire life in the city surrounded by people, noise and lights, she sighed contentedly, surprised to discover that she found the pastoral setting much more appealing.

Her sense of contentment ended with Jase's approach. Though he remained in shadows as he strode for the house, she could tell by the squareness of his shoulders, the deliberateness of his stride, that his mood hadn't improved since the picnic that afternoon. As he neared, she hugged her arms tighter around her knees, dreading the confrontation even as awareness fluttered to life low in her belly.

"What are you doing out here?"

Though his tone was anything but friendly, Annie forced a smile. "Waiting for you."

He snorted as he passed by her, climbing the steps. "It's late. I'm going to bed."

She caught the leg of his jeans, stopping him. "Sit down for a minute. Please?" she added, looking up at him. "I need to talk to you."

He hesitated a moment, then, heaving a sigh, swung around and dropped down on the step beside her. He dragged off his hat, swiped an arm across his forehead, then settled the hat back over his head. "Make it fast. I'm tired."

"I'm sure you are. You've been at it since dawn this morning."

"Yeah, well," he replied dryly, "there's always work to be done on a ranch."

"Yes, I'm sure there is." She caught the fabric of her robe over her knees and pleated it between her fingers, unsure how to broach the subject of his behavior. "About the picnic this afternoon," she began

He snorted and pushed to his feet. "I don't have time for this."

She caught the leg of his jeans again, stopping him. "Please hear me out."

Though she could tell by the tension he kept on the fabric that he wanted to avoid this conversation, he finally dropped back down and dragged off his hat, balancing it over his knee. "Say what you've got to say and get it over with."

"Are you aware that you hurt Tara's feelings this afternoon?"

He whipped his head around. "How the hell did I do that? I ate with y'all, didn't I?"

"Yes, but when I told you that the girls helped make your lunch, you just grunted."

He huffed a disgusted breath. "What was I supposed to do? Break out in song?"

"No," she replied, ignoring his sarcasm. "But you might have offered them a compliment or, at the very least, said thank you."

"Did *they* thank me for providing the food they prepared?" he returned defensively. "Did *they* do anything to help earn the money to buy that food?"

"Jase, they are children."

"So was I, once upon a time, but I worked right alongside my daddy on this ranch from the time I was six years old. Didn't seem to hurt me any."

"I think it did."

He turned his head to glare at her.

"You obviously never learned how to play."

He snorted and would have risen, but Annie stopped him by placing a hand on his arm. "Let them be children, Jase. They'll be forced to become adults soon enough.''

"They'll grow up lazy."

"No," she argued, "they'll grow up to be happy and well-adjusted adults.''

"Lazy," he repeated.

"Would you rather they be workaholics, like you?" she asked in frustration.

His eyes narrowed and darkened. "As long as there's work to be done, I'll do it.''

Knowing that she'd angered him, that she was growing angry herself, she took a deep breath, forcing herself to calm down. "You said yourself that there is *always* work to be done on a ranch," she reminded him pointedly. "If you don't take time for yourself, for your family, put off some of the work for another day, another time, you're going to kill yourself or, at the very least, alienate your children and wind up a lonely and bitter old man."

He stared at her for a long moment, his lips thinning, his eyes narrowing dangerously. "Are you through?"

She released his arm, sure that she'd failed in getting her point across to him. "Yes. I'm through.''

"Good," he said, rising. "'Cause I'm through listening.''

Annie glanced at the clock, then snatched the platter of fried chicken from the table and marched to the refrigerator.

"The coward," she muttered as she shoved the platter inside. Not coming in for lunch, and after she'd prepared a perfectly good meal for him, too. She knew it was Jase's way of avoiding talking to her, an immature and childish act, in her opinion. Not that she was foolish enough to believe that talking to him was going to change anything. She might only be a *girl,* as he liked to refer to her, but she wasn't a fool.

She'd known when she'd persuaded him to let her stay on as the children's nanny that she had her work cut out for her, the least of which was dealing with a rebellious teen. What Tara needed was love, attention and a firm, guiding hand, all of which Annie was more than willing to provide for the teenager. But Tara also needed her father, and convincing Jase to be more attentive, to express his love more openly to his daughter, as well as his other two children…well, that placed Annie right smack in the middle between father and daughter, an uncomfortable place to be, she was fast coming to realize.

Feeling the frustration building, she crossed to the sink, her gaze going instinctively to the window and the barn beyond where Jase had worked all morning. At breakfast, he'd ignored Annie, wolfed down his meal and left the house before the children even came downstairs for the day, choosing to hide out in the barn rather than deal with them or her.

Which left Annie to wonder if anything she'd said the night before had penetrated that thick skull of his. His children needed him. All of them, but especially Tara.

She caught a movement inside the barn and stilled, watching as Jase stepped out into the sunlight, shirtless and stooped beneath a heavy sack of feed he carried on one shoulder. Perspiration gleamed on his arms and chest and dripped from his chin as he strained to heave the sack onto the bed of the truck. She watched the muscles on his arms and back ripple at the effort…and swallowed hard, forced to admit that she needed Jase, too. Not in the same way as his children, but she definitely needed him.

No, she corrected, feeling the swell of longing rise as she watched him disappear inside the barn again. She *wanted* him, which was a totally different emotion from need. Need was a requirement, something vital to one's well-being, whereas want was purely selfish, and, in this case, purely physical, a desire of the flesh. A desire that he seemed to share, but one he seemed intent to deny as diligently as he fought to maintain an emotional distance from his children.

Her eyes sharpened, then narrowed as he stepped from the barn burdened beneath another sack of feed. What if she managed to somehow break down his resistance? she wondered. What if she were able to coax some of that emotion from him? The kind of emotion she'd witnessed and experienced firsthand when he'd kissed her that afternoon in the barn? Would it free him up to express more of his emotions and feelings? The ones he withheld from his children?

Could she teach him how to play?

Convinced that her theory was at least worth a try, she hurried to the refrigerator and pulled out the plate of fried chicken she'd prepared for their lunch.

Jase tossed the last sack of feed onto the bed of his truck, then lifted his hat and dragged an arm across his forehead, wiping away the sweat that dripped into his eyes, before settling the hat wearily back over his head. With a baleful glance at the sun and the unseasonable heat it was casting, he headed for the driver's side of his truck and climbed inside.

He revved the engine, cranked up the air conditioner a notch, then let out the clutch. The truck hadn't rolled forward more than a couple of feet when he heard a shout from behind. He glanced over his shoulder and saw Annie jogging toward him, jostling a basket in one hand, while waving the other frantically over her head.

Though tempted to make her eat his dust, he stomped on the brake, then leaned across the seat to roll down the passenger window. "What do you want?" he asked impatiently as she came to a stop beside the door.

"Lunch," she replied breathlessly, then smiled and lifted the basket for him to see. Before he could tell her that he wasn't hungry, she was climbing into the cab and forcing him back onto his seat with the basket she shoved onto the console between them. "Where are you headed?" she asked, clipping her seat belt into place.

"To put out some feed in the back pasture." He leaned across her and pushed open the door. "I'm sure you've got better things to do than ride along."

She smiled and pulled the door closed again. "No, actually, I don't." She dipped her head down to peer up at the sun as she rolled up the window. "It's a perfect day for a picnic, don't you think?"

"Picnic?" he repeated. "Again?"

"The one Saturday was such a flop that I thought you might need a little practice to get the hang of it."

"Look. I really don't have time for—"

"Cool," she said, distracting him by leaning to fiddle with the eight ball Clay had attached to the head of the stick shift. "Can I drive?" she asked, glancing up at him. "I haven't driven a standard transmission in years."

And if he had his way, Jase thought irritably, it would be another couple of years before she had the pleasure again. Scowling, he shoved her hand away and shifted into first with a grinding of gears. "No," he informed her with a little more force than necessary, then stomped on the accelerator.

The truck shot forward, throwing Annie back against her seat. She laughed gaily, kicked off her sandals and lifted her feet to prop them on the dash.

With her feet up in the air, Jase couldn't help noticing her toenails and the putrid shade of blue she insisted on polishing them. He waved a disgusted hand. "Why the hell do you paint your toenails that color?"

She wiggled her toes, admiring her polish. "It's called Wild Blue Yonder. Like it?"

"No." He shifted his gaze to glare at the road ahead. "Makes me sick to my stomach every time I look at it."

She stole a glance at him, her tongue tucked against the inside of her cheek. "Really? Then why do you keep looking?"

"Who could help but notice," he shot back angrily, "with you running around barefoot all the time."

She wiggled her toes, infuriating him further by drawing his gaze to her feet again, and the long stretch of bare, tanned legs. "But I like going barefoot. Don't you?"

"Wouldn't know," he replied, determined to ignore her. "Never done it."

She leaned to give his arm a playful punch. "Oh, come on. Surely you must have gone barefoot when you were a kid?"

He hunched his shoulder and drew his arm across his chest, avoiding her touch. "Can't remember that far back."

She settled back against the seat, seemingly unoffended. "That's too bad, because it's fun. And sensual," she added with a wicked grin and wiggled her toes again. "There's nothing quite like walking barefoot through grass when it's covered with early-morning dew. Or walking along a beach and feeling the wet sand ooze between your toes. You should try it sometime."

He braked to a fast stop and killed the engine. "I think I'll pass," he muttered dryly.

She sat up, dropping her feet to the floorboard, to peer through the windshield. "Are we there?"

"Yeah." He pushed open his door and hopped to the ground. The sound of the passenger door slamming echoed that of his. He glanced across the bed of the truck, frowning. "What are you doing?"

She lifted a hand to shade her eyes. "Looking for a spot for our picnic. Oh!" she cried, pointing. "Is that a creek over there by those trees?"

He followed the line of her finger. "If you want to call it that." He reached into the back of the truck and dragged a sack to the end of the tailgate. "More often than not, its nothing but a dry wash."

"But with all the rain we've had this winter, I'll bet there's water running in it now."

He lifted the bag of feed, straining as he hefted it to his shoulder. "Probably. Won't last long, though. In another couple of weeks it'll be dry as a bone."

With a huff of breath, she turned and planted a fist on her hip. "You are undoubtably the most negative person I've ever met in my life."

He crossed to a trough and dumped the bag inside. "I'm a realist," he replied and rammed a hand into his pocket, fishing out his pocket knife. "Easier to face reality head on, than try to avoid it by trying to turn everything into some kind of damn fairy tale."

Leading with her chin, she turned for the creek. "But not nearly as much fun," she replied airily, swinging the basket at her side.

He stared after her a moment, then dropped his gaze and stabbed the knife into the bag, ripping it open. "Damn fool *girl*," he muttered.

"I heard that!" she called over her shoulder.

He snapped up his head and was surprised to see that she'd almost reached the stand of trees that grew alongside the creek. Realizing that she hadn't bothered to put on her shoes, he shook his head as he watched her pick her way carefully through the tall weeds. "Better watch out for—" He winced when he heard her cry of alarm. "Stickers," he finished too late. He dumped the feed into the trough, tossed the empty bag into the back of the truck, then started after her. "You okay?" he called.

"No," she wailed. "I've got a sticker in my foot. Ouch!" she cried, then added miserably, "Make that both feet."

Standing with her toes pointed at the sky and her heels dug into the ground, she created a comical picture. As hard as he tried, Jase couldn't stop the smug smile that spread across his face.

"Don't you dare say 'I told you so,'" she warned as he drew near.

He lifted his hands in surrender. "Wouldn't dream of it, although I do feel obligated to point out that this is a prime example of one of the many dangers of going barefoot, which, I might add, I've been wise to avoid over the years."

"That's the same as saying 'I told you so,'" she grumbled, then squealed when he stooped and hooked an arm behind her knees. "What are you doing!" she cried as he swung her up against his chest.

"Carrying you."

"But our lunch," she began, stretching a hand toward the basket. She shrieked, flinging her arms around his neck, when he leaned forward, dipping her over it.

"Grab a hold," he ordered.

Pursing her lips, she shot him a frown, then snatched the basket's handle, clinging to it as well as his neck when he straightened.

She brightened when he headed for the creek and not back to his truck. "Does this mean we're going to have our picnic now?"

He plopped her down on a large rock beside the slow-moving creek and squatted down, catching her ankle and drawing her foot up to study it. "Soon as I dig these stickers out."

"Dig?" she repeated, her smile melting. "With what?"

He propped her foot on his knee while he worked his knife from his pocket. "This."

Her eyes widened when he flipped the knife open and the sun's rays struck a lethal-looking blade. Swallowing hard, she inched her foot back toward her hip. "But won't that hurt?"

"Depends on your tolerance for pain."

"It's low," she was quick to inform him, then caught her lip between her teeth and added nervously, "Really low."

He eased her foot back over his knee. "If you've got a weak stomach, you might want to look the other way."

"No," she replied, not trusting him. "I'll watch."

He lifted a shoulder and curled his fingers around her foot, angling it for better access. "Your call."

In spite of her intention to watch the proceedings, Annie squeezed her eyes shut, every muscle in her body tensing in dread as she waited for the painful dig of the knife.

"You might want to breathe," he suggested.

She flipped open her eyes to find him watching her, his gray eyes filled with amusement. "Oh," she murmured in embarrassment, then leaned to peer more closely at him, noticing the changes a smile made to his face. "You really should smile more often," she said without thinking.

He snorted a laugh and shifted his gaze to her foot. "Why?"

"Because...well, just because," she replied, flustered.

"Now *there's* a reason," he replied dryly as he probed the blade against the tender skin of her arch.

"Ouch!" she cried, jerking her foot from his hand.

"Sissy," he teased and held up the sticker for her inspection.

She rubbed her sore foot. "Easy for you to say."

He chuckled and reached to catch her other ankle. "Want me to kiss it and make it better?"

"And chance an infection?"

"Funny," he said and lifted the knife again.

"Yeah," she said, tensing for the probe of the blade. "About as funny as you." Determined not to make a sound, she was surprised when he held up the second sticker. "Hey!" she cried. "I didn't feel a thing that time."

"I could try again," he offered.

"No," she replied, laughing, pleased to discover that he had a sense of humor. "I think I'll quit while I'm ahead. Otherwise, you might decide to amputate."

Still holding her foot, he glanced up, his forehead creasing as he peered at her, the teasing fading from his eyes. "Do you really think I would purposely hurt you?"

She snorted a laugh and relaxed back against the rock, supporting herself with her elbows. "I think you'd do most anything to get me out of your house."

He frowned and glanced down at her foot, stroking his thumb thoughtfully along her arch. "You're young," he said, as if he felt he needed to justify his less-than-friendly treatment of her.

She rolled her eyes. "Oh, give it up, would you? It isn't my age that bothers you."

"No. But it's reason enough."

"For you, maybe."

"And it should be for you, as well."

"Look," she said patiently. "I'm an adult. I know how to take care of myself. And I don't need you, or anybody else trying to do the job for me. So why don't we just agree to disagree on the subject of my maturity level and go on from here?"

Jase stroked his thumb along her arch, from toe to heel and back again, his gaze narrowed thoughtfully on hers, wondering if she realized how far over her head she was when it came to dealing with a man as calloused as him. Thinking a lesson might be in order, he said, "All right. Sounds fair enough to me."

She sank back on her elbows. "By the way," she said and offered him a grudging smile. "Thanks for the massage. You've got good hands."

Frowning, he glanced down at her foot, unaware that he still held it, then looked back up at her, shaking his head as a slow smile chipped at one corner of his mouth. "You're welcome, though I'd have thought it would tickle to have your foot rubbed."

"Nope, but then I'm not ticklish. Are you?"

"A man never reveals his weaknesses."

"Which means you *are* ticklish."

"I didn't say that."

"You didn't have to." She sat up abruptly. "Take off your boots."

Startled, he barked a laugh. "Why?"

"Just take off your boots."

"I beg your pardon, ma'am," he said, feigning indignance, "but I'm not that kind of man."

She dropped back down to her elbows and smiled smugly. "You're ticklish, all right."

"It isn't wise to question a man's honesty when he's holding your foot."

"Why?"

He drew her toes to his mouth. "Because he might be tempted to take a bite."

Tensing, she gave her foot a tug, trying to free it, but he merely tightened his grip.

"You wouldn't dare," she warned, narrowing an eye at him.

"Wouldn't I?" His gaze on hers, he opened his mouth. But instead of biting her toe, he blew a long breath of moist, warm air along the arch of her foot. He bit back a smile when her leg jerked reflexively. "I thought you said you weren't ticklish?"

"I'm not."

"Then why'd you jump?"

"It was instinctive," she replied defensively. "An involuntary reaction to stimuli."

He smoothed his hand over her heel and up her calf, raising gooseflesh on her skin. "Maybe you better explain that in layman's terms," he suggested and drew her leg over his thigh as he shifted to sit on the rock beside her.

She stared up at him as he shaped his fingers around her calf and began to knead the muscle there. "Okay," she said, sounding a little breathless. "You're turning me on."

Five

Jase arched a brow, surprised by her bluntness. "I am?"

"Yeah," she said, her gaze shifting to his mouth as he leaned closer.

"And what do you think we should we do about that?"

She slicked her lips. "I don't know. What do you want to do?"

He puckered his mouth thoughtfully as if considering. "I suppose I could kiss you."

"Yeah," she said, releasing her breath on a sigh. "I guess you could."

"But that might be inviting trouble."

"For who?"

"Me. You," he added, his voice growing husky.

She slicked her lips again. "I'm willing to chance , if you are."

"I don't know," he murmured. "I—"

But before he could voice his doubts, she lifted her ead and pressed her mouth to his.

Though he fully intended to teach her a lesson, ommon sense told Jase to keep things light, to end ings before they went too far. But he quickly dis- overed he couldn't. Really didn't want to even try. heir previous kiss had haunted his dreams at night nd distracted him from his work during the day. e'd told himself that he'd only imagined the sweet- ess of her lips, that the years of deprivation had em- ellished his memories of her sensual response.

Anxious to prove his assumptions correct, he robed his tongue against the crease of her lips, ained entry, then groaned as her flavor poured rough him, hot and enticing, sweet and cloying, just s he'd remembered...and feared. Her tongue swept ver his, and he shoved aside all reason, giving in to e stronger need to explore.

Just one touch, he promised himself and slipped a and between them. He cupped a breast, molding his alm around its shape, and she bowed her spine, arch- g instinctively toward the pressure of his hand.

With a groan, he rolled to his back, pulled her over im, and took the kiss deeper. The rock's jagged sur- ce dug into his back, but he welcomed the pain for e greater reward of her weight, the softness of her ody stretched along the length of his.

"You're trouble," he murmured, withdrawing far ough to nip at her lower lip. "I knew you'd be ouble."

"Yeah," she said, sighing, then shifted to a more comfortable position on his chest and grinned. "Bu ain't it fun?"

He chuckled, then grunted, the breath whooshing out of him as she planted her hands against his ches and pushed to her feet. She grabbed his boot and pulled. "Hey!" he cried, propping himself up on hi elbows. "What do you think you're doing?"

The boot gave way and she stumbled back a step then grinned and tossed it to the ground before reach ing for the other. "Returning the favor."

He curled his toes inside the remaining boot thwarting her efforts to remove it. "What favor?"

"The massage."

He leaned to swat at her hands. "I don't want you massaging my feet."

She arched a brow, biting back a smile. "Why Are you ticklish?"

He scowled when, in spite of his efforts to keep i on, his boot slipped over his heel. "No, I'm not tick lish."

"Good, because you're getting a massage." Sh dropped the boot and picked up his foot. Slipping he hands inside the leg of his jeans, she smoothed he palms up his calf until her fingertips reached the elas ticized band of his sock. A shiver chased up his spin and she smiled knowingly as she slowly stripped th sock down his leg and off the end of his toes.

She sank down to the ground at the base of th rock and drew his foot onto her lap. "There's an ar to giving a good foot massage, you know," she saic sounding a little too pleased with herself.

Heat crawled up his neck as she drew her hand

from ankle to toe, her fingers drifting over the dark hair that dusted his instep, and between the joints of each toe. The contrast between his big, ugly foot and the graceful, slender fingers that cradled it was humbling, but no more so than having Annie sitting at his feet like a some kind of Grecian handmaiden. "No," he said, trying his best to ignore the sensual scrape of her nails along the bottom of his foot. "I didn't know."

"There is. I've studied a little about reflexology." She curled her fingers and dug her knuckles deeply into his arch, making every muscle in his body go limp as a wet rag. "There are pressure points on your foot that are tied to other parts of your body. For example," she said positioning her fingertips on the ball of his foot just below his little toe. "This area is connected to your shoulder. When I press here," she said, placing added stress on the spot, "you should be able to feel it in your shoulder. Do you?"

Jase felt something all right, but it sure as hell wasn't in his shoulder. "Yeah," he said, thinking it best not to tell her exactly *where* he felt the response.

She smiled, seeming satisfied, and resumed the massage. "The human body is a complex system of nerve and muscle, with everything connecting and responding to different stimuli."

Stimuli. There was that word again, he thought, frowning at her use of it. He wondered if she was purposely trying to turn him on, as she'd claimed he had her with his foot massage. He shifted his gaze to hers, expecting to find a coyness in her expression, or at the very least, a sly smugness. But he found only innocence in the depths of the green eyes that met his.

She smiled and curled her fingers around his foot, shaking it gently. "Relax," she scolded gently. "If you don't, you won't be able to enjoy the massage."

"I'm relaxed," he argued, though every muscle in his body felt as if it was caught in a vise and twisted tight.

She laughed and reached to pull off his other sock. "Yeah, and I can sing like Madonna." She stood and tossed his sock down to join his boots, then reached for his hand. "Come on," she said and gave him a tug, pulling him to his feet.

"Where are we going?" he asked as he high-stepped behind her, wincing as stones dug into his tender feet.

"Wading."

He stopped abruptly, drawing her up short, as well. "Uh-uh."

She gave his hand a tug, laughing. "Uh-huh."

"Uh-uh," he repeated more adamantly and tore his hand from her grasp.

Frowning, she propped her hands on her hips. "Why not?"

He jerked his chin toward the water. "No telling what's lying on the bottom of that creek."

"Chicken," she chided and turned for the bank.

"If you cut your foot or stub a toe," he called after her, "don't come crying to me."

"I won't." She waded out a few feet and shivered deliciously as the cool water struck her warm skin and lapped around her knees. She turned, smiling, and gestured for him to join her. "Come on in. The water feels wonderful."

He folded his arms stubbornly across his chest. "No thanks. I think I'll pass."

She lifted a shoulder and waded deeper, until the water reached the hem of her shorts. Laughing, she opened her arms wide, dropped her head back and spun in a slow circle.

"Watch out for rocks," he warned.

She drew her hair up on top of her head and strode farther out. "Worrywart," she scolded, laughing. Water rushed around her shoulders and filled her shirt, making it balloon out from her body.

Jase strained to keep an eye on her. "Annie! Get back over here before you drown."

She turned and grinned mischievously. "If you want me, you'll have to come and get me."

Jase took a step toward the water, then stopped. "Dammit! Get over here."

Annie's smile slowly gave way to incredulity as she saw the real fear in his eyes. "You can't swim, can you?"

"Who said anything about swimming?" he snapped. "I just want you out of that water before you hurt yourself."

Realizing that his concern for her was sincere, Annie started back for the bank. "I'm sorry," she said contritely. "I didn't intend to frighten—" Her eyes flipped wide as her foot slipped on a moss-covered rock and shot out from under her. She shrieked, dropping her hands from her hair in an effort to catch herself, but failed.

Jase was hip deep in the creek before her head

slipped completely beneath the water. His heart in his throat, he charged forward, fighting his way against the slow-moving current. When he reached the spot where he'd seen her go under, he dived his hands down into the water and fished frantically around. Not finding her, he glanced around and swore ripely when he saw her head bob to the surface a good ten feet downstream. She stood and swept her wet hair back from her face, sputtering water and laughing.

"You did that on purpose," he accused.

"I didn't," she said, still laughing.

"You damn sure did."

Annie sobered at the thunderous look on his face and started carefully making her way back toward him. "No. I swear. My foot slipped. Really."

"I told you not to go into the water, that you might get hurt."

She stopped, blinking water from her eyes as she stared up at him, stunned by the intensity of his anger. "But I'm not hurt. I just lost my footing."

"Well, you might have been hurt."

She laid a hand on his arm. "But I'm not," she insisted gently, hoping to reassure him.

With a growl, he shook free of her touch, started to turn away, then whirled back around and snatched her up into his arms. His mouth came down hard on hers, forcing her head back and stealing her breath. She tasted the fear on his lips, the anger, the desperate dig of his fingers into her back. He cared for her, she realized with a suddenness that had her heart slamming against her ribs. As hard as he tried to pretend otherwise, he truly cared what happened to her. Awe-

by the realization, she slowly wrapped her arms around his neck and drew his face closer to hers.

She was only slightly aware of his movements as he dipped to catch her beneath the knees. But as he lifted her to his chest and started for the bank, she smiled against his lips. "My hero," she murmured.

He jerked his head back and frowned down at her. "Don't kid yourself," he muttered and set her down on her feet on the bank.

Smiling, she caught her hair up in her hands and sank down on the soft grass at the edge of the bank as she twisted her wet hair up into a knot on her head. "And all this time I thought you were a mean old grizzly, when you're nothing but a big teddy bear."

He dropped down beside her and picked up a stick. "You must've taken in more water than I realized," he grumbled, dragging the stick through the wet sand and avoiding her gaze. "Made your brain soggy."

She bumped a shoulder against his, her smile widening at the blush that stained his cheeks. "Cut the macho act, wise guy. You might have fooled me in the past, but not any longer."

"Don't."

She laughed and caught the hem of her shirt between her hands, wringing the excess water from it. "Don't what?"

He dropped his gaze to the front of her shirt, then slowly brought it back to her face. Her smile slowly faded at the heat she saw in his eyes.

"Don't make the mistake of thinking I'm a nice guy," he warned. "I'm not."

Nerves danced to life beneath her skin as she

watched his face draw nearer. "I've never really cared for overly nice men," she said breathlessly.

"Don't say I didn't warn you," he said just before he crushed his mouth over hers. He forced her back against the soft grass and followed her down, pressing his bare chest against her damp one. Rolling, he pulled her over him.

He stiffened, groaning, when her pelvis bumped against his arousal. At the contact, he withdrew slightly and their gazes met with an awareness that had heat arcing between them. Suddenly the air seemed too thick to breathe.

Jase reached for her and captured her face between his palms, stunned by the intensity of the desire that swelled within him. Searching her gaze, he smoothed his thumbs beneath her lower lashes and watched the passion rise on her face, the heat spread to glaze her eyes. Slowly he lifted his head and claimed her mouth with his again.

He inhaled deeply as he swept his lips over hers as he drank greedily of her essence. The golden warmth of sunshine, the sweet scent of the grass crushed beneath him and tangled in her damp hair. He heard her soft whimper, felt the claw of her fingers against his bare flesh, and his need for her sharpened turned impatient. He rolled again, placing her on her back against the ground and moved to straddle her, his chest heaving with each drawn breath as he gazed down at her. "I want to touch you," he whispered and caught the hem of her wet shirt, shoving it up and baring her stomach. "And taste you," he said and dipped his head to press his mouth over the flat plane of her abdomen.

"Yes," she gasped, filling her hands with his hair. "Oh my, yes," she moaned as he dragged his lips up her rib cage. She sucked in a breath, arching, when he closed his mouth over her breast.

He swept his tongue across the budded nipple and groaned at the rich textures he found there, the added flavors.

Knowing he had to have her, he cupped a hand around her breast and slowly pulled it from his mouth. "I want to make love with you," he said, looking up at her.

Without a word, without a second's hesitation, she opened her arms in silent invitation.

He sank against her chest and dropped his mouth over hers, stabbing his tongue between her lips as he reached for the waist of her shorts. "Are you protected?" he asked, his voice as rusty as he feared was his technique.

When she tensed, he froze, then slowly drew back to look at her.

"Well...no," she said, her eyes wide as she stared at him. "Don't you have something?"

Groaning, Jase dropped his forehead against hers. "Not with me."

"Jase?"

He felt her fingers drawing small nervous circles on his back. "What?"

"I wrapped the fried chicken in plastic wrap. Maybe we could—"

In spite of his frustration, his disappointment, he found himself chuckling. Damn, but she was priceless. He rolled to his back and gathered her against his side. "I don't think plastic wrap would make a very effective form of birth control."

She pushed her mouth out into a pout. "Darn. And just when things were really heating up."

Laughing, he hugged her to his side. "It'll keep."

She lifted her head from his chest to peer up at him, her eyes filled with hope. "Later, then?"

"Yeah," he promised as he tucked her head beneath his chin. "Later."

Though it was pushing midnight, Jase stood at his bedroom window, a hand braced high on the molding. He stared blindly out at the night, waiting... wondering. Would Annie come to him? Though his body thrummed with need, and had since leaving her, he hoped she wouldn't. He feared, if she did, he wouldn't be able to resist her.

Later, he remembered telling her, and curled his hand into a fist against the wood, regretting the promise he'd made. What had come over him? he asked himself. He hadn't intended to get physically involved with her. Knew it would be a big mistake.

Annie, he reflected miserably. *She* was what had come over him. With that firm little body of hers. Those laughing green eyes. That sassy mouth. She'd teased him into remembering the pleasures a man could share with a woman, bewitched him into forgetting the hurt that would be inevitable if he allowed anyone to get too close. For the length of an afternoon, he'd let go of the memories, the fears, and had been ready to take advantage of what she freely offered.

The lack of a condom was all that had saved him

He heard the door open softly behind him and tensed, knowing it was Annie who had entered his room. Her scent reached him first, that subtle, feminine fragrance that teased his senses every time she was near. He felt the warmth of her hand on the small of his back, her touch light and reassuring on his bare skin. Then she was standing at his side, looking up at him, and he could feel the heat of her gaze on his cheek.

"Jase?"

He closed his eyes at the huskiness in her voice, praying for the strength to send her back to her room. But when he opened his eyes and looked down at her, saw the heat, the expectancy in her wide green eyes, he knew the prayer was wasted. There was no way in hell he could send her away. Not now.

Knowing this, he dropped his arm from the window. He crossed to the bedside table, opened the drawer and pulled out a gold packet. He nudged the drawer closed with a knuckle and stood there a moment, palming the gold packet, then angled his head to peer at her across the shadowed room. "You sure you want to go through with this?"

She hugged her arms around her middle as if suddenly chilled. "Do you?"

He stared at her a moment, then slowly nodded his head. "Yeah, though I have a feeling we're both going to regret it."

She took a hesitant step toward him. "Why? We're both consenting adults. We know what we're doing."

He snorted a rueful laugh and sank down on the side of the bed. "Do we?" Leaning forward, he braced his forearms on his thighs and shook his head, staring at the condom he held. "I'm not so sure."

Wondering at the cause for his hesitancy, Annie crossed to the bed and sat down beside him. "Are you not ready for another physical relationship? I mean...well...if you feel guilty because of your wife—"

He shook his head. "No. It isn't that." He inhaled deeply, then released the breath with a weary sigh and angled his head to look over at her. "But you hit the nail on the head when you said physical. That's all I'm looking for in a relationship. Just the physical. If you understand that, then we shouldn't have any problems."

Annie's heart broke a little as the moon chased the shadows from his face, revealing the bleakness of his expression. Though she hadn't expected anything more than a no-strings-attached relationship with him, it saddened her to realize that he thought he could exclude feeling and emotion from their affair, as well. To her, lovemaking was a form of expression, an act that demanded, in and of itself, all the emotions that he stubbornly chose to deny. It stripped people down to their most elemental level, leaving them vulnerable and exposed to exquisite joy...or utter despair.

But perhaps he did know that, she realized slowly. Perhaps that's why he'd offered the warning when he'd placed the choice of making love with him in her hands. Maybe he was trying to spare her any hurt.

But what he didn't know was that she'd made her decision long before coming to his room. Maybe as early as that first morning when he'd stepped into the kitchen after his return home and found a new nanny there. And she'd done so fully aware of the pitfalls that might await her, willing to accept the dangers in exchange for any rewards that might be gained.

She smiled softly and laid her hand against his cheek. "No need to worry," she assured him, stroking a thumb along the high ridge of his cheekbone. "I understand."

He stared at her a moment as if he wasn't sure he'd heard her correctly, then reached up to cover her hand with his. She felt the tremble in his fingers as he drew her palm to his lips and pressed a kiss to its center. Tears filled her throat at the tenderness in the gesture, the kindness in it. Though he wanted to deny his emotions, they were there, she knew, just waiting to be set free.

She rose, her back to him, and caught the belt of her robe, tugged it loose, then slipped the garment from her shoulders and let it fall to pool around her feet. Gathering her nightgown in her hands, she turned to face him and slowly pulled it up and over her head, shaking out her hair as she dropped it behind her. As he moved his gaze down her body, she had to will her knees not to tremble at the hunger she saw reflected in his eyes. But when he returned his gaze to hers and reached to take her hand in his, drawing her to him, she stepped boldly and willingly between his spread knees.

He stared at her for a long moment, then dropped his gaze to their joined hands, watching his thumb's movement as he stroked it slowly across her knuckles. "It's been a long time," he said quietly. "This might be over before we even get started good."

"We've got all night."

Jase glanced up at her in surprise, then, seeing the amusement in her eyes, smiled ruefully. "Yeah, I guess we do at that." He let his gaze slide down to her mouth and his sex swelled uncomfortably within his jeans as he stared at her lips, remembering the feel of them heated and moving beneath his. More than his next breath, he wanted to tug her down on the bed and cover her mouth with his, thrust himself deep inside her with a fierceness and an urgency that equaled that of the need swelling inside him.

Realizing how wrong that would be, how selfish, he tore his gaze from her mouth, and glanced away, shaking his head. "This is awkward as hell," he muttered.

"Why?"

"I don't know," he said irritably. "It just is."

"Perhaps because it seems so calculated?" she suggested softly. "So premeditated?"

He scowled. "Yeah. Maybe." He pushed to his feet, tossing the gold packet to the bed, and brushed past her to pace across the room. He stopped in front of the window and stuffed his hands into the pockets of his jeans as he frowned out at the darkness.

He heard the whisper of her feet against the carpet as she crossed to him, and tensed as her arms wound around his waist from behind. He felt the moist softness of her lips against his spine as she pressed a kiss there, and closed his eyes, fighting the urge to turn and drag her into his arms.

"Look at me, Jase," she whispered. When he didn't respond, she added, "Please?"

Unable to ignore the entreaty in her voice, he inhaled deeply and turned within the circle of her arms.

intending to send her back to her room before it was too late.

Before he could speak, she pressed a finger against his lips as if sensing his intent. "Empty your mind of everything. Pretend that we're a just a man and woman who are attracted to each other and meeting for the first time."

Shaking his head sadly, he lifted his hands and combed his fingers through her hair above her ears, then held his palms against her cheek. "If only it were that simple."

"Why can't it be?"

"Because it's been a long time," he said, his frustration returning right along with his need for her. "Dammit! I could hurt you."

She took a step closer, a tender smile trembling at her lips as she pressed her body against his. "You won't hurt me. You couldn't."

"You don't know what I'm capa—"

Before he could say more, she rose to the balls of her feet and covered his mouth with hers, smothering his argument. At the feel of her lips on his, he surrendered to the heat and desire he tasted there and, with a groan, pulled her hard against him. Capturing her face between his hands, he took possession of the kiss, drinking deeply, thirstily, greedily. Each new taste he encountered, each new texture he discovered, pushed the level of his need higher, making him forget his resolve to send her away, and he backed her toward the bed.

"Yes," she murmured as he hauled her hips roughly against his groin, bowing her back over the bed. He dragged his lips to her throat and forced her down, then followed, stretching his body out over hers.

"Oh, yes, there," she whispered when he found her breast with his mouth and closed his lips over its rosy center. He drew her deeply into his mouth, sweeping his tongue over her turgid nipple and she arched up hard against him.

"I want to touch you," she said as she fumbled feverishly for the snap of his jeans. Finding it and quickly releasing it, she dragged the zipper down.

He groaned when her knuckles chafed against his sex. "Slow," he ordered and rolled to his back, drawing her on top of him. "I want this to last."

Her face flushed, she pushed against his chest until she was sitting up. "It will," she promised and quickly divested him of his jeans. Moving to straddle him, she smiled coyly as she dragged a finger from the hollow of his throat down to his navel. "Remember? We've got all night."

He caught her finger before she could carry it farther. "Not if you keep this up."

She laughed and leaned to drop a kiss on his mouth. "Always thinking negatively," she teased.

Seduced by her smile, by the passion he was only just discovering in her, he drew her finger to his mouth. "No. I just know my limits." Keeping his gaze on hers, he drew her finger into his mouth and suckled, watching her eyes widen, hearing her breath catch in her throat.

He slowly drew her finger from between his lips and she released the breath on a ragged sigh. "Don't be so sure," she warned and rose to her knees. Finding the gold packet, she opened it and fitted the condom over the sensitive tip of his sex. He moaned as she smoothed it down his length with a frustrating and erotic slowness. Sliding her gaze to his, she shifted back over him, took him in her hand and, with a seductive smile, slowly guided him to her.

Jase flinched, gritting his teeth, as the tip of his sex met her slick opening, then groaned as she lowered herself and took him in. With his heart pounding wildly against his chest and heat pumping through his veins with the speed of a grass fire raging out of control, he reached for her, drawing her face down to his. "I want you," he murmured against her lips. "All of you," he warned, then set his jaw and thrust deeply.

He swallowed her startled cry of pleasure and held her hips against his as the velvet walls of her feminine canal clamped tightly around him. He clenched his teeth, struggling for control, stunned by the flood of emotion that swept through him. She was so open, so honest, he realized as he stared at her. With her feelings, her thoughts, her actions. She hid nothing. Held back nothing. She took with the same measure of enthusiasm with which she so unselfishly gave.

Her pleasure was obvious in the softness of her expression, in the satisfied purr that slipped past her parted lips, in the heat that flushed her cheeks and glazed her eyes. But he was aware, too, of her desire to please him in the fingers that stroked seductively down his chest, saw it in the soft, knowing smile that curved the corners of her mouth as she boldly met his gaze.

And in giving, in her desire to please him, she only made him want to please her more. Slowly he began to move within her, each stroke a testament of his awareness of her, of his determination to please her before he sought pleasure for himself.

Her breath quickened as she rode him, matching each of his thrusts with the rise and fall of hips that seemed to match perfectly with the fit of his, the rhythm that he set. He watched her eyes widen, her lips part on a strangled gasp for air, felt the painful dig of her fingers against his flesh as a second climax pulled at her.

"Again," he growled and thrust hard one last time against her, shooting her high and over the edge. She arched, her fingers opening over his chest, then clenching, and she dropped her head back with a low, guttural moan as he found his own release within her throbbing center.

Stunned by the intensity of her climax and weakened by the debilitating power of his own, he dragged her down to his chest and wrapped his arms around her, holding her against him. "Annie," he murmured and buried his face in her hair, inhaling her sweetness. "Oh, Annie," he said on a sigh as she snuggled closer, her purr of contentment vibrating against his chest.

With his heart pounding against hers and his sex growing soft inside her, he closed his eyes, sure that he'd never experienced anything like this in his life…and wondering if he'd survive it.

"Again," she whispered.

He flipped his eyes wide, then tucked his chin back to peer at her. "You've got to be kidding."

With a devilish smile, she rocked her hips slowly against his. "Dead serious."

Groaning, he dropped his head back to the pillow and closed his eyes. ''No way.''

''Way,'' she insisted and stretched to tease his lower lip with her teeth.

His response was immediate...and surprising. Feeling himself growing hard again, he hooked an arm around her waist and flipped her on to her back beneath him. ''Witch,'' he growled. He nipped at the bow of her lip, then dipped his head lower to catch a nipple lightly between his teeth.

She arched, knotting her fingers in his hair. ''Yeah, I know,'' she said, sounding pleased with herself, then dragged his face back to hers.

Six

Missing the warmth of the body that had curled against his throughout the night, Jase rolled to his side and flung out an arm, intending to draw Annie back to his side. When his hand met only cool sheets, he blinked open his eyes and swallowed back the moan of disappointment at discovering he was alone in his bed.

Sighing, he rolled to his back and stared at the ceiling, remembering the wild night of lovemaking, the passion he'd discovered in Annie, shared with her...but tensed when he heard pans clattering in the kitchen. He snapped his head around to peer at the alarm clock on the bedside table, then bolted to his feet, weaving drunkenly as he stared at the clock in dismay.

"Damn," he swore as he staggered to the bathroom. He couldn't remember the last time he'd slept this late.

Fifteen minutes later, he stepped into the kitchen, freshly showered and shaved.

Annie glanced up from the stove. "Good morning," she said, warming him with a secret smile. "Did you sleep well?"

Jase roamed his gaze down her body, noting each feminine curve and swell beneath her robe and remembering the feel of each beneath his hands. "Like a rock," he said and grinned as he returned his gaze to hers. "And you?"

"Never better."

"I slept good, too, Daddy."

Jase paled at the sound of his youngest daughter's voice and turned to find all three of his children sitting at the breakfast table, staring at him. Sure that they could see the guilt that stained his face, knew how he'd spent the previous night, he stammered, "Uh... that's good, dumplin'."

"Gee, Dad," Clay said, peering at his father curiously. "You *never* sleep this late. Are you sick or something?"

"No. That is...I—" Jase made the mistake of glancing at Annie, who quickly turned back to the stove, smothering a smile. Scowling, he crossed to the counter and grabbed his hat. "I put in a hard day's work yesterday," he growled as he rammed the hat over his head and reached for the doorknob. "Something you kids ought to try for a change," he added and slammed the door behind him.

"Yeah," Tara muttered resentfully, "like we never do anything around here."

"You *don't* do anything," Clay said, quick to come to his father's defense.

"And you do?" Tara shot back.

"That's enough," Annie warned from the stove.

Tara shoved back her chair. "Dude, I'm outta here," she muttered and stomped from the room.

With a sigh, Annie dropped the spatula and tugged off her apron. "Rachel, you and Clay finish your breakfast and get ready for school."

"Where are you going?" Clay asked as she headed for the door.

"To talk to Tara."

"What about?" Rachel asked.

"Eat your breakfast," Annie ordered, then hurried for the stairs. When she reached Tara's room, she found the teenager sitting before her vanity, smearing a dark mahogany lipstick over her lips.

"Planning on wearing that to school?" Annie asked as she moved to stand behind Tara and peer at the girl's reflection.

Tara met her gaze in the mirror. "What's it to you?" she asked spitefully.

Annie lifted a shoulder. "Just wondered." She plucked a tissue from a box and held it out to the girl. "Though something tells me your father wouldn't approve."

Tara's scowl deepened, but she snatched the tissue from Annie's hand and dragged it across her lips, wiping away the lipstick. "Like he approves of anything I do," she said bitterly.

Her heart going out to the girl, Annie picked up a brush from the vanity. "He cares for you," she said

softly as she stroked the brush through Tara's long
hair.

"Hey!" Tara cried, ducking from beneath Annie's
hand. "What do you think you're doing?"

Annie drew the brush back and lifted a shoulder.
"I was just thinking that you're hair would look nice
styled away from your face. Like this," she explained
and demonstrated by gathering a length of her own
hair and twisting it in a rope toward her crown.

Tara rolled her eyes. "Yeah, like my hair would
stay that way."

"Mine wouldn't either without clips. You can bor-
row some, if you like," Annie offered, then grabbed
Tara's hand and gave it a tug. "But we'd better hurry,
or you'll miss the bus."

Tara dug in her heels. "What kind of clips?"

"Rhinestones, sunflowers." Annie lifted a shoulder. "You name it, I've got it."

Though the teenager tried to maintain her sullen
look, Annie saw the gleam of interest that sparked in
her eyes.

"Okay," Tara said grudgingly and allowed Annie
to lead her from her room. "So long as I get to pick."

Annie waited until the children had left for school,
then dressed and went in search of Jase. She found
him out beside the barn, working on a piece of equip-
ment.

"Hey," she said softly, curling her fingers around
his neck as she bent over his stooped frame. "What
are you doing?"

He jumped, swearing, then tossed the wrench to the
ground and rose. Scowling, he tugged a rag from his

back pocket and wiped his hands, avoiding her gaze. "Working."

She bit back a smile. "I can see that. But that doesn't tell me what you're doing."

He waved a hand at the piece of machinery he'd been tinkering with. "I'm tightening the belts on the baler."

"Belts?" she repeated curiously and stooped to peer inside the machine.

His scowl deepening, he bumped his shoulder against hers, nudging her out of his way. "I don't have time to give a lesson in mechanics," he said, hunkering down in front of the machine again. "I've got work to do."

Arching a brow at his resentful tone, Annie took a step back. "I didn't expect one."

He strained to tighten the nut on the bolt. "Good," he ground out. "Because you aren't getting one."

"And I didn't expect to have my head bitten off, either."

He braced a hand against the baler and angled his chest, straining to reach deep inside the machine to test the belt's tension. "That's too damn bad."

Feeling the anger boil up inside her, Annie caught the collar of his shirt and gave him a jerk, making him lose his balance and sit down hard on the ground.

He was on his feet with his face shoved up to hers before she had a chance to regret the petty action.

"Listen to me, little *girl*," he growled and took a threatening step, forcing her back. "I've got work to do and I don't have time to play any of your silly little games."

Annie flattened her hands against his chest, stopping his forward movement. "Who are you really mad at? Me? Or yourself?"

His eyes narrowed and a nerve ticked at his temple. "Me," he growled and turned away, dragging the rag from his pocket again.

Annie dropped her hands and released a long, shaky breath. "Well, at least you aren't so blind that you can't see who is at fault here."

"I'm not blind to anything," he snapped. "Least of all your womanly wiles."

She arched a brow. "So now I'm a woman? A second ago, you were calling me a girl again."

He whipped his head around to glare at her, but Annie merely offered him a guileless smile in return.

With a huff, he looked away, bracing his hands low on his hips. After a moment, he dropped his chin to his chest, inhaled deeply, then puffed his cheeks as he slowly released the breath. "I'm sorry."

"I'm not."

He shot her a look over his shoulder. "Last time you said those words, I had just apologized for kissing you."

"Want to again?"

He stared at her a moment, then snorted a laugh. Tossing down the rag, he crossed to her. "Come here," he said, and tugged her against his chest. He wrapped his arms around her and buried his nose in her hair, slowly rocking her back and forth. "I was embarrassed," he admitted reluctantly.

"Because of the children?"

Frowning, he drew back and caught a lock of her hair to tuck behind her ear. "Yeah, the kids," he said, finally meeting her gaze.

"But they didn't know why you'd slept late."

"*I* did."

She laughed and wrapped her arms around his waist, rubbing her thumbs along his spine above his belt. "You shouldn't feel guilty," she scolded gently. "I doubt the children would suffer any emotional trauma if they were to discover their father was physically attracted to a woman. Not that I'm suggesting that we should openly flaunt our affair," she was quick to add. "But it might be healthy for them to see you interact with a woman."

He moaned and dropped his forehead to rest against hers. "Easy for you to say. They aren't your kids."

Annie felt a pang of regret at the reminder. "No," she said slowly, realizing how attached she'd become to Jase's children and how much she wished they were hers. "But I don't think I'd feel any differently if they were."

He shook his head and dropped his arms from around her. "I knew this was a mistake," he said, turning away.

Her heart froze in her chest. "What's a mistake?"

"This!" he cried and whirled to face her. "You and me. You're my kids' nanny, for God's sake! A good ten years or more younger than me. Hell!" he said, throwing up his hands. "There are probabl laws against a man having sex with his employee."

"Yes, and they were designed to protect wome whose employers tried to force them into grantin sexual favors. But you didn't force me," she re minded him. "I entered into this relationship with yo willingly and with my eyes wide-open, so you ce tainly can't blame yourself for seducing me."

"I don't," he shot back. "But that sure as hell doesn't mean I have to be fool enough to make the mistake of sleeping with you again."

Annie stumbled back a step, stunned by his anger, but even more so by his announcement that he intended to end their affair. She stared at him, praying that he would take it all back, that he'd realize he was overreacting. She searched for a crack in his stony expression, anything that would indicate regret for the angrily spouted threat...but found nothing but cold determination.

Left with nothing but her pride to sustain her, she turned for the house. "Fine," she said, telling herself the sound she heard wasn't her heart breaking. "And I'll certainly do my part to stay out of your way."

From the kitchen window, Annie watched the children emerge from the school bus. She quickly dabbed the dish towel at her eyes, not wanting them to know she'd been crying. She'd allowed herself a good, long pity party over the end of her relationship with Jase, but it was time now to set aside her sadness and put on a happy face. The children were home, and it was her job to take care of them, to add some sunshine to their lives. God knew they had enough to deal with without having to contend with a blubbering-feeling-sorry-for-herself nanny.

Glancing out the window again, she saw the sullen look on Tara's face as Clay passed his backpack to her, then watched Clay trudge toward the barn and his waiting chores. As she watched, something inside her snapped. She raced to the back door and flung it open. "Clay!" she shouted, waving a hand over her head.

He turned, frowning, to peer at her. "Yes, ma'am?"

The girls reached the door and she quickly herded them past her and into the house, then yelled, "Come here, please! I've got something I want you to do."

Clay glanced uneasily toward the barn, where he knew his father waited, then back at Annie. With a shrug, he headed for the house.

"What do you want Clay to do?" Rachel asked as Annie stepped inside the kitchen.

"Not just Clay," Annie replied, and forced a smile as she gave Rachel's pigtail a playful tug. "All of you."

"What?" Rachel demanded to know, her eyes growing bright with excitement.

"Can't tell. It's a surprise."

Tara pulled her head from inside the refrigerator and eyed Annie suspiciously. "What kind of surprise?"

"You'll see," Annie replied, smiling secretively.

Jase stepped outside the barn, wiping his hands on a rag, and looked toward the house, frowning. Clay should be home from school by now, he thought irritably. The boy had chores waiting.

Hearing a shout, then laughter, coming from the front of the house, he tossed down the rag. "If that boy's goofin' off when he's got work to do..." he muttered under his breath as he strode angrily for the house.

He rounded the corner of the front porch, then

ducked, swearing, when something struck him hard against the side of the face, knocking off his hat. He lifted his head as water ran down his face and dripped from his chin, narrowing his eyes on the four who stood frozen on the front lawn, staring at him in slack-jawed horror.

Clay immediately dropped the water balloon he held. "Uh, sorry, Dad," he said, taking a nervous step back. "It was an accident. I was aiming for Annie."

Jase lifted a hand and dragged it down his face, wiping the remaining moisture from his eyes and chin. "What the hell is going on here?"

"We're having a water-balloon fight," Rachel offered helpfully. "Me and Annie against Tara and Clay. Wanna play?"

Jase hauled in a breath, his chest swelling with rage as he turned his gaze on Annie. "A water-balloon fight?" he repeated. "You're having a water-balloon fight when you know damn good and well there's work to be done?"

Annie wasn't quite sure what made her do it, but as she watched Jase's face redden, saw the angry tick of a muscle on his jaw, she reared back and threw the balloon she held as hard as she could. It smacked against Jase's chest with a wet plop, exploding and shooting water up over his face and down the front of his shirt.

His eyes widened in surprise, then narrowed dangerously. "You're going to be sorry you did that," he warned as he took a threatening step toward her.

Annie thrust out a hand as if to stop him. "It's just a game, Jase," she said, laughing nervously. When he kept coming, she turned and ran.

He dived, catching her around the knees and taking her to the ground.

"I'll help you, Annie!" Rachel hollered.

Annie rolled to her back beneath Jase, her chest heaving, her heart pounding against her ribs. "It's just a game," she said again, then widened her eyes in horror when she saw Rachel lift a balloon above her daddy's head. "Rachel! No! Don't—"

But the warning came too late. The balloon split open upon impact, showering water over Jase's head and drenching his shirt.

But Jase never once moved his gaze from Annie's.

She stared up at him, her chest heaving, slowly becoming aware of the heat in his eyes, the desperate squeeze of his knees against her hips, the trembling in the hands that held her shoulders to the ground. She watched his gray eyes turn smoky, watched his gaze slide to her mouth...and had to swallow back the need-filled groan that rose to her throat.

Slowly he brought his gaze back to hers. Keeping one hand pressed against her shoulder, he lifted the other hand. "Rachel, get Daddy a balloon."

Annie's mouth sagged open. "You wouldn't dare," she cried, then shrieked and tried to wriggle from beneath him as he took the balloon Rachel passed to him and held it over her head. With a slow smug smile spreading across his face, he squeezed his fingers around the balloon, successfully bursting it and drenching Annie's face with water.

She sputtered, laughing, trying to keep the water out of her mouth. "Unfair!" she cried.

"Unfair?" he repeated, then held out his hand again. "Tara? Give me your balloon."

Tara glanced nervously at Annie, then reluctantly dropped the balloon she held into her father's waiting hand. He rocked back on Annie's stomach and held the balloon up, cradling it between his palms.

"Don't," she begged, still laughing. "Please."

"But I thought you liked playing games?"

"I do!" she insisted, then shrieked, when he popped the balloon and water rained down over her face a second time.

"Are you kids just going to stand there?" Annie cried. "Help me out here!"

Though Clay and Tara hesitated, Rachel didn't. She grabbed a balloon from the laundry basket filled with water bombs, then leaped on her daddy's back and smashed it over his head. With a low growl, he raised his arms, wrapped them around her from behind and dragged her over his head, flipping her to the ground.

Squealing in gleeful delight, Rachel tried to scoot away, but Jase quickly shifted off Annie and grabbed her by the ankle. "Traitor," he growled, before Rachel could escape. "You know what happens to traitors, don't you?"

"No, Daddy, please!" she squealed, laughing.

Out of the corner of her eye, Annie saw Clay stealthily approaching, both hands filled with water bombs. Not at all sure how this would turn out, she pushed to a sitting position and watched in silent wonder as Clay dumped the balloons over his father's head.

A split second later, Clay was on the ground, Rachel was up and scampering away, and Tara was leaping onto her father's back, her arms wound around his neck, squealing and laughing while Jase wrestled with Clay. Rachel skipped around the pile of humans, cheerfully rooting for her brother, then her father, her loyalties switching to whoever seemed to have the upper hand at the moment.

An incredulous smile spread across Annie's face. He's playing, she thought, almost giddy at the thought. Jase Rawley is actually playing with his children.

Awareness hummed in the kitchen like something alive, all but crackled and snapped each time Annie and Jase passed by each other as he helped her put dinner on the table. Flanked by the children as they ate their meal, their gazes would meet and instantly lock, heat pulsing between them until one or the other would find the strength to look away.

Sure that she would die from the need that swirled inside her, Annie prodded the children through completing their homework assignments, supervised Rachel's bath and shampooed the child's hair, then finally escaped to her room after seeing the three off to bed.

Hours later, unable to sleep, she prowled her bedroom, every nerve in her body attuned to the man who slept in the room below hers, wondering if he would come to her, telling herself that she couldn't possibly go to him. Not after he'd told her that he wouldn't make the mistake of sleeping with her again.

Determined to take her mind off Jase, she wandered her room, rearranging the knickknacks scattered along the top of the dresser and running her palm over the cool iron rungs of her bed's footboard. When she'd first moved in with the Rawleys, she'd promised her

elf that she wouldn't allow herself to grow attached
o this room, with its quaint iron bed and mishmash
f antique furnishings. She'd also promised herself
hat she wouldn't allow herself to grow attached to
he family she had been hired to take care of. The
esson not to form attachments had been learned long
go when she'd discovered that attachments, like
romises, were meant to be broken.

She sighed and turned to the window where moon-
ight spilled between delicate lace panels and pooled
n the wide pine planks of the floor, a circle of silver.
Yes, she'd promised herself she wouldn't become at-
ached to this house or the family who lived here, but
he realized now how foolish she'd been in thinking
hat she could keep that promise.

She loved this room, this house and the family who
nhabited it. And yes, she thought, feeling her heart
onstrict as she was forced to acknowledge her feel-
ngs for the man who stood at the head of it all.

She loved Jase.

Thankfully she wasn't foolish enough to believe
e'd ever be able to return her love. And, though she
ccepted that reality, she knew that when it came time
or her to go, she'd leave behind a large part of her
eart. Her eyes filling with tears, she stared out at the
ark landscape, wondering how many more pieces of
er heart she could afford to lose, before there was
othing left to sustain her.

The thought was fleeting, much too depressing to
ven consider, and she turned from the window to
scape it.

Pensive now, she crossed to the hallway and the
airway beyond. Keeping her tread light to avoid

waking the children, she headed downstairs and ou
the front door. She stepped out onto the porch and t
its edge, hugging her arms beneath her breasts as sh
drew in a deep breath of the cool night air.

Though she was dressed for bed, she wandered ou
into the yard, pleasure swelling inside her as she re
membered the war fought on the front lawn earlier i
the day. Though she hadn't planned the water-balloo
fight as a means to get Jase to interact with his chil
dren, she certainly didn't mind that things had turne
out the way they had. Seeing him play with his chil
dren had warmed her heart and given her hope fo
him and his family.

It had also eased her anger with him and left he
with a keen awareness of him that seemed determine
to keep her awake all night.

Sighing, she glanced back toward the house and t
Jase's bedroom window, the room dark beyond th
drapes that fluttered at the breeze's gentle teasing. Re
membering the night before when she'd slept there i
his arms, she wondered if he'd welcome her into hi
bed again if she were to find the courage to go t
him.

She wouldn't go to him, though, she told hersel
firmly and turned for the barn, and she wouldn't push
If Jase wanted her, he would have to seek her ou
For now, it was enough that he was interacting wit
his children.

Or so she told herself as she climbed the ladder t
the loft for a moonlight visit with the cat and her bab
kittens. Walking quietly through the tall stacks of hay
she made her way to the far corner where the mam
and her kittens had made their home.

She sank down to the loft floor near the animals, gathering her gown over her folded legs. Leaning forward, she whispered, "Hi, Mama Cat. Will you let me hold one of your babies?" Keeping a watchful eye on the protective mother, she eased a kitten from the animal's side and drew it to her breast, cooing softly. She nuzzled her cheek against the kitten's soft fur. "Hi, baby," she murmured. She held the kitten up to the moonlight that filtered through the high window and smiled as the animal opened its mouth and mewled softly, exposing a pink tongue and tiny, white teeth.

"Aren't you just the cutest little thing?" she said, admiring its tabby stripes.

"That cute little thing will probably give you ringworm."

Annie snatched the kitten to her chest and whipped her head around to find Jase stretched out on his side on a blanket spread over a long row of hay bales behind her, watching. Surprised to discover that he wasn't asleep in bed, as she'd thought, she asked, "What are you doing out here?"

He rolled to a sitting position and lifted a shoulder. "Couldn't sleep."

Biting back a smile, she returned the kitten to its mother, then rose. "Couldn't stand it, could you?"

He looked up at her as she crossed to him. "Couldn't stand what?"

"Thinking about the mama cat and worrying about whether she'd be able to leave her babies long enough to find food for herself."

He frowned and dropped his hands down to curl his fingers around the edge of the bale he sat on.

"Never gave that feline another thought after the day I first saw you taking pictures of her and her babies."

"Oh, really?" Annie said, and glanced pointedly at the bowls filled with fresh water and food.

She laughed when Jase's cheeks reddened. She draped an arm along his shoulders as she sat down next to him. "Like I said, Rawley, you're nothing but a big teddy bear."

"Yeah," he muttered. "You just keep thinking that."

She dropped an impulsive kiss on his cheek before tipping her forehead to rest against his. "Don't worry," she told him. "I will."

She felt the sigh that moved through him and the tension that slowly melted from his shoulders.

"Thanks for...well, you know," he said self-consciously.

"What?" she asked, deciding that it would make him stronger to admit what he was grateful for.

He angled his head to frown at her. "For nearly drowning me," he growled, then shoved her down on the hay.

She laughed as he stretched out over her, holding himself above her by propping a hand against the hay on either side of her face. "My, my, my," she said as she reached up with both hands to brush his hair back from his forehead. "What is all this about?"

He lowered his groin to hers, showing her. "You're lucky I was able to restrain myself earlier. If the kids hadn't been there this afternoon, I'd have taken you right there on the ground and out in broad daylight."

Shivering deliciously at the thought, she dragged her hands down his back, thrilling at the hard pads of muscle she encountered. "Seems as if I remember you saying something about this being a mistake."

He lowered himself more, slowly flattening her breasts beneath his chest as he gave her his full weight. "And nothing's changed my mind." He dipped his head down and nipped at her lower lip. "You're trouble," he murmured as he swept his mouth across hers. "Trouble with a capital T. I knew it from the first day I laid eyes on you."

"Really? So what are you doing here with me now?"

He pushed his hips more firmly against hers. "You have to ask?"

She laughed and cupped his hips, holding him against her. "Just remember. You started this. Not me."

"No. This is all your fault."

"Mine! What did I do?"

"Breathing. Existing. Seems that's all it takes."

He rolled to his back and hauled her over him. He dug his hands through her hair, his mouth seeking and finding hers in the dim moonlight. She tasted the hunger in him, felt the desperation in the hands that moved to roam her back, need in the thick column of flesh that lengthened and grew hard between them. She gloried in every touch of his hands on her, every groan that rumbled low in his throat, the heat that threatened to smother.

"You taste like sunshine," he murmured, nibbling at her lips.

"And what does sunshine taste like?"

"Golden. Warm." He swept her hair back from her face and held it against her head as he lifted his face

for another taste. "And honey," he added, testing the
flavor on his lips. "Sunshine and honey."

She laughed self-consciously and pressed a finger
against his bottom lip. "You make me sound like
something you'd order from a menu."

His gaze on hers, he caught her finger and drew it
into his mouth, closing his lips around it. Heat shot
through her bloodstream when he began to suckle,
stealing her breath. He smiled smugly, obviously
aware of the effect he had on her, and drew her finger
from his mouth. He placed her hand on his chest.

She felt his heart's wild pounding beneath her
palm, watched the smug smile melt slowly from his
face, the heat darken his gray eyes to midnight.

"I want you," he whispered, his voice husky with
need. "Even when we're apart, you're in my head
driving me crazy. I want you in spite of the fact that
I know I shouldn't. I want you," he said more em-
phatically. "Right now."

Even as he made his intentions known, he was
reaching for the snap of his jeans and ripping the fly
open. Within seconds the jeans were sailing across
the loft and she was beneath him, naked, her nightgown following the path of his jeans. He tore the
familiar gold packet open and sheathed his sex, then
with his gaze on hers, positioned himself over her.
Holding himself aloft with hands braced at either side
of her head, he swooped his head down, caught a
budded nipple between his teeth, then slowly drew
her into his mouth as he pushed inside her.

She arched, gasping, as twin points of desire shot
through her, slamming together low in her belly and
ricocheting out to every extremity, leaving her weak

Before she had a chance to recover, he was riding her, each thrust of his hips driving his sex deeper and deeper inside her.

Heat. It filled the loft, pressed down on her from every direction, slicked her skin with perspiration and sucked the oxygen from the air, making it difficult to breathe. Once her ally, heat became her tormentor, a wild, raging beast that roared its way through her, demanding release. She couldn't move or think for its mad pacing, only feel…and the hands that moved over her, seeking and finding her most sensitive spots, fanned the flames even higher. She felt shattered, fragmented, disoriented, lost in a sea of constantly churning sensations. She was desperate for something to cling to, to center herself with, a release that remained stubbornly out of reach.

Blindly, she grabbed for Jase, filling her hands with his hair, and drew his face down to hers. Before she could voice her need for him, beg him to take her, he closed his mouth over hers, swallowing her whimpered pleas. His tongue swept over hers, then stabbed deeply, matching the rhythm and intensity of his sex as he thrust wildly again and again and again.

A tidal wave of pleasure crashed over her, pummeling her senses and forcing the breath from her lungs. She tore her mouth from his with a startled cry and arched instinctively against him, her back bowing, her fingers digging into his scalp as the wave crested, flooding her body with sensation. Slowly, the tension ebbed from her limbs and her hands slipped to his back, and she soothed him while he trembled with his own release.

He drew in one last, deep shuddering breath, then

rolled to his side and gathered her into his arms and to his heart. Tucking her head beneath his chin, he pressed his lips against her hair. "You okay?" he whispered.

"Yes." She lifted her head to look up at him. "Are you?"

Jase stared down at her and smiled softly. "I'm with you, aren't I?"

Seven

If Annie had thought she'd known happiness before, she was mistaken. *This* was happiness, she decided as she flipped pancakes on the griddle. This irrepressible giddiness that seemed to bloom out of nowhere each time she thought of Jase, leaving her feeling buoyant and refreshed in spite of the little sleep she'd received the night before. Just thinking about the night of love-making in the loft and the hours spent cuddled against Jase's side on a bed of sweet-smelling hay made her sigh in contentment as she scooped golden pancakes onto a plate.

She felt a strong set of arms slip around her from behind and she melted back against a wide expanse of chest and muscled thighs.

"Good mornin'," Jase murmured against her ear as he closed his hands over her breasts.

"Good morning." Smiling, she angled her head for his kiss.

His lips were warm and achingly familiar, his freshly showered scent and his minty toothpaste taste as arousing as the hands that teased her nipples to attention.

"Kids up yet?" he asked huskily.

"Mmm-hmm," she murmured, closing her eyes against the heat that suddenly burned behind them. "They're getting dressed for school."

"After they leave, how about riding along with me while I check on the cattle?"

"On horseback?" she asked, flipping her eyes open to meet his gaze.

"We could, but I was thinking more along the lines of taking the truck."

"Oh," she said, unable to disguise her relief. "Sure. That sounds great."

Chuckling, he gave her breasts a squeeze before releasing her and taking a step back. "You don't like to ride horses?"

Feeling a little unsteady without his body to support her, she braced a hand against the stove as she began to transfer pancakes onto the plate again. "I wouldn't know. I've never ridden one."

"We'll have to fix that. But not today," he assured her when she whipped her head around to stare at him in alarm. He scooped his hat from the countertop. "You might want to pack us a lunch," he suggested. "And throw in a blanket, while you're at it." He shot her a wink as he headed out the back door. "My back's still itching from that hay last night."

Chuckling, she picked up the platter and turned

She jerked to a stop, her eyes widening in surprise when she saw Tara standing in the doorway that led to the hall. Quickly regaining her composure, she moved on to the table. "Good morning, Tara," she said in what she hoped sounded like a normal voice. "You startled me. I didn't hear you come downstairs."

"'Morning," Tara replied, eyeing Annie suspiciously as she crossed to the table and sat down. "What did Dad mean when he said that about hay scratching his back?"

Annie prayed that the embarrassing heat she felt crawling up her neck didn't make it to her face before she turned away. "Your father couldn't sleep last night so he went out to the barn and slept in the hayloft."

"Dad slept in the loft?"

Annie glanced up to see that Clay had stepped into the kitchen, catching the end of her and Tara's conversation. "Yes," she replied. "He couldn't sleep, so he went to the barn and slept in the loft." It wasn't a lie, she told herself. Jase *had* said he'd gone to the loft because he couldn't sleep.

"That's weird," Clay said as he took his seat at the table.

"What's weird?" Rachel asked as she skipped into the kitchen.

Annie rolled her eyes, wondering how many times she would have to tell the story. Tara saved her the trouble of repeating the lie yet again.

"Dad couldn't sleep last night," the teenager told her younger sister, "so he went out to the barn and slept in the loft."

"Oh." Rachel glanced over at Annie as she climbed onto her chair at the table. "Can I sleep in the hayloft tonight?"

Annie sputtered a laugh. "No, I don't think so."

"Why not?" Rachel complained. "Daddy did."

"Yes," Annie replied patiently. "But he's an adult and knows how to take care of himself."

Rachel pushed her mouth into a pout. "I'm big too, and I know how to take care of myself."

"Yeah, right," Clay replied dryly. "First time a coyote howled you'd be hightailing it to the house and screaming bloody murder."

"Would not," Rachel argued.

"Would, too," Clay and Tara said in unison.

And for once Annie didn't even attempt to put a stop to their innocent bickering. She was much too relieved that the focus of the conversation had turned away from Jase's—and her—night in the loft.

Sunlight filtered by the tree's canopy of leaves warmed Jase's face. The remainder of his body's warmth could only be attributed to the woman snuggled up against him. Shifting carefully, he rolled from his back and to his side, keeping his gaze on Annie's sleep-relaxed face. With the smattering of freckles high on her cheeks and on her turned-up nose, *cute* was probably a much better description of her, but he found the word *beautiful* stubbornly fixed in his mind.

She is beautiful, he argued silently. At least she was to him. And not just physically. It was her heart, her generosity, her goodness that made her so attractive. That, coupled with a sunshiny disposition and an innate sexiness that most women would pay good money to possess, made Annie a woman damn hard to resist.

And why should he try to resist her? he asked himself. He'd already tried and failed more times than he liked to think about. Besides, he'd laid out the ground rules from the get-go. A physical relationship. That was all he was interested in, and she hadn't seemed to have a problem with the restrictions he'd placed on their relationship. So why did he feel this niggling of concern now?

Because it isn't just physical anymore, you lunkhead. You care for her.

He tensed at his conscience's blunt prodding, then heaved a long, uneasy breath, knowing it was true. He did care for Annie. And if he wasn't careful, he could grow to more than just care for her. He could fall in love with her. It would be easy enough to do. She was so open and honest and warm and loving. And his kids seemed to idolize her. Even Tara, the hardest nut of the three to crack, seemed to genuinely like Annie.

Even as he thought this, Annie sighed in her sleep and snuggled closer to his chest, threading her fingers through the dark hair that curled there. Without thinking, he swept her hair back from her face and laid his palm against her cheek. A soft, sleepy smile curved her lips and she sighed again, her breath blowing warm against his chest, before she turned her lips against his chest and pressed a kiss over his heart.

Yeah, he thought, feeling the fear knotting in his gut even as desire tightened his groin.

If he wasn't careful, he could definitely fall in love with Annie.

* * *

Jase hated attending school events. Not because he felt guilty about all the work he was leaving undone on the ranch, but because his skin all but crawled at the curious looks his appearance at the events never failed to draw.

It had started years before when he'd taken over guardianship of his sister Penny, and a sense of obligation had forced him to attend the school events she participated in. People had stared at him then, some with pity, others with admiration for the task he'd taken on. But *why* they stared didn't matter to him. It was finding himself the focus of so much attention that had always bothered him, and that was the reason he usually found an excuse to avoid these functions, even when they included his own three kids.

But on this particular night Annie had refused to listen to any of his excuses and had bulldozed him into attending the Spring Fling at Rachel's elementary school.

Now he wished he'd stuck to his guns and stayed at home.

The surreptitious glances cast his way were beginning to get on his nerves. He wondered if these people didn't have anything more exciting to reflect on other than the activities in Jase Rawley's life. A couple of the single mothers who had, after his wife's death, gone out of their way to let him know that they were available if he should ever feel the need of female companionship, were busy eyeing him and Annie, as if they somehow knew their relationship was more than just that of employer and nanny. Others still

ooked at him with pity for the tragedies he'd suffered
n his life—first the loss of his parents, then that of
his wife. He figured he should be glad it was pity he
recognized in a few of the glances cast his way, rather
than the suspicious and jealous looks the single mothers were singeing him with.

But he quickly realized he wasn't the only one in
the gymnasium who was drawing a few stares. Annie
commanded a few of her own. Several of the men
were eyeing her hungrily, if covertly, which irritated
the hell out of Jase. He supposed he could have suggested that Annie wear something more appropriate
for the Spring Fling, something that didn't draw quite
so much attention her way. The yellow sundress she'd
chosen to wear, with its thin spaghetti straps and
flared, short skirt, begged every man in the room to
take a second glance at all that smooth bare skin, the
length of well-curved legs that the short skirt revealed.

Irritated by the men's admiring glances, he placed
a hand low on Annie's back and hustled her toward
the opposite side of the room and away from curious
eyes.

"What are you doing?" she asked, having to hurry
to match the length of his stride.

"I...I thought you might like some punch." He
grabbed one of the filled cups positioned on the colorfully draped table and shoved it into her hand.

Annie looked up at him in surprise as she accepted
the drink. "Why thank you, Jase. That's very consid-
erate of you."

He scowled. "Yeah. Well, I can be nice when I
want to be."

She sipped lemonade, smiling at him over the top of the cup. "Yes, you certainly can," she murmured suggestively, then laughed when his cheeks reddened.

"Mr. Rawley!"

Jase turned upon his hearing his name and bit back a groan when he saw Rachel's teacher bearing down on him. "Evenin', Miss Sharp," he said, giving his head a brisk nod of greeting.

"And you must be Annie." Miss Sharp grasped Annie's hand between hers and squeezed. "Rachel has told me so much about you."

Annie laughed gaily. "I hope it wasn't all bad."

"Oh, no," Miss Sharp was quick to assure her. "In fact, I expected to find a halo above your head and wings clipped to your shoulders. She simply goes on and on about how wonderful and talented you are."

Annie laughed again. "Well, I guess I've at least got Rachel fooled."

"And she's so excited about your upcoming marriage," Miss Sharp continued, beaming.

Annie's smile slowly melted. "Marriage?"

"Well, yes," Miss Sharp said, glancing uneasily toward Jase. "Oh, dear," she said, her cheeks growing pink at the thunderous look on his face. "I hope your engagement wasn't supposed to be a secret. Rachel was so excited, and she didn't mention anything about your and Mr. Rawley's plans to marry being a secret. I hope I haven't gotten the child into trouble for mentioning it. I'm sure she meant no harm."

Annie didn't dare look at Jase during the drive home. But she didn't need to look at him in order to judge his current mood. He was furious. Thus far

e'd managed to contain his anger, but she didn't sus-
ect that he'd be able to do so for much longer.
ddly, the children seemed oblivious to their father's
ark mood and were laughing and chattering in the
ack seat, still high from the festivities at the Spring
ling.

Once they arrived at the house, though, Jase
mmed the gear shift into Park, then threw an arm
ong the back of the seat and turned to glare angrily
 his children. Immediately the laughter in the back
at died, and the smiles melted off the children's
ces.

"Rachel, did you tell your teacher that Annie and
 were getting married?"

Annie turned to see tears fill Rachel's eyes.

"Y-yes, sir."

"And why would you tell her such a thing?" he
ked, his voice rising measurably. "You know that
 isn't true."

Rachel turned to look up at Tara. "But Tara said—"

"What did you tell her?" Jase demanded, turning
s accusing gaze on his older daughter.

Tara reached for the door handle. "I told her I
ought you and Annie liked each other, and that if
u did, maybe you guys would get married."

Jase grabbed Tara's arm, preventing her from es-
ping the car. "We're *not* getting married. Under-
and? Not now, and not anytime in the future. An-
e's your nanny. Period."

Tara twisted free from his grasp. "Yeah, like Annie
ould be stupid enough to marry *you*," she cried and
lted from the car.

A knife couldn't have penetrated Annie's heart and done any more damage. Whatever hope she had held for a more permanent relationship with Jase slipped quietly away as she stared at his shadowed profile. With tears burning her eyes, she turned to face the front and stare through the windshield.

With an uneasy glance at Annie, Clay opened the car door and caught Rachel's hand. "Come on, Sis," he murmured. "I'll help you get ready for bed."

Annie reached for her door handle, but froze when she felt Jase's hand on her arm, stopping her.

"Wait."

She dragged in a shuddery breath, blinking back tears. "What?" she asked, unable to look at him.

"You're not upset by all this, are you?"

It took all the effort she could muster, but she forced a smile as she turned to look at him. "And why would I be upset? You never promised marriage. A physical relationship, right? That's what we agreed to and that's all I expected."

Jase stood at his bedroom window, one hand braced high on the wall, looking out into the darkness his forehead furrowed with deep grooves.

He'd hurt her. He'd hurt Annie.

He hadn't meant to, had worried from the beginning that he would if he became involved with her had done everything in his power to avoid doing so

But he'd hurt her anyway.

Oh, she'd put up a brave front. Even smiled when she'd insisted that she wasn't upset over his denial of Rachel's claim to her teacher that he and Annie wer getting married. But he'd seen the crack in her smile, heard the tremble in her voice.

He'd hurt her.

The hell of it was, even knowing that, to his shame, he still wanted her. He wanted to slip out to the barn to see if she was in the loft with the cat and her kittens. Wanted to climb the stairs to her room and slip into bed with her.

He turned from the window, swearing under his breath as he raked his fingers through his hair. But he couldn't go to her. Couldn't hold her. Couldn't make love with her. Couldn't sleep with her cuddled against his body. Not ever again.

If he did, he'd only hurt her more.

The next few days were hell for Annie. It was difficult to maintain a smile when the children were home, present a veneer of normalcy when she was all but dying inside. More difficult still to avoid being alone with Jase, to keep from seeking him out while the children were at school. She desperately wished that she could go back to the day of the Spring Fling. If she could, this time she wouldn't force Jase to attend. If she hadn't made him go, then he would never have known that Rachel had started a rumor that he and Annie were planning to marry.

But if wishes were horses, she thought miserably, as a favorite phrase of her grandmother's came to mind, then they'd all ride.

With disappointment weighing heavily on her chest, she laid out the pictures she'd had developed, hoping to focus her thoughts away from Jase and on to potential sales she might make to magazines. In the weeks she'd worked for the Rawleys, she'd shot more than ten rolls of film; most of the children, some of the animals and plant life she'd discovered on the ranch during her wanderings.

But as she spread the prints out across the kitchen table, it was only one roll she focused on. The shots she'd taken of Jase while he'd been working with the calves in the corral.

She picked up one and sank down onto a chair, suddenly too weak to stand. He was so handsome, she thought tearfully, as she touched a finger to his face, tracing the familiar features. The high slant of cheekbones. The determined glint of flint-gray eyes. The proud lift of a square and noble chin.

She laid the picture down and selected another, this one taken in the loft when Jase had discovered her photographing the mama cat and her kittens. She'd turned the camera on him and snapped a picture of him, unaware, while he stared, mesmerized by the cat and her babies. His eyes were softer here, as were his features, reflecting the compassionate heart that he struggled so hard to hide.

Feeling the tears gathering in her throat, she glanced toward the window and the barn where Jase worked. God, she loved him, she thought, the pain of that love squeezing at an already bruised heart. But she could see the changes the revelations at the Spring Fling had left on their relationship, as well as on his relationship with his children. He was avoiding them all again. Her *and* his children. He rose before Annie even came down for the day, leaving the house and not returning sometimes until well after dark.

Though she'd planned to avoid him, he'd made the

task much too easy by first avoiding the house and her.

She'd leave.

The decision to do so was already there, in her mind and in her heart. And though it hurt to even consider leaving, she knew if she didn't, the children would lose what little part of their father they had managed to regain while Annie had been with them.

As she stood and began gathering the pictures, Annie thought perhaps she understood better Jase's sister's decision to leave the ranch. If Penny had stayed, then Jase would have continued to leave the children's raising up to her, just as he'd been willing to leave it up to Annie.

But knowing that didn't stop Annie's tears or lessen her pain.

Once again an attachment was being broken, another chunk of her heart ripped away. But this time, Annie wondered if she'd survive the loss.

From the safety and concealment of the barn, Jase watched Annie load her things into her car. She was leaving. He knew it, wanted desperately to stop her before it was too late.

But he didn't.

It was best, he told himself, as he watched her climb behind the wheel. If she stayed, it would only bring heartache to them all. To the kids. To Annie. To him. The kids would miss her, he knew. But they were young, resilient. In no time at all, she'd be just a fond memory. They'd survive the loss. They had survived others.

But would he?

Choked by tears, he watched the dust rise behind her tires as she drove down the long driveway, feeling as if his heart was being ripped right out of his chest and dragged down the road behind her. He stared until the dust had settled and her car had disappeared from sight, then dragged a hand across his eyes and headed for the house.

When he stepped into the kitchen, he saw her note on the table, propped up against the side of one of three Easter baskets filled with colorfully decorated eggs and candy. He picked up the folded note as he sank down onto his chair at the head of the table, flipped open the single sheet of paper and began to read.

Jase,

I think you know why I decided to leave, so I won't bother offering any excuses. I know it was cowardly of me to do it this way, but I honestly don't think I could bear saying goodbye to the children. I've grown to love them so much.

Since Spring Break begins at the end of school today and the children will have a week's vacation, I felt this would be the best time to make a clean break. With the twins home to look after Rachel, I'm sure that y'all can manage without me, plus it will give you a week to find a replacement. I left several casseroles in the refrigerator and instructions for reheating them, so I know you all won't starve in the interim.

Tell the children…well, tell them that I love them and that I will miss them. If they ask why I left, you can tell them that I found a teaching position in another city. It shouldn't be a lie—at least not for long, I hope. In the meantime, I've decided to do a little traveling. I might even put together a series on Texas wildflowers. Everything's in bloom now, so I should be able to find plenty to photograph.

I made Easter eggs for Rachel to hunt on Easter Sunday. They are in the largest basket. You can have Tara and Clay hide them for her. The other two baskets are for Tara and Clay. I've filled them with their favorite sweets and included pictures that I took of each of them.

Please don't think I blame you for what happened between us or think that I'm angry with you. I don't and I'm not. I knew the rules when we first began. Unfortunately, I discovered too late that my heart refuses to live by a set of predetermined rules.

I'm leaving a picture for you, as well. I took it that afternoon in the barn when you caught me photographing the mama cat and her babies. You want so badly for everyone to think you are heartless and uncaring. But look closely at the picture. I think you'll see your heart is reflected in your eyes.

Be happy, Jase. And take time for your children. They love you and they need you.

Annie

Jase dropped his hand to the table, his fingers convulsing on the single sheet of paper, his sight blurred by a swirling mist of tears. Gulping, he released the note and picked up the framed picture she'd left for him and stared at his reflection. But it wasn't his own image he saw beneath the glass. It was Annie, captured by his mind's camera just as she'd looked that afternoon in the barn when they'd climbed down from the loft after photographing the cat, her face flushed with color, her green eyes bright with excitement.

She found joy in such simple things, always smiling and laughing and making those around her smile, too. And she was so generous with her time, her energy and her love, making special treats for the kids, giving them hugs when they needed them, and gentle reprimands when they needed that, too.

They were going to miss Annie.

But no more than Jase would.

Choked by the emotion that clogged his throat, he dragged the note from the table and stuffed it into his pocket as he pushed himself to his feet.

It's better this way, he told himself, as he headed for the door and the work that awaited him.

With Annie gone, he couldn't hurt her anymore.

Eight

Rachel barreled inside the barn, followed closely by the twins. Jase glanced up from his workbench, then quickly back down when he saw the smile on Rachel's face.

"Where's Annie?" she asked, hopping impatiently from one foot to the other. "She made me an Easter basket and I've got to tell her thank you."

Inhaling deeply, Jase glanced over at his daughter, then shifted his gaze higher to look at the twins who stood behind her, their expressions hesitant, almost fearful, as if they suspected Annie wasn't just missing, but gone.

He dropped his gaze. "She left."

"Left!" all three cried in unison.

"Yeah, she...she got a lead on a teaching position

that's coming open,'' he explained, taking the cowardly way out that Annie had offered him.

"But she can't leave!" Rachel cried, her eyes already brimming with tears. "Annie belongs to us."

"Well, she *is* gone," he replied more harshly than he intended. "So you might as well gut it up and get used to the idea."

Tears spilled down Rachel's cheeks and she whirled and ran for the house, sobbing hysterically. Tara glared at him for a moment, then turned and ran after her little sister.

"You made her leave," Clay accused resentfully. "I knew you would. I told you that if you were mean to her she wouldn't want to stay around here very long."

"I wasn't mean to her," Jase argued, knowing he lied.

"Yes, you were! Annie liked it here. And she liked us, too. It's *your* fault she's gone. You always ruin everything. Everything!" Clay yelled angrily, then spun and strode for the house.

Jase had known grief before, had experienced it at a bone-deep level that most folks his age didn't even know yet existed. But he couldn't remember ever feeling this low, this lonely.

Annie's departure had left a void in his heart and in his home. A huge vacuum that had all but sucked the life from him, his children and his house. The kids dragged around all day looking lost and forlorn, and there was a silence within his home that was almost deafening. No more wild laughter or high-pitched squeals. No more sunshiny smiles greeting him in the

itchen of a morning. No more spontaneous picnics
r sensuous foot massages by the creek. No more
omfort in waking to find a warm body curled against
is in the night.

No more Annie.

Though he knew he should have driven into town
he afternoon she left and placed an ad for a new
ousekeeper and nanny to take her place, Jase hadn't
een able to bring himself to even attempt to write
he ad, much less make the drive into town to deliver
t to the newspaper. He had managed to survive the
veekend. Barely. But Monday morning had dawned
nd he wasn't any closer to adjusting to Annie's ab-
ence than he was when he'd discovered her note on
he preceding Friday. And he still hadn't made an
ttempt to find a replacement.

No one could replace Annie. Not in his home.

And not in his heart.

He sighed and turned from his window and crossed
o his bed. Though he knew that sleep would be a
ong time coming, he had to at least put himself in
he position to accept it if it happened to slip up on
im unawares. There was work to be done. A ranch
o manage. A house to run. Three kids to care for.
And how could he stand up under the strain if he
idn't at least try to get some rest?

He'd just dropped his head down on the pillow and
tretched out his legs when his bedroom door burst
pen. He jackknifed to a sitting position to find Clay
tanding in the doorway, his eyes wild, his chest
eaving.

"Come quick!" Clay gasped. "It's Tara."

Jase was on his feet and grabbing for his jeans. "What's wrong with her?"

But Clay was already running back down the hall.

With his heart in his throat, Jase followed, jerking up his zipper as he ran after his son. He bounded up the stairs and found Clay standing outside the bathroom door, staring at something on the floor inside.

Clay turned to look at Jase, his face drained of color. "I think she's dead," he said, then gulped, his eyes filling with tears.

Jase paced, holding a clinging and sobbing Rachel against his chest.

"It's okay, dumplin'," he soothed. "Tara's gonna be okay. She's gonna be okay," he repeated, and silently prayed he was right.

He glanced toward the row of curtained cubicles beyond the emergency room's glass doors and closed his eyes against the fear that gripped him, remembering Tara's ashen face, her limp and lifeless body as the ambulance attendants had wheeled the gurney she was strapped to beyond the door and into one of the cubicles, separating Jase from his daughter.

Please don't die, he prayed silently. *Oh, God, please don't let her die.*

"Dad?"

Jase opened his eyes to find Clay standing in front of him, his eyes dark with the same fear that twisted in Jase's gut.

"She's gonna make it, isn't she?" Clay asked, then gulped. "Tara's not gonna die, is she?"

Acting on instinct alone, Jase opened an arm and Clay stepped into his embrace, burying his face against his father's chest. With the arms of his youngest and his oldest wrapped around him, Jase tightened his own arms around his children, offering them the comfort he knew they needed, the same comfort he found in the arms that clung to him. "Tara's gonna be okay," he assured them. "She's gonna be okay."

"Mr. Rawley?"

Jase jerked up his head, his heart leaping to his throat when he saw the nurse standing in the doorway. "Yes?"

"You can see your daughter now."

When Jase started forward, still holding Rachel on one hip and with Clay hugged against his opposite side, the nurse held up a hand. "Just you," she said firmly. "The children will need to wait here."

Clay quickly stepped from beneath his father's arm and reached for Rachel. "I'll watch her, Dad."

Pride swelled in Jase's heart as he peered down at his son, realizing how much his son had grown, how much he'd matured, while Jase had been so busy ignoring his family. "Thanks, Clay," he said and shifted Rachel to his son's arms. He laid a hand on Clay's shoulder and squeezed. "I'll try to talk 'em into letting us all in," he promised.

With a reassuring smile for both his children, he turned and followed the nurse into the restricted area. As the nurse pushed back the curtain to the cubicle where Tara had been taken, Jase inhaled deeply, preparing himself for whatever he might have to face.

Tara lay on the gurney inside the narrow space, her eyes closed, her face as white as the pillow that cushioned her head. An IV was hooked to her wrist and tubes ran from her nose. A monitor beeped rhythmically somewhere in the room.

Jase swallowed back the fear that rose to his throat. "Is she…?"

"It was a close call," the doctor replied to the question Jase had been unable to ask, "but she's going to be fine."

The breath sagged out of Jase, leaving him weak-kneed.

"We pumped her stomach," the doctor explained, "emptying it of all the pills she took, and we're administering medication to take care of any toxins that managed to make it to her bloodstream. She'll need constant supervision for a few days, but she should be just fine."

"Thank you," Jase murmured, unable to take his eyes off Tara's pale face. With his legs trembling uncontrollably, he crossed to the gurney and took Tara's hand in his. "Tara? Baby, it's Daddy. You're gonna be all right, sweetheart. You're gonna be all right."

He felt the tears pushing at his throat, burning behind his lids, and swallowed hard as he watched his daughter's eyes blink open and slowly bring him into focus.

"Dad?"

His name was nothing more than a rusty whisper but Jase couldn't remember ever hearing anything that sounded so good.

"Yeah, baby. It's me." He gave her hand a hard squeeze. "You gave us quite a scare, but the doctor says you're going to be fine. Just fine."

Her eyes brimmed with tears and her chin began

o quiver. "I'm sorry, Daddy. I didn't mean to scare
ou."

Jase dropped down on the side of the bed and
moothed the hair from her face, his heart twisting
ainfully in his chest. "I know you didn't, baby."

"I just miss Annie so much."

"I know, sweetheart. We all do," he admitted
oftly.

"I thought if I...if I was sick, she might come back
nd take care of me."

"Oh, baby," he murmured and leaned to press his
ips against her forehead. He felt a hand slip around
is neck, the tremble in the fingers that curled there,
nd closed his eyes against the tears that stung his
yes. "I love you, Tara," he whispered, then leaned
ack far enough to meet her gaze. "I love you,
aby."

He saw the surprise flash in her eyes, and it was
s if a huge weight lifted from his chest, freeing his
eart. "I love you," he said again, a smile trembling
n his lips.

"I love you, too, Daddy," she said tearfully and
ugged him down to wrap both arms around his neck.

"Dad?"

Jase hefted the bale of hay high and tossed it down
o the truck below. "Yeah, son?"

"Do you miss Annie?"

Jase hesitated a moment, unaccustomed to sharing
is feelings, then firmed his lips, deciding it was well
ast time that he did. "Yeah, son, I do."

"I do, too," Clay said miserably. "And so do Ra-
hel and Tara."

"Yeah, I know," Jase murmured.

"Do you think she would come back, if we were to ask her? Maybe you could offer her a raise or something."

Jase snorted a rueful laugh as he lifted another bale from the stack in the loft. "I doubt money would be enough inducement to get Annie ever to come back here."

"Dad?"

He tossed the bale down to the bed of the truck. "Yeah?"

"Do you miss Mom?"

Jase froze, then slowly turned to peer at his son. "Yeah. Why?"

Clay lifted a shoulder as he dragged another bale to the loft opening. "I don't know. Just curious, I guess. I miss her, too, but sometimes...well, I don't think about her as much as I used to. You know? And it makes me feel kinda guilty."

Jase pulled off his work gloves and sank down onto the bale that Clay had dragged to the opening. He patted the hay beside him, inviting his son to sit beside him. "Yeah, son. I know what you mean. But I think your mom understands. She's a part of us. Always will be. But she's gone now and she wouldn't expect us to mope around, missing her and thinking about her all the time."

"Yeah," Clay said thoughtfully. "I suppose you're right. I know I wouldn't want y'all crying and grieving all the time if I was the one who'd died."

Just the thought of losing his son had Jase reaching over and slinging an arm around Clay's shoulder and hugging him hard against his side. "I'd miss you,"

said gruffly, "for a second or two," he added,
ping to tease his son from his melancholy thoughts.

Clay laughed and elbowed his dad in the ribs.
You'd better. Otherwise, I'd come back and haunt
u."

Jase laughed too and scrubbed his knuckles over
ay's head before releasing him. "What's got you
inking such deep thoughts?"

Clay rolled a shoulder. "I don't know. I guess be-
use of Annie." He glanced over at Jase. "I think
e was in love with you, Dad."

Jase's heart seemed to take a dive to his boots, then
mped back up to pound furiously against his ribs.
Maybe," he said uneasily.

"More than maybe," Clay said. "I could see it in
r eyes when she'd look at you. Kinda happy and
stful like."

"Now don't start imagining things that aren't
e," Jase warned.

"I'm not imagining anything," Clay insisted.
Tara noticed it, too. She even thought that you were
love with Annie."

"I cared for her," Jase admitted carefully, reluctant
completely bare his soul.

"Then why'd you make her leave?" Clay asked.

Jase pushed to his feet and paced away, slapping
work gloves against his thigh. "I didn't *make* her
ve. She just left."

"Because she thought you didn't want her to stay.
you'd told her you cared for her, I bet she would've
yed. I bet she'd even come back if you were to tell
r now."

Jase whirled, stunned by the suggestion. "Tell he
now?"

"Yeah," Clay said, rising, warming to the idea
"You could call her. Or better yet, you could go and
see her. She told you where she was going, didn'
she?"

"Well, no," Jase said slowly, his mind racing, try
ing to remember the details of the note Annie had
left. "Not exactly. She just said that she was going
to do some traveling and take some pictures of wild
flowers."

"We could find her. I know we could. The bes
place in the state to view wildflowers is the Hil
Country."

"Yeah," Jase said, thinking of the miles of high
way and country roads a search would entail. "Tha
it is."

"Well, let's go!" Clay said, slapping his dad or
the back. "We've still got a couple of days of Sprin
Break left, so it'll be like a family vacation. We'v
never taken one as far as I can remember."

"No, we haven't," Jase said and began to smile
"And it's about damn time we did," he added an
slung an arm around Clay's shoulders and headed hir
for the ladder.

"How much farther, Daddy?" Rachel whined fror
the back seat.

Jase glanced in the rearview mirror. "I don't know
dumplin'."

"I'm tired of riding in the car," she complained.

After two days of driving down mile after mile o
roadway, stopping at motels only when it became to

ark to see, so was Jase. And without so much as a
ngle, solitary glimpse of Annie. He was about ready
» call it quits.

As if sensing his readiness to admit defeat, Tara
rabbed a book from the duffle bag Jase had packed
or the trip. "Here, Rachel," she offered quickly.
I'll read you a story."

"Will you make all the sounds like Annie does?"
achel asked hopefully. "And make your voice
ound like all the different people?"

"Yes," Tara promised. "I'll make all the sounds."

Jase glanced in the rearview mirror and watched
ara release Rachel's seatbelt, pull her little sister
nto her lap, then readjust her own seat belt to include
achel as well.

"Once upon a time, there was a princess who lived
a castle far away—"

"That's not the way Annie sounds when she reads
e story," Rachel said, frowning.

Heaving a weary sigh, Tara cleared her throat, then
egan again, putting an old woman's rasp in her
oice.

Jase bit back a smile as he turned his gaze back to
e road. He had some great kids, he told himself as
e squinted his eyes against the bright sunlight. Three
eat kids.

Annie popped open her trunk and stored her camera
quipment inside, then straightened and stretched her
ms above her head to take the kinks out of her back.

She'd burned up at least six dozen rolls of film over
e last five days, driven a good eight or nine hundred
iles and waded through another hundred miles or

more of pasture and road frontage, taking pictures o
the fruits of Lady Bird Johnson's labors. Bluebonnets
Indian Blanket. Primrose. Purple Coneflower. Texa
wildflowers abounded on every spot of ground an
bloomed in every color of the rainbow, a rich canva
of botanical glory and history preserved and main
tained thanks to the efforts of former First Lady Lad
Bird Johnson.

But even the spectacular beauty of the fields o
wildflowers and the peacefulness of the pastoral set
tings Annie had spent her time in hadn't been able t
erase the memories of the Rawleys or ease the pai
of leaving them.

She felt the all-too-familiar sting of tears and fu
riously blinked them back. She wouldn't cry an
more, she told herself.

She'd already cried enough tears to keep a fleet o
ships afloat.

But as she settled behind the wheel of her car, th
tears remained in her eyes, blurring the last rays o
sunshine as she steered her automobile from th
shoulder and back onto the country road. Prepared t
drive until exhaustion promised a good night's slee
she switched the radio on to a rock station, hopin
the loud music would drown out thoughts of Jase an
his children.

Bone-dead tired, but unable to sleep, Jase stood a
the window of the dark motel room, looking o
across the parking lot and to the highway that ran i
front of the motel's office. Occasionally a car woul
pass by and he would follow its movement until he'
determined that it wasn't Annie's.

Sighing, he braced a hand against the wall, shifting
s gaze to the coils of the neon Vacancy sign, watch-
g it flash red, then grow dark, and wondering how
uch more of this driving the kids could stand before
ey went stir crazy. At the moment, they were all
leep—Tara and Rachel in one bed, Clay in the
her, sprawled across the entire bed, leaving no room
r Jase. But after two days of being cooped up in a
ir together, all three had had about all the closeness
: feared they could stand.

As he stared blindly at the Vacancy sign, an auto-
obile pulled up beneath it, stopping in front of the
otel's office. Jase straightened, sure that he recog-
zed the car.

Couldn't be, he told himself as he waited for the
r's single occupant to alight. But when the car door
ened and a woman stepped out, Jase felt as if some-
ie had whipped a length of steel around his chest
d winched it up tight.

Annie.

He watched her disappear into the office, afraid to
ink, afraid to move, for fear he'd lose her again.
nd when she returned to her car moments later, a
ender strip of plastic in her hand, he turned for the
or.

"Dad? Where are you going?"

Jase stopped at the sound of his son's sleepy voice
d turned to peer at the shadowed bed. "Can't
eep," he said quietly, trying to keep his voice low
d calm, not wanting to build false hope in his son
· telling him he'd spotted Annie, for fear Annie
ould send him packing. "Thought I'd take a little
alk. Keep an eye on your sisters for me, okay?"

"Okay," Clay mumbled. He yawned, then rolle
to his side and pulled the sheet over his head.

Jase opened the door and stepped outside, closin
it softly behind him. He quickly spotted Annie's c
and headed for the stairs.

By the time he reached the parking lot, his brea
was coming fast, his hands slick with perspiration. H
stopped in the shadows and watched as she dragge
an overnight bag from the back seat of her car, the
waited until she approached a door on the first floc

When she inserted the plastic card key into the slc
he stepped from the shadows. "Annie?"

She whirled, her eyes wide with fear, looking as
she were ready to bolt. "Jase?" she said, saggir
when she recognized him. "What are you doir
here?"

He took a step closer. "Looking for you."

Her overnight bag slipped from her fingers ar
clunked against the concrete walk. "For me?" Sl
peered past him. "But…where are the children?"

He gave his head a jerk toward the stairs. "In
room upstairs. Asleep."

She whipped her gaze back to his, as if just rea
izing the impossibility of his knowing her locatio
"How did you know where to find me?"

He stuffed his hands into his pockets and rolled
shoulder. "Didn't. Been driving country roads for tv
days looking for you."

"But…why? Is something wrong?" she asked, ta
ing a step toward him. "Has something happened
one of the children? Is Tara…"

"She's okay. Or at least she is now."

He watched her face pale, her eyes darken wi

ar. Realizing that he was frightening her unneces-
rily, he pulled the card key from her hand. "Let's
lk about this inside," he suggested and unlocked the
or. He shoved it wide, then picked up her bag and
epped back, waiting for her to enter before him.

With her gaze frozen on his, she passed by him,
it stopped just inside the room. "Jase. Please.
ou're frightening me. What's happened?"

He flipped on a light and dropped the bag inside
e room before closing the door behind them. "We
id a little scare several days ago," he explained,
but everything's okay now," he assured her.

"Tara?" she asked, her voice quavering.

He stuffed his hands into his pockets again and
ew out a long breath, remembering that night. Tara
ing on the bathroom floor. Her face white. Her lips
ue. Her breathing thready, labored. The fear. The
one-chilling ride in the ambulance. "Yeah. Tara.
ie took a half bottle of pills."

Annie dropped her face into her open hands. "Oh,
)," she moaned. When she lifted her head, her face
as ravaged by guilt, her eyes gleaming with tears.
It's my fault."

"No," he said quickly and stepped to close his
nds around her upper arms. "If it was anyone's
ult, it was mine."

"No," she argued tearfully, shaking her head. "I
ouldn't have left. I knew how fragile her emotions
ere, how devastating it would be for her to feel as
she were losing someone again. I should have
ayed."

"Yes," he said, effectively halting her tears with

his quick agreement. "You should have stayed. Bu
not for the reasons you think," he added quietly.

She stared at him, her chin quivering, then sh
firmed her lips and jerked free of his grasp. She turne
away, hugging her arms beneath her breasts. "I di
what I thought best at the time. What was best for u
all."

"The kids didn't think so. In fact, they were plent
mad when they discovered you'd left without tellin
them goodbye."

She angled her head to look at him, tears floodin
her eyes, her voice thick with them. "I couldn't sa
goodbye to them. It would have been too hard."

"Was it any easier leaving the way you did?"

She dropped her chin to her chest and the tear
slipped down her cheeks and dripped off her chi
"No," she murmured miserably. "I miss them."

"And they miss you."

She covered her face with her hands. "Jas
please," she begged pitifully. "Don't do this."

"Do what?" he asked in confusion. "All I sai
was that the kids miss you."

She jerked her hands from her face. "I can't g
back," she cried. "I won't."

"Annie—"

She took a step away from him, pushing out a han
to stop him. "No, please," she said, sobbing nov
"Just go. Please. Just go."

He stared at her, wanting to argue, to take her i
his arms and comfort her, to tell her he loved her,
coax and cajole until she agreed to come home wit
him…but found he couldn't. Not when confronte
with her tears and knowing he'd caused them. N

when faced with the dark circles that lay like bruises beneath her eyes and realizing that she hadn't slept any better than he had since they'd been apart.

Not when he realized how much pain just seeing him and talking to him again caused her.

Not when reminded of how much he'd already hurt her.

Not when he feared that in her present exhausted and emotional state, she might refuse him.

"Okay," he murmured reluctantly and backed toward the door. "I'm going. But we're heading home tomorrow. If you want to come with us, you'd be welcome." He opened the door, then glanced back. "If you need me," he added quietly. "Or feel the need to talk. I'm here. Room 216 at the top of the stairs."

Nine

It took hours for Annie to finally fall asleep. And when she did sleep, she did so fitfully. After Jase had left, she'd considered climbing right back into her car and driving away, fearing that she might accidentally bump into one of the children the next morning when she checked out. Or, worse, give in to temptation and climb the stairs to room 216.

But exhaustion had kept her from leaving, and fear had kept her from going to Jase.

She knew she'd done the right thing in leaving the ranch. Remaining in Jase's home when there was no hope of a future with him, other than as his employee, was too painful to even think about.

But, oh, the children.

It had been so difficult for her to leave them, even though she'd known they were better off without her

If she'd stayed, Jase would have continued to ignore them, just as he had for years.

And now, because they'd tracked her down, and Jase had invited her to return to the ranch, she felt as if she was being forced to leave them all over again. His offer to return to the ranch with them had been tempting. Much too tempting, she thought, tears filling her eyes. And if he'd even hinted that *he* was the one who wanted her to return, that he cared for her, and had not hidden behind the needs of his children, she might have seriously considered returning with them.

But not once during their late-night conversation had he revealed his feelings for her. Only those of his children. Which meant nothing had changed. *Jase* hadn't changed. And if she were foolish enough to return to the ranch, Annie feared Jase would slip right back into his old ways, ignoring his children and leaving their care up to her. And the children needed their father and his time and attention so much more than they needed that of a nanny.

But, mercy, she missed them, she thought, sniffing back tears as she forced herself from the bed and into the shower. Tara. Clay. Little Rachel. She'd grown to love them all so much.

But most especially Jase.

Tara waited until she heard her father's footsteps clanking on the metal stairs outside their room, then hurried to the window and pushed back the drape an inch to peek outside. She craned her neck to watch him climb into their car. "Dad's acting weird," she said, gnawing a thumbnail.

Clay folded his hands behind his head and stretched his legs out on the bed, his gaze and his attention riveted on the TV screen. "Dad always acts weird."

Tara shot him a frown, then peeked through the slit in the drapes again. "Yeah, but this is different." She shivered as a chill chased down her spine. "He's acting *really* weird. Yesterday he was in a pretty good mood, but this morning he looks all depressed, like somebody died or something."

"I wanna watch 'Scooby Doo,'" Rachel complained from the opposite bed.

Clay frowned, but punched the remote, surfing through channels until he found the cartoon show Rachel requested. "He's probably just tired," he said to Tara. "He couldn't sleep last night."

Tara whipped her head around to peer at her brother. "How do you know that?"

Clay lifted a shoulder and tossed down the remote, resigned to watching cartoons with Rachel. "'Cause I heard him open the door and I asked him where he was going."

"Where'd he go?"

"For a walk."

"In the middle of the night?"

He lifted a shoulder. "Yeah."

"Weird," Tara murmured and turned her face back to the window. She watched until her father pulled out onto the highway, started to turn away, then whipped back and shoved the drape wide. "Clay!"

"Would you clam up? Me and Rachel are trying to watch TV."

"Clay! Come *here!*"

Muttering under his breath, he heaved himself from the bed. "Whadda you want?" he groused.

"Look," Tara said, pointing. "Isn't that Annie's car?"

Clay frowned and moved closer to the window. His eyes widened in surprise. "It sure as heck is."

The twins turned to look each other. "Do you suppose—?" they began in unison, then tripped over each other as they both bolted for the door.

"Come on, Rachel," Tara yelled.

"I don't wanna go," Rachel whined, reluctant to leave her Saturday-morning cartoons. "I wanna watch 'Scooby Doo.'"

"Annie's here!" the twins screamed at her. "Hurry!"

Rachel rolled off the bed and to her feet, blinking twice. "Annie? Where?"

"Downstairs. Now come on!"

Annie stuffed her hair dryer into her overnight bag and zipped the lid closed. Turning, she glanced around the room, checking to make sure she hadn't left anything behind, then picked up her bag. A soft knock on the door had her shoulders sagging in frustration.

Sure that it was Jase outside, she whispered a fervent prayer. "Please don't make this any harder than it already is."

Dreading another confrontation with him, she crossed to the door, dealt with the security locks and pulled it open. She stumbled back in surprise when she saw Rachel, Tara and Clay standing on the narrow walkway. She glanced behind them, then quickly looked back at the children. "What are y'all doing here? Where is your dad?"

Rachel grinned up at Annie. "He went to get us sausage biscuits from McDonalds. Hi, Annie."

Annie lifted trembling fingers to her lips, then sank weakly to her knees and opened her arms. Rachel raced into her embrace, nearly knocking Annie over with her exuberant hug. With Rachel clinging to her neck, Annie grabbed for Tara's hand and, laughing, pulled Tara down for a hug, too. "Mercy, but it's good to see you guys," she said, sniffing back tears as she squeezed them to her. She unwound Rachel's arms from her neck and stood, smiling tearfully at Clay. "Don't I get a hug from you, too, big guy?"

His cheeks flaming in embarrassment, Clay stepped forward, gave Annie a quick hug, then stepped back and ducked his head, grinning sheepishly.

Annie placed a hand over her heart, looking at each of the children in turn. "I can't believe this," she said, then laughed. "Does your dad know you're here?"

"No," Tara replied. "And he won't believe that we found you. We've been searching for you for days."

"Days and days and days," Rachel said, rolling her eyes dramatically. Then she caught Annie's hand and beamed a smile up at her. "But we found you now, and you can come back home and live with us again."

Annie dropped to a knee in front of Rachel. "Oh, no, sweetheart, I can't."

Tears welled in Rachel's eyes. "But Daddy said."

Annie glanced up at Tara.

Tara lifted a shoulder. "Dad really did say that we were going to find you and bring you back home with us." She glanced at Clay for confirmation and he quickly nodded his head in agreement.

"But I can't!" Annie cried.

"Why not?" Clay asked.

"Kids."

At the sound of Jase's stern voice, all four turned to stare at the open doorway.

"What are y'all doing down here? I thought I told you to stay in the room?"

Rachel ran to grab Jase's hand and tug him inside. "We found Annie, Daddy! See? She's right here."

Annie slowly pushed to her feet, smoothing her palms nervously down her thighs. "Good morning, Jase."

He glanced her way, his scowl deepening, then away, and focused on the wall behind her. "'Mornin'. Sorry the kids bothered you." He put a hand on Rachel's shoulder and turned her for the door. "I'll just clear them out of your way."

"Dad, no!"

Jase shot Clay a warning look. "Come on, son. I'm sure Annie's anxious to get on the road."

"But we can't just leave, Dad!" Clay cried. "We want Annie to come back home with us."

Jase glanced at Annie. "I've already asked her and she said no."

"But did you tell her—"

"Clay," Jase warned, cutting his son off.

"But, Dad!"

Tara flopped down on the bed, stubbornly folding

her arms over her chest. "I'm not going anywhere. I'm staying right here with Annie."

Jase sucked in air through his teeth. "Tara Michelle Rawley..."

She jerked up her chin. "I'm not going, and you can't make me."

Rachel pushed out her lower lip and fisted her hands stubbornly at her hips. "And I'm not going if Tara's not going."

"Dad, if you'd just tell Annie that you love her," Clay begged.

Jase whipped his head around to silence his son with a threatening look.

Tara rose slowly from the bed. "Daddy loves Annie?"

Clay squared his shoulders, boldly meeting his father's furious glare. "Yeah, he does. He told me so himself."

Tara took a step toward her father. "And you never told her?"

Jase felt the heat climbing up his neck. "Well... no...not exactly."

"Dad!" Tara cried.

Jase glanced at Annie, saw the tears glimmering in her eyes, the tremble in her chin. "I wanted to," he said. "I really did want to."

Tara gave him a shove in Annie's direction. "Well, then do it. Tell her now!"

Jase stumbled to a stop, frowning. "It's not something a man wants to do in front of an audience."

Tara grabbed Rachel's hand and dragged her sister toward the door. "Come on, Clay," she ordered impatiently, then called over her shoulder as the three hurried out the door, "Don't worry about us, Dad. We'll be in our room watching TV. Take as long as you want. Checkout time isn't until noon."

The door slammed and the sound echoed loudly in the suddenly quiet room. Slowly Jase turned to look at Annie. "I'm sorry. That isn't exactly the way I'd hoped this would go."

Annie stared at Jase, her heart lodged firmly in her throat, not daring to hope, but helpless to do anything else. Clay had said Jase loved her. Did he? And if he did, she thought stubbornly, he was going to have to say the words himself. She'd accept nothing less from him than an all-out admission. "How what would go?" she asked, then held her breath.

"This!" he cried and tossed a hand up in the air. He turned and paced away, then whirled back around. "I'd hoped to sweeten you up a little first. With roses and chocolates. They're probably wilting and melting on the front seat of the car at this very minute." He tossed his hands up in the air again. "But who the hell could hope to pull off a romantic rendevous with three kids underfoot, messing everything up all the time?"

Annie took a step toward him, then stopped, clasping her hands together at her waist. "They're wonderful children."

Jase huffed a breath, then glanced her way and had to bite back a smile. "Yeah, they are, aren't they?"

"The best."

His smile slowly faded as he was struck again by her beauty, by the pureness and goodness of her heart. "I love you, Annie. More than I can ever begin to tell you."

She took a step toward him, then stopped, her chin trembling. "But you never told me. Last night you stood right here and never said a word about how you feel. All you said was that the children missed me."

"I know," he said miserably, wanting to go to her, but fearing he'd never get around to saying all he had to say if he dared touch her. "I wanted to. Intended to. But you were so upset after I told you about Tara. It just didn't seem like the right time."

"But what if I had left?" she cried, panicking as she realized how close she'd come to doing just that. "I considered it."

"Figured you might. That's why I sat out on the steps all night."

Her eyes widened in surprise. "You sat out on the steps all night?"

"Yeah. Planned to stop you if you tried to sneak out."

Annie felt the tears building as she saw the dark circles under his eyes, his exhaustion in the weary slump of his shoulders, proof that he'd kept a vigil all night, watching her room. She lifted her hands to press her fingers against her lips. "Oh, Jase," she murmured tearfully.

"Panicked a bit this morning when the kids woke up and wanted breakfast, because I knew there was a good chance you'd slip out while I was gone." He stuck a hand in his pocket. "So I bought myself a little insurance."

Annie's mouth dropped open when he pulled out a spark plug. "You didn't!"

Ducking his head, he said, "Yeah, I did. Couldn't take a chance on losing you again." He slipped the spark plug back in his pocket, then lifted his head to meet her gaze. "Marry me, Annie," he said softly. "Marry me and put me out of my misery."

Though stunned by his proposal, she sputtered a laugh. "Put you out of your misery? What kind of marriage proposal is *that?*"

He crossed to her and took her hands, squeezing them within his. "An honest one. I've been lost without you, Annie. Miserable. More miserable than any man has a right to be and still be alive to tell it."

Laughing, she tugged her hands from his and lifted them to his cheeks, drawing his face to hers. "Many more of these pretty words and phrases, Jase Rawley, and you're likely to sweep me right off my feet."

He slipped his hands around her waist and drew her hips to his. "I love you, Annie," he said again, then brushed his lips across hers. "I love the way you look. I love the way you smell, the way you walk. I love your heart, your hands, your feet. I could even probably grow to love that blue nail polish you favor so much."

Laughing through tears of joy, she flung her arms around his neck. "And I love you."

Groaning his relief at hearing her declare her love for him, he hugged her to him, swaying with her, his cheek pressed tightly against hers. "Marry me," he said again and drew back to meet her gaze. "Marry me and be a part of my family."

Tears slipped over her lower lashes and streamed unchecked down her cheeks. "Oh, Jase. I've always wanted a family."

He thumbed a tear from beneath her eye. "Then marry me and share mine with me."

Hiccuping a sob, she flung her arms around his neck again. "Yes, yes, a thousand times yes!"

Laughing, Jase lifted her off the floor and, hugging her against his chest, spun around and around and around. "I'll make you happy. I swear I will."

"You couldn't possibly make me any happier than I am right now."

His legs bumped against the side of the bed and he tumbled down, landing on his back on the mattress. Holding Annie against his chest, he tucked his head back to meet her gaze. Smiling, he framed her face with his hands as he thumbed tears from her cheeks. "You make me happy," he told her. "More happy than a man as mule-headed as me deserves to be."

"Oh, Jase," she murmured tearfully. She rolled from his chest to lay beside him and rested her head in the curve of his shoulder. Smiling up at him, she stretched to press a kiss against his cheek, then rubbed the tip of a finger against the spot as she settled back, doubts suddenly crowding her mind. "Do you think the children will accept me?"

He reared back to look at her in surprise. "You've got to be kidding! The kids are crazy about you."

She lowered her gaze and smoothed a hand across his chest. "I know that they accepted me as their nanny." She tipped up her face to meet his gaze again. "But what about as their mother? Not that I'd ever try to replace their real mother," she added quickly.

Chuckling, Jase gave her a reassuring squeeze. "I know you wouldn't. And the kids know that, too. They love you, Annie. Never doubt that."

Sighing her relief, she snuggled closer. "Should we go and tell them?"

He turned to his side and dipped his head to brush his lips across hers. "They're busy watching TV. Besides," he said and slipped a hand beneath her blouse. "Checkout time isn't until noon."

A shiver chased down her spine as he closed a hand over her breast. "No, it isn't, is it?" she said breathlessly.

He smiled and threw a leg over hers, drawing her closer. "Nope. And I know just how to fill those remaining hours."

*   *   *   *   *

*Be sure to look for the next book
from Peggy Moreland.
Don't miss MILLIONAIRE BOSS,
coming next year from Silhouette Desire®.*

SILHOUETTE
DESIRE

AVAILABLE FROM 16TH NOVEMBER 2001

CHRISTMAS WEDDINGS

MONAHAN'S GAMBLE Elizabeth Bevarly

Sexy Sean Monahan aimed to make Autumn Pulaski break her no-man-for-longer-than-four-weeks rule. And when the four weeks were over, her rule had been replaced...*by wedding bells?*

A COWBOY'S GIFT Anne McAllister

Rugged Gus Holt was sure he could win over his pregnant ex-fiancée. Mary *would* be his by Christmas—if he could just work out how to gift-wrap forever!

FIRST LOVE, ONLY LOVE

A SEASON FOR LOVE BJ James

Men of Belle Terre

Maria Delacroix had been forced to flee her home and leave her first love. Now she was back, but someone was determined to destroy her. Could the tall, dark Sheriff protect her and give them a future—together?

SLOW FEVER Cait London

Freedom Valley

Returning to her home town meant that Kylie Bennett had to face Michael Cusack, her first love—who'd never shown any interest in her...*until now*. Had his passion been simmering for all these years?

JUST ONE TOUCH

THE MAGNIFICENT MD Carol Grace

Sam Prentice, prestigious MD, had been Hayley Bancroft's first love until they'd been cruelly driven apart. Now he was coming home, and time hadn't dimmed the memory of Sam's loving touch and fiery kisses...

THE EARL'S SECRET Kathryn Jensen

Just one touch was all it took for Jennifer Murphy and Christopher Smythe to feel an intense passionate attraction. But this union could only be temporary, unless the Earl could divulge his secret...

1101

MONTANA
BRIDES

0901/MB/RTLb